A CAROLINA CROSSFIRE MYSTERY

SIDE HUSTLE

WENDY GEE

ISBN: 978-1-95386592-2 (Paperback)
ISBN: 978-1-95386593-9 (eBook)

Library of Congress Control Number: 2025924347

Books Fluent
3014 Dauphine Street
New Orleans, LA
70117

For Linda,
who loved this story from its inception,
yet sadly is not here to see it realized.
I miss you. Always.

1

Three more police cruisers were wedged at sharp angles against the curb. Bewildered neighbors clustered nearby, riveted to the growing fleet of first responders. A relentless pulse of red and blue lights caromed off the lavish Coosaw Creek homes, casting an eerie pall over the usually serene neighborhood. It was one thing when a large police and firefighter turnout happened elsewhere. But it became a whole new ball game when that activity happened close to home.

Ever the broadcast professional, Sydney managed to look both harried and glamorous as she emerged from the van emblazoned on every available surface with Action 7 News. Her station's E350 spearheaded the convoy of media trucks that added to the traffic knot. A foil wrapper crinkled in her pocket, a reminder of the hastily devoured Waffle House BLT she'd wolfed down en route to the spectacle. She took a final swig of her Diet Mountain Dew, then folded a stray curl of shoulder-length chestnut hair behind an ear.

Her photojournalist, a man who could find the perfect angle in a room full of obtuse angles, was already setting up his camera near the imposing POLICE LINE barricade tape circling a yard. A pair of magnolia trees towered nearby, blissfully unaware of the unfolding drama. Sydney adjusted her earpiece, a gesture that was part habit, part preparation for her upcoming live shot. She surveyed the scene with the practiced eye of someone who'd seen it all, yet always hoped for a twist worthy of the six o'clock news.

A veteran reporter from Eyewitness 13—and constant thorn in Sydney's well-manicured paw—offered her patented frothy smile. "Hey, Syd. I heard they have explosives and machine guns inside that house."

Sydney pretended to listen to her rival's drivel as she studied the two-story brick Georgian. The residence seemed better suited for a warm and fuzzy Christmas movie set. Not the kind of place to harbor bombs, guns, or even a tweaker in-law. "Sheesh, Julia. We're in the 'burbs, not on the front lines," Sydney said.

"This is *North* Charleston, Sugar. They play by their own set of rules way up here."

Way up here was only a thirty-minute drive from the Holy City's cobblestoned lanes, horse-drawn carriages, and pastel antebellum houses. But a century removed from its grandee neighbor. The South Carolina legislature, hoping to add more pizzazz to the state's third largest city, once toyed with a name change to Upper Charleston. Denizens objected when they considered potential nicknames, such as Upper Chucktown, which shorthanded to *Up Chuck* in urban vernacular.

Up Chuck wasn't blessed with the chicest Lowcountry zip codes. Yet the city possessed several fashionable neighborhoods that helped elevate the tax base. Among them was Coosaw Creek Creek—a five-hundred-home golf and country club community generally immune to serious crime.

Until now.

The crowd thickened along the length of the barrier tape while Sydney continued to scrutinize the Georgian. The house backed onto the sixteenth fairway, a lush expanse lined with towering loblolly pines and majestic oaks. She was familiar with the golf course, having played in a few celebrity events there.

Her mind wandered to those easy days that remained untarnished by a veteran reporter's weary viewpoint. She even smiled as she recalled the marshy water hazard that split the par 5's fairway, causing headaches for club members. Though she couldn't see the marsh from her location, her mind's eye remembered an osprey nest balanced atop a utility pole, waiting for the community's most famous residents and their new clutch to return for the season.

A youthful NBC reporter spoiled her thoughts. "I know Julia's exaggerating, but what's really going on, Syd? My producer can't tell me nothin.'"

"Waiting for the press conference, same as you."

Julia gave her bleached mane a well-practiced tousle before pressing her palms together. "C'mon, you're always the first to know any scuttlebutt. Throw us a bone. A scrap. A morsel."

Sydney was enjoying one of those days when she could tolerate the groveling from her opposition. After all, they were right about her ability to pry open the tight-lipped law enforcement community. She'd already tapped a coveted source at North Charleston's police department who provided valuable information regarding an EMS crew presumably being held against their will inside the Georgian. That accounted for the ambulance parked in the driveway next to a beat-up Ford Focus that likely belonged to the unidentified male who'd placed the 911 call summoning the ambulance.

At first glance, the beater reminded Sydney of a guy on her street who used to fix cars in his garage when she was a kid. Her mom always complained about his mess, citing distressed property values and abominable curb appeal. But Sydney had been taken in by the grease and specialized tools. Digital wrenches for torquing fragile cast housings. Tubing straighteners. Deburring gadgets. Exhaust pipe cutters. And her favorite—pickle forks.

Despite few confirmed details from her police source, Sydney knew this event qualified as a genuine *lulu* according to genteel Southern ranking standards. One rung below *brouhaha*, yet noticeably ahead of *kerfuffle*, *humdinger*, and *doozy*.

She dabbed on a fresh coat of lip gloss but didn't bother glancing at her notes before offering her colleagues a solid nugget. "Better settle in. Might be here a while. Two paramedics are being held hostage."

"Omigod, how awful," the NBC guy said.

Before she could comment, Sydney's cell phone vibrated with

an incoming text from her producer, indicating the Georgian was owned by a high-level executive at an area insurance company. Obvious follow-ups ping-ponged in Sydney's head, such as the name of the executive, for starters. She felt confident the production team would provide that information soon.

She shielded her eyes from the bold pre-summer sun riding high overhead and noted the time. A little after two.

She wasn't about to settle in.

Questions were piling up faster than answers.

Now was the time to uncover the rest of the story.

2

Sydney crabbed over to the Dorchester County sheriff's tactical van and hunched below a screened vent choked with an assortment of cords and cables spooling out. She squinted through a crack and could barely make out her pal, Detective Lieutenant Draymond "Dino" Bernadino, from the Charleston Police Department.

Dino adjusted a set of headphones and closed his eyes while focusing on whatever he was listening to. A few beats later, he snapped his fingers. "Is she dead? Bind his hands and feet."

The undersheriff moved into view. "Huh?"

"Two voices. Part of the MAYDAY before it cuts out." Dino lobbed the headphones to the sheriff's number-two man, then continued, "I'm glad that EMT had the presence of mind to activate the panic button on his radio. Gives us ten seconds maximum duration of a hot mic signal."

The undersheriff jutted his lips in and out while he listened. "This is indeed confirmation of a hostile act. Medic 6 is under duress. Ops dig up anything on the homeowner?"

"Piper Kingston. Phone company provided an unlisted landline." Dino cleared his throat. "Ms. Kingston may be injured—or worse."

Sydney gasped and her pulse quickened.

Piper Kingston was a kind-hearted woman she'd dealt with during her own insurance business at Lansing Group. Divorced with a college-aged son, Piper came across as a firm but fair negotiator. The two managed to strike up a friendship, and Sydney understood Piper hated dickering with desperate people in their hour of need, as though monetary restitution could replace a lifetime of lost baubles and memories.

Sydney strangled her cell phone in a clenched fist, then forced herself to stay cool. She knew hostages ramped up any crisis. But this event had become personal.

"You run him to find if anything dredged up?" Dino asked.

"He's clean," the undersheriff said.

Sydney took that to mean the cops knew the name of the man behind all the hubbub and were working up an offender dossier. A steamy gust made her sweat and shudder at the same time.

Dino moved to a window positioned above her eavesdropping spot.

Sydney pressed herself against the van, hoping the lieutenant couldn't see her. She heard him flipping the shades, and he likely spotted NCPD officers muscling the press corps and lookie-loos down the block, expanding the security perimeter. With her back to the van and camouflaged by a leafy oleander, Sydney eyed firefighters from North Charleston's fire department evacuating residents away from the Georgian while sheriff snipers flattened themselves on lush lawns and rooftops across the street.

Sydney knew all too well this was when the neighbors' initial flurry of excitement would give way to a grim reality—an unmistakable transgression had punctured their tiny cocoon, and now would be a good time to curl up with arms wrapped tight around cinched knees. No amount of money, or education, or fame insulated those good people from full-blown catastrophe.

When she heard Dino move away from the window, Sydney re-chinned herself on tippy toes and watched him pass the phone to another deputy.

"Redial every two minutes until we find out what's going on in there." Dino keyed the command vehicle's loudspeaker, causing Sydney to jump. "This is Lieutenant Bernadino, CPD. We're going to talk sooner or later—you might as well answer."

He made a grand arm gesture for the deputy to dial again.

When the assistant signaled no response, Dino re-keyed the

loudspeaker. "Everyone okay? Anyone need a doctor? I can help."

Crickets.

"Look, do me a favor and pick up the damn phone so I can stop using this bullhorn. I'll call one more time."

Dino signaled the uniformed deputy to put the call on speaker.

A man answered on the third ring. "Fuck you." The guy disconnected without further fanfare.

The sheriff's team barked with laughter while Sydney muffled a giggle. Nothing particularly funny about crime or criminals. Yet gallows humor helped ratchet down tense and morose conditions without erasing the concern everyone held for Piper or the EMS team. Besides, a well-placed f-bomb galvanized everyone's attention.

Dino shook his head and thumbed the loudspeaker. His voice held no trace of the irritation showing on his face. "Thanks for breaking the ice."

3

For Sydney, media callouts were as predictable as an old TV detective's trench coat—interviews, press conference, followed by either a live report or a pre-recorded package. All brisk and efficient. But today, the standoff moved with the urgency of a slow pan.

Sydney was still leaning against the police van when another of her sources, this one from the DMV, came through with vital information gleaned from the old blue Ford's license plate. The car was registered to Josh Andrews. Sydney surmised he was the hostage-taker whom the cops were already profiling. She texted the name to Mandy Reynolds, the station's researcher and her best friend, then shinnied into a tree for a better vantage into the tactical van while concealing herself from the snipers.

Two uneasy hours passed.

During that time, Mandy texted that she'd come up empty in her quest for additional information about Josh. Sydney continued to work other sources while fretting about Piper's health status and the captured EMTs. She cursed the hostage-taker for reasons that required no explanation, and herself for choosing such a rotten hiding spot. Her legs and arms numbed from being pinned up a tree. That led her to resent the SWAT snipers trained on the Georgian. She was marinating in sweat as she rearranged her position, the reward an unpleasant poke in the derrière from a stray branch.

Finally, someone inside the house phoned the command van, altering the dynamics.

'Bout damn time, Sydney thought. She was hungry and had to pee.

The wait had been an excruciating exercise in patience. Family and friends used lots of words to describe Sydney, but *patient* was never one of them. She wobbled out of the tree and over to the vent.

"Put it on speaker," Dino said to the deputy. "Hey, buddy. My name's Dino. May I call you Josh?"

"Sure."

Dino teed up a satisfied grin. "Work with me, Josh."

Sydney pumped her fist—at long last confirming Josh Andrews's role. "Booyah," she mouthed.

Dino continued. "This isn't only about you. Lots of other people are involved. Folks living 'round here need to get moving again."

"Don't come in," Josh said. "I'll hurt 'em."

Dino's grin evaporated. "Let's talk things through, okay?"

"I want this to be over. I swear I didn't do anything to her."

Up the block, Sydney caught a glimpse of a man walking a dog. He was quickly confronted by a cop on perimeter patrol. The man seemed taken aback, like he hadn't noticed the commotion.

Dino nudged the conversation forward. "You called 911, Josh. Do you remember?"

Josh began blubbering. "I'm not thinking straight. I hurt all over. Please send those SWAT guys away."

"Then, talk to me. Better yet, come out. Hands in the air."

"What am I gonna do? I got nobody . . ." His voice trailed off.

Sydney heard shuffling as though Josh was moving about the thirty-five-hundred-square-foot mini-mansion. She was pretty good at reading people, but without laying eyes on the alleged hostage-taker, the jury was still out. A thin crack in the sidewalk caught her attention. Too much water in the concrete mixture, she surmised, then shoved aside the stray thought.

"You made it bad in here," Josh said. "We got no air conditioning. No lights."

"I can fix that," Dino said.

Josh didn't speak for a long minute.

Dino let the silence hang in the air.

Sydney could barely stand the wait.

Josh broke the quiet with a sigh. "You guarantee my safety?"

"Yes, I can," Dino said. "How 'bout you send out the EMTs first? They're okay, right? You haven't hurt anyone else?"

"I'm done talking to you. I wanna speak to a reporter. Better tell my story in case something goes wrong and you mess up." Josh disconnected.

The portly undersheriff flapped a series of animated gestures, then moved near Sydney's vent. "What do you recommend?"

Dino said, "My first instinct is to say 'no' until he gives us something. On the flip side, we could use this as a chance to send in a decoy. Move a cop inside with a camera. No weapons of course, but we'll suit 'em up for protection."

Sydney scrunched her lips to one side. Why wouldn't Dino leverage the skills of an actual reporter—like her?

A phone rang in the command post.

"It's our guy. Let me work this out." Dino answered the call using the speaker feature. "Hey, Josh. Trying to get approval on the interview you asked for."

"Send the brunette from Channel 7," Josh said. "You know who I mean. The pretty one. She's the only person I'll talk to."

Sydney covered her mouth with a hand to hold back a *whoop* of excitement.

"C'mon, Josh," Dino said.

"Send her, or I'll kill a paramedic. You hear me?" Josh disconnected.

Dino eyed the undersheriff. "He's escalating. Wants Sydney Quinn."

The officer-in-charge of the situation shook his head. "No way."

"You heard him. Says he'll kill one of the guys."

"Dammit, I hate ultimatums." The undersheriff spun toward his heavily armed SWAT captain. "Ready to move?"

"Forcible entry could be a cluster for the hostages. I can't guarantee a successful outcome."

Dino checked his watch. "Sydney can do it. I'll vouch for her."

"I won't put a civilian in danger," the undersheriff said.

"Trust me. I have your back." When the big boss acquiesced, Dino phoned Josh. "I need a little time to see if she's here. Give me ten minutes."

"Make it five. And turn the electricity back on."

Sydney edged behind the van and sprinted through backyards to the corner where the press was huddled. She grabbed the digital camera from Eric, her photo guy, then ducked behind a row of her colleagues. She spotted Dino push open the van door, then saunter toward the press pool. He planted his feet and made a show of asking for a volunteer while searching the crowd. She watched in amusement as her colleagues tripped over themselves for a shot at Dino's special assignment.

At thirty-five, she'd done most everything on her bucket list except write a bestseller, race in the Indianapolis 500, and climb Mount Fuji. Those had to wait until she won the lottery. Oh yeah, that was on her list, too. More practically, as far back as Sydney could remember, she'd wanted to be a highfalutin TV correspondent for moments like these. Never wanted to be a princess or anyone who had to wear a tiara. She preferred baseball hats.

Sydney knifed through the reporters and signaled Dino.

He was tall, maybe six-three, with ropy muscles accentuating a rich African-American complexion. Only a handful of years older than Sydney, his jet-black hair was beginning to show some graying at the temples, though he gave the impression he could handle himself in any situation. He wore black commando pants and a black T-shirt stenciled with NEGOTIATOR in neon yellow letters on the front and back.

Dino waved her over, and they marched up the block amid boos and catcalls. "I don't think your peers like you right now."

"If you ain't got haters, you ain't poppin'," she said.

"Part of your journalism school curriculum?"

"Nah, I've been watching gangbanger videos all morning. Busting out my new vocabulary."

"Stick with the old one so I can understand you."

They climbed aboard the van, and Dino parked at a table littered with cardboard coffee cups and wadded candy wrappers.

Sydney snuck a peek at her hidey-hole and realized she'd been well-concealed while snooping. "Never expected to see you here. You're a little out of your jurisdiction."

"Lending a helping hand while the sheriff's crisis negotiator is on vacation in Daytona." Dino shook his head. "Man, is he gonna be hopping mad. The guy takes his first vacation in three years and misses the lulu."

Sydney made a pretense of seeking information. "What have you learned about the hostage-taker?"

Dino glanced at his watch and reset the timer. "Guy's name is Josh. He's holding two paramedics at gunpoint. Demanded to speak with a reporter. We declined at first, but then I thought, you'll do."

"That's a ringing endorsement." Sydney smirked. "Asked for me by name, didn't he?"

"Maybe—" Dino motioned for another deputy to help her don a ballistic vest. "Besides, you're the only one I trust for the job."

"Which is what?"

"Could be a minefield. But we need you to gather intel."

Sydney cinched the straps of the Kevlar vest. She enjoyed working with Dino. His primary job was homicide detective, but she knew he loved flexing his skills as a negotiator. She'd also learned from experience that he wasn't prone to jumping to conclusions, nor did he tolerate those who did.

The SWAT captain injected himself into the conversation by squaring off in front of them. "I coordinated with Ops for tactical entry in case things go sideways." The solid hunk of granite pointed to a crude drawing of the Georgian's open-concept kitchen, dining, and great rooms. "First, we'll break and rake the kitchen window for deployment of tear gas and diversionary devices—it'll tip the scales in our favor. Then, breach through Alpha and Charlie doors using delayed entry to avoid crossfire. This won't be a level playing field. We'll use overwhelming force to apprehend the suspect and secure the hostages."

Dino tried to wave him off, but the SWAT boss continued to throw his weight around.

Sydney conjured an image of the Special Weapons and Tactics team, a paramilitary organization that possessed the same bravado as the Marines she'd embedded with in Iraq. The emergence of SWAT would mean an end to her participation before she even established a beachhead. She glanced at Dino; half a smile crept across his face. She read his expression as a signal Granite-guy was hoping to intimidate her into bailing.

The SWAT boss fixed a menacing glare that could melt a popsicle in Fargo. In January. "Use of deadly force is authorized."

The line floated without reaction.

Sydney imagined plenty of lowlifes had tossed in the towel after being subjected to Granite's well-rehearsed scowl. She found it comical and choked back a snicker.

Dino let a moment pass before checking her. "So, you ready to do me this little favor?"

4

Sydney welcomed being thrust ahead of the field, the most ideal position to score a bona fide scoop. Being first on-scene, getting firsthand information, and being first to report the particulars were undisputable coups in broadcast journalism.

Secondhand implied second-rate.

"Oh, yeah. Let's do this," she said.

Dino plastered on the other half of his smile and continued giving instructions as the SWAT captain skulked away. "Syd, move your camera around so we can see what we'll be facing if they decide to breach. A five-man tactical team will be hunkered at the back door, with another tac team out front ready to move on command. Our technicians will stream your video here to the command post. Give this guy a few minutes for chit-chat, then get the hell out. We'll take it from there."

"I hear you. No warmth or compassion. They give me a rash, anyway."

"I knew you'd be perfect for this."

"Seriously, any dos and don'ts?"

Dino raked his fingers through his tight, dark curls. "No time for a tutorial on hostage negotiation, but I'll tell you the most important thing—never lie. It's a cardinal rule."

Sydney didn't argue. "Makes sense. A lie breaks rapport, along with any illusion of trust and cooperation."

"And no promises. You can't deal anything. No food, transportation, or money."

"Yeah, that might lead to a lot of compromising."

"Dammit, Syd." Dino slapped his beefy palm on the table. "This is a high-risk, vulnerable situation. I went out on a limb for you.

There could be a dead woman inside."

Sydney jerked.

After a deliberate exhale, she debated whether to tell Dino she knew Piper. But she didn't want to miss an opportunity to square off against the lug nut who might have killed her friend. She opted not to give Dino any ammunition for picking someone else for the coveted assignment.

"High risk—got it," Sydney said. "I promise to use my dulcet tones."

Dino arched his eyebrows. "Lastly, I know this'll be hard for you. But you need to follow his instructions. As though your sweet life depended on it."

"Do I have a safe word? Some sort of code to let you know if I slide off the rails?"

"*Help* always works for me." Dino blew out a jet of air. "Avoid prolonging this by asking dumb questions, Ladybug. It doesn't matter what he has to say. We're only interested in the pictures."

"Wow! You want to switch places? Sounds like you've considered all perspectives."

Dino continued, unfazed. "Anyone ever tell you you're a pain in the ass?"

"All the time."

"And?"

"I ignore 'em." Sydney jotted a few notes on her spiral pad and dumped it into her purse. She accepted his wit as proof of the situation's seriousness. "Thanks for the pep talk."

She'd made her bones steering toward conflict, rather than dodging it. Even so, she hated to admit feeling an extra tinge of excitement. Sydney forced her face to remain unimpressed, though inside, her stomach was cartwheeling.

Dino placed a hand on her shoulder. A flicker of understanding passed between the two colleagues. "Please be careful."

"Where's the fun in that?"

•

At 5:27 p.m., Sydney ducked under the police tape rimming the yard and bulldozed her way into the residence. Since the air conditioning had been cut to ramp up discomfort, the place sagged with repulsive odors. She resisted an urge to fling open the curtains and raise a window.

Instead, she squeezed her grip around the camera. "Hi, honey. I'm home." She felt a rush as she called into the dark. "Sydney Quinn, Action 7 News. Which one of you is Josh?"

In the next instant, house lights popped on as power was restored.

Sydney zigged in time to avoid a sickening pool of crusted blood on the floor near Piper's body. She recoiled from the sight, yet quickly retreated into a more clinical posture so she didn't vomit. She felt Piper's neck for a pulse. Finding none, she stared at the dead woman, graven against the gorgeous hardwood floor. That was a heck of a thing to notice under the circumstances, but the opulently appointed house seemed totally unsuited for the deadly struggle that had occurred.

Sydney refocused.

Piper's swollen mouth skewed to the side, and her wide eyes seemed to track the reporter in haunting fear. A whiff of rusty copper slapped the back of Sydney's throat as she lifted waves of salt and pepper hair with a pen so she could inspect the side of Piper's head. Didn't take a genius to deduce the ugly gashes had been caused by the bent four-iron tossed nearby.

Crime scenes were never pleasant sights.

But Sydney hadn't expected to see Piper covered in so much blood from hideous head trauma. Instead of basking in a big scoop, she wanted to hold Piper's hand until the woman's corpse could be ceremoniously removed by the coroner. She eyed Piper again and knew that'd be an image she could never erase. The best Sydney could hope for was to tamp it down without her brain trying to compare the newest terrible experience to all the other bad ones she'd accumulated.

She fanned away a tear and straightened with a new resolve. She'd promised Dino intel photos and understood exactly what the situation demanded. Lives were depending on it.

Sydney placed the camera on the dining room table where the EMS pair was seated, then wiped a cheek with the back of her hand. "Humidity—weather you can wear. Am I right, fellas?"

The paramedics' mouths flinched into sour puckers.

She winked, hoping to convey assurance. "You guys look like you need an enema."

No one spoke.

"C'mon, no humor in the room?"

The lanky EMT with sand-colored hair whispered, "You gonna get us outta here?"

She bobbed her head.

"I'm Andy. He's Danny."

"Keep it together. Help is nearby." Sydney made a slight tilt of her head toward the rear door, then spotted Josh leaning against the big island separating the kitchen from the great room and dining area. At least she assumed the man was Josh by virtue of her superb powers of deduction. White, thirty-ish, with a solid head start on a potbelly, the guy clutched the island as though he might topple over if he didn't hold on.

She passed by him and moved to the fireplace in the great room, sweeping the camera to show the location and status of Piper near a sofa, the two EMTs in the dining room, and Josh in the kitchen. When she finished, she placed the camera on the mantel. Next, she mentally matched the actual layout to the SWAT captain's crude drawing and made a quick inventory. On her far left, a grand spiral staircase corkscrewed its way to the second story. To her right, bloody shoe prints crossed toward the kitchen and down a hallway to that side of the house. In the massive great room, splotches of dried blood dotted the white linen sofa. And a double row of oil paintings hung off-kilter.

In her thirteen-year career, she'd conducted many tough interviews, but the stakes had never been so high. Two people's lives were tied to her ability to appease the hostage-taker while tac teams made final preparations for storming the residence. Then, Dino and the SWAT crew would handle whatever came next.

Josh shielded his face with a brawny palm to stifle the camera's blinding light. He placed a handgun on the counter and rubbed his temples with the heels of his palms. As his head lolled forward onto his chest, Sydney and the two paramedics eyed the unclaimed weapon with surprise.

Danny, the thicker EMT, made a brash attempt to lunge for the gun. Instead, the duct tape binding his ankles and wrists to the chair caused him to face-plant onto the floor.

Sydney rushed over and helped him right himself.

Josh digested their slack-jawed expressions and placed his hand over the pistol. "I'll use this for real, if I have to." A few puzzling beats later, he trundled off-balance into the great room. He propped against a recliner, rearranged the cockeyed suspenders of a compression back brace, then grimaced. His feet rooted to the floor, seemingly paralyzed by pain.

"Are you okay?" Sydney moved toward him.

Josh slumped into the chair and rested the pistol in his lap.

Sydney sat across from him and pondered his stoic silence. She folded her arms across her chest, finding it hard to take her eyes off the gun. "Let's start by you telling me what's going on."

"What's it look like?" Josh's accent was hardcore Dixie, and his eyes bugged out when he spoke.

Sydney concentrated on him with a genial smile. "No one can speak for you, but you."

"Will you believe me?"

"Gotta be honest. I doubt everyone's story initially. It's an occupational hazard. I'm programmed to look for the bad in people. But

I'm not immune to truth. If your story checks out, I'll do everything I can to help you." She glanced at her notes and opted to skip ahead. "Show everyone you're not a monster by letting the paramedics go."

Josh folded his massive hands as if in prayer. "I made a big mistake. What am I gonna say to my boy?"

Sydney was elated at the chance to poke around a new topic. "Tell me about your family."

"Me and June, we'd only been dating a few months when she told me she was preggers. Wasn't sure the kid was mine. I mean, we did the deed. A lot. But I knew she played around with other guys." Josh's face pinched tight and his cheeks reddened. "I'm no deadbeat. Was taught to take responsibility if something ever happened with a girl. You know . . . a girl I'd been with."

This wasn't how Sydney imagined the interview would wend, but as a professional, she needed to adjust. "Do you have a picture? I'd like to see who all this fuss is about."

Josh stood on wonky legs and fished his wallet from a front pocket. "This is my favorite. Greatest day of my life. Last fall, before the injury." He tossed the wallet onto a side table.

Sydney eyed a photo of Josh and his kid at the beach. She could almost feel the hot sand between her toes. The kind of heat that reminded her how good a cold Diet Dew tasted. "What do you do for a living?"

"I'm a firefighter. At least until I got hurt." Josh had a thick neck to go with large hands. His skin filmed with sweat. "I'd only been out of work three days when my wife packed up and moved to Myrtle Beach."

"Sounds like an understanding gal."

"Haven't seen my little dude in over eight weeks. I really miss him." Josh rearranged his posture, and his face contorted as he bit back pain. "When my disability ran out, pals from the firehouse chipped in—but they're barely scraping by themselves. Working two jobs to make ends meet. Lately, I've been taking meals at the church. Now, I'm drowning in debt from medical bills. The bank is about to foreclose on my house in Wadmalaw. I packed my stuff into cartons—ready to move. But I have nowhere to go."

"What meds are you taking?" Sydney asked.

"Nothing illegal, and no money to fill prescriptions."

Sydney rerouted the conversation to the key point she wanted to address. "How do you know Piper Kingston?"

5

Sydney waited for Josh to find a comfortable position.

"Ms. Kingston is my insurance rep or whatever," Josh said. "I received workers' comp for a couple of months, then bam—my checks stopped. I called Lansing Group and was told I didn't need it anymore. She told me, 'Get a job, quit living on the dole.'"

Now they were getting to the meat of the coconut, but that tone of insensitivity didn't sound like Piper. "Is that a direct quote from her?"

Josh's shoulders drooped and he shook his head. "Ms. Kingston could see I was hurting. I told her I wanted to work, but some days I can't even get out of bed. I pleaded with her to extend my benefits, so I could get well enough to return to the firehouse."

Sydney peppered him with questions, and all the while, he kept repeating he'd never asked Piper to break any rules. He thought she was on his side. He'd trusted her to help him. Sydney found Josh authentic, without guile.

Josh pulled a small Bible from his pocket and squeezed it with both hands. "All I want is to see my son. How much jail time will I get for this stupid stunt?"

"No idea," Sydney said flatly. "How'd you hurt yourself?"

"Yanking some lard-ass from a burning MVA."

"MVA?"

Danny chimed in. "Motor vehicle accident. You think this one's bad? Those scenes are the worst."

"Let them go," Sydney whispered.

Josh dismissed her with a low wave of his hand. He scooched his chair closer and unloaded the rest of his story. "I have spinal stenography, or whatever, from two ruptured discs. I waste what little money I have on cheap booze just to stop the hurt. And the MVA gives me nightmares. Wish I could un-see things."

"We all have nightmares, Josh." Sydney meant it as a statement—not criticism. Despite her bluster, she too hid many fracture lines below the surface and understood his sentiment. All at once, her mind spooled to visions of the deadly ambush in Iraq. She became stranded on the riverbank—pinned down by withering enemy fire.

Fighting for her life.

Beads of perspiration formed on her upper lip.

Nothing snuck up on you like inconsolable grief.

From his seat at the table, Andy seemed to read her ballooning anxiety. "Hey, Syd. You're safe here."

She came out of her thoughts and exchanged a kindhearted glance with a guy who knew *the code*.

Andy worked his jaw. "Believe me, I understand how you and Josh are dealing. I've been there. Hell, I'm still climbing out. And since I'm about to die at the hands of a fellow firefighter drowning in more self-pity than me, I could really use a finger of bourbon."

Everyone followed his gaze to the nearby bar cart.

"What the heck—two fingers. Haven't had a drink in a couple of years. I could get lit on two fingers. And a beer chaser."

Josh stirred in confusion. Then, a sad smile crossed his lips.

Andy shook his head. "What's my number, Danny Boy?"

"Seven-hundred sixty-two days sober. Right, partner?" Danny winked.

"One grueling day at a time. Especially with you nagging me."

"Nagging? Damn, bro—" Danny laughed it off. "You can do this. I got you."

Andy sat ramrod straight. "For me, it started by celebrating the saves. Then, I got so I celebrated end of shift. Anything that let me crawl into a bottle to dodge the pain from the bad calls."

Sydney's brief episode, combined with Andy's confession, seemed to draw everyone closer. A shared experience. She noted even Josh seemed more relaxed, gently crossing his ankles and resting back in the cushiony recliner.

She tapped her pen on the notebook's spiral loop and pushed ahead. "I can't promise you'll get your son back, but we should start to undo this mess." She'd sidestepped Dino's advice to keep the interview succinct and wondered how much longer her favorite cop would allow her to continue. "Why did you come here—to Ms. Kingston's residence?"

Josh furrowed his brow as though he'd been asked to solve complex differential equations. Something foreign and incomprehensible. "The reception desk lady at Lansing Group handed me a note on my way out. Uh, typed. Yeah, typed. In all caps. Note said to meet Ms. Kingston at this address. One o'clock."

His story seemed straightforward, though Sydney lasered in on Josh blaming Piper for troubles with his terminated compensation benefits. Clear motive, in police parlance, explaining why he may have beaten her or wanted her dead.

But Dino had taught her guilty people acted guilty. And something in Josh's demeanor convinced Sydney he was telling the truth.

She craned her neck toward Piper's body. "A cold person did that. I'm betting it wasn't you, Josh. But there's more to this than you're saying. Maybe you were talked into doing something you didn't want to do. Anyone threaten you?"

He shook his head.

Sydney said, "Walk me through it."

Josh's system seemed to spike with adrenaline. His eyes flared, and she wondered whether he might hyperventilate. He caught his breath before speaking. "When I first arrived, Ms. Kingston acted surprised to see me. But she let me in the house . . . I think. Everything's pretty fuzzy." Sweat dripped down his face like a parade of ants. "I woke up in another room." He pointed down the hall. "Had to wriggle out of . . ." Josh made a motion around his wrists.

"Handcuffs?" Sydney offered.

"Torn cloth, not real metal ones." He rubbed the back of his head, then glanced at his bloodstained hands and clothes. "I noticed the house had been ransacked. Drawers were pulled open and stuff was tossed on the floor. I tried not to freak out. Wanted to step outside and wait for the cops to arrive, but I'm a firefighter. We help people." He rubbed his neck again. "I tried to help her—but I didn't have my rescue kit. I couldn't stop the bleeding. Jeezus, it was awful. So. Much. Blood."

"Why do you keep rubbing your head?" Sydney asked.

"I'm pretty sure I got conked right after I came in."

Sydney frowned. "You lost consciousness? If so, you need a doctor to rule out internal bleeding."

"Yeah?" Josh said. "Maybe later."

She'd done plenty of research on traumatic brain injuries, the signature wound from the second Gulf War. Doctors classified all concussions, whether you lost consciousness or not, as TBIs. All had a deleterious effect on short-term memory, vision, and balance that might explain Josh's confusion over specifics. She knew his mental fog might last a week or so, along with headaches.

"Do you still have the note?" Sydney asked.

"I sorta remember making good time on Maybank Highway," Josh said. "Arrived early, so I stopped at McDonald's to grab a bite. The one near Dorchester and Ashley Phosphate. I ate, tossed the note, then headed here."

Sydney scrutinized his facial expressions and cemented her conclusion that Josh was a lug nut. But not a duplicitous lug nut. "How'd you get through the neighborhood's security gate?"

"The guard knew Ms. Kingston had sent for me."

She nodded toward his lap. "Did you bring that gun with you?" If so, Sydney believed that'd go a long way toward proving an act of premeditation.

Josh cocked his head toward the kitchen. "Found it on the

counter. I intended to hand it to the cops, but EMS arrived first."

"Why hostages?" Sydney asked.

He faced the paramedics. "Be honest . . . You guys thought I killed her. I had to buy time. Think things through." He scrunched his nose. "Sorry, fellas."

"You threatened to harm them." Sydney gathered her purse and signaled the two EMTs. "C'mon, we're leaving."

Josh waggled the handgun. "Before she left me, my wife said, 'You're no good anymore. No good to us.' She wrecked my heart." He muttered a few obscenities under his breath, then tried to hide an embarrassed frown.

Josh must've been born and bred in the South, because he maintained good manners for a guy committing multiple felonies. Moreover, he seemed determined to avoid appearing rude in front of the woman who might be able to help him out of his jam.

Sydney backed away. "Cops want everyone to leave here unhurt. Nobody has to die today."

Four sets of eyes shot a quick glance at Piper's crumpled corpse.

Sydney sighed. "Okay, poor choice of words. Do you know who killed Ms. Kingston?"

Josh shook his head and pleaded, "I didn't do it. Please tell them I didn't do it. When the paramedics arrived, I was in so much pain. I knew how it must've looked." His voice sounded an octave higher than normal. He drew a sleeve across his brow to mop perspiration.

"If what you're saying is true, you can't be blamed for this," Sydney said. "Your fingerprints won't be on the murder weapon."

Josh glanced at the four-iron. "Comes from a set of old Callaways I keep in my trunk."

Sydney's Scottish ancestors had used quaint names for their golf clubs like cleeks, niblicks, and baffing spoons. Stark contrasts to modern bold names like Launcher drivers, Slingshot metals, and White-Hot putters.

They called four-irons *mashies*.

Since Josh seemed to be recalling more and more details, Sydney surmised the conk on his head had likely disoriented him for less than a minute or so. Begging the question, how did the killer have time to find a golf club in Josh's car, then use it to thrash Piper during such a short window of opportunity? If Josh hadn't done the thrashing, as he claimed, Sydney wondered whether he and/or Piper had been incapacitated with a sedative of some sort to knock them out. Or render both unable to defend themselves.

Josh limped into the kitchen and leaned against the island. He eyed Sydney with a vacant expression, then rubbed his aching back—thick fingers clawing at knotted muscles.

Sydney pointed. "You didn't touch anything else besides the club, did you? And whose footprints are those?"

Josh peeked down the hallway, then stared at his rust-stained shoes, apparently tallying up his mistakes. His chest heaved and his eyes misted over. Raw emotion pulsated.

Sydney sensed the denial of his claim extension had tossed him into a deep, rancid pit—his own personal abyss. He'd lost his wife. His kid. And his career was toast. All from an on-the-job injury.

Josh pulled a sheaf of papers from his back pocket and passed them to her. She began skimming the first page before he rested his hand atop the pile as though making a sacred trust. "You can read 'em later."

A faraway look filled his eyes.

For a moment, Josh seemed at peace, and she worried he was planning to harm himself. Her eyes blurred with a rage she attributed to Lansing Group's temerity for denying his claim. Greedy SOBs—palms up to demand premiums but shoved in deep pockets whenever anyone needed them to pay. Sydney understood Josh's frustration, because she was facing litigation against LG regarding a contentious property claim of her own.

Dino's voice boomed over the loudspeaker. "Josh Andrews. Come outside. Hands in the air where we can see them." He no longer employed the soothing undertones of a late-night disc jockey. His calm and mellow timbres were replaced by a high-voltage, matter-of-fact current. The signal was obvious; SWAT was prepared to breach.

Sydney waved at the camera before turning toward Josh. "I have to leave, but I promise to look into what you've told me."

"You coming back?" Josh's eyebrows knitted into a single fuzzy line. "Don't know how much longer I can last—"

"I'll do my best." She re-eyed the paramedics before settling on Josh. "In the meantime, don't hurt yourself. Or them."

Sydney dashed to the command van, having left the camera behind so Dino could maintain a visual inside the house. She hoped that'd persuade him to delay extrication. She cornered him and pitched her case. "Look, I know it goes against protocol. But this hasn't been a by-the-book negotiation. I'm certain you want to get Piper out and crime scene techs in. But this guy is wrapped as tight as a thermal crochet stitch. I wanna help him off the ledge and ensure this ordeal ends without a violent outcome that'll stain your permanent record."

Dino scratched his chin. "Ladybug, I've let you yank my chain so many times—"

"I need to do this," she said with special emphasis.

He tucked his thumbs inside his web belt. "How much time?"

"Three hours. Tops." Sydney registered Dino's rejection in his tight lips. "Okay, two."

He tossed her the keys to his Mustang.

She exhaled with relief, then hugged him. "Keep an eye on Josh, and don't let SWAT take him down while I'm gone." Sydney flew out of the van and sprinted for Dino's car.

In the next two hours, she hoped to prove Josh Andrews hadn't killed Piper Kingston.

And maybe find out who had.

6

Sydney thrived on a ticking clock the same way a jazz musician did on improvisation. Deadlines kept her heart racing and her mind sharp. However, in their haste, some reporters treated accuracy like an accessory, something to be tossed aside in the mad dash for a scoop.

But not Sydney.

In her world, errors were as unwelcome as a rainstorm at a picnic. And her reputation for precision made Action 7's producers a whole lot of happy.

Despite the time constraint, Sydney intended to pursue at least four investigative priorities: One—recover the note, Josh's explanation for being at Piper's. Two, three, and four—obtain vital exculpatory information from Lansing Group, the insurance conglomerate responsible for terminating Josh's claim; Medic 6, where the EMTs worked; and the Cooter Ferry Fire Department, Josh's former employer prior to his job-ending injury. She calculated she could only accomplish the first two in person due to logistical limitations. Phone calls would have to suffice for the latter, along with any additional discoveries made during the initial stops.

A little more than five hours after Josh had entered Piper's home for an alleged one o'clock appointment, he was engaged in a stalemate with Dino and the Dorchester County Sheriff's Department, waiting on Sydney to perhaps save his life.

She phoned her producer with an update from outside the McDonald's. After she disconnected, she silently berated herself for not obtaining specific information regarding which bin Josh had used for trash disposal. The place had three public exits, with two bins at each door. Plus, another bin by the drink dispenser and one near the menu kiosks. Maybe more. Sydney rummaged through the two nearest the door she'd entered, but quickly abandoned the chore. She took it upon herself to persuade the manager to cordon off the dumpster and trash bins until evidence techs could conduct a more definitive search.

Following a time-sucking thirty-minute drive, Sydney exited the freeway when she spotted concrete gargoyles roosted atop The Golden Crust's welcome sign. Home to Charleston's toniest neighborhoods, the island featured an exclusive enclave of boutique shopping, premier golf courses, colossal neo-plantation homes, and a bevy of private schools.

Lansing Group's sprawling complex consisted of six brick edifices surrounding a sparkling pond with an ornate bird sculpture spitting water in every direction. She invented a parking spot on the sidewalk outside the Azalea Building and dashed inside.

Corporate money was on full display with an industrial-glam, three-story wall of tinted glass lending a green cast to the cavernous entry. A circular reception desk in the center of the foyer symbolically clogged several arteries leading to the rest of the building. Behind the reception desk, turnstile chutes led to five glass doors. Each turnstile sported keypads, magnetic card swipes, and fingerprint biometric readers, while mirrored domes in the ceiling hid a collection of cameras and other security devices.

Sydney convinced the receptionist to let her through the layered security and raced toward the executive suite. She skittered into the massive ante-office and spotted a woman of rather dull plumage planted at an impressive desk. "Sydney Quinn, Action 7 News."

"I recognize you," the woman said in a raspy voice. "In addition to being on TV, you're an LG client. I'm Grace Rogers, Mr. Lansing's executive assistant. How may I help you?"

Sydney pegged the woman as a chronic smoker. And maybe a fangirl the reporter could exploit to her advantage.

Grace's lips curled into something resembling a smile. Could've been a sneer—the skinny redhead was hard to read. Either way, the woman's smugness suggested Sydney would owe something in return for being accommodated after normal business hours.

Sydney said, "I want to see Gavin Lansing regarding a workers' comp client. Rather urgent."

"That won't be possible. He stepped out." Grace began sorting mail according to envelope size. Smaller ones on top. Medium in the middle. Larger ones relegated to the pile's bottom. Odd-shaped parcels seemed to earn special scorn. "Why don't people simply use standard legal envelopes?"

Sydney pressed, forgoing her usual polish. "Josh Andrews is being framed for the murder of Piper Kingston."

Grace's hands flew to her face.

Sydney wasn't proud of her inelegant behavior. But she was operating on a strict timeline. "Do you recognize the name?"

"Of course, Piper works here."

"I meant Josh Andrews."

Grace flicked a cigarette from a fresh pouch with chewed nails, but didn't light it. "That man is emotionally unstable."

"Go on."

"Security had to remove him from the building. He was a terror."

"When?" Sydney asked.

"This morning."

"Let me get this straight. You saw Josh here this morning? What time?"

Grace tapped the unlit cigarette with a little pucker of distaste. "Around ten. Maybe closer to ten-thirty."

So far, Josh's story added up. "He says Piper invited him to her house."

"She'd never. Except—" Grace rolled the cigarette in her fingers. "She has a soft spot for strays."

Sydney often judged people by their annoying habits. At that moment, she wanted to crush the darn cigarette. Or better yet, film a PSA for the no-smoking bloc. "Any idea what time Piper left for lunch?"

Grace hiked her shoulders in a manner that suggested she didn't know. Or wouldn't say.

Sydney turned her attention to generating an alternate suspect pool for Piper's murder. "Josh was a firefighter injured in the line of duty. He's struggling because his disability insurance was canceled. He's unable to work and feels abandoned. I'm guessing Josh isn't the only person with a similar situation. Can you think of other disgruntled former clients who might have it in for Piper?"

"Lots of people become upset when their claims are denied, but none have resorted to physical violence." Grace's tone not only closed the subject—it slapped a lid on it.

"How do you explain dropping his coverage?" Sydney asked. "Josh wears a back brace. Experiences crushing headaches and an occasional seizure."

"I have no idea what you're talking about."

Sydney leaned in. "I believe you."

Grace snorted. "I'm certain you have a pending claim against us. Doesn't that constitute a conflict of interest in your reporting?" She plugged her mouth with the unlit cigarette, and it flopped around as she spoke. Lipstick served as the glue keeping the darn thing from dropping out.

Sydney stared for a moment in fascination, then responded to Grace's question. "Hardly. It helps me better understand Josh's frame of mind." In reality, the situational ethics were murky, and she hoped to skate around the point. She pulled a document from her pocket and passed it to Grace. "May I get a copy of Josh's complete claim? He signed a release."

Grace retreated to her computer. A few keystrokes later, a block of paper spooled from the printer behind her desk. She butted the edges, squaring page corners, before handing the file over. "Is Piper really dead?"

Sydney rocked on her heels and nodded.

"I hope that bastard gets what's coming to him," Grace said.

Sydney checked the time. Only seventy minutes left. Not enough time to persuade Grace that Josh wasn't the bastard who killed Piper. "Thanks for the record."

She backtracked to Dino's Mustang and reflected on what she'd learned. Sydney half expected LG to pose a roadblock, yet Grace's eventual cooperation made her feel like a Grade A, pain-in-the-keister louse for forging Josh's signature on the release. She was thankful she didn't have a camera crew in tow, since according to her plausible deniability credo, if a transaction wasn't on video, it never happened.

In the car, Sydney thumbed through Josh's case file. Medical reports diagnosed herniated discs and nerve impingements. Prognoses: grim and dire. She skimmed a journal listing each contact LG personnel had made with others connected to his case. The last entry was Piper's note regarding a verbal encounter with a *disappointed Josh Andrews—former client.* Piper made no mention of feeling threatened or inviting Josh over for tea.

Sydney flipped a page to locate entries made around the timeframe his benefits had been terminated.

MAY 6—PI Jenkins has video of JA violating Dr. order. Despite, PK recommends continuation of benefits.

MAY 7—GL terminated policy.

Sydney ran a highlighter over the two dates, then finished scanning the remainder of the pages before circling back to the highlighted section. She didn't need a decoder ring to decipher JA meant Josh Andrews, PK was Piper Kingston, and GL was Gavin Lansing. But what about PI Jenkins?

She fished out her cell phone and called Mandy, who answered on the second ring. "I'm at LG and on the clock. Run a name for me in their employee database."

7

Sydney waited as Mandy tried to identify PI Jenkins, the apparent Lansing Group employee who possessed video evidence that had contributed to terminating Josh's benefits. She didn't have time to meet with that person and walk through the details, but she hoped to view their video tomorrow after the hostages had been released.

She used the lag time to peruse the pages Josh had handed her. The collection included an apology note to his family, along with a life insurance policy, solidifying her concern he might kill himself or engage in suicide-by-cop. Either scenario added urgency to her mission.

"No one by that name in their rolls," Mandy said.

"You sure?"

"Double checked. I'm doing a White Pages search for South Carolina phone numbers. Hmm—lots of Jenkinses. But no PI."

"Just spitballing, but what if those aren't initials? Rather, job title." Made sense an insurance company would employ a private investigator to explore suspicious claims in hopes of curtailing fraud. Sydney put the car in gear and exited the parking lot. A few miles later, she banked the Mustang onto a stretch of road she knew well.

"Found a Hank Jenkins who might fit. He has an office in Harleyville," Mandy said. "Need the address?"

"Phone number will suffice."

"I'll connect you." A few beeps later, Mandy said, "Okay, it's ringing." She disconnected.

"Jenkins Investigations. Hank here."

Sydney introduced herself and sketched out her main concerns. "Josh Andrews's file says you have a video of him violating doctor's orders. What exactly did he do?"

Sounds of drawers scraping open and rustling papers filled the Mustang's comfy cabin.

Hank said, "I remember him 'cuz I was tailing three backs that week."

"Backs?"

"Sorry, I have a bad habit of calling my cases by their injuries. Backs are notorious for scams. Two men were milking it. Genuine douchebags. But your guy was the real deal."

"Keep talking." Sydney took the Aviation Boulevard exit and settled on a well-established route through the airport to cut off a few miles.

"Mr. Andrews had been ordered to avoid lifting more than ten pounds. I tailed the guy for over a week—an actual gimp."

"But—"

"One day, a woman drops a kid off at his house. I guessed she was the wife, though I'd never seen her or the kid before. Anyhow, after the woman leaves, Mr. Andrews takes the kid out front to play with plastic golf clubs. Guy seemed like a good father. Lots of laughter."

"Hate to cut you off, but are you getting to the point?"

"Coming 'round to it. As I said, Mr. Andrews had been watching his son play. Then they decide to head out for ice cream or whatever. I snap a few pictures and prepare to give this guy a clean bill. When out of the friggin' blue, the kid has trouble climbing into the car seat. This guy gives the kid a final boost. Damn—the kid's gotta weigh thirty pounds or more. Made me sick to my stomach. But I keep the video rolling."

"And?"

"After he straps the kid in, the guy drops to his knees. He's in agony. Wails and rolls onto his back. I run over to him. He's stiff as a board. Eventually, I help him to his feet. He can't lift his arms. The kid's crying. Mr. Andrews is sobbing like a wounded animal. Man, I felt like a dickhead when I forwarded the video to Ms. Kingston."

Sydney pulled onto Dorchester Road, about five miles from the hostage scene, with a sense of mounting excitement. "You think Josh could swing a golf club over his head a couple of times? Like chopping wood."

"Oh, hell to the no. I tell you, made me sick when I learned they'd terminated the guy's coverage."

"No fraud, right? You'd swear to it."

"None whatsoever. Somebody at LG did him wrong."

"File says Ms. Kingston agreed with you," Sydney said.

"Damn glad to hear it. I always knew she was a straight shooter. Perhaps she'll help with Mr. Andrews's appeal."

Sydney wheeled into the parking lot at the fire station housing Medic 6 and killed the motor. "Unfortunately, she was murdered earlier today. Cops think Josh did it."

"He must be the world's most unlucky sonovabitch. I'll be glad to repeat what I said—if it'll help."

"Thanks." Sydney used the fob to lock Dino's car. "Josh will be pleased to know someone else is on his side." She disconnected and stabbed at her cell phone to call the Cooter Ferry Fire Department, where Josh had worked. She was passed to a battalion chief who knew him.

The chief offered his version regarding the day Josh's disability benefits had been terminated. "We were all livid. Losing his insurance destroyed what was left of the man. Josh is the very definition of permanent line-of-duty injury."

Sydney slammed a fist in the air. "But now he's in an awful mess. Do you think Josh is emotionally unstable?"

"Aren't we all?" the chief hooted.

Sydney creased her brow and measured her next question. "In your opinion, would he intentionally hurt anyone?"

The chief didn't answer immediately, which she took as a good sign the man was thinking it through. "He swore up and down he'd make someone at Lansing Group pay for their costly mistake. But I never took it to mean physical harm. No ma'am. I don't believe

Josh would ever hurt another person. You can bet on it."

Sydney pressed the issue. "What about himself?"

Another lengthy silence. "Couple months ago, I would've been able to answer that with a definite 'no.' But today? Who can say?"

Sydney ended the call and checked the time. Only thirty minutes remained. She texted Dino to expect her return within the allotted window.

A North Charleston fire department captain met Sydney at the station door. The woman was compact and powerful in her duty uniform, blonde hair pulled into a ponytail. "I'm Sela Ross. I understand you've been inside the residence where Andy and Danny are being held. Are they okay?"

Sydney's career was all about façades. And she'd been at it so long she'd almost forgotten how to act authentic. This time, she mustered sincerity. "Your men are focused on ensuring they get out unharmed." She bobbed her head as she spoke, hoping to encourage understanding.

"Those two are the backbone of our station."

"I don't mean to be curt, but I need help regarding on-the-job injuries." Sydney launched the first question and allowed the captain to explain everything needed to solidify a case on Josh's behalf, such as strenuous physical fitness requirements for firefighters and the dangers of suicide resulting from traumatic events they encountered. She also learned South Carolina firefighters responded to more medical emergencies than fires. So, being called to an MVA was right in their wheelhouse.

Captain Ross sighed. "It's an open secret Andy is a recovering alcoholic. Stress from this incident might catapult him off the wagon."

"I understand. I'll be sure to suggest he seek help when this is over."

"We all need help. Every paramedic, firefighter, and cop on the job has some degree of traumatic stress from bad calls. They add up."

8

By the time Sydney returned to the Georgian, a silky twilight had draped itself over Coosaw Creek. She threaded her way through the tangle of cop cars to the command van with seven minutes to spare.

Inside, Dino and his team were plugged into their headphones, eyes glued to a six-panel matrix of computer screens. The screens displayed multi-shots of the house's interior, each angle more unflattering than the last. It was like watching a reality show where the contestants were furniture with bad lighting.

Sydney smirked, thinking that if the house had a personality, it'd demand a better agent. But for now, it was the star of the show, and she was ready to capture its best—or worst—side for the late news.

She dropped into a chair next to her hunky pal. "Short version, plenty of evidence points to Josh that I read as a textbook setup. But I think I found proof of his innocence in Piper's murder."

"Even so, he'll need to answer for taking the hostages," Dino said.

"Where do we stand?"

Dino placed his headphones on the table and launched into a truncated version of the events that'd transpired in her absence. The most interesting: SWAT had deployed sophisticated cameras and listening devices inside the front and back of the house to complement Action 7's video, watching and listening to the three men inside.

Dino shook out his arms and legs. "Josh keeps apologizing for holding the EMTs. Says he made a big mistake. The Ops boss thinks he means killing Ms. Kingston."

"Did he admit it?" Sydney asked.

"Nope." Dino rubbed the stubble on his cheeks. "Tell me what you turned up."

"If a blunt-force thrashing killed Piper as I suspect, Josh couldn't do it."

"Explain."

"He's unable to lift his hands over his head or swing a golf club with enough force to bruise a peach, let alone dent a human skull. I have at least two people who'll swear to it." Sydney turned a page in her notebook. "I think the big mistake he's referring to was lifting his three-year-old son into a car seat. That event led to his loss of coverage."

"Any new suspects?"

Sydney shook her head. "Nothing specific. Several hostile clients. And you'll need to rule out a break-in. I also asked the McDonald's manager to hold the dumpster contents until techs can search for the note Josh says he tossed."

"Already on it. You prepared to talk him down?"

Sydney smiled at Dino. "Oh, yeah."

He phoned into the house. "Josh, I'm sending your reporter back in, but she only gets five minutes. We clear?" He disconnected and signaled for the Kevlar vest.

Sydney snugged the Velcro bands before she reentered the house by way of the front door. She met Josh and the EMTs in the dining room. All three appeared wiped out.

"Fellas, time to wrap this up," she said.

"Did you find anything to help him?" Andy asked with what sounded like earnest concern.

Sydney eyed Josh. "I believe you didn't beat Ms. Kingston. Surrender, then find yourself a lawyer who can argue your physical limitations. You even have grounds to appeal your workers' comp claim for reinstatement of benefits. But you can't drag this out any further. These guys want to go home."

Home.

For different reasons, neither Sydney nor Josh had a home.

At least Josh wouldn't need one right away, since he was headed to jail for holding the paramedics.

Josh toed the floor. "My son?"

Sydney waited for his gaze to meet hers, sensing a great deal of empathy for a guy she barely knew. "You won't want him to see you like this." She sliced the tape binding Andy and Danny before facing Josh. "Here's what you're gonna do. I want you to shout your name and what you're wearing. Then say, 'I'm unarmed and coming out.' Now, give me the pistol."

Josh hobbled to his feet and handed Sydney the gun.

She ejected the magazine and made sure the chamber was empty before placing the weapon on the table. "Go ahead. Keep your hands where the cops can see 'em. They're going to handcuff you and it'll hurt. You play nice. We clear?"

Josh shuffled through the front door, and a pair of SWAT officers wrenched his arms behind his back. He let out a pained cry as they ushered him to a patrol car.

Sydney pilfered loose papers from Piper's briefcase, open on a sideboard, and stuffed them into her purse before a dozen uniformed cops swarmed the residence. Outside, a couple of North Charleston's finest hurled a spool of crime-scene tape across the front porch. The Medic 6 captain threw an arm around her two paramedics before hustling them to a waiting ambulance.

Sydney sat on the porch swing, trying to reconcile the afternoon's events. A swarm of flies peppered the screen on Piper's front door, instinctively aware a body inside had begun to decompose.

Dino sidled up. "Need a tissue?"

Sydney shook her head and attempted to act with a reporter's sterile emotions. Yet a bubble of irritation fizzed inside. She thought Dino knew better than to mollycoddle.

"You nailed a successful extrication," he said.

Sydney pulled her hair back and wiped sweat from her neck. "That means a lot, coming from you."

Dino wasn't much for dishing out compliments, yet she felt

a certain unease about his praise. Not out of false modesty, but because she wanted to keep the record straight. Her contributions had been overstated before.

Deputies erected a tent in the front yard so evidence technicians could work out of sight from the public. Sydney felt certain the hostage standoff would stick with the neighbors. Some might even feel compelled to move, the horror of Piper Kingston's murder too much for them to stomach.

"Did you remind the undersheriff to place Josh on suicide watch?" Sydney asked.

"Yup," Dino said.

"The man is desperate and thinks he's worth more to his family if he's dead—a dangerous combination. Also, can you ensure they complete a drug screen?"

Dino eyed her with curiosity. "Anything specific in mind?"

"Just a hunch I'm working."

A deputy waved them inside.

Dino said, "C'mon, let's see what they've turned up."

In the great room, Sydney fixed her attention on Jean Gilliard. Dressed in denim jeans with a knife-edge pleat and a green T-shirt stamped with CORONER across the back, Jean had earned a reputation for handling the deceased with dignity. She was also every detective's first choice for helping close the most challenging homicides. The veteran coroner pulled two paper bags from her kit and carefully placed them over each of Piper's hands.

Sydney swayed, slightly off balance, as if a gust of wind had caught her broadside.

Dino cradled her hands to steady her.

Okay, a little coddling—under the circumstances.

"I told Sydney not to move the body," Dino said with an air of authority.

Jean's hair sprouted in every direction. "Syd's been at enough of my scenes. She knows what'll happen if she touches any of my corpses. As for you, Lieutenant Bernadino—lookin' good. Hot date later?"

Dino seemed to ignore the pass. "Have a cause of death yet?"

"I'm guessing it has a lot to do with that dent in her head, but you know I never make a field judgment."

Dino asked the crime scene techs if they'd taken enough pictures while he donned latex gloves. They gave him a thumbs-up, so he examined the bent golf club near Piper's body.

"Might be the weapon," Jean said, sidestepping an obvious conclusion. She offered him a paper sack.

Dino placed the club inside with the same care Sydney supposed he'd done with vital evidence many times before. He sealed and initialed the sack, then handed it to the coroner. "Techs will collect prints and fibers. I trust their magic assortment of lab work."

Sydney crouched beside Jean and peeked at the gashes near Piper's left eye again. After a moment, she backed away to afford the professionals more room.

"Yo, Syd." Jean flashed a toothy grin. "I'm guessing exclusive access didn't score any points with your fellow newsy buds, huh? All the same, no pictures on TV until I notify the family."

Sydney knew the drill. She blotted her cheek and followed Dino back to the front porch. "There's a little something I should've mentioned earlier; Piper was my friend."

Dino removed a pad from a cargo pocket on his pants leg. He jotted a notation, then considered her for a beat.

Sydney had worked beside him long enough to know his mind was grinding, trying to form a scenario of what might've happened to Piper now that he'd seen the layout for himself.

Her eyes leveled with his. "Piper isn't the story I envisioned for tonight's lede. All I wanted was to help you with the rescue. See, my contract expires—"

"I know."

"Lately, my station manager's been—Oh, it doesn't matter."

Sydney clamped her mouth shut, suspecting her rambling made her sound like a jerk.

"Tell me about Piper." Dino's tone was purposeful. Reassuring.

"We met at Krav Maga class a couple of years back. We hit it off—one thing led to another."

He suppressed a grin. "Is there something I should know about this, uh, relationship?"

"Do you usually get good results with absurd questions?"

Dino scrawled in his book to avoid eye contact.

Sydney was regaining her balance. "Anyway, Piper told me Lansing Group could be a good fit for my insurance and investments." She wondered aloud why anyone would want to kill Piper. "I can't believe she's gone. She doesn't deserve this."

"Few people do," Dino said. "What did her job entail?"

Sydney's mind wandered to the last time she'd seen Piper—four days ago. They'd met for lunch to discuss a new settlement offer concerning her torched house. Sydney hadn't even asked about her friend's son. She wondered if she should offer to accompany Jean to break the bad news to him.

Dino snapped his fingers. "Her job?"

Sydney pressed her temples with the heels of her hands. "Piper is in charge of high-risk insurance management. You know, settling big claim disputes."

"You mean she determined if LG was going to pay after a questionable event?"

Sydney flexed her fingers. "I suppose. Of course, she has people below her who do the administrative heavy lifting."

The front door flung open.

The coroner's team rolled a dark body bag strapped atop a Stryker gurney from the house, then into the rear of their van. Piper's remains would be taken to the Medical University of South Carolina's morgue for autopsy before being released for her funeral and final disposition.

Dino sat on the swing beside Sydney and cradled her hands again. "I've worked a lot of gruesome scenes. Homicides. Domestics. And stomach-turning vehicle accidents. I carry them all with me. No one ever has it easy after a bad call."

Sydney wilted from exhaustion as the adrenaline-fueled situation drew to a close. She laid her head on Dino's sturdy shoulder. "How do you cope?"

"Police officers never talk about these kinds of cases with friends or family—the ones that get to you. But life has taught me I can't save 'em all. And my training teaches me to stay focused. Be ready for the next call."

"Repress and move forward?"

"Sort of." Dino kissed the top of her head. "When an officer needs assistance, we come Code 3—lights and sirens. I'll always be here when you need me."

9

Action 7 News was located east of the Cooper River on a sliver of land cleverly called East Cooper. Actually, the TV station was in Mount Pleasant, but the tightly packed suburban community required further definition. Aging antennas and satellite dishes surrounded the peeling, green-brick, two-story building. Sydney whipped a haymaker at the punching bag hooked inside the back door, followed by a left cross for good measure. Two interns shot a quick glance in her direction before manufacturing interest in the purring Associated Press printer located behind the senior producer's desk.

Sydney trudged to Editing Bay 5—her inner sanctum. When the soundproof door snapped shut, a savage twinge of bitter memory stabbed under her rib cage. She flipped the on-air switch and covered the side window with its withered paper sash to avoid interruption. She slumped onto the stool to compose herself. After a minute, she cleared her eyes with a napkin, then called up the video package Eric had created for the late-night broadcast.

The footage opened with a wide shot of Piper's house, panned to the command van and collection of emergency vehicles, then pushed in on Josh's DMV photo for wallpaper. Sydney reset the digital timer and played the segment again, sifting through a preliminary script in her head.

Forty seconds of video. Eric had edited the best footage to fit their assigned window. Sydney replayed the video again. No sound. Only moving pictures without any detail or context.

Her job was to match a script to the video. Tell her audience what the pictures meant.

Ensure people cared.

Sydney cared.

•

A little past 2:00 a.m., Sydney's Civic roared with a defiant whine as she goosed the gas pedal, tearing west down a desolate stretch of Savannah Highway. It stretched out before her like a ribbon of uncertainty, leading past Parker's Ferry and into an inky void toward Beaufort, or perhaps nowhere at all.

The mascara streaks on her cheeks told a story of their own. They were the war paint of an over-caffeinated journalist who'd seen too much and slept too little. She squeezed the steering wheel, knuckles white against the padded cover.

The lonely road shimmered with an oily sheen as the Civic's wheels gulped asphalt.

Two miles.

Five miles.

Sydney pinned the pedal to the floor mat and buried the needle near one-hundred miles per hour. The tachometer shivered as it licked the red line. Thankfully, the road was empty. Otherwise, she might've run over something in her path.

She blew through a series of red lights near Rantowles Creek, raced over the Harriet Tubman Bridge at ACE Basin, then flicked through the tiny town of Jacksonboro. Her dark auto was unremarkable—no racing stripes or markings that might cause it to stand out.

A couple of weeks back, her mechanic had dropped the front struts so the ultra-light rice burner—a derogatory term for Asian imports—could hug the road better. But she could feel the rear tires drifting. She released her grip, shifted into neutral, and eased her foot off the accelerator. The car floated to a stop—straddling the center line. Her headlights caught a half-dozen whitetail deer clotting the tree-lined median and glaring their disapproval.

The drive was supposed to offer an escape from the relentless undertow of Piper's murder, the recent death of her favorite cameraman, and her house fire.

It didn't work.

Overcome, she silently mouthed her mantra—the names of Marines she knew who'd been killed in action: *Crandall. Reed. Slater. Townsend. Walters.*

Shaking violently, she doubled over onto the steering wheel and choked it tighter with each convulsive sob until nausea erupted. Sydney flung open the door, folded to her knees, and retched on the fractured pavement. Her cell phone skittered across the road like a hockey puck and netted itself in the marsh.

She wiped her mouth with the back of her hand, then shouted, "Crandall. Reed. Slater. Townsend. Walters."

A puff of jasmine wafted overhead.

And in the wind, a voice that sounded like Echo Company's gunnery sergeant whispered, *"All your fault."*

10

Tendrils of sunlight leaked through cracks in the blinds of Sydney's temporary abode—a luxurious ninth-floor suite at the Francis Marion. The legendary King Street hotel was one of the tallest buildings in Charleston, rising twelve stories above the Historic District. The place had opened in 1924 and hosted plenty of A-list celebrities and political functions.

Sydney limped into the shower. Hot water pounded her shoulders. As steam enveloped her, she pondered yesterday's hostage situation. Josh, the paramedics, and Dino were probably nursing their own post-event hangovers, each dealing with the aftermath in their own unique way. She imagined Josh asleep in his cell. The paramedics swapping war stories over coffee. And Dino? He was probably glued to a screen, analyzing every pixel of the drama.

For Sydney, recovery proved a more delicious affair. She knew that after a supercharged event, the human body needed time to bounce back. In her case, that meant indulging in chocolate-smothered crepes and a side of *huevos rancheros* from the Blue Pelican. It was a breakfast fit for a queen—or, at least, a journalist who'd survived another day in the trenches of breaking news.

As she stepped out of the shower, she felt a renewed sense of determination. Soon, she'd have a full stomach and a fresh perspective, ready to tackle whatever the day had in store.

Sydney dressed in cotton slacks and an airy blouse, lodged sunglasses on the bill of her RiverDogs baseball cap, then rode the elevator to the spacious lobby.

At exactly 8:30 a.m., she burst through the door at Market 159, a convenience store she frequented around the corner from the hotel.

The pubescent cashier handed her a stack of newspapers and a

Diet Mountain Dew. "Here's the *New York Times* and *Washington Post* you asked for. And the local rag. Anything else, TV dudette?"

Sydney grabbed a bag of pretzels and slid the guy sixty bucks. "Do you have cell phones?"

"We carry a pre-paid model." The guy rounded the counter and jerked a package from a rack stand near the bread. "This should do the trick."

Sydney didn't waste time haggling. "Enough there?"

"You have change coming."

"All yours. I appreciate the enthusiasm."

Sydney crossed King Street, sat by the fountain in Marion Square Park, and pulled out the new phone. She keyed in a few contacts, then sent each a quick text with her new number before studying the headlines. She was reading a blurb about yesterday's standoff on page three of the *Post & Courier* when the cell phone chirped. Caller ID indicated Olivia Hampton—her senior producer.

Sydney punched the call to voicemail.

A minute later, the phone chirped a second time. Olivia again. Voicemail—again. Sydney continued scanning the rest of the local paper before grudgingly fetching the phone when it chirped a third time.

"Sparky, thanks for picking up," Mandy said. "Please hold for Olivia."

"We'll talk later about you ignoring my calls," Olivia said. "Anyway, I know I said you could have the day off, but something fishy is going down, and I wanted you to know."

"You hooked me at fishy."

"Folks at Lansing Group are holding a press conference."

"About Piper?"

"They want to discuss a missing laptop with names and vitals for a hundred or so local clients."

"Oh, great—I'm a local client," Sydney mused. "On top of everything bad happening there, you know this can't be good. What time?"

"Ten. Can you make it?"

Sydney's plan for the day involved sinking her teeth into the internationally bougie breakfast, then meeting her realtor to visit several houses on the market. She could reschedule both.

•

Sydney returned to the hotel and changed into a sage silk blouse and black pencil skirt. Then she arranged to visit her favorite resident at the Ralph H. Johnson VA Medical Center before the press conference. The center was only a short drive west on Calhoun Street. She waved to a nurse peering over her bifocals and a stack of metal charts as she strode to the private room at the corridor's end.

Third-floor rooms were arranged like mini bachelor pads for long-term residents. Room 325 was painted a serene saffron with a light blue ceiling. Last fall, the ladies' auxiliary had added sailboat wallpaper over white beadboard wainscoting on one wall. Other nautical accoutrements from a party store luau kit—a fishing net festooned with starfish, conch shells, seahorses—were sprinkled on the wall to the door's left. Despite the room's cheap distractions, a peculiar blend of institutional disinfectant and Old Spice welcomed Sydney like a grandfather's warm embrace.

"How's my top dog?" she asked.

Commander Bob Hargrove, retired Navy intelligence officer, Vietnam War vet, and former globe-trekking accordion player, held up an iPad. "Give me a sec. My poker buddy in Arizona drew to an inside straight. We're negotiating his winnings."

Sydney pointed at the gaudy wall. "Let him have the starfish."

Bob seemed to consider the idea, then clicked off. "I watched your broadcast last night, Doll. That hostage situation must've been a ballbuster."

"Josh said he didn't kill Piper, and I found a solid lead his attorney can use in his defense. But you know what bugs me most?" She hesitated. "I have a lot in common with the guy."

"How so?"

"Something bad happened to me, my insurance company won't cover the damages, and I'm houseless. Josh Andrews is probably not the only hero first responder in a similar predicament."

An unexpected jolt crushed her against imaginary rocks.

Bob's eyebrows shot up. "Hey, Doll. I wasn't with you at the river ambush. But I've been with you nearly every day for the past seven years. I know you get scared sometimes."

Sydney rubbed her hands together, the one way she dealt with her . . . condition. "Let it go, Dr. Phil."

Bob's gaze met hers. "It doesn't take a prime-time psychologist to comprehend that you think about your Marines every day."

His words stung.

"Spare me the pity party," she said.

"Then it's gut-check time, Dollface. Quit moping. You're in a prized position to change things around."

"How?" Sydney squeezed her lips together, hoping to quash the unpleasant sizzle in her tone. She loved the old coot and hadn't meant to offend him. Matter of fact, she'd come here seeking exactly the prescription he was peddling—a full dose of no-nonsense. With a sprinkle of bootstrap pulling. And a dash of get-your-act-together.

Bob bubbled, eroding her hard edges. "You're an honest-to-goodness celebrity. Use it to raise awareness and money for those in need. This could be your next war to fight."

Sydney changed the conversation's direction to one that didn't require internal analysis. Now wasn't a good time for a session. Maybe later. Maybe never. "Lansing Group has more problems. Someone stole a company laptop loaded with client business."

"How bad is it?"

"I'll find out at ten. Could mean identity theft. And my personal information might be in the pilfered database."

"Sounds like a world of hurt. But whoever is responsible picked a battle with the wrong person. No one messes with my gal." Bob gazed out the window while they sat in stroppy silence. After a full three minutes, he raked his fingers through snowy hair. "Quit listening to me about a new mission. You're undoubtedly too busy to take on something so monumental."

She kissed him on his wizened cheek. "As usual, you've given me plenty to consider. I'm already warming to your idea."

Bob cast a sideways glance at Sydney and grinned. "Wish I could be more help, but I'll leave you with a bit of wisdom. The whole world is a narrow bridge. Your job is to drive on, delightfully unafraid."

11

Sydney maneuvered her Thunderbird into Lansing Group's massive palmetto-tree-lined parking lot and scavenged the closest spot. She sauntered into the Delphinium Building, hoping to catch a friend in Client Records before the presser.

"All rise, your favorite broadcaster is here."

Two expressionless women added to in-baskets choked with cardboard folders. Velma, the supervisor and Sydney's pal, was the imposing one seated farthest from the door. Her arms were tightly folded across an ample chest.

Sydney waved. Velma didn't wave back.

Instead, she leaped from behind her desk like a calico. "Come here." Velma grabbed Sydney's elbow and ushered her into the hall-way. "You can't up and show your TV-self in my office on press conference day. Lordy, you sure got a pretty face, but no sense for the drama that's about to unfold." She turned on Sydney with a grimace that could set off a smoke alarm. "You really should take better care of your secret informants."

"You're a source, not an informant. The differences are subtle, but I'd be delighted to go through them with you."

"Blah, blah, blah. You'd be wasting my time and yours."

Velma hustled Sydney to the employee coffee shop off the lobby and purchased refreshments. Once they claimed a table, she prattled about being only eight years from retirement. Afraid she'd lose her job on account of Piper's murder.

"Why?" Sydney asked. "You didn't do it, did you?"

"That woman was in my office yesterday morning. We exchanged a few—" Velma pushed a wooden stir stick through whipped cream and caramel in her iced decaf mocha latte and whispered, "confidential files."

"Why are you whispering?"

Velma held a finger to her lips. "Keep your voice down so the whole world doesn't know my business. I'm saying, Piper downloaded privileged records."

"I'm listening."

"You gonna eat your donut?" Velma slid the plate over before Sydney could respond. "Piper sat at my desk, and I showed her where to access archived client accounts. She used one of those thumb thingies."

"Flash drive?"

"Right, a flash drive. Piper had a sparkly pink one with a cartoon cat on the side. She thought it was cute." Velma shook her head. "Butt-ugly, if you ask me."

"I didn't." Sydney made a whirling motion with her fist to encourage Velma to fast-forward.

Velma took another sip from her drink. "We were in the middle of copying files when she received a phone call. Got really mad at whomever she was talking to."

"Hot damn." Sydney pounded the table, nearly knocking over Velma's latte. "But you buried the lede. Tell me more."

Velma beamed impishly. "I may have overheard Piper say they 'had to act fast because people were going to find out.' She tried to hide her anger, but I could see she was hot and all."

Sydney let out a long whistle. "Any idea who was on the other end of that call?"

Velma shook her head. "Had to meet my supervisor. When I returned, Piper and her flash drive were long gone."

"Anything else?"

Velma blotted donut crumbs with her thumb. "Now my computer has death cooties."

Sydney scrunched her lips to one side. "Who does the stolen laptop belong to?"

"Did I mention I asked one of my girls to keep an eye on Piper before I left the office?"

Sydney sat forward. "You may be the worst secret informant ever."

"The girl I asked to watch Piper—"

"Yeah?" Sydney's irritation spiked.

"Name's Deleisha."

"She in? I want to speak with her about Piper."

"Her laptop is the one that's missing. And she's gone, too." The expression on Velma's face registered a full-blown, code red panic. She reached for the reporter's hand. "Oh, heavens, Syd. Please help me. I'm in big trouble."

•

Following Lansing Group's lackluster and weirdly short seven-minute press conference, Sydney returned to the TV station to craft a script regarding their apparent data breach. Gavin Lansing, the firm's chief executive, tried to downplay the situation since his company wasn't the first to mishandle personal information, or likely the last. Over the past few years, one corporation after another had been forced to alert customers when computers were stolen or hacked. Like the others, if LG's client information became available through unauthorized retrieval, a thief could exploit stolen identities by tapping banking and investment accounts, applying for credit cards, or selling info—creating a costly mess for all concerned.

Despite numerous personal concerns, Sydney acknowledged more pressing issues. Like, why had Piper downloaded client files? What happened to her flash drive? And how were Piper's murder and Velma's missing employee, Deleisha, tied to the stolen laptop—if at all?

Sydney distilled a tag for her story—Lansing Group was in a pickle.

She kicked off her shoes and curled her legs to one side while nestling into the overstuffed recliner in her cramped cubicle. She mulled over whether to share with Dino what she suspected about LG's transgressions or keep them to herself. The present dilemma felt akin to the first time she'd tried to outfox him.

Years ago, she'd tumbled onto a tip from a friendly prostitute regarding a shipment of drugs and guns coming from somewhere in the Northeast straight to a Walterboro gang that trafficked in all things depraved. Back then, Sydney believed *cooperation* between law enforcement and the press came from mutually disingenuous transactions. Not from either party's conscious lack of scruples. More like an inherent conflict between missions—the pursuit of "justice" versus exposing the truth. Her lack of boots-on-the-ground experience made the first seem cynical, the second a righteous crusade. So, she went at Dino sideways with a few hints to keep him off balance, hoping to score essential law enforcement details no other reporter had gleaned.

Dino saw through her play and manipulated his answers to feed her ferocious ambitions. The result for Sydney: a painful lesson in journalistic integrity and an enduring friendship with Dino.

Sydney dug her fingers into the chair's buttery-soft leather and opted to let the incongruous Lansing Group matters percolate until she could explain to Dino what they all meant.

Mandy rounded the corner, waving her arms as though she'd walked through a cobweb. "I read your copy for tonight. Are you concerned your private info might be out there?"

"Should I be?" Sydney knew the answer but lobbed the question for her bestie.

Mandy jacked her hands on her hips. "Haven't I taught you anything about computer protection?"

"I recall one or two lectures on the subject. Seems to me, you double-encrypted my laptop with some sort of cyber-condom. Besides, Gavin Lansing said they didn't find any data compromises."

"Regardless, you should freeze your credit and notify your banks."

Sydney sat a little taller. Not exactly the advice she'd expected.

"Will it interfere if I decide to make an offer on a new house?"

"Freeze. Unfreeze. Freeze. Like bacon." Mandy perched a hip on the corner of Sydney's desk. "Do me a favor and run through Josh's story again."

Sydney repositioned the framed photo of Reggie, her recently deceased cameraman, atop her desk. "I think Piper's killer is the same person who ensured he received the invitation to her house—a setup. Josh's head gets scrambled, affording enough time to drag him into the guest room. There, he was probably drugged, bound and gagged, then tied to a bedframe. The killer finds a golf club in Josh's car. Anything that'd incriminate the poor guy. Then things spiral out of control."

Mandy's hands flew to her face. "Sounds awful, but how does the stolen laptop fit in?"

Sydney continued with her theory of the crime. "After Piper is dead, the killer ransacks the house. But the offender doesn't have much time. No telling how long Josh would be incapacitated. I believe the killer tossed the place searching for Piper's hot-pink flash drive."

"Why?" Mandy asked.

"Velma told me Piper downloaded client archives for some reason. Maybe the killer knows it contains damning info. When he can't find the USB, he thinks maybe a company laptop is loaded with the same vital files. He chooses to end her life and frame Josh in the process. That makes finding her flash drive and the laptop vitally important, since they could ID her killer."

Mandy nodded in approval, then added, "What about the handgun Josh used to hold the paramedics hostage?"

"Said he found it on the kitchen counter." Sydney exchanged glances with Mandy and reconsidered withholding her ideas from Dino. "I'd better check in with my favorite lieutenant."

12

Sydney parked by Dino's Kona-blue Mustang at the Law Enforcement Center on Lockwood Street. In addition to headquartering the city police department, the facility hosted several municipal courtrooms. She breezed through the front door and beelined for the front desk, flashing her press credentials. The sergeant offered a visitor's badge and a nod of approval for her part in yesterday's hostage rescue.

A minute later, Dino sauntered into the lobby. "I expected you sooner."

"You aren't my only beat," she said. "Spoke with the Dorchester County sheriff leading the Kingston investigation. He must've banged his head on something because he still thinks Josh looks good for Piper's murder. Locked in, despite obvious evidence to the contrary. Think he's willing to explore other alternatives?"

Dino held a heavy metal door as Sydney slid past. "You mean, like rounding up the usual persons of interest?"

"That expression doesn't exude the same panache as Claude Rains's line in *Casablanca*, but yeah. I believe that would be a good strategy." In Dino's office, Sydney looped her purse over a chair, then flipped open a spiral-top notepad. "I'm simply asking, since it's a fresh investigation, will he keep his eyes wide open?"

"When you've worked as many scenes as the undersheriff and I have, the picture focuses fast." Dino slid a can of Diet Dew to her, then climbed behind his desk. "Sometimes when it appears straightforward, it's dead bang. A no-brainer. Slam dunk."

Sydney wanted to fume but held herself in check. "I'm telling you, Josh didn't do it. He's not the guy."

"No need to go all Stockholm on me." Dino rested his chin

on a fist. "Truth is, I'm pretty disappointed the undersheriff didn't subscribe to Homicide Rule 1—like I taught you."

She understood what he meant. "It's always the spouse."

"Bingo, a classic." Dino fired off his trademark two-handed index-finger pistols. For good measure, he blew away an imaginary puff of smoke before holstering the guns.

Sydney glanced at the ceiling to check if he'd ever accidentally misfired into the acoustic tiles. "How does it work if Piper was divorced?"

"Then Rule 1A applies—it's the ex."

Sydney snapped her fingers. "You might be onto something."

"Even though Piper Kingston isn't my case, I trust your physical assessment of Josh Andrews." Dino affixed a sly grin. "So, despite the guy having means, motive, and opportunity—the holy trinity for proving guilt—I don't want Rule 1, or rather 1A, to bite the undersheriff in his ass."

"And?"

"I freelanced. Rode along with Jean when she made a death notification to Aaron Kingston this morning. He's the vic's ex-hubs. Get this, the guy lives in an abandoned school bus on a spit of land past Megget. Down near a Toogoodoo River tidal creek."

"Sounds cozy, but a long way from Piper's Coosaw Creek estate. I'm guessing there's more to the saga."

Dino bobbed his head. "Any reason you'd expect a guy who lives all Spartan like that would keep a real Gauguin stashed under the hood? I mean literally—a painting wrapped in a beach towel, crammed next to a frayed fan belt in the engine compartment."

The image was so ludicrous, Sydney had to stifle a laugh. "Maybe he has a hankering for primitivism style. Or he likes to gawk at Tahitian boob art. Though I can see how his ridiculous presentation of the piece offended your artistic sensibilities."

"I love when you twist things to find a new angle."

"Thank you, I guess." Sydney pooched her lips. "I'll bet the painting was pinched from Piper's house. And it probably wasn't the only purloined goody you found on the bus."

Dino nodded.

"Let me guess. Piper's former hubby offered some lame excuse for how those items came into his possession. Maybe even accused Piper of some misdeed to sweeten the pot in his effort to mitigate Rule 1A."

"Damn, Ladybug. You nailed it."

"Even the misdeed part? I only added that for giggles. What sort of poison did the dirtbag spew?"

"Embezzlement."

Sydney reflexively flinched. "Ouch."

"What's your take? Any chance Piper might've dipped into company funds?" Dino was angling in dangerous waters by accusing her dead friend of anything illegal. He seemed to sense Sydney's aversion. "Look, I'm a cop. I have to ask."

Sydney gripped the armrest in protest. "Piper would never—"

"You could be wrong."

"I don't make it a habit."

Dino hooked a thumb inside his belt. "The guy made a solid case. Told me Piper recently handed him a pile of loot if he promised to leave town."

"But he hung around." Her voice took on a surprising quiver. Sydney tapped her pen with artificial nonchalance as she regrouped. "What else did he say?"

"Big surprise, he owned up to other legal problems." Dino removed a pencil from the top drawer and bounced it off the eraser. "The way I figure, the ex-hubby was successful at shaking Piper down. Then, thinks maybe he deserved an extra helping. When she doesn't come through—"

"Whoa." Sydney slid back on the chair. "Why kill your personal ATM?"

"Here's where it gets janky. I downloaded her bank statements.

Piper was capital-*B* broke. Then, I pulled papers on the ex's spanking new truck and bass boat—he paid cash. The guy's been unemployed for two years and lives in a friggin' bus. Where else would he get the smack for those big-boy toys?"

"Did you check your list of unsolved bank robberies?"

"I'll admit the guy's a schlub—a deadbeat who sponged off his ex-wife. But here's what sealed the deal for me. She was months behind on alimony—"

"Wait . . . What?" Sydney rocked forward again. "She was paying him?"

"These are modern times, Syd." Dino drummed the pencil. "Convenient how she reeled in an unexpected windfall to catch up and buy him off, wouldn't you say?"

Sydney ignored Dino's second go at an embezzlement accusation. "I want you to put Schlub away, but you're missing the big picture. Piper's murder is connected to LG's laptop theft. Any chance you recovered that device on the bus?"

"Didn't see one." Dino scratched a note on his ink blotter. "C'mon, Ladybug. You know what it means when money troubles are involved."

"Not always," she said defiantly.

"Nine times out of ten."

Sydney wanted to pound the desktop. "Piper was my friend. She didn't steal any money. Maybe she sold a painting or two. She has an extensive collection, as you saw with your own eyes."

"Suppose for a moment . . ." Dino tossed his palms up in surrender. "Show me how you'd play it in TV-land. And don't make the undersheriff look like he dropped the ball. He's a great guy who'll get it right with Josh Andrews once he reviews lab results and medical reports."

Sydney took a long pull on the Diet Dew as her brainwaves swirled like a cyclone. She cobbled together an imaginary outline—aware she was taking Dino's bait. "Alrighty. Shooting a spectacular four-minute package, most reporters would begin with a perp walk, thinking they'd found the hook. Sucker bet. I'd focus on the eye-popping amount of money in Lansing Group's coffers. Then, set the hook with a fresh voice-over regarding what would happen to LG's clients if private information from the stolen laptop has been hacked. Real people. Genuine problems. And I'd put the camera on a tripod. Not that shaky stuff any idiot can shoot with a phone camera and a selfie stick."

Sydney waved her arms as she crafted the story with broad brushstrokes. "Two minutes left. I introduce details about Piper and the dirtbag ex-hubby who claims he knows a little something nasty about her. Maybe he even has a secret or two of his own. Cut back to LG's clients. Then, punch the pedal with sound bites from the undersheriff telling of his action and reaction to what is unfolding. You know, how you law enforcement guys always poke around close to home when a peccadillo has been committed. I'd also provide my own interpretation of Rule 1, or rather 1A. Then, wrap with a close-up of Piper, noting the inconvenience of her death, and how she won't be able to refute Schlub's allegation."

Sydney was drenched in satisfaction. Her silk blouse clung to every curve. "A piss-cutter package, if I say so myself." She caught Dino before he could speak. "You may think it's formulaic, but you'd be wrong. It's a raging wildfire. Viewers are hooked. Can't turn away. The payoff comes when they watch my next segment, and the next, waiting for a possible court case or other resolution. That's when I give them a kick in the teeth—the truth. Piper and Josh are the victims here."

"Not bad," Dino said. "You should produce."

"I respect their work. Without a capable producer, Watergate would've been a simple burglary. Or so I hear. I wasn't born yet. Though Woodward and Bernstein can be credited with my journalistic eminence."

"How so?"

"Because of them, my mom suggested I join the school newspaper instead of putting all my hopes on playing first base for my beloved Detroit Tigers." She tipped the soda can and emptied its contents.

"That stuff is like rocket fuel to you." Dino moved over to the window. "Reminds me . . . Our Gang Squad swept up about twenty college kids last night. Part of the street racing scene. Their roving party took over I-26 around Aviation. Caught the whole shebang on surveillance cameras—muscle cars, low-riders, even a couple of Japanese models."

"Why tell me?"

Dino offered his best cop stare. "I'm famished. You eat yet?"

To the untrained eye, his penetrating gaze might've been disarming. But Sydney sat unaffected. She wasn't buying into his patented bait-and-switch routine.

"Swear you're not involved," Dino said.

13

Sydney remained silent, her mind a whirlwind of thoughts as she processed the lieutenant's warning.

Dino added, "Street racing is reckless. Syd—you could be killed. Like the driver of a Scion. He smashed the back of a Camry, spun out of control, and slammed into a utility pole before being ejected."

"Sorry to hear." A cool shiver raced down her spine. Every death ripped a piece of her soul away. Sydney closed her eyes and pictured her late-night Jacksonboro thunder run, knowing a high-speed crash could've involved her. "Let's stay focused on Piper."

Dino returned to his chair and rested his elbows on the desk. "Stop playing coy with me, Ladybug." He glared for a beat, likely to drive home his point.

Neither person said anything for the next several minutes until Dino broke their pigheaded silence. "I have Mr. Kingston in the box. Ready to meet him?"

Sydney cried *uncle* under her breath, grateful he'd offered a way out of the corner she'd backed into. "May I see Josh first?"

"He's on suicide watch for seventy-two hours at Big Al's Casa." Dino was referring to the massive detention center on Leeds Avenue named after former Charleston County Sheriff, Al Cannon.

They ambled down to the bank of holding cells located on the first floor. Dino leaned against the door. The shaggy-haired Aaron Kingston, aka the *Schlub*, was thick enough around the middle to put his filthy Bass Pro Shop polo to a stretch test. He held onto the cell's metal bars, seeming comfortable in his surroundings, as though jail were nothing new for him. His veiled attempt at menace reminded Sydney of the SWAT commander's scowl—over-rehearsed and ineffective.

Sydney stepped forward. "I'm a friend of Piper's."

"She always did good in that department." Schlub wiped his mouth with a sleeve. "You look even better in person than on TV."

Sydney shot him an angry glance, which he must've mistaken as confusion.

"You gotta know you're hot. Am I right? I'm always right." Schlub made a mock pucker. "Mind if I touch your hair? I'm a hair guy. And those green eyes."

"Are you familiar with hashtag-MeToo and the perils of sexual harassment?"

"Oh, you're shittin' me. I'm only kidding." He hunched his shoulders. "Oops, is swearing still okay in mixed company?"

She believed men with limited vocabularies had other *short*comings as well. "Why'd you tell the detective Piper had her hand in the cookie jar at work?"

Schlub's eyes narrowed. "Lawyer."

"Do you really want a lawyer, or would you rather clear this mess up?" Sydney asked.

"What do you wanna know?"

"I want to hear why you did it."

"I did not kill her."

She threw her head back. "Ha, your emphasis on *not* is a good effort to try to deflect guilt. Keep practicing. I mean, why'd you shame Piper?"

"Wanted to hurt her, like she hurt me."

Sydney rubbed one eye with a knuckle. "Boohoo—you're breaking my heart."

"If you must know . . ." Schlub placed an elbow on the metal bar separating them and cradled his chin in his palm. "One day, Piper comes home and finds me in the sack with a bleached-blonde kitten half her age. Piper calls me an asshole. Tells me to get out—never come back. 'You've given me nothing but hell,' she says."

"So, you lied about her embezzlement to get even." Sydney stated it as fact for Dino's benefit. "Where were you when she was killed?"

Schlub's eyes began to well. Sydney read sincere grief, even though he might have murdered Piper. "Out fishing 'til two. Then, me and a couple of buddies drove over to Shem Creek—Gator Bait Saloon. Ran out of beer money around nine and bounced."

"We'll see." Sydney backed away, then Dino escorted her to the lobby.

She tapped her pen on the notebook. "You never told me what you're doing about Lansing Group's stolen laptop."

Dino shook his head. "Someone else is working that. I'm homicide, Ladybug."

Or rather, he worked in the succinctly named Crimes Against Persons bureau responsible for investigating assaults, robberies, and domestic violence—in addition to the occasional homicide.

"You can't overlook the fact that Piper's murder and the laptop are linked." Sensing she wasn't moving the needle on her theory, Sydney tried grasping. "What's the purchase date on Schlub's car and boat?"

Dino thumbed through a notepad he pulled from his shirt pocket. "April 26th. Want my advice?"

"Not particularly."

"Sit this one out. Let the undersheriff do his job." Dino twirled a pencil between his fingers like a drum major. "He's working the case the same way you did. Talking to people, collecting alibis and evidence. If Josh didn't do it, the sheriff will drop the charge."

Sydney tucked her pad into a purse pocket, then braced herself, arms akimbo.

Dino splayed his hands out in front. His reaction seemed heartfelt. "Hold on a sec. You haven't listened to a word I said."

"I always listen. I don't always comply."

"*Never* might be a more accurate account. Whatcha got planned?"

"A lady never tells."

"Yeah?" Dino winked. "What about you?"

14

Sydney wasn't about to let Dino put a hitch in her plans. Tunneling into her work meant recovering Piper's missing flash drive. Locating LG's stolen laptop. And ferreting out Velma's AWOL employee. Any or all of those things would surely go a long way toward unearthing Piper's killer.

But first, she needed to find a place to call home.

She met her realtor, Eve Martel, at a Mount Pleasant office. The woman's passion-red sundress matched her Escalade's paint color. Sydney wondered whether Eve had a whole closet full of clothes to match the car, or whether her garage was filled with expensive cars matching her wardrobe. Either way, finding a home courtesy of Charleston's Luxe Properties was going to be pricey.

Eve showed Sydney several nice houses at major golf courses, like Dunes West, River Towne, and Wild Dunes. The massive residences enjoyed breathtaking views of tidal marshes or sculpted fairways. But they reminded Sydney of Piper's super-sized place at Coosaw Creek and didn't match the cozy vibe she was seeking.

Maybe nothing ever would, because it wasn't just a cozy vibe Sydney sought; it was *her* vibe. Something akin to the effortless tranquility of her house at the old shipyard, the first place she'd ever owned. And the one by which all others would be measured.

She pondered whether she should settle for a bland rental for a while, a rebound house, so to speak. Like dating a less-than-perfect guy because you didn't want to meet Mr. Right when you were grieving Mr. Gone Forever.

Frustrated with Sydney's inability to reach a decision, Eve called it quits for the day. Passing Shem Creek, Sydney suggested a stop for drinks at the Gator Bait Saloon. The respite would allow her to discuss future showings and also afford the chance to check out Schlub's alibi.

Wide docks ran along both sides of the waterway for about a hundred yards, splitting allegiance between working fishermen and tourists. Shrimpers who'd cast off in the middle of an outgoing tide would take their day's haul to a pair of seafood wholesalers located around the bend in Hog Island Channel. Tourists had their pick from a half-dozen bars and restaurants.

The Upper Deck sat atop the Gator Bait. Both establishments were owned by two brothers unable to agree on a cohesive vision for the place, but who accepted an intersection of clientele. The Deck's cocktail bar catered to white-collar professionals awash in expensive whiskey, tequila, and rum. Unlike the *experience* patrons received upstairs, the Bait's saloon operated in a different universe with dim lighting and sticky floors. Its flavor profile included notes of skunky beer, hints of armpit slammers, and traces of month-old cigar smoke melding with the lingering aftertaste of deep-fried foods.

Sydney and Eve sipped cold sodas and nibbled from a plate of fried clams while watching dolphins loll in the creek. Their waitress knew Aaron Kingston and remembered him and his posse being at the Gator Bait on Monday during the approximate hours Schlub had offered to profess his innocence.

That meant he probably hadn't killed his ex-wife. But he still had to explain to Dino how he possessed a valuable painting, presumably looted from Piper's collection.

As they departed the saloon, Eve said, "I know I've been showing country club homes, but I have a few downtown properties you might like. Care to take a peek?"

Downtown? Why hadn't Sydney thought of that? Her heart skipped a few beats as she imagined easy access to food and drink, a convenient commute to the station, and a place within walking distance to Mandy's, her bestie.

"Sure. Let's do it," Sydney said.

They toured a magnificent sampling of quaint houses in Charleston's French Quarter, near the iconic Waterfront Park and City Gallery. Sydney fell hard for an immaculate three-bedroom, three-bath number located on a charming cobblestone street beside the Cooper River, a half block from Rainbow Row.

Nine North Adger's Wharf, named after shipping magnate James Adger, had been built within the original walled city and had no history of flooding, according to its disclosure document. Sitting high and dry was a bonus for the notoriously low-lying peninsula. The place had been converted from a cotton warehouse and factor's office into a residence sometime during the 1940s.

The reporter and realtor breezed through the ground floor's bright living area and stunning kitchen. Sydney didn't cook but knew a kitchen that looked that good held a certain vivacity. The primary suite, with a huge walk-in closet and spa bathroom, encompassed the entire second floor. As if the private courtyard off the dining room wasn't enough, the highlight of the property was a third-story rooftop terrace. What struck her most was the spectacular panoramic view of Charleston's historic downtown and harbor.

Sydney could already see herself living there and made a generous offer on the spot. The only thing preventing her from occupying that wonderful residence was Lansing Group's stubborn attorneys, who had yet to pay her insurance claim.

She returned to the TV station to share the exciting news with Mandy.

Her tale was interrupted a few minutes before 4:00 p.m., when an intern dashed to Mandy's cubicle waving a hot wire-story. Charleston police reported they'd located LG's stolen laptop—at Lansing Group.

Perhaps Sydney had goaded Dino into action after all.

She quickly prepared a script for the evening broadcast from the wire's facts.

In short, Charleston police received an anonymous tip regarding the whereabouts of the laptop. An LG spokesperson expressed relief and apologized for any inconvenience to their clients. Even so, a pair of local consumer action groups demanded LG tighten obvious gaps in their security protocols.

Sydney handed the copy to Olivia to serve as a placeholder for the top story.

Since breaking news traveled at warp speed, Sydney knew she'd be able to uncover more in the next 120 minutes before going on the air. To do so, she and Mandy raced to Lansing Group.

•

A pair of police cruisers with strobing light bars blocked LG's parking lot. Sydney flashed her press creds, and an officer waved her through. She spotted Julia Mayfair, her sparring partner from Eyewitness 13, recording a stand-up on the front steps of the main building. Sydney offered Julia a thumbs-down signal as she waltzed past.

Julia stuck out her tongue.

Classy.

Physical security at Lansing Group—the area's leading private employer—seemed tighter than the skin on a snare drum. Begging the question, if they took protective measures so seriously, how had a company laptop become lost, stolen, or misplaced?

The Action 7 duo negotiated their way through a knot of employees crowding the lobby.

"We're in a high-tech Garden of Eden," Mandy whispered.

The receptionist spun his chair in their direction. He was neatly dressed in khaki pants and a light blue, long-sleeved shirt, embroidered with Lansing Group on the right sleeve. "May I help you?"

"Sydney Quinn, Action 7 News. Gavin Lansing, please."

"Are you expected?" The young man's pretentious tone sounded so dry, you could spank dust off it.

"I know the way."

"Not so fast." He held up a palm, then ushered the two women into an interior conference room off the expansive lobby. Mandy fussed with the video camera, then handed Sydney a stick mic.

After seven dull minutes, a side door to the conference room opened.

Grace Rogers, the prickly executive assistant, made a sour face when she spotted Sydney. "You again? Follow me." She strode importantly down the hall, smoke trailing from her mouth like a leaky chimney.

"Quick question," Sydney said. "Do you think Piper stole money from the firm?"

Grace established a position in front of her desk like a bulldog standing its ground. She folded her arms and produced a stare that could vaporize most opponents without hesitation. "Is it important?"

15

Sydney debated whether to fire verbal artillery or try flattering Grace. She opted for something down the middle. "I'm nervous about my money and suspect you're in a position to help me. Also, there's a rumor that IDs may have been pilfered along with the laptop. So yeah, it's important."

"Only if you don't tell anyone this came from me," Grace said.

Sydney made a zipping motion across her lips, sensing this was Grace's prerequisite for sharing.

Grace pushed away a tumbled lock of flame-red hair. "A police detective asked me that same question. He was quite insolent. Name was Burn-something-or-other."

"Bernadino? Draymond Bernadino?"

Grace squared a cache of magazines on her desk. "His manners need retuning."

Sydney suppressed a laugh. "I'll mention your concern next time I see him."

"Anyway, I told him Piper was solid. She'd never steal from LG. Then, he barged into her office and pawed her things like a lech. Between you and me, I didn't say anything about her personal life."

"Oh? Such as . . ."

Grace glanced sideways. "Such as whose slippers are tucked under her bed. And who didn't abide that arrangement at all."

More ugly gossip Piper could neither confirm nor refute.

"Relevance?" Sydney asked.

"You tell me." Grace's five-pack-a-day gravel voice sounded as friendly as a spool of barbed wire.

Sydney played along. "Okay. Who owned the slippers?"

"Ted Armstrong, our software guru. Piper was playing footsies with him prior to her divorce. The affair may have even precipitated her split. Definitely the impetus for her paying alimony to that polecat ex-husband."

"And who didn't like Ted's cozy relationship with Piper?"

Grace glanced toward Gavin Lansing's door.

Sydney tugged at her watch. "Juicy motive. That makes it imperative I speak with Mr. Lansing."

"He's on the phone."

"What about Ted Armstrong? Where can I find him?"

"Haven't seen him since . . ." Grace's voice cracked. "You know." She sat at her desk and turned her attention to a *Wired* magazine, occasionally peeking over the top to gauge Sydney's mood.

As each droplet of condensation trickled down Grace's water glass, Sydney's blood pressure ratcheted up until she sizzled like an egg on firecracker-hot pavement. Eyeing Lansing's open door, Sydney grabbed Mandy's arm, and they darted past Grace into the commodious inner office. A bank of windows on the curved exterior wall offered a killer view of the river. Other walls combined mahogany and buffed stainless-steel paneling, draped with numerous oil paintings and etchings. If these were the trappings of success—then he'd made it.

Gavin, late forties Sydney guessed, stood when the two women approached his mammoth desk. His thinning head of auburn hair grayed at the temples. "May I help you?" He sported a harsh New England accent.

"Sydney Quinn, Action 7 News. Mind if I record this, Mr. Lansing?"

He motioned for Sydney to sit. "Call me Gavin."

She signaled Mandy to begin recording.

He said, "I suspect you want to talk about the laptop."

"Why was it reported stolen if it never left your complex? Could it have been merely misplaced? And who found it?"

Her questions flew like spears.

"Hey, Syd," Mandy said. "Maybe you could slow down and let him answer."

Gavin affixed a trained smile, but his tired-looking brown eyes seemed empty.

He added little more about the laptop than Sydney had pulled from the wire. He didn't have any idea whether the device had been misplaced or stolen, whether it had any connection to Piper, or who had made the anonymous tip leading police to the laptop. Gavin tried to close by stating his firm was cooperating with authorities.

But Sydney wasn't finished yet. "Why are companies like yours reluctant to share information about data breaches? Seems like a best practice to get in front of such issues."

"Simply put, pesky disclosures risk lawsuits and affect stock prices."

"What's your policy on co-workers sleeping together?" She didn't expect him to discuss a possible jilted relationship with Piper, but she wanted to poke a stick in the vicinity of his heavily fortified beehive.

Gavin scoffed. "The business of consenting adults isn't news, Ms. Quinn."

"But finding the person responsible for Piper's murder is top-notch. Did you kill her?"

"You can't be seriously suggesting—"

"Well, not seriously," Sydney said with mock credulity. "More half-hearted. Tongue in cheek. A real thigh-slapper."

"No need for your station to trash the victim." Gavin smoothed his sleeves. "Piper was an important member of this firm. I attribute any stress she encountered to her teenage son."

"She adored Lionel."

"Of course. But Piper always had a full plate. There simply weren't enough hours in the day for her."

"Or you?"

"Ugly rumor." Gavin twisted his wedding ring. "I'm happily married."

"As I suspected." Sydney waited for an inner voice to caution her. Hearing nothing of the sort, she plowed ahead. "What about the purported embezzlement Piper's ex-husband implied?"

"This is the first I'm hearing of that allegation." Gavin moved to put a cork in the interview by ushering Sydney and Mandy toward the hallway.

Sydney didn't believe him. Corporate embezzlement was exactly the kind of aberration a CEO would pounce on. She banked his denial in her notepad and took a leap to steer the conversation in a new direction. "What can you tell me about cybercriminals?"

Gavin paused a beat. "Not my bailiwick. Why do you ask?"

"I'm concerned whether LG can be hacked."

He launched into a well-rehearsed company tagline. "The Lansing Group manages over 80,000 clients and $700 million. We employ best-in-breed cybersecurity measures to protect our systems, data, and client information. Of course, no system is impenetrable, but we deny thousands of attack-attempts each month. That's why this laptop snafu is such an embarrassment."

"What a relief." Sydney reflexively wiped her brow. Perhaps her own money and personal information were safe after all. "This snafu, as you call it, might be construed as an inside job. If so, could any of your programmers hack encrypted client records on the misplaced laptop?"

"What would be the point?" Gavin pressed his lips together and glared. "To be clear, we neither hack nor employ those who do."

"Who's your best programmer?" Sydney asked.

Gavin pointed at the squat, middle-aged man in a black suit and police handcuffs. "Him."

16

Sydney eyed Dino marching with another plainclothes cop she didn't recognize. They led Lansing Group's top programmer through the spacious lobby. She turned to Gavin. "Who is he?"

"Ted Armstrong." Gavin shifted in confusion. "Excuse me, Ms. Quinn. I'd better find out what's happening."

Mandy yanked the video camera from its case, then chased after Dino and his quarry.

Grace sidled up to Sydney. An unlit cigarette dangled between her lips. "I overheard you ask about cybercrime. Is it for a story? Are you working on anything specific?"

"Not exactly." Sydney backed a step away to dodge the stale odor of nicotine lingering on Grace's breath. "This attempted breach hit close to home, and I discovered a gap in my education."

Grace continued her irritating tendency to smirk. "Most companies have employees who are hack victims waiting to happen. They are unsophisticated about common phishing schemes like scam emails that can unleash malware into a company's network or provide backdoor access to cybercrooks."

"Sounds eerily like squatting on a proverbial hand grenade."

"Coders are a fierce lot, Ms. Quinn. If you start probing into those who write viruses, you may be venturing out on a ledge. Be sure you have a safety net."

Sydney offered an insincere salute. "Thanks for the advice."

In the next instant, a good-looking man burst into the lobby at full speed and rushed over. "Where'd they take Ted?"

"How would I know?" Grace's smugness grew tiresome. "This is Mason Sterling, our new security consultant."

Sydney's jaw slackened and an unexpected rush surged through her.

Mason was everything she remembered, despite a fourteen-year lapse since their last encounter. He wore an expensive, neatly tailored charcoal-gray suit with chalk pinstripes, crisp French blue shirt, crimson necktie. Trademarks of a guy who'd tumbled off a *GQ* cover, and a 180 from his typical college wardrobe of jeans and a bowling shirt.

Grace continued. "And this is—"

Mason outstretched both arms. "Sydney Quinn, in the flesh. Stop my beating heart."

Grace gawked. "You two know each other?"

"What network are you with?" Mason asked.

Sydney's words sounded timorous to her ears. "Where did you—"

"Let's have dinner tonight. I'll explain everything."

Mandy raced back, clutching the camera. "I have footage of cops with the perp. Hope you can use it as B-roll."

Sydney never shifted her attention from Mason. "Lens cap off?"

"Of course, my favorite reporteress. I'm not a moron. I've been tested."

"So, dinner?" Mason said.

Mandy's glance bounced between the two.

"Bad idea," Sydney said. "Might be seen as a conflict of interest."

Grace sniped, "Mason, she might conflict with your agenda, too."

He continued ogling Sydney. "Eight o'clock. City Marina. You know it?"

"Seven," Sydney said.

"But I won't be free until—"

"Action 7 News. Here in Charleston. Perhaps you should make plans to eat alone." Sydney signaled Mandy with a tidy wave. "C'mon, we have work to do."

As the two women rolled away from Lansing Group, Sydney phoned Dino. "The LG boss's gal Friday doesn't think much of your interview tactics. Said you were a lech."

"I've been called a lot of things, but never a perv," Dino said.

"Did you arrest Ted Armstrong for Piper's murder? I didn't even have him on my radar."

"Collar belongs to Sergeant Cash."

"Because?"

"He's working with the Secret Service." He paused. "I'm not at liberty to divulge any more on the subject, Ladybug."

"At least tell me why CPD took credit for recovering the laptop rather than the feds?"

"Because we found it."

"But if it's a Secret Service case . . ." Sydney left the statement hanging, chumming for more.

A lengthier pause suggested Dino was weighing how much to offer. "We shared jurisdiction. See, Secret Service gets involved anytime a nitwit steals personal information to create fake IDs or credit cards. Or when a thief uses looted information to drain bank accounts or run up huge credit card purchases. Or whatever else suits 'em."

"How come you never told me about this sharing arrangement?" Worse, how come she'd never rooted out the cooperative venture on her own?

"I don't disclose all police business to you."

Sydney chuckled. "May I interview a very special agent?"

"Feds work out of Columbia's field office, but they deputized Mike Cash to honcho task-force business in our area. And they often place undercovers in the company they're investigating."

An undercover operative would explain the so-called anonymous tip regarding the laptop.

"That means LG is being investigated by the feds," Sydney said.

"Your conclusion, not confirmation from me."

"Seems a little too convenient. Aren't anonymous tips the hallmark of a frame-up?"

Sydney tended to avoid anonymous sources—squealers were always a gamble. Either they had an axe to grind or were reluctant, for whatever reason, to come forward publicly.

"Look, Ladybug. I disclosed more than I should've because you need closure on Piper's murder."

True. There'd be no more of her friend's sharp wit, warm smiles, or any insane ideas about food fusion.

Sydney tried to clear her head, but the finality of Piper's death had hit a bull's-eye on the grief-o-meter. "Don't go there. I have a story to tell—pure and simple."

"Murder is never simple," Dino said. "And I suppose I'm wasting my breath if I demand you stop interfering, right?"

"Piper was my friend. And I made a promise to Josh."

"Be careful, Syd. A notepad won't stop a bullet."

"I hear you, though I'm adding Ted Armstrong to my killer suspect pool. You should, too." Sydney jabbed the disconnect button.

Mandy followed Sydney with the wild eyes of someone who'd opened the door to a jam-packed closet—before everything spilled out. "Are we gonna talk about *him*?"

"Dino?"

Mandy shook her head. "He's a hunk. But I'm interested in 'City Marina, eight o'clock.'" She tried to impersonate Mason's baritone, giggling at her attempt.

Sydney admired how Mandy's brain worked. "Mason was eons ago."

"What happened?" Mandy wrapped a spool of blonde hair around her finger. "Any reason you've never mentioned him?"

"Stop gushing. He's history."

Mandy rubbed her palms together. "Methinks this is spicier than expected. Was it serious?"

"Everything's serious when you're twenty-one." Sydney drummed her thumbs on the steering wheel. "Two months from graduation and—*poof*. Mason disappeared. No fighting. No ugly breakup. He simply walked away."

Her mind ricocheted between old and new.

Mason was a former lover who'd shattered her heart into a gazillion tiny pieces, though the pain he'd inflicted was long gone. Her current prospect: Cooper Bellamy, a hotshot ATF agent, specializing in arson investigation and mending shattered hearts. She'd met Coop when someone tried to burn up Fleet Landing, a historic Charleston neighborhood. But Coop worked out of the Charlotte field office, and they only saw each other when their hectic schedules permitted.

Sydney tilted her head. "College romances have a way of being carefree. No consideration for any consequences. Let's just say Mason's father disapproved. I wasn't up to snuff, since we Quinns weren't clubbish snobs. His parents were hoping for . . . a more appropriate woman."

17

Sydney ducked into the station locker room before the evening broadcast. After considerable hair fussing and a dab of fresh lip gloss, she leaned against her producer's desk, an institutional shrine perched aloft a raised platform dubbed the altar. She hooked a finger through the slingbacks on her heels and tossed them over a shoulder.

One popular television adage claimed those with a *face for radio* were doomed to produce. Olivia Hampton was an exception. An African American with breathtaking physical attributes, the senior producer was a former Miss Sweet Potato Pie and third runner-up for the more prestigious Miss Dixie Diva.

"Your contract extension is on Pete's desk," Olivia said. "Frog's butt is watertight, if you know what I mean. And here I thought the on-air talent was only hired to be fired."

"Pete canned me three times last month," Sydney said. "I never take him seriously."

Pete Conroy, Action 7's cantankerous station manager, often reminded Sydney of her late father, who'd paid her to pull dandelions when she was a kid. Dad coveted a weed-free lawn, and Sydney pocketed spending money for baseball cards. He'd double her salary if she ever found an elusive four-leaf clover. Being a TV reporter resembled the yard work of her youth. Prior to the big hostage scoop, she'd aired a lot of dandelions and other assorted weeds.

Mandy surveyed the massive assignment board behind Olivia's workstation. "Any leftovers from your upcoming identity theft piece, Sparky? I'll add it to your blog."

"Miss Q. has a blog?" Olivia asked Mandy, ignoring Sydney.

"I call it Sydney Quinn's Tips for Better Living. *Q-Tips*, for short."

"Nice—aside from possible trademark infringement," Sydney said. "How long have I been blogging?"

"Couple of months." Mandy uploaded the blog page on Olivia's desktop.

Olivia pointed at Sydney's picture on the screen. "In my pageant days, I opted for extensions. Nothing like the natural beauty of your long brown hair."

Sydney twirled her tresses. "My hair isn't brown. This is Medium Ash 5A—and I'm worth it."

"I'm 8RB," Mandy said. "And Nick thinks natural curls run in my family."

"I can dig it," Olivia said.

Sydney laughed. "It's official—we're the new *Mod Squad*."

Mandy struck a runway pose, hand on hip, shoulders back. "One blonde, one Black, one beautiful. Now, go report the news."

Sydney took her place in Studio Control, a tiny area carved out at the edge of the frenzied newsroom. A wireless, interruptible fold-back earpiece lay in a plastic box. She pushed the IFB in place and waited for her cue following the opening montage.

"Sydney, what can you tell us about problems at Lansing Group?" the anchor asked from his seat in the main studio.

She focused on a camera mounted to the wall. "Here we go again, Nick." Sydney recapped what she'd learned about the laptop's theft and recovery, chalking the whole thing up to bad housekeeping. She suggested a potential thief was probably more interested in the computer than sensitive data on its hard drive. Sydney ended the segment with, "Thankfully, this seems, as Shakespeare put it, much ado about nothing."

The anchor teed up a scripted follow-up question. "What do we know about identity theft?"

"Identity thieves are ruthless, savvy, and not choosy," Sydney said. "The Federal Trade Commission estimates more than 16 million Americans each year are victims of the fast-growing crime, accumulating annual losses totaling more than $55 billion. And your personal information is waiting for thieves in more areas than you can imagine. The most common form of theft results from misuse of a credit card. But the Internet makes it faster for today's cybercriminals to comb your computer for passwords, accounts, and other personal information they can sell, creating misery for innocent victims, merchants, and banks caught in the crossfire. We'll stay on top of this and bring details as they develop. Sydney Quinn, Action 7 News."

•

Five minutes before eight, Sydney turned onto Lockwood Boulevard and began ruminating as though cast in a rom-com she had no interest in starring in. She mentally scolded herself for even considering hearing Mason out. She'd moved on, and she didn't need him or his flimsy excuses cluttering her life.

Mason had been a wuss, plain and simple, for walking away when things got tough. She wasn't interested in any wussy explanation he might offer, no matter how eloquently he tried to dress it up. In her mind, nothing he could say would make up for what he'd put her through all those years ago. It was like trying to put a Band-Aid on a bullet wound—pointless and a little insulting.

As she navigated the evening traffic, she chuckled to herself, imagining Mason's excuses as bad movie trailers: "Coming soon to a theater near you: *The Apology You Didn't Ask For*, starring Mason as the man who couldn't commit."

With a shake of her head, she resolved to keep her focus on the road ahead, both literally and metaphorically.

But a warm feeling hiked into her head.

She looped back at Broad Street.

A block from her destination, she changed her mind again and sailed past the marina.

Definitely not having dinner with a wuss.

Sydney continued north, passing the VA Medical Center. After crossing under US 17, she hung a left into Brittlebank Park and circled the lot until the car pointed south again.

Well, maybe drinks.

Who's the wuss now?

Sydney veered into the marina and parked next to a palmetto tree. She'd listen to his version of the disappearing act. Then, swing by Waffle House for a nosh before returning to the TV station for the late broadcast.

Time-worn brick and hurricane-tested mortar enveloped the Ashley River Yacht Club's two-story headquarters. Even the old gal's earthquake bolts had rattled on more than one occasion. Recent hard times, however, forced the stately club to lease unused space on the second deck to a real estate firm. By contrast, the adjacent marina was a spiderweb of modern floating docks branching off two stanchioned piers. The grid created fifty permanent boat docks and an equal number of day slips. *Miss Adventure*, Mason's 145-foot, neatly stacked tri-deck was moored at the head of the main pier in the deepest water.

Sydney wasn't surprised Mason owned a fine yacht. He'd spent years navigating the Great Lakes. Sailing in the Detroit Regatta. Crewing for family friends in the Chicago-to-Mackinac-Island race. Traversing the Soo Locks.

She sauntered down the long pier, dodging rope coils trailing from cleat hitches. The tangy smell of saltwater interspersed with a pungent bite of diesel exhaust from some wing nut moored at the foot of the pier and not hooked up to shore power. Sounds of lapping water and creaking boat fenders reminded her of those days when she used to hang out with other sunburned lake rats hoping to hitch a ride or water ski.

She boarded Mason's sleek yacht using the aft brow with the stinging realization he might not be aboard, since she hadn't accepted his dinner offer. She felt a pang of relief when he emerged from the salon balancing an iced Diet Mountain Dew in crystal stemware on a mahogany tray.

"I decanted this only a minute ago," Mason said. "I trust this remains your color."

"Awfully sure of yourself."

"Hardly. As I recall, you suggested I dine alone."

"Plans change." Sydney funneled the Dew, held back a belch, then blotted her lips with the back of her hand. *Always a lady.* "One more, barkeep. This is purely a curiosity tour for me."

Mason sported a troublemaker's grin, yet he seemed as suave and debonair as a matinee idol. "Would your curiosity extend to the menu for tonight's elegant repast?"

He'd always made her feel like royalty. Sheesh, he even looked edible in tight-fitting khakis.

Sydney cocked her head. "Answer one question, and I'll stay for appetizers."

"I'll answer as many questions as you want, if it'll keep you onboard." He poured another Diet Dew and dropped onto the sumptuous, cushioned sofa.

"Where did you go?"

Mason flipped his palms up, the universal sign for stalling. "It's complicated."

"C'mon, you can do better. Kinda hard to marry a guy who bails before I graduate. At least you left me at the Language Arts lab—"

"Rather than the altar?" he grinned.

"I'm not joking."

"Me neither." Mason seemed to consider his plight. "I had to leave."

Sydney blotted her lips again. "Explain."

"I . . ." He froze for a ten-count. "I found myself in a little trouble."

"What was her name?"

"No-ooh-ooh. My trouble was money." His face flushed. "I didn't have any. And I owed a lot of people."

"So, goons broke your kneecaps, and you've spent the last decade or so in the hospital?"

"You think I wanted to leave?" Mason cleared his throat. "Swear to God, I wanted to call."

"I'm glad you didn't," Sydney shot back. "I made a clean break. Carved a niche for myself without having to drag a poor anchor along for the ride. Now, I'm kind of a big deal."

Mason bobbed his head in agreement. "I asked around. You are a pillar here."

18

Sydney studied Mason for hints of deception. Alarm bells hammered in her head.

"What a crock." She swept her arms across the boat's expanse. "You come from big money. If you owed anyone, that debt would've been an easy check for Daddy to write. I'll give you five seconds to set the record straight, or I'm outta here."

"My job—" Mason stood and steepled his fingers. "Had to drop out of sight."

"You were a graduate teaching assistant. TAs don't need to disappear."

Hmm, she thought. *What kind of job requires you to go off the grid? Witness protection? International spy?*

Then, an idea hit her like a blinding flash of the obvious. He was the agent that the Secret Service had planted at Lansing Group, as Dino had alluded.

Sydney sought corroboration. "LG seems to have money and data troubles. So, they hired you as a—"

"Security consultant."

"Sure, let's call you that." She sipped from her glass before setting the expensive stemware on a teak table. She sank onto the couch and patted the cushion for Mason to join her, growing comfortable with his company, the luxury yacht, and the promise of food. "I'm thinking their money woes, laptop loss, and murder of a top employee are related. Perhaps even an inside job. Sounds like something the Secret Service might look into. Is that your assignment?"

Mason maintained a contented smile. "Are we off the record?"

"I'll go background. For now."

"Okay, off the record and on deep background—" He sucked in

a huge gulp of air before slowly exhaling. "I can neither confirm nor deny any problems related to money managed by Lansing Group."

"I'll take that as a yes." Sydney felt like a cat cornering a frightened mouse. "Is it true a Secret Service financial crimes task force is prying into LG's business practices?"

Mason offered a vague nod. "Classified."

Sydney mirrored his steepled fingers. "Welding A plus B tells me you're working undercover to identify which LG employee is up to no good."

"If you say so."

"Also explains why you disappeared fourteen years ago. That indicates you probably think you can waltz in and pick up where you left off."

"Any chance?"

"Yeah, slim and none." Sydney reached for her purse to remove a notebook, then remembered they were speaking on background. "Wait . . . I get it. You were working undercover on campus. Though it doesn't explain why you never reached out when you eventually came up for air."

"Whoa." Mason waved his hands in surrender. "You're making giant leaps based on faulty assumptions."

She wanted to kick herself for not outing him as a secret agent. Of course, it'd taken a few years on-the-job to hone her Spidey skills. Back then, he'd successfully misled her, prompting her to question everything. Their infatuation. His facile proposal.

Did you love me—even a little?

Sydney glanced into his watery blue eyes. Had they always been that bright?

She shook it off and returned to the conversation. "Faulty assumptions? If you say so."

"Let's eat." Mason jumped to his feet and opened the slider leading into the salon. "You must be hungry. As I recall, you were always hungry, because you never cooked."

He escorted Sydney to the table stylishly arranged for dinner. He moved aside the chafing tray cover and plated baked rice and shrimp purloo—a concoction of bell peppers, onions, celery, tomatoes, and saffron.

"Everything smells divine," she said. "Food here is so different from our Midwest roots. Mom's idea of a fresh herb is a new jar of spice mix." She licked a spoonful of lemonade pie. "For the record, many people have eaten my cooking and gone on to lead normal lives."

The strain of lost years erased from her conscience.

Mason sat beside her and took her hand. "I know it's just shrimp, but where do we stand?"

"We have a history. I won't be neutral. If LG is dirty, I'll find it and report it. Classified or not."

"To be clear, I was asking about us."

Sydney winked. "I know."

Mason forked a bite and grinned.

They melted into happy talk, and thirty easy minutes passed before Sydney helped him tote dirty dishes to the galley. "Thank you for dinner. And I like your boat."

"You never told me where you live?"

Sydney pictured her torched place at the old shipyard versus the plush hotel room. "It's complicated."

Mason arched an eyebrow. "C'mon, aren't we beyond hemming and hawing?"

She explained about her house fire and the suit she'd filed against LG. She didn't mention making an offer on the Adger's Wharf property.

Mason bonked his forehead with an open palm. "I have a great idea. You can live here. Until you sort everything out."

"No way. We aren't—"

"I'm living in a house I inherited on Kiawah Island." Mason held out a keychain with a single key attached. "This opens the salon door. She's all yours. Long as you need. No strings."

The key reminded Sydney of the one he'd given her to his apartment years ago. Always a gentleman, only once a jerk.

She wanted to shout a full-throated 'yes,' but tempered her enthusiasm by pinching her leg. "Are you sure? I've been a little mean-spirited tonight."

"Nothing more than I had coming. Let me do this for you. Please."

Sydney reached for the key. "Well, if you insist."

Came for dinner. Stayed for the excuses—and earned a magnificent yacht.

•

At midnight, Sydney slid open the thick glass doors and stepped onto *Miss Adventure's* roomy aft balcony, feeling like a femme fatale, albeit one with a penchant for late-night snacking. She inhaled a handful of cherry tomatoes dunked in ranch dressing while she waited for the Chinese delivery guy to bring her Mandarin beef— culinary choices that'd make any nutritionist raise an eyebrow.

She stared out over the water, the moment suspended in time.

The sky was a canvas of luminous jewels, with stars twinkling like the eyes of a mischievous accomplice, partially hidden by high-scudding clouds. A velvety breeze teased her face, playing with the loose wisps of her hair.

The boat basin was alive with a symphony of nocturnal sounds. Oysters clicked in the pluff mud like tiny castanets, a great blue heron offered a rusty squawk that could have been mistaken for a disgruntled saxophonist, and halyards clanged against aluminum masts like church bells. Hypnotic waves lapped against fiberglass hulls, though the rusty tub nearby continued to fart diesel fumes, adding a touch of gritty realism to the scene.

Sydney had many bad habits, but falling hard for an old beau wasn't one of them. Even so, accepting the yacht might've been flirting with disaster. She promised herself to be smart about Mason.

Keep him at arm's length—or farther.
    But dammit . . .
    Tingly feelings were finding their way back in.
    And she liked it.

19

Sydney spilled out of bed around eight-thirty, nursing a mild headache and craving mushroom and spinach quiche. She opened the aft deck slider to survey the morning. Two shrimp trawlers and an oyster boat were making their daily pilgrimage down the Ashley River. Every ounce of color on the horizon looked as if it came from an artist's palette—an eye-popping mix of cerulean sky with thin, cheeky pink clouds.

Her mind shifted into work mode, especially since her investigation into Piper's murder had stalled.

Police investigators could easily discard their two likeliest suspects, Josh Andrews and Aaron Kingston. Gavin Lansing and Ted Armstrong both made Sydney's list, though she had little to connect them besides gossip. She pinned her hopes on finding who'd taken Piper's flash drive, unless something better popped up.

She checked her phone on the way to the galley for a Diet Dew and discovered a voicemail from Mandy. Ted had been released last night after police finished questioning him about the recovered laptop and potential data breach. Mandy arranged for Sydney to meet him later. Instinct told her Ted should be able to shed new light on Piper's murder along with Mason's covert employment.

She dressed in a pair of navy capris with tiny white anchors and a silk blouse. After swinging by the Francis Marion to retrieve her valise and check out, she made the drive over the bridges to The Golden Crust's most trendy eatery.

The Golden Crust was a hybrid *boulangerie-pâtisserie* located next to a Food Lion supermarket, four blocks from Lansing Group. They specialized in artisanal breads and scrumptious pastries. Casual lines of patrons weren't unusual, but today an unexpected throng, three abreast, snaked past the café's storefront.

Sydney flagged a young couple wearing khakis and white polos seated on the curb. "Is this line for the French bakery?"

The male in khakis waved a sheet of paper. "Free quiche coupons."

She'd memorized the bakery's quiche-of-the-day menu but wasn't clued in on any coupons.

He added, "Came in an email. I normally delete spam. But, hey, it's free food."

Sydney circled the block and found a car exiting the Food Lion. She jockeyed for the vacancy ahead of a Range Rover. Leaving the top down on her T-bird, she hefted her newspapers and glided to the head of the bakery's long line.

Cutting was a perk of celebrity.

Rhapsody, the harried assistant manager, ducked behind the counter and called into the kitchen. "Slice the mushroom quiches smaller. The coupon says they get a free one, doesn't say what size." She tossed fistfuls of coupons into a plastic box. "How much longer on the asparagus?"

Sydney elbowed her way behind the counter. "Seems like poor form to offer free quiche without letting me know."

"Finally, a friend." Rhapsody threw her arms around Sydney. "I'm tearing my hair out. The owner isn't here yet and didn't leave word about a coupon promotion. We've been swamped since I opened the doors. Any ideas?"

"I can help take money."

Antsy customers grew edgier. A few mumbled obscenities.

Sydney faced the crowd. "C'mon, people. You'll get what you came for. The staff is doing their best to serve you. Let's cut 'em some slack." She moved to the coffee machine and held up a take-out cup and a *pain au chocolat*. "How much are these?"

"Coffee is four dollars, plus tax," Rhapsody whispered. "Croissants are five."

Sydney shouted, "Okay, folks. I'm serving hot coffee. Ten dollars, and I'll throw in a chocolate croissant, in lieu of quiche, if you hand over your coupon and leave quietly. Any takers?"

The line surged forward waving sawbucks, eager to accept the new offer.

It took twenty minutes to thin the herd, after which Sydney sauntered to a small booth at the café's rear, carrying a plate piled with mushroom and spinach wedges. She'd paid full price and was savoring every bite. The Paris Saint-Germain football team was playing Bayern Munich on a large, wall-mounted, flat-screen TV. A shelf next to the television held an assortment of PSG memorabilia, including a team banner, Mbappé action figure, and scarf.

Rhapsody dashed over, even more frantic than she'd seemed during the quiche rush. "The owner just arrived. Help me explain to him what happened," she pleaded.

Sydney pointed at the newspapers. "I'm catching up—"

"He thinks I'm responsible for the mess. Please?" Rhapsody was on the verge of sobbing but managed to wrangle Sydney's elbow and tug her toward the kitchen.

Sydney was overcome with a new wave of hunger when she spotted the rear prep area piled with assorted breads, fruits, and cheeses. She reached for a strawberry before making a quick tally. The kitchen included a high-end commercial stove and oven, and a small walk-in cold storage anchored with those heavy vertical blinds—both fun and creepy to push through.

The owner, Hugo Dupont, a man she knew well, was thin with a stubborn jaw elongated by whiskers shaped carefully into a point. Emerging from a tiny office adjacent to the built-in dishwasher, he pushed up silver-framed glasses. "Sydney, what are you doo-eeng?"

The song-like quality of his accent was always pleasing to her ear. Wiping her mouth with the back of her hand, Sydney dropped the strawberry's leafy top into a garbage bowl. She glanced over her shoulder, but Rhapsody had disappeared. "I'm here to answer questions about this morning's coupon crisis, Monsieur Dupont."

The owner wet his lips. "Is this for your Action 7 News? The station that begins their broadcast with 'Good Evening,' then proceeds to tell you why it isn't." A wide smile broke across his face. "No funny business, right, *mon ami*?"

"Right."

After a moment, his bright eyes flickered—a decision had been reached. "Please, call me Hugo. Come, I have something *très dommage* to share with you." He motioned Sydney into the office. "This morning, you helped sell my croissants and coffee, *oui*? You made money for my bakery despite people stealing my quiches." He shook his head. "I didn't send coupons."

Hugo pointed at the computer and raised his voice. "You tell me—is the *bête* who sent coupons also the same *bête* who did this after my morning rush?"

Sydney settled in an uncomfortable chair and jiggled the computer's mouse. The screen filled with a strange message: *YOU'VE BEEN BIZNAPPED.*

Hugo tapped his finger on the screen. "What is biznap? I don't understand. And all my registers are locked up. Nothing works. I can't access my payroll file, my menus, my inventory." He patted his head. "You click mouse and see what happens next."

Sydney did as he instructed. The screen changed to a message containing instructions for paying a ransom to obtain some sort of password that would purportedly unlock Hugo's hijacked computer. The cost for the password—eight grand.

She felt an instant rage that his business was being targeted. "I've never seen anything like this. Did you call the police?"

Hugo slapped his palm on the desk. "Message say, 'no police.' I must pay eight thousand to get my files back. Golden Crust is dead without files and inventory."

"But if you pay the ransom, there's no guarantee whoever is behind this will give you the password," Sydney protested. "Or whether the password will even work. I think your business is being electronically robbed."

"Robbery same as *biznapped*?"

"I think it's like kidnapped," Sydney said. "Biz—short for business." She drummed her fingers on the desktop. The bogus coupon and biznapping scheme were likely synchronized to disable Hugo's business. And the $8,000 ransom was two grand below the transaction threshold triggering mandatory reporting by reputable banking establishments.

Sydney captured a screenshot of the ransom instructions with her cell phone's camera. She'd find a way to involve the police without harming Hugo.

He asked, "What are you thinking? You have a plan?"

Computer viruses were outside of Sydney's considerable expertise. "Your computer has been hacked. Do you have any idea who would do this?"

Hugo shook his head. "Many friends here, just like you, *mon ami*."

"Do you know what happens if you don't pay?"

"Files lost. Tax problems. *Très mauvais*."

"Very bad," she agreed. "But how can you be certain the hacker will send the crypto key you need?"

Hugo took a plate from the sous chef and slid a mushroom quiche with a generous side of strawberries in front of Sydney. "This isn't the first time this happens."

"What?" Sydney choked on the forkful filling her mouth.

"I know others who pay. And now, they're okay." He told Sydney about three other delis and restaurants on The Golden Crust and two in North Charleston he knew that'd been hijacked.

Sydney jotted the names and contacts. "How can I help?"

"You figure out who is the *bête*—and put them out of biznap biz."

She acquiesced.

"Good quiche, no?"

"*Très bien*." She blew a small chef's kiss. "You have a little time until the ransom is due. That gives me a chance to bring in an expert to look at your system." Sydney swept the last of the quiche crumbs into her mouth. She knew the restaurant industry was challenging enough without being extorted.

By 3:00 p.m. tomorrow, she'd know exactly how this story would shake out.

20

Sydney never liked to admit she was punching above her weight class, though she recognized the critical need for a cyber-guru. Even if it meant taking her focus temporarily off Piper's murder.

She headed to Grand Oaks Station in West Ashley. The row of boutique stores consisted of seven high-end profit machines painted a rainbow of cheery sherbet colors like lemon zest and tangerine mist. All Geek to Me occupied the key-lime center unit.

The store's concrete floor and exposed ductwork redefined unassuming retail. Industrial showroom shelving displayed scads of new and refurbished electronics. Posters encouraging people to recycle, save the planet, and reduce waste lined the walls. Sydney hailed a twenty-something wearing saggy blue jeans and an Earth Day 2015 T-shirt.

"Moose Barton, at your service. Man, you're a looker."

"Thanks, I guess."

"I saw your report about the laptop. You were right on the mark. Everyone knows the only reason to steal a device is to pawn the hardware. You gotta know hackers can pirate IDs or forage proprietary information without physically possessing hard drives."

"Precisely the angle I'm working," Sydney fibbed. "Brings me to today's challenge. I need info regarding the black web."

Moose blurted out a laugh. "Dark web."

"That's the one. How do I access it? Do I need a sherpa?"

"Only a Tor browser."

"Huh?"

"Tor is free software for anonymous Internet communication. It's intended to protect users' privacy. Anything else?"

Sydney scrunched her lips to one side. "At the risk of sounding redundant, how do I do it?"

"Simply download a verified Tor browser. But be careful. Plenty of frauds out there waiting to infect your system. My best advice is to register using a strong alias. Something like venom—but spell it capital V, number 3, lower case n, zero, lower case m. And never ever give your actual name or anything personal. Besides those guardrails, the dark web's perfectly safe and an important tool for reporters such as yourself." He suggested a pair of sites for her to explore.

Sydney was still confused but suspected Mandy had the know-how to help her with access. She pointed to dozens of used laptops, processors, and monitors haphazardly arranged. "What are these?"

Moose hitched his pants. "Trade-ins or drop-offs. Customers score a discount when they bring in old stuff. We recycle or ensure proper disposal to preclude all those lithium-ion batteries and mercury-laced motherboards from corroding landfills and leaching into our drinking water." He recounted how the store repaired and rebuilt components, then gave them to lower-income kids. "Most come from people discarding old gadgets. Many companies in town donate, too. I suppose they take a tax write-off, though we aren't a non-profit. Recycling is a whole lot better than dumping. The dumps already contain over a million tons of e-waste."

"Ever come across any stolen devices?"

He pulled a stool from behind the counter and offered Sydney a seat. "I always check serial numbers through the tri-county stolen property database. As I said, anything of value would be pawned." He smoothed his sideburns. "You know, a week ago, some lanky dude carrying a federal badge scared the crap-arooni out of me. Asked to see my intake files looking for a specific laptop. Lucky for me, my business partner and I do everything by the book."

Sydney nodded like a dashboard bobblehead doll.

Either the feds were psychic or Velma was the worst secret

informant ever. Sydney had to wonder whether Velma had intentionally misrepresented how long the laptop had been missing. And if so, why?

Sydney purchased an original Simon, the 1978 Milton Bradley memory game, for Mandy. The piece would fit nicely beside her Atari Pong unit. The toys weren't antique in the classic sense. According to Mandy though, they were technology relics. Sydney preferred collecting a Magic 8 Ball or an Etch A Sketch.

Moose added, "You'd be surprised what people leave on hard drives."

Sydney raised an eyebrow. "Such as?"

"Outrageous stuff. I found student records on old school equipment and a mess of customer credit card information from a department store laptop they were tossing. Totally wicked. But I ensure nothing goes outta here unless it's wiped slick."

"Know anyone into ransomware?"

"Not my jam." Moose shoved his hands in his front pants pockets. "Bad juju."

•

Sydney returned to the TV station at ten-thirty and discovered Olivia had dispatched Mandy on assignment. She'd have to figure out the intricacies of Tor and the dark web on her own.

She scanned the newsroom, the place she'd worked for nearly eight years. Action 7 had five editing bays lining the back wall—six-by-six-foot soundproof booths crammed with ancient recording and temperamental playback equipment. From there, a reporter could record simple tags or prepare packages without tying down a camera operator or sound technician.

She moved into Editing Bay 5, her inner sanctum, and admired the wallpaper, the city's iconic double diamond bridge image along with a soaring bald eagle, the ubiquitous logo for Eagle News Network, Action 7's parent company. As much as Sydney loved a live broadcast, she welcomed spending time in the trenches. She plugged an Internet cable into her laptop and dug in with a quick tutorial.

Tor was an acronym for The Onion Router, initially developed by the US Navy. Their goal had been to prevent anybody from watching what sites a user visited, affording relative anonymity by bouncing communications around a distributed network of more than seven thousand relays wrapped in complex and random layers of encryption—like an onion.

The folks who created the network had a wonderful sense of humor.

Nowadays, anonymity needed a big ole asterisk next to it, since trying to conceal online activities and Internet protocol addresses came with a whole slew of caveats. Using Tor or Virtual Private Networks—called VPNs by the cool kids—made IPs hard to track, but not impossible.

Next, Sydney discovered the Internet was really comprised of three parts she pictured like an iceberg. The most visible above-the-surface web was easiest to access for day-to-day activities, using standard search engines and web browsers that didn't require special configuration.

The largest chunk hiding just below the surface was called the deep web. It wasn't indexed or accessible by ordinary search engines. Users required specific addresses to find websites or services. Many deep-web sites supported applications the general public used every day, such as social media or banking websites, but didn't need to access.

A tiny bummock on the bottom of the berg was home to the dark web. That secretive place, largely unregulated and requiring specialized software to access, became infamous for criminals and other malicious actors buying and selling drugs, weapons, malware, and stolen data. Even so, Sydney was relieved to learn network news organizations also operated on the dark web to protect confidential sources.

She rubbed her jaw with the heels of her hands. She hadn't realized she'd been clenching her teeth during the preliminary research. What she planned next was perfectly legal, but it felt like she was about to touch an ethical third rail. It'd be easy for a newbie like her to flounder in virtual quicksand or get zapped.

Sydney checked her notes before downloading a Tor browser, then established her profile using the *V3nOm517* username suggested by the Geek store salesman. She invented a longer, more complicated password combining random numbers, letters, and symbols. She typed in a dot-onion address with the cautious calm of a second-story cat burglar.

Sydney quickly stumbled into a sketchy private chat forum where she received a vulgar initiation. After weighing the risks, she eventually set up a meet with someone willing to provide a legit local street address.

The dark web: the *anti*social side of the Internet.

Sydney closed the Tor browser, then wiped the application from her laptop.

Next, she conducted a search for past ransomware attacks and learned it was big business, both in terms of losses and paid ransoms. Victims ranged from small organizations to giant conglomerates in nearly every sector of American commerce and government, including pharmaceutical, energy, automotive, advertising, municipalities, hospitals, movie studios, and colleges. Massive breaches like at Garmin, Canon, and Carnival Cruise made headlines. But most attacks occurred with little fanfare.

Such was the case at The Golden Crust.

21

Sydney needed to clear her head, so she decided to meet Dino at The Midway, a place that was part amusement park, part therapy session. It boasted an assortment of arcade games, go-karts, and a driving range, the kind of place where you could lose yourself in the chaos and maybe find a little mental clarity between rounds of Skee-Ball.

The Midway was known for its chili dogs, a culinary delight that could make even the most hardened journalist smile. But this afternoon, Sydney wasn't in a chili dog frame of mind. She was more in the mood for a side of introspection with a dash of humor, the kind that only Dino could provide.

The batting cage was her favorite activity. With a bat in her hands, she could leave problems in the rearview and take a swing at whatever the day had in store, one baseball at a time. She plunked a handful of tokens into the machine and set the pitch speed at seventy miles per hour. Sydney tucked her hair up under a helmet and took a few practice swings before pressing the button to engage the hurler. The first pitch came at her like a freight train. She swung and missed.

Grumbling a host of her favorite expletives, she steadied. The next ball crossed on the outside of the plate, so she slammed it into pretend bleachers in right field. The cage was equipped with laser sensors measuring ball flight and distance. Fake crowd-roar sounded when Sydney slammed the third pitch over the center wall for another homer. She doffed her helmet, pretending to round an imaginary third.

"Two in a row." Dino leaned against the cage. "Let me see you do it again."

"No problem."

He moved to the control panel. "How 'bout a little extra salsa?"

The pitch screamed past Sydney at eighty-eight miles per hour—a decent college fastball. She let it go without taking a cut. She settled into the batter's box and gritted her teeth but swung late and fouled the next ball off.

Sydney flexed her fingers on the bat.

Another one came low and away—sucker pitch. She let it go without swinging. The mechanical pitching arm reloaded and sent the ball belt-high across the plate. Sydney took a hefty swing and computerized fans roared approval.

She signaled Dino to pause the machine so he could climb in the cage and take a few cuts. He selected an aluminum bat.

She scoffed, then handed him a thirty-three-ounce Louisville maple gem. "Aluminum is for middle-schoolers. You need real lumber."

Dino situated his helmet and stepped into the box. "If you say so."

When he nodded, Sydney switched on the machine. The first pitch came inside. Dino swung and fouled the ball high into the netted cage. The next pitch came right down the pike. He lofted a long ball and the synthetic crowd cheered. He tugged his helmet and readied himself. "Child's play," he said.

"We'll see about that." Sydney jacked the machine to ninety-three miles per hour—an indisputable major league fastball.

Dino never stood a chance.

As the pitch steamrolled toward the plate, Dino stuck out the bat in defense. The ball kicked the darn thing clean out of his hands and knocked him off his feet.

Sydney scrambled to press pause before another ball tore his head off. "Sorry, I thought you could handle it."

Dino brushed at a patch of road rash on his elbow, seeming eager to change the subject. "I spoke to Piper's son—"

"Lionel."

"Drove over to College of Charleston. Took me a while, but I finally caught him between classes to give him the bad news about his mom."

"How'd he handle it?"

"Asked me who killed her—his dad or her boss?"

Sydney hiked an eyebrow. "Interesting."

"And there's more regarding the dirtbag ex," Dino said. "The guy won't shut his yap about their bitter split. Keeps repeating neither of them was the happily-ever-after kind. Both alley cats, like he told you. Came and went as they pleased."

"I guess the clean, dirty, and otherwise finds its way into the sunshine after you're gone." Sydney disliked gossip, especially about someone she respected. "What about Gavin Lansing?"

"No reason to suspect him. The undersheriff has Josh Andrews dead-bang. Remember?"

"Yeah, right. Still waiting for him to correct that travesty of justice."

Dino said, "Before coming here, I met with Sergeant Cash, our task force liaison. He gave me copies of several financial statements from LG. See, he's conducting a forensic audit and thinks at least $60,000 has disappeared. Matches what Piper's ex-hubs said she gave him."

"Not what I expected, though I still don't believe she misappropriated any money." Sydney yanked off the batting helmet and fluffed her hair. "Did you know the task force started searching for LG's laptop at least a week before your recovery?"

Dino's frown deepened. "Wasn't aware they'd been at it so long."

"But you knew they were involved and didn't tell me?"

"Yeah, I'm funny like that," he said. "Here's a heads-up. No attribution or release."

"I hate when you say things like that," Sydney protested. "Tell me."

"Crime scene techs found Ted Armstrong's prints on the laptop."

"You should confront him with that incriminating evidence. See if he cops to Piper's murder."

"Can't connect the two events with only stray prints." Dino cleared his throat. "The lab also recovered Josh's prints on the four-iron. No surprise, since he didn't deny that it's his club. Lastly, Josh's DNA was found under Piper's nails. Tells me she tried to fight him off."

Sydney skewed her mouth to one side. "Josh said he tried to help her. That's when she scratched him."

"One version." Dino glared at the pitching machine. "Just wanted you to know, Mike Cash will give Piper a fair shake on the embezzlement claim."

"Suppose you could set up a meeting?"

He rubbed the back of his neck. "Am I your errand boy?"

"If you insist." Sydney plopped down on a picnic table and changed the subject. "Know anything about ransomware?"

"Definitely out of my strike zone, but I'm aware gangs are overtaking the web—organized criminals hell-bent on illicit financial gain. Not to mention the Nigerian and Ghana scams."

"Superstars in the web's underground."

"You hoping to expose players from the dark web?" Dino asked.

"You bet, especially when they're operating in my coverage area."

"Whoa, you can't drop a bombshell like that without elaboration."

"I'm working with the owner of The Golden Crust. His business was hacked. The hijacker locked his computers and threatened to erase everything unless he pays eight grand."

"I knew ransomware was a common threat."

"If you're targeted, you have to go through a complicated process of paying criminals using untraceable cryptocurrency without any certainty you'll be rewarded for obliging the extortion."

Dino said, "Our department doesn't have a cybercrime unit. I'd have to contact SLED or the financial crimes task force."

Sydney knew SLED was short for State Law Enforcement Division, a South Carolina agency comprised of more than three hundred agents, criminalists, and technicians. SLED provided local cops with expertise across the board—from human trafficking to background checks.

"Sounds like another job for Mike Cash," she said.

"Yeah, he'd know where to plug in." Dino shook his head. "Forgot to mention, I'm supposed to back off talking to Armstrong."

"Why?"

"One, because it isn't my case. And *B*, Cash is probably flipping him to uncover more about the bogus money issues at Lansing Group."

"Are you at least warming to him as a possible suspect for Piper's murder?"

"Only saying I hate being benched—for any reason."

Sydney winked. "Good thing I'm not a cop."

Dino eyed the stack of bats. "That last one—"

"A Verlander changeup," Sydney said, referring to her favorite former Detroit Tigers ace. "You'll catch it next time."

"Doubt it. But I can drain a three-pointer from anywhere on the arc."

22

Sydney returned to The Golden Crust for her appointment to meet Ted Armstrong, armed with new information from Dino. She spotted Ted slumped at a table along the back wall as she snaked her way through the late lunch crowd.

Ted gave Sydney a quick, impulsive handshake. "Saw you at LG last night. Hoped maybe you could help me." He wore blue jeans and a wrinkled Member's Only jacket partially obscuring the graphic design on his T-shirt. "What did Gavin say when the cops yanked me out? Did he seem surprised?"

Sydney ignored the small talk and dived in, hoping to throw him off balance. "I understand you two were rivals for Piper's affection."

Ted shifted in his seat.

The tension in his jaw signaled she was losing him, so she chose a different tack. "Gavin told me client money is safe at LG, but law enforcement officials have discovered at least $60,000 is missing."

Ted didn't flinch.

Disappointed, Sydney added, "They think Piper took it. Cops matched it to her ex-husband's claim she recently gave him fists full of cash in overdue support." Though Sydney felt sure of her friend's innocence, she had to concede that Piper's financial windfall didn't look good on paper.

Ted flopped his head against the wall and rested his hands on the table. "I've done a lot of stupid things. I even have a police record— that'll come out eventually. But I swear I didn't steal the laptop."

"Your fingerprints were on it."

Ted's eyes widened. "I'm being framed."

"By whom?"

"I told the cops I had no idea how or why the laptop was found in our workshop. I didn't steal it. Honest truth, Mrs. Quinn." Ted hung his head, his voice saturated in desperation.

"Call me Sydney." The *Mrs.* label reminded her she owed her mom a phone call. She continued to press. "Where were you when Piper was killed?"

"You make it sound like I need an alibi."

"It's probable."

"Okay, I left work around noon. Was headed to Piper's . . ." The realization of placing himself anywhere near the scene of her murder registered in his blinking eyes. He tried to pull out of a looming death spiral by whacking his forehead. "Wait. I'm getting boggled up. I didn't kill her. I worshiped Piper."

Sydney knitted her hands.

He turned his head as if struggling to control his grief. "Got a call to meet my business partner. Didn't get home until after seven."

"How about the anonymous tip regarding the laptop?"

"We have piles of hardware. No one would notice another laptop in our workspace. I'm being set up."

"Why?" she asked.

Ted shifted in his seat again and bit his lip. "You can't believe how hard this is. I've been making funeral arrangements with Lionel. You coming?"

Sydney searched his face for sincerity.

He took a breath and laid his palms face up on the table, which Sydney interpreted as a sign he wasn't afraid to be vulnerable. "I miss her." Ted dropped his gaze.

"Me too," Sydney said with the ghost of a smile. "Do you know who killed her?"

"Lionel picked out a nice casket. A walnut number with pink velvet inside. Carnations and roses for the spray."

She refused to buy into the distraction. "It wasn't her dirtbag ex-schlub. Am I right?"

No one spoke for a minute. Then Ted said, "How should I know?"

"Because I believe you know who killed Piper," Sydney said. "And for someone who claims to care about her, you don't seem too invested in helping find her killer or the laptop thief."

He blinked. Then his shoulders sagged again. "That isn't true. I phoned Moose once they released me. He's swinging by LG after everyone leaves tonight so we can check security video."

"Met a guy named Moose at a computer store this morning."

"That's him. He's my business partner and a coding prodigy. Even better than me at his age. He did the art for this." Ted removed his jacket, revealing a shirt covered in ones and zeros. "These are the lyrics to The Beatles' *White Album*. His high school AP computer project. Moose also created concert tees for Placental Gush, Toe Jamz, and Navel Lint."

Sydney felt out of touch. When did bodily functions become super chill names for garage bands?

"I can't read binary code," she said. "But I bought a Simon game from Moose's store."

"Solid purchase," Ted said. "Lots of unused memory. It'll triple in value in the next couple of years. You a gamer?"

Sydney shook her head.

Ted hesitated before advancing the conversation. "Do you know the story of the Trojan horse? Or 'Aeneid?'"

"Why?"

"No reason." He pointed to her soda can. "Had to give up caffeine. Stuff burned a crater in my stomach." Ted took a slug of water, then put his hands over his face. "Piper was never flush with money—she intended to put it back."

Sydney leaned forward. "You're lying."

Ted looked away. "Gavin hopes to raise operating capital for an expansion, so he's taking the firm public. Piper and I have plenty tied up in future shares. We planned to leave LG right after cashing in on the IPO."

Sydney pounded her hand on the table.

Ted jerked back. "Sydney, I—" He broke off. Wouldn't let himself speak. He wiped the back of his hand across his nose. "Piper would be pleased, you taking up for her. You're right—she never stole any money. I don't know why I said that. I gave her cash from my savings. Wanted her ex to leave us alone."

The newest version of his story was the one Sydney wanted to believe. Of course, it didn't explain the missing sixty grand from LG's coffers. Or why Ted was offering ricocheting explanations about the money.

"No way to come at this sideways," Sydney said, "so, I'll ask straight up. Are you working with Sergeant Cash as an informant? Perhaps in return for immunity."

Ted's voice tightened. "He asked for my help."

Dino had guessed right.

"More please," Sydney prodded.

Ted hunched his shoulders, and Sydney understood he either couldn't or didn't want to divulge any more regarding his federal connection. Probably so he wouldn't risk whatever advantage he was receiving in return.

Sydney said, "Let's rewind to the frame-up you mentioned. Who do you think is behind it?"

"They'll kill me."

"Who? Aren't the feds protecting you?"

Hugo, the bakery's owner, placed a hand on Sydney's shoulder. "What is all this commotion?"

Sydney maintained a lasered gaze on Ted.

Hugo continued. "This is computer expert to fix my biznap, no?"

Sydney snapped, "No! I mean—"

"What's *biznap*?" Ted asked.

"Biznap is terrible," Hugo said. "You join me in my kitchen—now." He pulled Ted to his feet and elbowed his way toward the office with Sydney in their wake.

Sydney nudged Ted toward the uncomfortable chair. "Gavin

said you're his best programmer. What do you think about this?" She wiggled the mouse until the *YOU'VE BEEN BIZNAPPED* message appeared.

Ted rubbed a hand over his bristled jaw. He tapped a few keys but the computer didn't respond. He clicked the mouse and the ransom instructions filled the screen. "Do you have any other computers hooked up to this network?"

Hugo pulled a laptop from a briefcase beside the desk, and Sydney could sense Ted's wheels turning.

Ted booted up the laptop and found the same messages. He locked his fingers behind his head and tipped back in the chair. "I've seen this before. What are your intentions?"

Hugo and Sydney glanced at each other.

Sydney spoke first. "Against my advice, Hugo wants to pay the ransom and reclaim his files."

Ted eyed Hugo. "No guarantee you'll receive the crypto key—"

Hugo waved a hand. "I know. Key may never come. Key may not work. I have to try, no?"

Ted sat up straight. "Do you have your ISP bill?"

Hugo scrunched his lips. "What is ISP?"

Ted's tone grew confident. "ISP—Internet Service Provider."

Sydney translated for Hugo. "He needs your Three Rivers Communications bill."

Hugo pulled out a copy from a desk drawer and slid it over. Ted grabbed the landline and phoned Three Rivers's customer assistance. After a little jockeying for information, he scribbled a series of numbers on a scrap of paper.

Sydney asked, "What's the plan?"

"I'm going to add a patch of code," Ted said. "I'll attach a tracer worm to the ransom payment and see where the money gets routed. Odds are, it won't work. But it's worth a try. Could lead us to the hacker's IP address."

Sydney considered that for a moment. For all she knew, Ted

harbored the skills to transfer Hugo's ransom payment directly into his own account, leaving the bakery high and dry. Yet he'd proffered a tried-and-true investigative technique—follow the money.

"Can we trust you?" she asked.

Ted made a placating gesture toward Hugo. "I'll front the ransom. Your café won't be out a nickel."

Hugo clapped him on the back and smiled at Sydney. "*Je t'aime bien* this biznap expert."

Ted smiled and finished keying in essential information, then Hugo shooed them from his kitchen.

In the dining room, Sydney placed a hand on Ted's arm. "Thanks for what you did for Hugo."

He spread his hands. "Just remember, Piper isn't mixed up in any of this mess. In return, please keep her name out of it."

23

After meeting Ted, Sydney was buzzing with adrenaline. Leads were piling up faster than a stack of pancakes at an all-night diner, and she was ready to chase them down.

Her next stop was The Seafood Company, a popular Gullah restaurant in Awendaw, a tiny coastal fishing village. It was the kind of place where the fish was always fresh, the gossip was fresher, and the ambiance came straight out of a Conroy novel.

The address had come from her dubious dark-web contact, a shadowy figure who probably spent more time in front of a computer screen than in the sunlight. Sydney couldn't help but chuckle at the thought of meeting such a character in a quaint fishing village. It was like expecting a supervillain to show up at a school's bake sale.

As she drove, the road wound through marshlands and past weathered shacks, the scenery as atmospheric as a black-and-white film. She could almost hear a sax playing in the background, setting the mood for whatever intrigue awaited.

With a smirk and a steady grip on the wheel, Sydney recalled a story from a year earlier, when two lug nuts tried to hole up near there after spree-robbing a series of convenience stores. They'd hidden aboard a fishing trawler but were discovered by the shrimper's crew the next morning, passed out—plastered on Bud Light and covered in nacho chip crumbs. The crew had balled the pair in a net, hoisted them over the side, and dunked 'em in the briny. The soggy thieves proved an easy arrest for Charleston County's sheriff and an exquisite visual for TV news.

This time, she came for an assignation with an alleged black-hat hacker she'd met in a sketchy chat room. The hacker had insisted the interview take place off the record. Despite the regrettable stipulation, the hacker promised to provide background and a glimpse into cybercrime's shadowy underbelly. Or as the source put it, "Deep, deep, deep—underlined, with an exclamation point—deep background."

Sydney wasn't one to always toe the line. Even so, she didn't have a lot of back-room or dark-alley experience. Her street smarts were strictly suburban: more boulevard or cul-de-sac. But she understood what motivated a source's caution and generally complied with their initial demands to learn what they had to offer.

Not every informant delivered the goods.

But if they did, her goal was to encourage them to reveal themselves and their subject matter on camera.

Adhering to the hacker's specific instructions, Sydney glided through The Seafood Company's dining room and entered a short, dark hall. The heady aroma of Caribbean seasonings emanating from the kitchen drew her attention. Her mouth watered as she imagined yummy plantains and shrimp.

She continued down the hall, past voices coming from a narrow dining area adjacent to the stockroom, then exited out the screened rear door. Sydney held her purse to shield her face as her eyes readjusted to the crippling sunlight.

The restaurant backed up to serene marsh waters. Trawler masts and crane arms stretched above the reeds. Sydney eased down the slanting dock and clambered aboard *The Collective*. The fishing boat entertained a certain nautical allure.

Sydney tiptoed around seining-nets and empty bait boxes crowding the deck. The hatch was open, and she wasn't sure whether to have a secret handshake ready or ramble in as though she were Julius Caesar crossing the Rubicon. She opted for the latter.

Three twenty-somethings were punishing laptop keyboards at the galley table. They made no attempt to hide their skepticism of her, their eyes never staying too long in one place. Sydney shoehorned a seat on a bench next to Sneezy, who kept wiping his nose on a shirtsleeve.

Doc reached in his pocket and tossed Sneezy a box of Claritin. "I thought Dale told you to have those allergies tested."

Sneezy, who sat as pale as a Goya portrait, squeezed two pills from the foiled package. "For real, bro?"

A guy built like a bomb shelter emerged from someplace below deck. He marched directly to Sydney, then jerked her from the bench like clean linen from the dryer. After a moment of silent appraisal, he dropped her back on the bench. The bench protested, and Sneezy, Dopey, and Doc nervously abandoned keyboarding.

Sydney considered throwing a hissy—but her cautionary defenses mushroomed. She couldn't be certain whether the situation might grow more dangerous if she played it wrong. She welded on a tight grin. "Ever get the feeling the world's a tuxedo and you're a pair of brown loafers?"

Doc's laugh ratcheted down the testosterone level. "She's cool."

"Yeah, dude," Dopey said. "Quit acting like our breed ain't domesticated. She might get the wrong idea."

The big guy shifted his considerable weight. "Go ahead, news lady." A smile played across his lips. "What do you wanna know about hacking?"

His question was unvarnished, and Sydney relished the efficiency. "Let's talk ransomware."

The four men howled with exhilaration. Sydney blew out a breath, relieved she'd struck the right chord.

"You've come to the right place." Mr. Big passed Sydney a business card that read: Dale Lawson—Discreet Cyber-Searcher.

"Is Dale your real name?" she asked.

"Depends."

"I can work with that."

Dale slid a stool next to her. His hair was yanked back in a tight wad. Gray hairs ran amok, choking out what remained of the darker ones. "A ransom hack is pretty sophisticated, because I can think of at least two ways to get busted."

Sydney offered what she knew. "Sending the message and collecting the ransom."

He nodded. "And it doesn't matter whether you're an elite or a noob, there's always a trail."

She clapped her hands. At least a portion of Ted's explanation synched. "How would you go about sending a tainted message to launch an attack?"

The four men exchanged furtive glances.

Sneezy spoke first. "Phishing is a super easy way to drop dirty script. Hacker dangles something bogus—"

"Free food, for example?" Sydney asked.

"Exactamundo," Doc said. "Anything to pry open the system's backdoor and steam past firewalls."

Sneezy continued. "Dirty script hijacks the operating system. Locks up the target's data. Then demands a ransom to unlock it."

Sydney deliberated whether to press the point, not knowing how much to trust Ted's supposedly helpful actions. She opted to plow ahead. "Can you trace a specific ransom attack for me?"

Dale rested an elbow on the table with the confidence of a nuclear physicist about to split an atom. "Lady, you asked the wrong question—it isn't whether we *can*."

Sydney was entering uncharted territory as murky as a public swimming pool. "*Will* you?" She quickly added, "I have a hundred bucks."

The offer broke her cardinal rule about buying information. Though the little voice in her head suggested she was purchasing a service—and hopefully solving a crime.

"Make it three bills, and we'll work it," Doc said.

Sydney pulled three crisp C-notes from her pocket and fanned them on the table. "The Golden Crust. The attack was Monday or Tuesday. The ransom was paid today."

Sneezy and Dopey rattled their laptops.

Doc inspected the bills, then slid them to Dale, who palmed the money like a pro.

"Should've never paid," Doc said. "Fewer than twenty percent of targets are able to decrypt their files. And 100 percent of the time, they wind up on the hacker's shit list."

"Meaning?" Sydney asked.

"Payers always get slammed again."

Seconds later, Sneezy said, "Looks like the café's firewall stopped at least twenty attacks over the last two years before being breached. But their encryption is so last-week. Pathetic. They deserved to be hacked."

"I'm in," Dopey shouted. "I accessed their network's journal registry to scan all incoming and outgoing emails. Found one sent to over a thousand addresses."

"I see it," Doc said. "Fucker didn't even scrub the headers or use a VPN."

Sydney knew more about cars than Internet protocols. When mechanics talked about headers, they referred to performance-enhancing exhaust manifolds. Installation of a header increased horsepower at the expense of amplified noise and emissions. But she sensed these guys were talking about a computer nameplate, of sorts.

Dale said, "Probably a dumbass script-kiddy too cool or too stupid—but a bad mistake to leave headers unmasked." He poked Sydney's arm. "Watch this." He hammered his knuckles on the table. "Attention, fellas. I have an extra fifty for the first one to tell me the sender's name and IP."

The guys worked themselves into a frenzy. The blinding speed with which they unraveled the dark web of deceit boggled Sydney's mind. Clearly, hackers were smarter and faster than she'd given credit. And the trawler, their clandestine lair, crushed every myth.

The guys were into it now—firing solutions in short bursts.

Sneezy slammed a fist in the air. "IP address is from a Lansing

Group server—"

Doc added, "Address is assigned to—"

"Ted Armstrong," Dopey, Sneezy, and Doc shouted in unison, before smashing empty R*Ampd cans on their foreheads.

<h1 style="text-align:center">24</h1>

Sydney sank back. "You mean Ted sent the phishing email initiating the café's ransom attack?"

Dale reached in his pocket, peeled off three fifties from a wad, then tossed the bills on the table for his crew.

"Holy shit," Dopey said. "Same IP is on the crypto key. What a dumb fuck." He jutted his arms out, wrists together.

Sneezy snapped imaginary cuffs around them.

"Guys, take a peek at the malware run," Doc said. "I see extensions."

Dopey and Sneezy eyed their screens.

Sydney's chest burned. "What is it?"

Doc zeroed in on her with concern. "Everyone who opened the free food email has become part of a botnet."

She scrunched her nose in confusion.

Dale offered interpretation. "A botnet is a network of infected computers, numbering in the hundreds or even thousands. They connect to the criminal's command-and-control server like zombies. I'll bet Lansing Group's server farm is being used as a proxy, and they don't even know they've been hijacked."

"Ted works at LG," Sydney blurted out, though he'd never mentioned any server or malware problems when they'd met. "He can access the servers. He's in charge of them."

Sneezy shook his head and beaded locs tumbled across his shoulders. "Total dumb fuck."

"That changes things," Dale said.

"How so?" Sydney asked.

"Once a botnet is in place, it'll do the most damage. Like denial-of-service attacks, keystroke pilfering, and RATs."

Sydney threw her palms up.

Dale said, "RAT stands for Remote Access Trojan. It's sophisticated malware enabling the hacker to gain control of a target's computer remotely and surreptitiously. They can prowl around undetected until they find what they want. Like something ripe to use or sell—"

"Examples?"

"Credit card numbers, classified and proprietary information, bank accounts."

Something clicked in her head, and Sydney recalled Ted asking about a Roman poem. "Is there a program called Aeneid that is a RAT bot?"

The hackers groaned.

Dale held up a fist. "RAT and bot—two different bad dudes. Bots are smaller than RATs with a limited range of commands. And I never heard of a RAT or bot called Aeneid. But we'll look around."

Sydney's newfound understanding of Ted's involvement in the bizarre biznap scheme sent an icy chill down her spine. She tended to see the worst in people, a bad habit she never tried to break. But this had caught her flat-footed and forced her to revise her theory regarding Piper's murder.

Perhaps Piper had discovered Ted using the powerful Lansing Group servers to electronically infiltrate businesses for extortion and other transgressions. They argued, then Ted killed her to cover up his malicious software ploy. Embezzlement allegations against Piper merely served to distract from Ted's tangled mess.

But why would he take such illicit action with a lucrative IPO hanging in the balance? And what was Aeneid?

Then again, maybe Ted wasn't the dumb fuck behind the ransomware. Maybe the virus was another piece of the frame-up pie, like he'd claimed. If so, he could be leaving breadcrumbs.

Mulling over those opposing positions left her with a catchy tagline for tonight's broadcast: The World Wide Web—used and abused.

She rose to leave.

Sneezy wiped his nose on his sleeve again. "Ruh-roh, there's more. And it's super nasty."

"Out with it," Dale said.

"I'm chatting in a private forum. There's a bounty on our TV lady."

"A hitman?" Sydney clutched her chest. "Someone wants me dead?"

Dale appeared amused. "They're after your digits, babe. Targeting your personal emails, bank accounts. Your complete online presence. Hope your social accounts smell good—unlike those deviant Sony executives."

"What do I do?"

"Change all your passwords—stat. We'll create additional firewalls and security protections, but if you've already been hacked—get ready for major-league blowback." Dale asked earnestly, "Any idea what's next?"

"That's a loaded question," Sydney said.

"You can say that again."

"That's a loaded question."

25

Mandy was pacing in a tight circle near the front door when Sydney swung by the TV station to pick her up. She flung open the car's passenger door. "I found an unlisted number for Lansing Group's missing employee."

Sydney's mouth gaped with genuine astonishment. "You're kidding?"

Mandy handed her pal a slip of paper with a neatly printed phone number after she climbed in.

"I mean," Sydney cleared her throat as she pressed her cell's keypad. "Never doubted you."

Deleisha answered on the first ring, and Sydney grilled her with pointed questions.

During the short, and somewhat terse, conversation, Deleisha detailed being placed on administrative leave due to the missing laptop. She'd been away for a week, upstate, with her boyfriend. That information synched with Moose's claim that the feds had been searching for the laptop prior to the Lansing Group CEO making the public announcement. But it didn't jibe with Velma's assertion Deleisha had been working the day Piper was killed.

Sydney disconnected, then climbed out of the car. "You drive while I continue working the phone."

"Where to?" Mandy dashed around the hood and slid into the driver's seat.

"Lansing Group. Velma has some 'splaining to do. Wonder what else my secret informant is holding out on."

During the ride, Sydney phoned Olivia to recap her meetings with Ted and the hackers, hinting she was working two rabid stories. Next, she called Moose to cross-check Ted's alibi. He said they hadn't met, meaning Ted was laying pavement for a proverbial wild goose chase. It also left him without a motive—but no substantiated alibi during Piper's murder window.

Sydney formulated scripts for the evening broadcast in her head. One story focused on the discrepant timeline between LG's apparent laptop theft and their public notification. She didn't yet understand the significance of the delay and hoped Velma could fill the gap. Her second story, The Golden Crust's ransom attack, was pricklier.

When the two arrived at Lansing Group, they pushed into the Records office. "Mandy, point the camera directly at Velma and hit record."

Velma caught sight of the red light. Her face registered the predicament. She waved her hands. "Get outta here."

"This is Sydney Quinn, Action 7 News." She moved near Velma's desk. "Why did your company delay in reporting the laptop theft to the public?"

Velma pleaded as Mandy closed to within three feet. "Go away."

"What kind of cover-up is this firm perpetrating?"

Velma slid below her desk.

Sydney tapped Mandy on the shoulder and jerked a thumb for her to stop recording. "The camera is off. You can come out."

Velma's eyes flared with fear as she peeked over the desk.

Sydney asked again, "Why did LG wait?"

Velma collapsed into her chair. "They told me to keep quiet. I swear."

"Let me get this straight—"

"Said I'd lose my job for sure. But it didn't seem right. So, I needed you to provide a little muscle."

"Who told you this?"

"Sergeant Cash, that federal cop. Don't you think his name is perfect for his job? On account of he works with money."

Sydney clapped her hands. "Focus."

Velma rubbed her forehead with her palms. "I figured you'd take a look-see at what he was poking into, and I could keep my job. Win-win."

The only thing Sydney hated more than being wrong was being used. "Let me give you a little friendly criticism. I promise no one will know this came from you, but it doesn't close the book on your little plot to deceive me." She was starting to loathe secret informants. "By the way, we located Deleisha. In good health. On paid vacation. You are truly bad at your job."

"I knew you'd find her." Velma heaved relief. "All the same, there's no way you'd have known how long the Fee-bees been hunting after that little ole laptop without me."

"What else have you lied about?" Sydney asked.

"Not about death cooties."

•

When Sydney and Mandy returned to the parking lot, Mason slid off the hood of her Thunderbird. Sydney beamed and turned to Mandy. "I'd like to formally introduce you to Mason Sterling, owner of the yacht where I'm presently residing."

Mandy arched an eyebrow before shoving a hand in his direction.

Mason kissed it with a flourish. "You must be the remarkable Mandy Reynolds. Syd speaks highly of you."

"And you must be the Mason Sterling I've heard practically nothing about."

"Alright," Sydney said. "Enough pleasantries. We're headed to the VA Medical Center. Why don't you join us? I'd like you to meet my favorite guy."

Mason manufactured a pout. "You mean someone else enjoys that distinction?"

Mandy smacked her lips. "She wants to show you off to the nursing staff."

He seemed to savor the notion of being eye candy.

When they arrived in Commander Bob's room, Sydney tossed her purse on the hardwood floor and stared at him in disbelief. Of all the pants in the world, his were the tackiest. Mandy burst out laughing, signaling her approval for his multicolored paisley slacks. Then she taped large sheets of poster paper to the wall.

Sydney faced her trusted trio. "We only have an hour before I'm needed back at the station. I want to run a few ideas by you with regards to my pesky prime suspect in Piper Kingston's murder."

"Rats and maggots." Bob jerked his leg and waggled the lime-green tennis shoes Sydney had given him.

She knew the old man wasn't losing his mind. He often uttered incoherent babble around people he didn't like. Sydney followed his gaze to the only new person in the room, having forgotten to make introductions. "Bob, this is Mason. I expect you two to play nice."

"*Huevos verde* and pig parts," Bob said.

"Green eggs and ham?" Mason asked.

Bob saluted. "Roger, control. Cleared for takeoff."

"That should settle things." Sydney smoothed her hair. "As you know, the undersheriff still has Josh Andrews in custody for Piper's death. I'm confident he's not the guy. I brought Mason here because he can offer an insider's perspective while we brainstorm."

Mason's chiseled jawline tightened. She took it to mean he feared she might let the proverbial feline escape from the sack regarding his undercover assignment. She raised a palm in reassurance. "Because he works at Lansing Group."

Bob raked his hair to one side, seemingly satisfied with the explanation. "This Josh fellow . . . Wasn't he the one who pointed a gun at you and the hostages?"

Sydney exchanged a fleeting nod. "But he was framed for the murder. Mic drop."

"What makes you so certain?" Bob asked.

"Because the killer is most likely the person who sent Josh the note. Explains everything."

Mason sat on a stool. "What note? I'm not aware of any note."

Bob clapped him on the shoulders. "Watch and learn. Syd is the brains of our outfit—a true professional."

Mandy giggled. "I know we aren't supposed to be having fun, but this is similar to what they do on *Cold Justice*."

Sydney realized she owned a lead Mason and the task force didn't have. "Josh received a note from a receptionist before he departed LG the morning of the murder. He thought it came from Piper, who'd invited him to her house, presumably to talk about appealing the termination of his benefits."

Mason eyed Bob, and they shook their heads.

"We men aren't buying it," Mason said. "Sounds like an elaborate ruse."

She blew them off with the wave of her hand. "I call it a solid clue."

Bob said, "Even if LG wrongly stopped Josh's benefits, Piper didn't deserve that beating. Based on the pictures, she never stood a chance. Plenty of spatter and blood pool. And the size of her head gashes . . . Yuck."

"Sheesh, Bob. You made it real." Mandy bounced tented fingers together and faced Mason. "Did the police find any other useful clues at the house?"

Mason frowned. "I can't say."

Bob cackled. "One more time 'round the dance floor."

Mandy and Commander Bob glared at Mason with a collective sense of distrust.

Sydney came to his defense. "We should ask the sheriff's office since they're honchoing the investigation."

Mason pointed at Bob. "Syd, how do you work with this senile old codger?"

Bob stabbed a finger at him and grinned. "I'm not senile. I'm eccentric."

They glowered at one another for nearly thirty seconds before Bob burst out laughing.

"You played me?" Mason slapped his thighs. "I love it. Gosh, you three are fun. Eccentric. Rhymes with—"

"Oh, we don't rhyme," Bob said. "Not ever. Too cheesy."

Mason started to speak, then shook his head. "I see, no time for rhyme."

Bob waggled the lime-green sneakers again. "If not Josh, who else has a motive to harm Piper?"

"Were you a Navy cop?" Mason said. "You ask perfectly pointed questions."

"Are you trying to butter my toast, or are you always this nice?"

They both snickered as though they shared a secret.

Sydney jumped in. "Glad you two have bonded. But let's do this my way."

26

Sydney meticulously detailed her thoughts on Piper's murder to the group, her voice a blend of urgency and determination. Her eyes flickered with intensity as she painted a vivid picture of the events, weaving together clues and suspicions with the precision of a seasoned investigator. Each word was carefully chosen, each pause deliberate, as she guided her audience through the labyrinth of mystery surrounding the case.

The room was silent, all eyes fixed on her as she unraveled the tangled web. "First, let's create a timeline using the coroner's suspected window for the time of death—between noon and two."

Mandy suggested narrowing the timeframe to encompass when Josh said he last spoke with Piper at the house and when EMS arrived on-scene to find her unresponsive. That left them with a TOD window of one to one-forty.

"Does that help, Nancy Drew?" Mason asked.

Sydney wagged a finger. "Don't make fun of Nancy."

"Quite a competent investigator, our Miss Drew," Bob added. "She's solved every case."

Mason threw his hands in the air and laughed. "I guess Nancy Drew knew which clue to pursue."

Bob nudged him with an elbow.

"Alright, fellas," Sydney said. "My top suspect is Ted Armstrong. He's unmistakably connected with Lansing Group, so it's plausible he knew Josh visited Piper on Monday. Probably spotted him in the building, then generated the note for Josh to meet at her place."

Sydney penned *Ted* atop a poster page and listed all the reasons he might've killed Piper or wanted her dead. The list included: Piper's history of infidelity, deceit about the sixty grand, and lying about where he was during the TOD window, thereby not having a solid alibi.

Sydney added, "His prints were on the stolen laptop, and he claims to have a mysterious police record that may or may not be related."

The group haggled a few points, though everyone seemed satisfied with the evidence against Ted.

A nurse practitioner banged through the door, pushing a cart topped with medicine cups. She surveyed the posters, then wrinkled her brow. "Y'all planning a little somethin' somethin' here?"

"Working the old noggin," Bob said. "Don't want to catch old-timer's disease."

"Alzheimer's," Mandy corrected.

"You say potato, I say tater."

"Ooh, I say tater too," Mandy cooed.

"Afternoon visiting hours are over," the nurse said. "Wrap it up."

"We'll be gone before you finish your med run," Sydney said.

Mandy closed the door behind the nurse. "Where were we?"

Sydney shot Mason a glance, hoping he'd divulge spanking-new, privileged information. He shook her off, so she pressed forward. "In conclusion . . ." Her phone vibrated, and she removed a half-dozen reporter notebooks from her purse before retrieving it. "Hey, Dino."

"I called Mike Cash to set up your meet," he said. "Mike told me about more weird doings at LG."

"Such as?"

"They have north of $88 million in cash reserves. But during his forensic audit, Mike found several instances of millions missing one minute. Then, the next time he checked—the money was back."

"Millions?"

"Sounds squirrelly, right?"

"Well, we're only halfway through the calendar, but I'd call *squirrelly* one of the year's top understatements. By the way—you corroborate Schlub's alibi?"

"I released him an hour ago. But he still owes me an explanation for the painting."

"What about Ted Armstrong's suspect status?"

"I asked the undersheriff to let me take a run at him just to see what shakes out. Said he'd get back to me. I'm not holding my breath."

Sydney clicked off and eyed Mandy and Mason. "Who could make money disappear, then reappear?"

Mandy took the marking pen and added a bullet point to Ted's list. "A great coder."

Mason reached for the pen and wrote GAVIN.

Sydney said, "Are you serious? All I had on Lansing was tawdry rumors."

Mason rubbed his chin. "Gavin doesn't know the difference between media, application, or system code. But he could hire someone with mad coding skills to leach his own firm. Like Ted."

•

In the bustling newsroom, Sydney made her entrance through the rear door, taking a swift swipe at the speed bag, a habitual gesture that signaled her arrival. Her presence was a whirlwind of energy and purpose, cutting through the clamor of ringing phones and clattering keyboards. She marched to her cubicle and flung herself into the well-worn recliner. The chair embraced her like an old friend, its familiar creak a comforting sound, before she tackled the next challenge with her trademark tenacity.

"Quinn, get in here," the station manager yelled.

Sydney threw her hands in the air, her brief respite spoiled. "What now?"

Pete Conroy enjoyed a TV news career spanning the better part of four decades. An award-winning foreign correspondent back in the day, he'd hired Sydney and her former camera guy, Reggie, while they were with Golf Channel. Pete improved her interviewing skills and taught her to fight for a story by digging deeper, asking better questions, getting superior answers. But like his waistline, Pete's interviewing skills were long gone.

Sydney moseyed into his office. "You bellowed?"

"Where are the big stories you promised Olivia?"

"I met new sources today. And I haven't verified the task force's action regarding laptop theft reporting delays or possible bank fraud."

"No need for verification," Pete said.

"Huh? Thought I was supposed to identify leads, nail down facts. You know, basic journalism."

"Wednesdays are notorious for flaws and retractions. Unlike newspapers, TV operates in an era of fast and dirty. A sound-bite jungle. Your job is to feed the beast. Lob a grenade if you have to. We can always issue a correction tomorrow."

"You sure? I'm certain the two-source rule remains best practice."

"Here's a solid practice—do what I tell you. Drop the laptop story. There's not enough meat there to make it worth gnawing at the bone. Find me something fresh for tonight." He grabbed a putter from the edge of his desk and rehearsed his grip. "Take a few chances. Get out of your comfort zone. Not everything that stinks is a massive conspiracy."

27

Sydney didn't have time to piece together a brand-new package. So, she phoned Andy Bates, the Medic 6 crew leader who'd been held hostage only two days earlier, for a follow-up. He and Captain Ross greeted her at the Lowcountry Rehab Station, located in a former North Charleston shopping mall.

Andy shook his head when Sydney reached for a camera in her trunk. "This is a private and safe place for our brothers and sisters."

Sydney latched the trunk. "You caught me on the only day when I'm inclined to follow the rules."

Though she understood the sanctity of safe places, she was a little miffed she wouldn't have fresh video for her segment. She texted Eric to pull EMT action footage from B-roll files.

Captain Ross handed her a swag bag filled with department patches and a rehab station coffee mug. "By design, visitors aren't typically welcome here, but Andy insisted on presenting you with goodies from the fire service, police and sheriff's departments, EMS, and emergency call center."

Andy reddened and placed a hand over his heart. "We also prepared a special program for you. One I'm sure you're gonna enjoy."

Sydney spread her arms, palms up, ready to take it all in.

The main meeting room of the cramped center was awash in bright colors. And even though the place catered to all first responders, it was outfitted with comfortable furnishings designed to mirror familiar firehouse accommodations—rows of comfy recliners, big-screen TVs, and computer workstations. A plaque, carved from an old-growth bottomland bald cypress, reminded everyone they weren't alone in their fight for survival and long-term recovery.

"Hey," Andy shouted over the din. "This is Syd. You might

recognize her from Channel 7. She promises to be on her best behavior, if you'll do the same."

A few whistles erupted from the group of about twenty.

Sydney raised a hand and grinned. "Full disclosure. Never promised."

The group *whooped* with delight.

Captain Ross guided Sydney through the rest of the station. Areas were designated for therapy, dining, chapel, fitness, and recreation. A fragrant current of tomatoes and garlic wafted from the kitchen area.

"I probably sound like a brochure," Captain Ross said. "But nearly all first responders experience some sort of job-related stress or anxiety. For most, symptoms wear off in a few days."

"Yours is an exceptional job," Sydney said. "I suspect you see some pretty awful situations."

"Most of us have a calling to serve others," Andy said.

"More like a pathological need to fix things," Captain Ross added. "While we protect the community and each other, we run the risk of burnout. Constant exposure to stress and trauma wears on even the strongest individual."

Andy said, "Exactly why we have this station. Folks need a place to get their shit together before the next call. Others need professional services to avoid self-medicating with food, drugs, or alcohol."

Captain Ross bobbed her head in agreement. "Social support and peer intervention are the most important protective measures we offer. As dangerous as our jobs are, we risk losing crewmembers from suicide rather than in the line of duty."

"I embedded with a Marine battalion years ago," Sydney said. "The brass was split on whether asking for help showed a sign of weakness. That stigma became a roadblock. Probably cost a few Marines their lives before a dramatic change in the leadership's perspective."

"The captain will tell you the clinicians we hired had the same worries," Andy said. "However, professional organizations, like the International Association of Firefighters, stepped in to encourage participation. They call *reaching out* a sign of resilience."

Sydney flickered with hope. "I want to help."

Andy said, "You could let people know we exist. I know firsthand what a difference the rehab station makes. Getting the word out will help reach guys like Josh Andrews who need this place."

"Should this program be higher on the funding totem pole?"

Captain Ross swung her head side-to-side. "Area counties treat us with respect. They've funded an expansion twice. However, post-pandemic expenses sucked up earmarked money. Not coming at you with our hand out, but the chaplain who manages the station wouldn't discourage public contributions. Especially since our lease here is expiring soon, so we'll need a new space."

Sydney agreed. "Speaking of Josh, what did you talk about when you were alone?"

"Mostly, how to make ends meet on skimpy salaries. Danny works at the Rec Center. I'm a weekend concierge at The Renaissance. Where do you unwind?"

An alarm sounded two short blasts before she could respond. She paled, thinking the first responders were being called to a fire or other emergency.

Andy put a calming hand on her arm. "Supper is ready. A true firehouse chef made his signature chili and cornbread. Hungry?"

Sydney beamed with delight. "Show me the way."

They ambled through the service line, then found seats at a picnic-style table. One bite, and Sydney's mouth was ablaze from the spicy combination of jalapeno, poblano, and habanero peppers. "Wa. . .ter." Her throat tightened and her lips burned. Thankfully, she was surrounded by firefighters.

"Cow juice. Stat!" Andy shouted.

The chef heaved a half gallon of two percent milk. Andy fielded it like a line drive to third base and poured a tumbler for Sydney.

She chugged the milk to dilute the smoldering capsaicin, then wiped her lips with the back of her hand. "Sheesh, you should warn a gal."

Everyone in the dining room doubled over.

"Oh, I get it." Sydney's eyes darted around the crowd. "Initiation."

Andy bowed and the group applauded.

She raised her glass to honor her hosts. "Does the cornbread fight back too?"

"Nah," the chef said. "But you might get a cavity from all the brown sugar in my batter."

Laughter and garrulous chatter caromed off the walls, and Sydney didn't want to believe anyone here was hurting. Yet she knew firsthand how people camouflaged their pain.

After they ate, the group adjourned to the meeting room, where pet-therapy volunteers had arranged a dozen or so dogs, cats, puppies, and kittens awaiting needy hands.

Sydney was mesmerized by the animals' soft fur and playful innocence.

"A purring kitten reduces blood pressure and anxiety." Andy eyed her. "We never run into a burning building by ourselves. You don't have to deal with your trauma alone."

She knew she'd never forget the river ambush, though those frozen memories of excruciating loss begin to thaw as she hugged a golden puppy. "Thanks for the peppers. How are you doing?"

"I have a great wife and family, a terrific work partner, and the best captain in the department. I'm living the dream." Andy cuddled a calico kitten. "I'll be okay."

28

Sydney zoomed back into the newsroom like a whirlwind, with little time to spare before the evening broadcast. Every editing bay was crammed with assistant producers and reporters, all frantically making final cuts from raw footage. The air buzzed with the sound of rapid-fire keyboard clacks and the occasional exasperated sigh. Every night, it was the same chaotic routine—producing a piece that lasted sixty seconds or fewer required an effort that could rival a Herculean labor. Sydney often joked that if they put this much energy into solving world hunger, they'd have it sorted out by lunchtime on Day One. But for now, Action 7's mission was clear: make the news happen, one frantic edit at a time.

The subject of her segment centered on progress and purpose at the rehab station. She made sure her packages always entertained and informed, since she could conceptualize better than most.

Sydney worked fast, arranging details from previous research about post-traumatic and acute stress disorders. She understood more than enough to add context and authority to rally public support for hero first responders.

She polished her piece by sprinkling in a few solid facts about brave police, fire, and rescue personnel. Such as, more than eighty percent experienced traumatic events during their careers. And they were four times more likely to be injured on the job than in any other profession. She capped her package with Captain Ross's words of encouragement when she aired her segment from the main studio. Eric's video added a brilliant touch.

By the time she returned to her cubicle, Mandy and Josh were waiting.

Josh pushed out his palms. "I came by to let you know the under-sheriff dropped the murder charge. A public defender managed my release."

"Have you seen your family?" Sydney asked.

He shook his head. "Waiting for a judge to give permission. Until then, I'm all yours. What do you need me to do?"

"Josh says he's pretty handy with computers," Mandy added.

"A lot better than I am with emergency medicine," he said. "I started taking classes for IT certification after I was injured. Had to stop when the money ran out."

"I'll keep that in mind," Sydney said. "Right now, I have all the sources I need. But we'll call if anything pops up."

Josh nodded with a hint of palpable disappointment. "Figured I owed you something since you helped raise money for my bond."

"I didn't—"

"Yeah, you did." Mandy signaled with flailing arms and an impish grin. "She's generous that way."

Sydney gave her pal, the obvious do-gooder, a wink. "Mandy played a huge role."

Mason rounded the corner and peeked into the crowded cubicle.

Sydney placed her hands on her hips. "I thought we were meeting at the marina?"

"Plans change." Mason eyed Josh. "Am I interrupting?"

Josh thrust out a beefy hand. "Josh Andrews. Just leaving."

"Josh—" Mason returned the handshake before the glint of name recognition hit. He puffed out his chest in some sort of macho protective mode. A vestigial reminder of days gone by.

Mandy giggled her nervous chortle. "Back off, big fella. Josh comes in peace."

Mason stared long and hard in Josh's wake. He spun toward Sydney. "What was that about?"

She brushed aside the question.

"You need to up your game, Syd," Mason said. "Start hanging

out with a better class of people."

Sydney folded her arms. "Oh, really?"

He smiled to diffuse the mess. "Let's skedaddle before any news blips across the wire and spoils our evening."

•

Sydney maneuvered her car into the marina parking lot and spotted Captain Morgan's catering van on the pier. She hoped Mason's menu wasn't too spicy, since she hadn't recovered from her nasty encounter with the pepper triumvirate.

Mason helped the caterer set up in the salon, while Sydney changed into a casual, green-and-white sleeveless knot dress for dinner. She claimed a seat, and the caterer dished two plates of scallops, kale salad, country ham, and sweet corn coulis before leaving.

"Tell me about your EMS visit," Mason said.

She didn't like discussing work, but she indulged him. "Commander Bob encouraged me to raise money for first responders. Americans donate roughly $300 billion a year. I'm hoping to redirect a little toward our heroes."

"Does the city do enough for them?"

"They provide compensation for responders killed in the line of duty. And the state pays workers' comp to cover medical bills. However, the law allows insurance companies like Lansing Group to apply a weird formula to calculate disability pay, resulting in paltry benefits when folks are out of work. And their families incur unreimbursed expenses, too."

Wrinkles of surprise appeared on his brow. "Bloody hell, are you thinking of changing the law?"

She shook her head emphatically. "One step at a time before I go charging off to Columbia. Mandy donated an office building she owns that was vacated during the COVID shutdown. We also made a couple calls and received seed money from several wealthy locals. Lastly, I'm still putting the pieces together to host a fundraiser, but Mandy assures me daylight fireworks are a must-have. Care to contribute?"

"Put me down for five thousand."

Sydney's eyes bugged.

"Not enough?" Mason said. "What am I thinking? Round up my donation to ten grand."

She threw her arms around his neck and kissed his cheek. "And thanks for joining our murder board this afternoon."

"Totally impressed with your friends. And you blew me away when you mentioned Piper's note to the suspect."

"I'd rather you call him Josh, since he's no longer a suspect."

Mason held up a hand. "Anyhow, the note came as news to me. Changes the whole dynamic of why Josh was at her house in the first place."

"Makes you want to believe the rest of his story, right?"

"What about the hostages?"

"Sheesh, you commit one felony, and all of the sudden cops want to slap cuffs and a pejorative label on you."

"They're funny like that."

"Including you."

"If you say so."

Sydney cleared the table and spooned leftovers into plastic containers. Her rhythmic scraping triggered a headache and a sudden rewind to Iraq.

Heavy rain had unexpectedly flooded Tent City and turned ancient sand into stinky mud. Once the rain ended, the troops were treated to a steady dose of dry air, intense heat, and blinding dust storms. Her unit operated in the US-controlled International Zone. Later called the Green Zone, the heavily guarded diplomatic area in central Baghdad was surrounded by chain-link fencing and razor wire. Only a year or two older than the youngest barefaced Marines, Sydney's job was to paint the full picture of life in unfamiliar surroundings far from home. Gunny Walters made her wear a flak jacket and helmet everywhere. That meant routine headaches.

Sydney rubbed away the weight of her memory. Now wasn't a good time to dwell on Gunny. "Tell me about Grace," she said.

"Grace who?"

"The bulldog guarding Gavin Lansing's office."

"Oh, her." Mason's face pinched. "She rubs me the wrong way."

"I'll bet she chafes everyone. Think she's covering for Gavin regarding Piper? The laptop's timeline discrepancy? Or whatever the reason you have his company under surveillance?"

"Could be." He moved closer to Sydney. "Never gave her that much thought. She's a new hire." Mason flashed his teeth and kissed her. Sloppy, wet kisses. "Come with me. I made arrangements to borrow one of the marina's Boston Whalers for a sunset cruise."

29

Sydney rested a loose grip on the windshield as Mason maneuvered the Whaler around the Battery, where the Ashley and Cooper Rivers met to form the Atlantic Ocean. Ritzy tourists lined Charleston Harbor's quay wall, anticipating a postcard-worthy sunset. Kids spilled from bustling seafood restaurants ahead of their parents, saluting as the Whaler lazed past and headed off to tangle with the harbor's outgoing current.

Sydney's hand moved to return the salute, much as her Marine gunner had done. Back then, cheering Iraqi kids pressed against the perimeter fence every time a platoon departed.

Once the Whaler cleared a rocky shoal fortifying the peninsula's antebellum mansions against hostile tidal surges, Mason revved the twin outboard engines. The boat pitched through the first trough, dumping Sydney into a cushioned captain's chair. Sea spray pelted her. She drew her knees to her chest and relived the last time she'd taken a similar pounding.

Staff Sergeant Sam Townsend, a fifteen-year Marine Corps veteran, careened the battered Humvee alongside the Tigris River while Sydney rode shotgun on her ninth mission outside the wire. A rare shamal breeze helped tame August's sweltering desert. But she didn't enjoy the shamal, Townsend, or anything else for that matter. She was pissed at him for scribbling *routine patrol* in the command duty log before they rolled out.

Routine patrol—what a dumbass expression.

Thunder Runs, as they were known in-country, were high-intensity adrenaline kicks. Driving under cover of darkness. Dodging roadside bombs. Knowing the Taliban might strike at any moment, without notice.

They were shadowing a convoy about sixty clicks from Al Kut in Wasit Province, traveling southeast on Highway 6—Iraq's most notorious stretch of road from Baghdad to Basrah. Sydney checked her watch—0218—then tore open the envelope she'd pulled from a sleeve pocket and slid a new SD card into her camera. She thumbed the setting for video and shook off an uneasy feeling.

"I'm getting too old for this shit." Townsend guzzled the last of his Maalox before tossing the empty bottle over his shoulder. "How much time you have left in the sandbox, Ms. Quinn?"

"Two more months with all you bozos." She pasted on a sardonic smile and forcibly exhaled. "Once I'm stateside, I won't skimp on any comforts—hot showers, clean sheets, and meals that aren't ready-to-eat."

Townsend ran the back of his hand across his lips. "Remember when you first crawled off the plane? I thought, Jeezus, I have jockstraps older than this chick. Now look at you—one of the boys."

He meant it as a compliment. She'd shaken the *outsider* tag.

The radio crackled, drawing their attention.

"Townsend," Gunny Walters barked. "Get your hillbilly hajji-rod back into position."

"Up yours," Townsend shot back, without keying his mic. He turned to Sydney and winked, then stomped the gas pedal, and the vehicle lurched.

Sydney's camera toppled to the floorboard, and her knees pounded against the metal dash in the Humvee's cramped compartment, adding to a dull headache she sported from the weight of the Kevlar helmet. She managed to wedge the camera between her feet, then patted her vest pockets, searching for her Motrin stash.

A heartbeat later, a sudden *whumph* rocked the Humvee as the lead vehicle in their heavily armed convoy detonated an improvised explosive device. Sydney's head slammed against the side of the vehicle.

When Mason cut the engine, it jerked Sydney back to the

moment. Alert, yet a little terrified. She fought through the panic, reflexively recalibrating her heart rate as her stomach turned over.

The boat glided onto Morris Island's sandy beach, an 840-acre uninhabited environmental refuge. During the Civil War, the fortified island had been the site of the Union Army's ill-fated assault to capture Charleston. The bloodbath of the 54th Massachusetts Volunteer Infantry, an all-African-American regiment, was depicted in the film *Glory*.

Insects hummed an electric current as the sunset's wild beauty streaked across the watery expanse. Puffy clouds swept overhead.

Mason threw the anchor over the side and removed his shirt. "Care for a little swim?"

Sydney wetted a finger to smooth untamed strands of hair. She forced a steadiness she didn't feel into her voice. "Didn't bring a suit. Besides, what creatures are lurking in the water?"

Mason dropped his pants and splashed over the side. "The sexy, two-legged kind. Come on in, the water's fine."

Sydney stood in the middle of the boat, clutching her purse like it held the crown jewels. Might be true if the monarchy placed any value on a dozen reporter's notebooks, three tubes of lip gloss, and fifty dollars in cash.

She remembered he could charm the pants right off her. And he'd usually gotten his way with a minimum of fuss.

But was she ready to move to the next level? Reopen her heart to the one who ran away?

The risks were enormous.

Maybe she should play it safe—maintain her distance.

"Oh, what the hell." In a war of head-versus-heart, her head lost the first skirmish. She slinked out of her dress and eased down the ladder. "I should get a swim in, since I missed my Krav Maga training tonight."

Mason playfully grabbed her from behind and pulled her close. The pressure of his tongue and hands prickled her skin. Despite years of separation, they were two familiar lovers—hungry for each other.

After a session of energetic lovemaking, followed by tender canoodling, they floated together, him with one hand on the ladder and one in her hair. Sydney wilted her head onto his chest.

"I've missed this," she said. "I mean you. I've missed you. Doing this." So much for taking things slowly. But at that moment, she wasn't worried about being careful. Maybe keeping things physical, without any emotional attachment, suited her just fine. Perhaps she'd break his heart this time around. "I'd love for you to do it again."

"Whoa there, little lady. This buck isn't as young as he'd like to think. I may need a little more time before rolling the ole rocket out to the launch pad again."

"Are you taking a ride on the mismatched metaphor train?"

"I'm a space cowboy." They drifted ashore, and Mason leaned on his elbows, his taut body pressed against hers. He caressed Sydney's tangled hair. Happily, she wasn't the kind of gal bothered by wind-whipped and sand-crusted curls. "You make me feel like a Triple Crown stallion," he said.

•

Mason maneuvered the Boston Whaler back into the marina alongside *Miss Adventure*. Twinkling lights and laughter from the yacht club's patio filled the night air. His big yacht dwarfed the neighboring *Three Maple Leaves*, a thirty-seven-foot sailboat. The boat was home to a delightful Montreal couple and their dog, who intended to stay a month before continuing their holiday down the Intracoastal Waterway.

Sydney and Mason snuck aboard *Miss Adventure* like teenagers eager to resume what they'd started.

"What suite are you using?" Mason asked.

Sydney hesitated for a Carolina second—about the equivalent of a New York minute. Maybe longer.

The sleek yacht had five generous staterooms. She'd taken up residency in the owner's cabin on the upper deck because it had two johns and a bathtub large enough to swim laps. Plus, the other suites were clad in baby-poop yellows and moldy greens that didn't do anything for her complexion.

"The blue room at the top of the stairs. Will you join me, or would you like to stay in one of the ugly rooms?"

Mason gave a long, high cackle, then shoved his hands in his pockets. "The guest quarters didn't earn your seal of approval?"

"Nope." Sydney weaved her way through the salon, shedding clothing as she climbed the teak spiral staircase connecting the suite with the main deck and upper wheelhouse. "C'mon, rocket man."

30

The next morning, Sydney flung open the blinds in the yacht's luxurious stateroom, letting in a cascade of sunlight. Three days had passed since the grisly murder of Piper Kingston, and life had somehow wobbled back to a semblance of normalcy—or, at least, as normal as her life could be on a floating palace. She left Mason tangled in a knot of sweaty sheets, resembling a burrito with a penchant for channel surfing and multitasking phone calls.

Meanwhile, Sydney pranced to the galley, her stomach leading the way like a divining rod for snacks. She rummaged through the galley with the enthusiasm of a treasure hunter, half-expecting to find a map guiding her to buried chocolate. However, the cupboards were empty, and she felt discomfited that Mason would discover she'd eaten all the grub he'd provided. Sydney moved to the rear diving platform for a firsthand weather check before dressing. Flags atop the yacht club hung limp, though the flawless, azure sky could've been painted by the Chamber of Commerce for a photo shoot.

She snagged the last bag of pretzels, wrote out directions to the nearest Waffle House for Mason, then placed the note next to him on the bed. In the shower, she made mental plans to continue tightroping another day with Ted as they dealt with the café's biznap ransom hustle. She reserved the right to point an accusatory finger at him for Piper's murder once that adventure was over.

Mason sidled into the shower.

Her knees weakened with anticipation as he wrapped his arms around her. "Am I to understand *Headline News* turned you on?"

"Nothing hotter for me than newspeople all lathered in—" He inhaled the scent of her shower gel. "Lavender suds."

•

Ten minutes later, Sydney sat at the vanity, dabbing makeup and lip gloss. Her fabulous black-and-tan sundress would be ideal for the day's agenda. She wrapped an oversized belt around her waist while Mason caressed her neck.

She spun toward him and pushed him onto the bed. "Today, I'm nailing the dipstick behind a small business ransomware scheme. Is your task force working on that?"

The plush bath towel around Mason's waist drooped open. "I don't know, sounds a little dangerous. Will your pal Dino assist, or do you need me to supply the muscle?"

"Have you met me?" Then a flash of ugly truth blindsided her. He really didn't know she was a professional badass. She swept away the thought, then tried not to stare under the towel. But what was a gal to do under those conditions? "Are you kidding? We can't talk shop while you're—" She pointed at his nether region, then reached for her hairbrush.

He draped the edge of the towel over his thigh. "I know. I have a distinct advantage."

Sydney stuck out her tongue.

Mason grunted approval. "Any chance you plan to involve the firm in future exposés?"

"Why do you care about Lansing Group? Someone may have committed financial fraud. It's what you're there to expose. Right?"

"Look, I won't deny the investigation is big league. But hear me out." Mason tracked Sydney's gaze in the mirror. "Do me a favor and quit pursuing the laptop." He gave her a non-flirtatious wink.

She spun around. "Something in your eye?"

"It's a bad time to disclose that clients were being fleeced."

"Were? Past tense?"

"Oops." Mason drew a symbolic finger to his lips. "I'm less sure-footed when I'm being ogled by an attractive woman."

"Last night you alluded that Grace was new to the firm.

How new?"

"Slip of the tongue." Mason scrunched his eyebrows. "Feel free to go after Ted with both barrels. But leave Gavin to me."

"What do you have on him? Anything I can report?"

Mason dropped the towel. Sydney stopped combing her hair as he undressed her.

Welcome to the big leagues, kid.

•

Sydney arrived at Piper Kingston's funeral service with the kind of timing that'd make a Swiss watchmaker blush. Not technically late, but in her world, anything less than ten minutes early was practically a scandal. She noted the good-sized crowd Piper had drawn—work colleagues, church parishioners, and a smattering of other friends—all gathered to pay their respects.

Sydney slid onto a chair beside Grace Rogers and asked, "How long have you been with Lansing Group?"

"Long enough," Grace said. "By the way, I remembered something else about Ted and Piper."

"Okay, let's hear it."

"Last Friday, I overheard them talking about a virus called Aeneid."

"What do you think it means?"

"I'm hardly in a position to know. But I get the feeling you and the undersheriff are only concerned about her murder, when in fact, there's probably more at stake."

"And you think this Aeneid bug—"

"As I said, I'm not the one you should ask."

Sydney racked her brain for the hint Grace was dropping. "Gavin?"

Grace offered a conspiratorial wink. "We're on the same page."

They both turned their attention to the service, where the eulogies were as heartfelt as they were long-winded, proving that even in death, Piper could hold a room.

The service concluded with Genesis 3:19, ashes to ashes. Sydney recognized that one, despite a glaring lack of religion in her upbringing. She placed a bouquet of yellow daylilies on Piper's casket before it descended into the ground.

Lionel, Piper's son, broke away from a clutch of college friends. "Thanks for coming, Syd. I hoped to catch you."

"Of course. Whatever you need. Your mom was pretty special."

He glanced slyly over his shoulder.

"Everything okay?" Sydney asked.

"I think Mr. Lansing is involved in Mom's death."

"Oh?" She matched his volume, a low whisper.

Blaming Gavin was becoming a popular theme.

Lionel continued. "He told me some ugly things. Made me think he didn't trust her anymore."

Sydney allowed the claim to hang there in hopes he'd continue if uninterrupted.

Lionel scratched a line in the grass with his toe. "You think Mom did something wrong and got herself killed?"

Now she was on the hook for a direct response.

Since Sydney didn't know the full truth, she could hedge in a not-so-hurtful manner. "Accusations have been made about your mom 'borrowing' money from Lansing Group." She hated making dumb air quote doinks with her fingers, though it seemed like a good time to avoid the word *embezzlement*. "The rumor is being investigated by professionals."

He puckered his lips inward. "Explains why a detective asked about my tuition expenses."

"I know this'll sound lame, but forget about gossip. I'm more concerned with finding the dipstick who—"

"Me too. Glad Mom has you on her side. Hit me up when you solve it. Please?"

Once Lionel returned to his pals, the empty place in Sydney's court was filled by Ted Armstrong.

"I want to come clean," he said. "I stole the sixty Gs."

"Another version? How many more do you have?" Sydney cocked her head. "I bet money is what you and Piper argued about the day she died. She said you 'had to act fast.'" Sydney regretted using the doinks again.

"Stupid, I know. Even desperate. Her ex was always begging for handouts. Threatening to expose a crazy video they made."

"Sex, drugs, and rock and roll?" Sydney asked.

"I told her nobody cares. I intend to pay LG back."

Sydney took a deep breath. "Let me get this straight. Piper used money you stole to pay off her ex-husband. In exchange, the schlub would skip town and destroy a compromising video."

"Kinda the idea," Ted said.

"How do you intend to reimburse LG?"

"From the IPO."

"I'm supposed to believe you stole money, but not the laptop?"

"What can I say?"

"I don't think either of you stole any money from LG. Though I'm not sure why you insist on spinning that yarn." Sydney jotted a few notes on her pad. "What about the café's ransom? Were you able to track the payment?"

He shook his head. "Bounced through more than a hundred routers. I lost count. But at least the café received a crypto key to restore their system."

Yeah, from you or someone who cloned your IP address, she thought.

"Were any LG client identities stolen?" Sydney asked.

"That's a minor problem compared to the malware attempting to corrupt our server farm and fleece accounts."

"Aeneid?"

"Perhaps."

At long last, an acknowledgment of malware.

Sydney made a quick recap in her head. According to Ted, Lansing Group was on the brink of hemorrhaging money and sensitive client information. That prompted her to wonder if he'd really taken every precaution to secure the company's infrastructure, or whether he fronted a criminal conspiracy as a side hustle to siphon valuable information. She needed to run it by Mason, LG's so-called "security consultant."

Dammit, she'd mentally used the air quote doinks again.

Ted continued. "The hack attempting to breach my security measures will be hard to wipe."

That sounded a lot like The Golden Crust's biznap troubles.

Sydney said, "I'll need more details if I'm going to put you on TV. And what should I tell the police?"

"We're a long way from TV, Syd."

"I have to put you on—"

"This is more like background, or whatever you people call it. And no cops. You can't tell anyone about the company's breach."

"I have to report it. You've made me an accessory after the fact."

"Please . . . Give me a day to sort out LG's malware so I can save the IPO. Then I'll say whatever you need for your story. In the meantime, focus on Grace—everything she says and does is important."

"Why? What's her role in all of this?" Making a deal with a potential source, aka criminal, sullied every journalistic bone in Sydney's body. "Ted, be straight with me. Did you kill Piper?"

His face puckered in grief. "No way. Don't even think that."

"The cops will want more than your word on it. By the way, did you and Moose get a chance to examine the security recordings yet? Anything suspicious?"

He glanced away.

Sydney came back to an old area of inquiry, trying to trip Ted by ignoring Mason and Pete's directive. "Your fingerprints were found on the laptop. Care to change your story?"

"I told you; I'm being framed." Ted held up a palm, cutting off her objection. "Okay, my hands are dirty, legally speaking. But stop hounding me. Give me a day, and I'll help you build an airtight case against the conspirator."

"Conspirator? Do you mean Grace? Or Gavin? And what about the embezzlement claim against Piper? You need to clear her name."

"I'm trying."

Ted walked away before Sydney could fire off another question.

31

Following the funeral, Sydney made her way back to the city, the skyline looming ahead. Her mind was an eddy of thoughts, each one a piece of the puzzle she was determined to solve. She needed to cultivate information from the task force, something that required the finesse of a diplomat. As she navigated Charleston's bustling streets, she prepared her arsenal of charm and wit, ready to extract every nugget of intel she could.

The federal building was located on the corner of King and Mossy Oak Streets. The cement-colored eyesore at the extreme upper end of the design district was often scheduled for modernization, only to have the project scuttled by lack of funds. Nearly every building in the district, including that one, had been officially conserved by either the National Trust or Preservation Society of Charleston—the fruits of living in a city founded nearly four centuries ago.

Sydney's peep-toe pumps clacked on icy marble tile as she skated across the lobby. She flashed press credentials for the dark-haired guard stationed in a cocoon of bulletproof glass. He set aside the toothpick dangling from his lips to cram the last bite of a Twinkie into his mouth.

"I'm here to see Sergeant Cash," Sydney said.

The guard wiped his lips with a sleeve before lifting the desk phone's receiver. A moment later, she wrenched a laminated visitor's badge from the fishbowl's tiny opening.

A flat-nosed guard materialized and positioned himself between Sydney and the stairwell as she edged through a hulking body scanner. The behemoth blocked most of what looked like a mural of Charleston circa 1860. A third security guard rested one hand on his government-issued Smith & Wesson 9mm Compact while he yanked her purse off the conveyor belt as it exited an imaging booth.

She shifted her weight when he unzipped a silk bag containing personal hygiene items. Once the lug nut realized he was pawing tampons, he signaled her through. Shouldering past Flat-nose, she barreled up the wide, blood-veined marble stairs two at a time to the second floor, then pushed a doorbell outside the first office.

Cash jerked open the wooden door. Up close, he resembled a character you'd read about—a thin man with a razor-sharp part in his hair and firm jawline. He looked about forty, with wrinkles around his eyes as though he spent a lot of time squinting. He wore jeans, a polo shirt, and work boots.

"Sydney Quinn, Action 7 News."

"Lieutenant Bernadino called," he said. "Mentioned you intended to stop by. Didn't think he meant quite so soon."

"My producer hates when I waste time." She moved inside the office. "I'd like to know what evidence you have against Piper Kingston."

He zipped his lips.

"C'mon," Sydney said. "I'm sure Dino told you I can be trusted."

"Never came up."

Sydney braced her hands on her hips. "Did he mention I wouldn't leave until I got what I came for?"

Cash manufactured a genial smile. "I do recall similar words. Follow me. I'll show you some of what I've uncovered."

He ushered her past a conglomerate of tables and desks piled with computer monitors and stacks of three-ring notebooks. He fetched a blue binder from a heap of blue binders. "I reviewed the corporate banking statements and the accounting ledger with a fine-tooth comb, and I detected an undocumented $60,000 disbursement, which has since been traced to Piper Kingston. There is clear and compelling evidence she embezzled this money from her employer, Lansing Group." Cash hesitated, likely for dramatic effect. "And that's not all."

Sydney tried to scrub away thoughts about Piper's involvement in any illicit scheme. After all, according to Ted's latest narrative, he'd taken the money.

Cash continued. "Special electronic monitoring detected several instances where other large withdrawals were spontaneously transacted in what are commonly called SQL injection attacks."

"You think Piper embezzled *more* than 60,000?"

"Not exactly," he said.

"Then who spontaneously injected money?"

Cash scrunched his nose, creating a deep cleft in his brow. "Actually, the firm's balance sheet is within acceptable limits. So, they aren't in deep kimchi."

"*Kim* who?"

"Kimchi, a killer Korean delicacy. Oh, never mind. Let me back up."

"Twizzle all the way back to electronic monitoring."

He shook his head. "I can't throw back the curtain on our counter-surveillance techniques. Suffice it to say we find things bad guys are hiding."

Such as Tor Internet users' IP addresses, she thought.

Sydney leaned against the desk. "If LG accounts were electronically pirated, how come the books balance? I'm no certified accountant, but that seems improbable. Even asinine."

Cash bristled at her presumption. "What makes you think—"

"My finger is on the pulse."

"Well, your butt is on my notes." He swept his hand to move her away, then thumbed through a legal pad to find the page that pressed his point. "Microattacks aren't new. The balanced ledger, however, is quite a fresh twist on the embezzlement game. I'll continue researching this anomaly. I also subpoenaed Lansing Group for associated program code and executables. Their lawyers are having a fit, suggesting I'm trying to disrupt commerce."

Sydney believed LG's corporate lawyers clearly didn't know the feds—that was to say, Mason—had already infiltrated their staff.

She asked, "Can your undercover agent at LG covertly obtain what you need without a subpoena?"

Cash cocked his head. "What undercover agent?"

Sydney touched her nose in a conspiratorial gesture. "Oh, I get it. You can't confirm or deny."

"If you say so."

She registered his non-denial and moved on. "Are you at liberty to provide a detailed explanation of the attacks based on your considerable expertise?"

If she thought a shameless play to his ego would get him to reveal sensitive information, she'd made a big, fat mistake. He sat stone-faced. The hard silence hung there uncomfortably longer than anticipated, like he was trying to run out the clock.

And just when Sydney thought Cash might never speak again, he said, "Malicious software, or pestware, is designed to secretly access computer systems as a virus, wiper, worm, or spyware."

"Is this a malware lecture, or did you make an actual discovery?"

That question roused him. Cash shot to his feet and his boots hit the floor with a thud. He moved across the room and leaned against the wall near a bookcase stuffed with printouts and notebooks. "I've concluded LG's operating code has been penetrated, and their servers are hosting a potent virus."

Sydney's eyebrows shot up, despite having already heard that item from Ted. "Yikes. Tell me more."

"The way I figure, sophisticated electronic pirates remotely embedded the malware. That is to say, black-hat hackers are capable of writing a script so infinitely concealed, it nearly avoided detection. And their code may be resistant to disinfection."

"Why pirate LG?"

Gavin Lansing had assured her that her investments were safe at his firm. But Ted, and now Cash, had identified a big malware problem. While Mason hoped to tie Gavin to whatever conspiracy the task force was investigating at Lansing Group.

"Simple answer," Cash said, "they have quite a lot of money ripe for plucking. But it's likely LG isn't the malware's only target. Hackers widely distribute worms and viruses to see what other domains and organizations they can infect."

32

Sydney's eyes widened in a mixture of shock and frustration as she faced Sergeant Cash, her voice quivering with intensity. "What I'm hearing is that things may not be so bad, or that conditions at Lansing Group could be even worse than advertised."

Sergeant Cash frowned, then nodded.

Though she couldn't untangle the previous mess, she wanted to keep him talking. She knew the answer to her next question from a tutorial with Dale and the three dwarfs. "How big do you think the malware's reach is, and what happens if all the safety nets fail?"

Cash pushed off the wall and trapped a sliding binder before righting the shifting mound. "The Internet is a powerful economic and social tool, putting the whole world at your fingertips."

"Tell me something that isn't common knowledge."

"Pirates redirect traffic by tweaking the numerical language of web addresses. Then they install a rootkit to modify the host's operating system. If the malware stays hidden from view, crooks can launch a sniffer code to determine what sites or applications the cybercriminal enterprise wants to attack. Once the sniffer finds what it's looking for, other malware apps attack the target. In this case, seizing money from LG client accounts."

Sydney sought clarification. "And you think Piper was behind all this rooting, sniffing, and attacking?"

"Too soon to say. My job is to uncover evidence of criminal activity, then identify and apprehend suspects. Remember, I still have thousands of lines of code yet to review. So far, we're relying on a patchwork of security fixes." Sydney took a moment to ponder whether he'd been drawn to a technology-imbued career because he was hardwired. Or had years of immersion in drab financial statements and computers turned him into a droid? She felt kind of sorry for him and wanted to find out. "How'd you become interested in this line of work?"

A gleam of genuine enthusiasm lit his eyes. "Ever hear of the Hack Pack?"

Sydney shook her head.

"Notorious OG hackers. Cybercrimes's match to Willie Sutton."

"He's the guy who said he robbed banks because they had the money."

Cash nodded.

"What about Ted Armstrong?" she asked.

"What about him?"

"I have it on good authority he's a solid suspect in Piper Kingston's murder. But local law enforcement isn't allowed to touch him while he's working as a federal confidential informant."

"Is there a question?" Cash hid behind an expressionless mask. His face betrayed nothing. No hints. No clues. No confirmations.

"Is he?" Sydney asked.

"A solid suspect? You'd have to ask the sheriff in charge of the murder investigation."

She crossed her arms. "Your informant?"

That earned a tight-lipped smirk from the sergeant, who wasn't likely to give up any confidential information to her.

Sydney opted to pivot again. "What about ransomware? Same motives?"

He offered a little finger wave, and they moved to a neighboring room, where he pointed to a detailed flowchart attached to an easel. "Ransomware generally starts with unsolicited email designed to trick a victim into clicking on an infected attachment or website. The malware leverages flaws in an operating system, forcing it to run dirty code. It encrypts important files on the system, then demands a payment, generally using cryptocurrency. Extremely malicious software targets misconfigured or unpatched computers to replicate itself and spread around the network."

"Any local activity?" The question further served to calibrate Cash's truth-telling, since she already knew the answer.

"We've seen a rash of significant and tenacious cyberattacks on businesses in the southeast. Most have been thwarted before any critical or sensitive data was stolen or compromised. But a couple of cities in Florida were hit and paid out significant six-figure ransoms. And you've heard of the Colonial Pipeline and JBS meat production hacks. They made a big splash."

Sydney managed a punch of laughter. "So, the cybercrime underground is only after money?"

"Mostly, but they can also be phishing for closely held corporate information by using the façade of a legitimate company. Or espionage, hoping to steal national security methods and secrets. Our task force treats most cyberattacks as bank fraud."

Sydney knew the Secret Service hadn't thwarted The Golden Crust's hack. "You're telling me the hacker doesn't even have to live around here?"

That question earned the rictus of a grin. "A talented hacker with nimble fingers can initiate an attack from anywhere in the world. On the web, a single hacker or crew can commit fifteen thousand bank frauds a day from their mother's basement or dirt hut. They're hard to identify and nearly impossible to catch."

"In the case of a ransom attack, what do you recommend businesses do?"

A sober tone blanketed Cash's clipped delivery. "First and foremost, they need to let us know they've been hacked. All forms of cybercrime leave a trail, electronic crumbs we can track in hopes of putting a stop to the hackers. Two, never pay the ransom. Lastly, businesses should ensure everyone uses long and strong passwords."

"But they're such a pain."

"Complex passwords are even more of a pain for hackers. Also, users should create a different password for each website they visit.

Change passwords every three months or more frequently. And avoid common words—even if you add symbols and numbers. At home, install antivirus, anti-spam, anti-phishing, anti-spyware protection. Ensure you employ an active firewall. And by all means, back up your data."

Sydney rolled over the points for Mandy's inclusion in her blog. Then she swung for the fence. "Could LG's troubles be the work of Russian or Chinese state-sponsored hackers?"

Cash winced. "They certainly have the brio. But I can neither confirm nor deny."

•

Upon leaving the federal building, Sydney tapped the voice recorder app on her phone and dictated notes and questions. According to the Secret Service Task Force's local detective, Piper had stolen $60,000 or more from Lansing Group. Yet Sydney refused to believe Piper had abused her position and embezzled from the firm. It seemed more likely that whoever had killed her had also framed her. And what, if anything, was Ted Armstrong's part in Piper's murder, the misplaced laptop, and the SQL attacks? Or Gavin Lansing's role in the snowballing saga?

A part of her mind was still organizing specific questions for Ted and Gavin as she sauntered to the car. Satisfied with her progress, she phoned Mandy.

"Where have you been?" Mandy shouted.

Sydney held the phone at arm's length. "Leaving the federal building. Why? What's shaking?"

"Did you do a little late-night swimming, dare I say, bareback?"

"Mason and I may have done the hey-diddle-diddle in the ocean. How'd you guess?"

"I searched your name, like I do every day, to find out what people are writing about you online. Imagine my surprise when I saw a photo link to Face Place."

"What's Face Place?"

"A 'Page Six'-style gossip site where you upload naughty pictures and video clips to share."

"Pictures?" Sydney vibrated on full alert.

"A buck-naked keister," Mandy said.

Sydney leaned against the car. "Yeah, right. Quit jerking my leg."

Mandy continued. "You're climbing into a boat, I think. The images are kind of grainy."

In the grand scheme of things that could upend her universe, prurient photos weren't something Sydney had ever contemplated. "You sure it's me? What if they pasted my head on someone else's butt? They can do that, you know."

"Yeah, Sparky. I'm acutely aware of the technological marvels available with Photoshop. I can only tell you what I saw. On the upside, you're viral."

"Have to die of something, right?" The words stuck in Sydney's throat.

Several pedestrians gave her sideways glances. Recognition? Or worse, pity?

Mandy said, "I mean, you have over twenty thousand hits. The number will quadruple by tomorrow."

"Make them disappear. Mrs. Quinn can't have her daughter's butt as some wing nut's screen saver." Sydney made a quick net assessment. Even if the photos were real, her temporary embarrassment wouldn't lead down a path of no return. She could always play the contempt card and deny they were her. Or she could own it. Suck it up and carry on 'til the gossip blew over. Though any level of intrusion into her private life left Sydney feeling a little violated.

Mandy continued, "Especially since you have other redeeming qualities. I'll check into getting the photos deleted from the site."

As Sydney merged onto the Crosstown Expressway, she phoned Mason.

"How's it going?" he said. "Making a big impression today?"

"Making an impression on a lot of people." For a moment, she imagined wrapping her hands around the mystery photographer's throat. Taking and posting those pictures had been cheap. Low-class. And tacky.

"What do you mean?"

"Apparently, my rear end is plastered all over Face Place from our little interlude last night."

Mason hooted.

"It's not funny," she said.

"Kind of," he said. "No worries. I'll use my clout to take 'em down."

Sydney clicked off and crammed her phone into a console slot.

At a stoplight, she pulled on a baseball cap and tucked in her hair. She snatched a pair of oversized sunglasses from the glove compartment, confident her techno-freak best friend and man-pal were working to yank the pictures. With luck, the twenty thousand people who'd already seen her hind end all lived in an Eastern European country and never watched Action 7 News.

33

Sydney executed a stealthy entrance through the station's back door. She slinked through the newsroom, dodging colleagues. Her destination: Mandy's cubicle, a place known for antiseptic cleanliness and order, along with an impressive collection of novelty mugs.

When she reached Mandy's desk, the researcher was engrossed in her computer screen, oblivious to the world. Sydney whispered, "Show me."

Startled, Mandy nearly spilled her coffee. "You need to wear a bell." She turned the monitor, then patted her rear. "One more item of yours I have to envy."

"Oh, sheesh." The photo was unquestionably Sydney.

Next, Mandy did something she'd never done. She slid onto the corner of her desk, hiked one leg up like a smoldering noir movie starlet, then loaded a fresh stick of gum in her mouth. "You know something, Sparky? We need to talk. Aren't you moving a little fast with this Mason character?" She angled her head toward the computer.

"Depends on your definition of fast. We've known each other for almost fifteen years."

"I'm your friend. Don't treat me this way." She spit the juicy cud into the wastebasket. "You *knew* each other fourteen years ago. There's a big difference. What do you really know about him now?"

Sydney could feel Mandy's eyes dissecting her. She gulped down a mouthful of caffeine. Mandy was right. She'd jumped in without a solid exit strategy.

Mandy continued. "Let me sum it up." Her tone sounded professorial with a touch of humor. "You drink too much Diet Dew.

You cuss. And you have questionable morals. In other words, you're everything I'm not—which makes you the perfect best friend."

"But you think I'm in over my head?"

"Probably. So, I'm counting on you to act like *Sydney Quinn*."

"Instead of . . .?"

"Look, I won't presume to tell you what to do—except be yourself. Ferocious and unstoppable. The Syd I know doesn't take shit from anybody. She'd fillet whoever snapped those pics. Okay, maybe not commit actual violence, but you get my drift."

Sydney roared her approval. "Channeling your inner football coach?"

"You know it—because I never swear. Curse. Or use profanity."

Mandy became a veritable thesaurus when nervous.

In her thirty-five years, Sydney had endured a handful of less than shining moments. This was another of those unalterable historic times.

Mandy opened a fresh stick of gum. "How's Coop?"

Leave it to Mandy to remind Sydney she had another man in her life.

Sydney said, "He mentioned he'd scored a big assignment. Won't be around for a few weeks. Why do you ask?"

"Mason? Coop?" Mandy tipped her palms up and down like a scale.

Sydney puffed out her cheeks. Her relationship with Coop was still in its infancy. More like long distance and without a firm commitment for exclusivity. In other words, complicated. And unconsummated. Mason's reemergence could alter its dynamics—and not in a good way.

"By the way, Pete asked to see you," Mandy said.

Sydney skulked to the station manager's office.

Pete was stooped over his putter when she entered. "Close the door."

"Wanted to see me?" she asked.

"Already have. That wasn't exactly what I had in mind when I told you to take some chances." The edges of his lips curved upward in a sullied sort of way. "I know plenty of great reporters, but you have to turn away when they're on camera. Others, all they have going for them is their looks. You—you're the whole enchi-mama. Hell, I saw beyond the pretty face the first day I met you."

She rubbed goose bumps from her arms.

Pete knocked a golf ball into an overturned glass. "You have the chops. And a great caboose. Makes me proud to be an American." He let his voice trail off. "Those pictures really you?"

"'Fraid so."

"I'll get our lawyer to sue whoever is responsible." Pete placed the putter on his desk. "Now, let's talk about your first-responder fundraiser. What should I expect in terms of visuals?"

"My usual highfalutin soirée. I'm thinking infomercial meets telethon." Sydney snapped her fingers. "And daylight fireworks."

"Nice."

"The money we raise will go toward building adapted homes, providing living expenses, and funding college scholarships. And I intend to relocate and re-outfit the Rehab Center."

He examined the putter's grip. "You're like a daughter to me, so I wanted you to be the first to know. I'm leaving Action 7."

She pointed at the putter. "Joining the senior tour?"

"Retirement. I mean it this time."

Sydney didn't believe him. The newsroom was in his bones. "Because of my photos?"

"Just not having fun anymore." Pete blew out a tired breath, then waved her out.

Sydney wandered to Olivia's desk atop the altar, carrying a heavy lump of guilt over Pete's likely departure. She couldn't veil her culpability. "I need a little pep talk."

"Right church, wrong pew, if you know what I mean." Olivia's attention was focused on the bullpen, surveying the glut of reporters and assistant producers hard at work finalizing packages, honing story pitches, and nailing down sources.

Sydney pooched her mouth in frustration. "But—"

"No pep talks for you." Olivia placed her hands on narrow hips. "You're my rock. And rocks don't need pepping."

"I only—"

She held a shushing finger to Sydney's lips and shooed her away with the sweep of a hand. "Go rain sunshine someplace else. I have to knock a few sound technicians upside the head."

Sydney pushed through the newsroom before collapsing in her recliner. She couldn't wrap her brain around Pete retiring. Nah, that was never gonna happen. But if he was serious, wouldn't that be a kick in the shin? She quirked an eye toward his office.

If he left, the newsroom would never be the same.

She wanted to believe the tribe would always stay together. Yet they were evolving. And there was nothing she could do about it.

Mandy sidled in and handed her a Diet Dew. "Mason called. The pictures are all gone. Any idea who took 'em?"

Sydney pressed the cold can to her forehead. "Some wing nut with a telephoto lens and nothing better to do."

"How'd they know you'd be there?"

"Just lucky, I guess." Sydney snapped the pull tab on her soda. "Nothing else makes sense. Unless . . ."

"Unless what?"

Sydney dredged up a grin. "I must be close to breaking a big story. First, the photos. Second, someone put a digital bounty on me. Those things might drive other reporters away. But not me."

Mandy thrust a fist in the air. "Not the ferocious and unstoppable Sydney Quinn. Even so, let's change all your passwords—stat."

They moved to Mandy's desk. She pattered the keyboard, and her screen flicked from one site to another. Mandy was a skilled race car driver on the Internet autobahn. She passed Sydney a scrap of paper with an elite password, an odd combination of letters, numbers, and special characters. "This'll work on your accounts. Tonight, you change them all again using something new. Enter a different code for each account. Promise me you won't use a dupe."

"I pinky swear," Sydney said.

"What's next, my favorite reporteress?"

"I started down this road earlier, but let's take one more run at ransomware attacks that hit the big-time."

Mandy nodded, and it didn't take long for her to locate several recent breaches. The first, at a huge gaming company. Experts labeled the ransom attack *an IT incident*. A trite euphemism for more deep kimchi.

In another security bungle, an oil company employee claimed to have lost his laptop containing names and vitals of Gulf Coast residents who'd applied for compensation from a damaging oil spill. Once the company paid off the hackers, they'd revealed the ransom demand.

Even an international banking organization had been extorted, and a department store conglomerate had had their own credit financing operation hijacked, along with information from every shopper who ever used a bank-issued card in their stores. The feds traced stolen information to an organized crime syndicate, who then parsed information to other criminals for looting bank accounts and fraudulent credit card purchases, in addition to a seven-figure ransom.

Hackers were profiting in so many ways, even they had no idea where the stolen info wound up.

Sydney rerouted her eyebrows. "Hey, get a load of this."

34

Sydney passed her laptop to Mandy.

"Says here, Moonshine Clothing, the co-opted department store, used ID Rx, a Charleston-based identity restoration company," Mandy said. "The judge cited a proactive contract with ID Rx likely mitigated millions of dollars in additional liability."

Sydney re-keyed her laptop and continued to find other references to the local restoration company. "Seagull County School District, west of here, hired ID Rx when they forgot employee and student information on computers destined for the salvage heap." She sprang from her chair and did laps around the cubicle. "The Geek Store guy, Moose, was involved in that school's debacle. Said he discovered student data while scrubbing hard drives. Wonder if ID Rx can assist Lansing Group or The Golden Crust? Get me everything on ID Rx."

"Already on it." Mandy's hands blurred across her keyboard. "Whoa baby, their website has slick graphics. Come to Momma. ID Rx gives good GIFs and JPEGs."

Olivia poked her head in the cubicle. "What in the world are you working on?"

Sydney brushed away the knot forming in her stomach. "Mum's the word."

Olivia leaned in as if anticipating a salacious secret. "Part of your promised barn burner? Why hold back?"

"I'm on a short leash with the Secret Service."

Olivia threw up her arms. "Let me know when I can put you on the storyboard. The schedule is full unless you break a major one."

After Olivia left, Mandy admitted being dead-ended—finding nothing about the ID Rx corporate structure. "I'll make a few calls."

Sydney withdrew to her desk and phoned her contact at Lansing Group's Records Department. "Working hard?"

"Glad I'm working at all," Velma sighed.

"Any idea if LG is choosing an identity restoration company to preempt a lawsuit over possible stolen IDs?"

"Hmmm, why do you ask?"

"Because it's my job. And you owe me."

"Wow, you're a little cranky today." Papers rustled on Velma's end. "Okay, here we go. We set aside $2 million for a company called ID Rx. But that's strictly on the down-low."

Sydney disconnected, then dialed Seagull School District's administrative offices and was pleased to find an employee familiar with their ID Rx contract. The district had paid nearly a half-million dollars. From the Moonshine headquarters in Raleigh, North Carolina, she learned their contract cost a hair north of $3.5 million. ID Rx had netted a cool 6 million bucks from these three clients alone.

That left Sydney with more questions than answers.

And she hadn't uncovered anything concrete to broadcast.

She meandered to Editing Bay 5. Inside, she flipped open an unfinished to-do list stapled to a folder. First item on the list—Ted's arrest record. In all the hubbub, Sydney hadn't confirmed that important detail.

Mandy tapped the door before poking her head inside. "Anything for me, Sparky?"

"Locate Ted's police record from your collection of public data sources. Or use a second cousin-in-law from your never-ending family tree if you have to." Sydney pressed her lips together. "And what do you know about Trojans?"

Mandy giggled. "Condoms or Southern Cal?"

"Get creative."

Mandy reappeared fifteen minutes later wearing a frown. "No police record for Ted."

Sydney's jaw dropped. "Must be a mistake? He told me he has one."

"Can't help you there. But I have info on a not-so-empty giant horse."

Sydney flattened her chin on a fist. "Let's hear it."

"After ten years of war, the Trojans were tricked by the Greeks into bringing a huge wooden horse inside their city walls. They considered it a kind of victory trophy. Boy, the look on their faces must've been priceless when Greek soldiers spilled out from the hollow belly."

"Thanks for the history review. Relevance?"

Mandy staged a shoebox on the tiny workstation. "In today's parlance, the expression Trojan horse is a substitute for *ploy*. You know, when a foe invites themselves into an opponent's secure space. I also took the liberty of researching *Aeneid*. It's an epic poem about a Trojan who traveled to Italy." She sighed. "You think there's a connection between Ted's police record, *Aeneid*, and Trojans?"

"Oh, yeah. What's in your box?"

Mandy removed the lid. Inside were DVDs of *Castle*, *Monk*, and *Murder, She Wrote*. "I'm calling it the Rockford kit. We need to refine our investigative skills if we're going to solve whatever Ted is doing."

"But I'm a professional interviewer. That's almost like being an investigator."

"Except you can't spot a tail, conduct a stakeout, and don't own a nifty plaid jacket."

Made sense she'd toss that one in. Mandy's favorite color was plaid.

"Oh, forgot to mention," Mandy said. "I discovered ID Rx is a shell company under the J&W Enterprises umbrella."

"Then get me everything on J&W."

"Feelers already out among my clan."

They moved to Sydney's cubicle. With a sigh, she sank into her recliner. "Next topic—the Hack Pack."

Mandy's hands batted around with excitement. "Oh, wow. The Pack is legendary. They were a driving force in stealthy, web-based piracy. That dynamic duo gained epic status in the hacking community." She remained fish-eyed, checking a text on her phone. "Luis Gaston has the dubious reputation of receiving the largest hacker sentence ever dished out in federal court. Of course, he was also fined and paid gonzo amounts of restitution."

"Can we imply Ted was a member of the notorious Hack Pack? And he changed his name from Luis Gaston?"

"Nope. I read Luis died a year or so after leaving prison. But the other purported member was Jake Bishop. He has a sealed juvie record in Virginia because he was a minor when he got caught hacking." Mandy's phone beeped and she glanced at the screen. "Here we go. My contact at the state business bureau texted that Jake Bishop owns J&W Enterprises."

That meant it was plausible that Ted was really Jake, and he'd been a member of the notorious Pack. Did Gavin know? Did Piper?

Sydney sat forward in the recliner with an uncomfortable intuition. "If Ted and Jake are one and the same, it's a game changer. And now Ted owns ID Rx. That would certainly explain the laptop's disappearance."

Mandy considered the point. "You think Ted stole the laptop simply as a means to hawk his identity-restoration services?"

"Could be, but he denied taking the laptop." Postulating conflicting scenarios was fun but reckless. Sydney needed to nail down facts. And figure out how it could've resulted in Piper's death. "If Ted was framed, like he claims, where does that leave us?"

"In an awful mess," Mandy replied.

Sydney phoned Ted for confirmation, but the call went to voicemail. She didn't leave a message. Pushing back in the recliner, she said, "Tell me more about the Pack."

Mandy seemed eager to spill what she knew. "Rumor has it, the pair hacked NASA in the early 00s. Probably for kicks. Trying to upstage one another. Like, 'Hey, look what I did.'"

"My guess is their snooping escalated."

"The two code geniuses quickly graduated to hacking-for-profit."

"Who'd they victimize?"

"The Pentagon and phone companies were lucrative targets back in the day. As well as ATMs."

Sydney laced her hands behind her head. "I'll bet the Defense Department didn't roll over quietly."

Mandy's excitement grew. "The Pack crashed top-secret DOD sites. And they attempted to sell battle plans and weaponry blueprints on the black market."

"Please stop your geeky admiration for the crew. Who finally busted 'em?"

"Secret Service raided Luis Gaston after he formed a splinter sect called the Keebler Elves."

"Dumb handle for marauding computer crooks."

Mandy stacked her wrists on the desk and began drumming her fingers. "Legend is—Luis saw himself as a cyber-Fagin."

"You mean the dude from *Oliver Twist*?"

"Righto. Instead of being a gentleman pickpocket, Luis hoped to pass on what he'd learned to next-gen hackers."

Sydney's journalistic instincts churned at high speed. She felt a pulse of unease—and liked it. The tickle was a good sign she was onto something important. Unease drove questions. Questions meant pursuit. And reality often sent her down an unexpected path.

Unforeseen. Scary. Fortuitous.

Truth was her guiding star—no matter what side she hoped to land on.

Sydney said, "Better set DEFCON 5 if Ted has resurrected Hack Pack 2.0 and is back in the game with Aeneid."

35

Puffs of white clouds jostled for space over the Ashley River, casting playful shadows on the water below. Ribbons of orange unfurled from the receding sun and painted the sky with a masterpiece of hues. In the Michigan suburb where Sydney grew up, such a day would've been a quintessential slice of Americana. Moms hanging clothes on the line, the crisp linens flapping like flags of domestic triumph. Kids dancing barefoot in the freshly cut grass, their laughter mingling with the scent of summer. In short, the kind of day where the ice cream truck's jingle became the soundtrack of joy.

Sydney phoned Mason from the car. "Confirm for me that Ted Armstrong was once formally known as Jake Bishop."

"No can do. That's privileged."

"C'mon. I'll let you do that thing you like."

He responded without hesitation. "Not for attribution, but yeah."

She would've let him do that special thing even without confirmation, but she loved to barter. Sydney disconnected, then turned her attention to the evidence mounting against Ted, monumentally pissed she'd made a deal with him to wait until tomorrow before going to the police. That deal was certainly worthless now, since Mason—a federal copper—knew all that she did, and undoubtedly more.

Despite his dogged pursuit of Gavin Lansing.

Since Ted's freedom from apprehension was closing fast, Sydney needed to speak with him before the Secret Service shuttled him away. She wanted him to clear Piper of any accusations of pilfering once and for all before he cut a deal. Since Sydney wasn't involved with the evening broadcast, she phoned Dino to join her.

Ted lived near the Military College of South Carolina, known simply as The Citadel, in an uptown section of Charleston prone to flooding. A hand-forged wrought-iron fence and ornate gate marked his property. Palmetto trees lined the front yard, strung with tiny white lights roping from one tree to the next. Sydney studied the sidewalk, salvaged brick laid in a herringbone pattern, as Dino unfolded from his Mustang. The detective looked downright urbane in a pullover and dark pants.

"How do you want to play it?" he asked.

"Since you're prohibited from arresting Ted for Piper's murder, let me see if I can coax him to confess on camera before the feds toss him in a hole or give him immunity."

"There's a pissing contest brewing over jurisdiction for Ted's apprehension. Glad I'm out of the fray." He rang the doorbell. "Give me a dollar."

"I'm kind of short—"

"Pretend."

Sydney passed an empty palm to him.

"You just hired yourself a bodyguard," he said.

She squared her shoulders. "Didn't know I needed one."

"Serves as an excuse for my being here off duty."

Ted's face was as tight as a Ziploc seal when he opened the door and eyeballed Dino. "What am I being charged with?"

"Besides bad grammar?" Sydney said.

Ted clawed the stubble on his scruffy face.

She pushed past him. "Thanks for inviting us in. Glad you recognize my bodyguard."

Sydney surveyed Ted's home furnishings. His personal style tended toward gray on gray, punctuated by stainless steel. Just what she'd expect from a computer pro.

The three sat at a brushed-edged kitchen table. Ted made no effort to disguise his confusion, and Sydney was elated he didn't ask for a lawyer. Dino allowed her to speak first—kind of a cute-reporter, stud-cop/bodyguard tag team. She hoped Ted's incriminating responses would tumble out during the conversation.

"Let's review." Sydney ticked off the summary of damning evidence on her fingers. "Lansing Group's missing laptop was found in your office with your prints all over it. Folks with personal information in the laptop's database are conveniently funneled to your identity restoration company to abate identity theft issues. And there's still the matter of big money missing from your firm. Ready to come clean about Piper's murder?"

Ted screwed up his face as he measured the impact of what he'd heard. "I vehemently deny having anything to do with the stolen laptop."

"What about the missing sixty large?" Sydney needed Dino to hear it from Ted to expunge Piper's record.

Ted avoided eye contact. "Can we keep this out of the press? You only have supposition and innuendo."

Sydney skated over the point for the moment. "Remind me where you were when Piper was killed. Moose didn't substantiate your claim."

"What's the use?"

"How about this new wrinkle? Your IP address was found on both the spam message and crypto key used in The Golden Crust's ransom attack. Care to deny it?"

Ted made an expression like a guy who'd been sucker-punched. He ran his finger around his collar a couple of times. When he did it again, Sydney found it seriously annoying.

By this time, Dino's eyebrows were scrunched so tight they nearly touched. His glance darted between Sydney and Ted without settling on either one. He jumped from the table. "Can I use the latrine?"

"First door on the right." Once Dino was clear of the kitchen, Ted said furtively, "You agreed to give me until tomorrow. Why'd you spoil everything by getting him involved?" He jerked his thumb toward the living room.

"Dino isn't your problem. The feds are ready to move in. And remember, you told me you stole money—not Piper. Unless you provide irrefutable evidence to the contrary—"

Ted pounded his fist into his palm. "You have it all wrong."

"Then tell me what I'm wrong about. The truth has to come from you. And what's with the other financial hocus-pocus?"

The edges of his mouth cracked, showing signs of discomfort. "What do you mean?"

Sydney took advantage of his indecisiveness and pounced. "A forensic audit of LG uncovered the missing $60,000. Same audit also revealed large sums gone one minute and back the next. A software glitch, maybe? Part of the server bugs you alluded to? Aeneid?"

Dino returned to the kitchen and tossed a hot-pink flash drive on the table.

Ted reeled from his chair as though the device were radioactive. "Where'd you find that?"

Sydney recognized the flash drive. "That's Piper's. What are you doing with it? Talk to me and help yourself. Or you're going to prison for the murder of Piper Kingston."

"Better idea." Dino drew himself up to his full six-three and thrust a finger in Ted's chest. "Let's play tornado and trailer park. You're the park."

Ted spoke slowly, editing each word. "That flash drive isn't pertinent."

36

Sydney stomped her foot. "Of course, Piper's flash drive is germane. You've lied so many times, I've lost count. And your arguments? The sophistry is mind-blowing. Let me break it down. Piper found out you stole money from LG and were involved in even bigger shenanigans you probably ginned up from your old Hack Pack schemes. You killed her, then conveniently put the blame on computer woes at LG's server farm infested with malware and sniffles as a cheap distraction."

"Infected," Dino corrected.

Ted offered a correction of his own. "Sniffers."

Sydney flicked open the notes from her interview with Sergeant Cash. She snapped the page. "Yup, malware. Like I said."

Ted wrenched his face. "I told you; I've been monitoring the server's glitches. And I'm compiling new code to enhance encryption and wipe the virus."

"What about the embezzlement?"

Ted's eyes moistened as the tension in the room mounted.

Sydney said, "Piper wasn't responsible. Right?"

Ted nodded. Sydney eyed Dino to make sure he understood that Piper was clean.

She continued to come at him from all directions. Pedal to the mat. Her confidence bolstered by progress. "Who killed Piper?"

Ted's tie-dyed T-shirt sagged in defeat. He fingered the flash drive. "Aeneid."

Dino rested an elbow on the countertop, flicking glances between the two. Then, his eyes fired up, and he moved for the door, fumbling his cell phone. "Gotta grab this call. Let me step outside."

When the front door slammed shut, Sydney turned on Ted.

"You want me to accept that a super RAT-bot bug killed Piper? How? When she learned you were using the firm's servers to launch Aeneid for the Hack Pack?" She grabbed the flash drive, and heat flushed her cheeks like a controlled burn. "I was darn close to taking your side."

Sydney hated saying that phrase out loud, since her job shouldn't involve taking sides. She collected details. And reported them in an unfiltered context. That way, the public could draw their own conclusions. Form their own opinions based on facts.

Even though Sydney felt confident Ted had played a role in Piper's murder, she refused to grandstand in a broadcast to fulfill her self-interests. But that didn't stop her from putting a figurative heel on Ted's throat.

She needed to score a confession.

Sydney took a deep breath. "And I almost believed an unknown entity had you in their crosshairs. Why all the unnecessary subterfuge?"

"Look, I need you to trust me. I've been set up." He pointed at Sydney's video camera. "Go ahead and record my statement, but if you air it before tomorrow—I'm a dead man."

Ted's fear was palpable. Talk about a game changer.

Sydney took his death threat to heart, but she wanted rock-hard proof. In a blink, a plausible motive came to her. She said, "Let me roll this out. You were coerced into creating Aeneid. Even pressured to co-opt LG's servers. Maybe strong-armed in other ways."

Ted straightened as though she'd hit the bullseye. "I'll tell you everything."

He was a drowning man who seemed to want to set the record straight, as though his life truly depended on it.

Sydney placed a wireless omnidirectional microphone on the kitchen table. Then she arranged the camera on the counter and squared it on Ted before pressing the record button. "Where do we start?"

"This may sound like a movie script," Ted said. "A tale of unbridled greed and deception. But I assure you, Hollywood never imagined what's over the horizon."

Sydney settled back. "Talk to me about Aeneid."

"It's a good one, as far as cyber-extortion schemes go. A former world-class hacker, hell-bent on destruction, hatches a calculated plan to drain the national treasury in a breach so massive—" Ted flung his arms out wide. "I bet you didn't know Charleston has become the epicenter of wire fraud."

"And Aeneid is the destructive malware?"

"Yeah—nasty little shit."

Sydney's head was spinning. "Did you write Aeneid?"

Ted waved her off. "A colossal nightmare is brewing simply because our government failed to take basic steps to secure its financial infrastructure. And don't get me started on porous international systems."

Sydney was concerned he was getting preachy and moving out of frame. But she didn't want to slow him down.

He paced a tight circle. "Sure, sure—government weenies deploy intrusion detection software and other high-tech trip wires. But their organizations are constantly bleeding sensitive information and find themselves in a sprint to catch up."

"Details."

"In general, they've been too slow or too weak to address system vulnerabilities. And hackers exploit vulnerabilities."

She motioned for Ted to sit. "Does this hacker have anything to do with The Golden Crust's attack?"

Ted slunk onto a chair. "The ransomware hits are mere noise—a side hustle. This hack is about retribution, along with siphoning huge amounts of money. The public has cyber-hack fatigue, and stuff like a viral pandemic, partisan bickering, and royal-baby news take law enforcement's eyes off the dark web."

Sydney tapped a pen on her notebook. "Are you the master

hacker behind this scheme, Jake?" Sarcasm and calculated insinuation dripped from her question.

Ted ignored the use of his birth name. "US companies lose more than 70 billion bucks each year to computer viruses, spyware, and online fraud. And I have the battle scars to prove it."

Sydney reflexively rubbed her right shoulder—her own battle scar.

Ted said, "But here's where the rapacious thief made a rookie mistake. Cloaked *my* IP address and tipped off authorities." Ted rapped his knuckles on the table. "In a cyber-war, trust is ephemeral—the tide is turning. Mark my words."

Ted's ranting seemed off base, if he was the one behind the attack. Sydney needed him to quit orating about an amorphous thief and be specific. He needed to own it.

"C'mon, talk about noise. Aeneid isn't on anyone's radar." She tried to appreciate the enormity of the alleged scheme, though Ted was omitting key pieces of information. Really important stuff such as *who* and *why*. Sydney attempted to fuse his ambiguities. "Tell me about the Hack Pack."

Ted said, "I *was* in the Pack. Not anymore."

"Any proof?"

Ted faced the lens and said flatly, "Grace, tell Sydney what you know." He pushed his chair back and flipped off the camera.

Sydney gave Ted the side-eye. The interview wasn't a prospective Emmy winner. It wasn't even quality journalism. She clenched her jaw. "That's it?"

"Yup."

She ticked off points on her fingers. "You were too cryptic. You never tackled whether you are involved in Aeneid. You didn't clear Piper's reputation. And you didn't reveal who wants you dead—a significant loose end in the alleged coercion plot. Then you toss in Grace's name without specifics." She glared at him before adding, "Lastly, I know you don't owe me any favors, but I didn't hear a confession."

His whole timbre changed in a heartbeat. "Relax, Syd—things could be worse."

A bolt of irritation stormed through her body. "I need more. Details I can verify."

Ted crossed his arms, signaling an end to the discussion. "Now, unless you're arresting me—"

"Most importantly, you didn't tell me who killed Piper."

"You'll figure it out."

Sydney reached for the camera. "C'mon, Jake, this thing is off."

"You have everything you need."

She flipped her purse strap over a shoulder.

Ted opened the door to show her out. "Please, I'm begging. Don't air anything until tomorrow evening."

Sydney met Dino on the sidewalk next to his car and held up Piper's flash drive. "Does this look butt-ugly to you?"

"You bet. Why?"

"Nothing in particular. Hey, why the quick getaway? I could've used your vaunted urban-chameleon skills in there."

Dino widened his stance. Big. Authoritarian. "You trying to piss me off?"

Sydney opened her trunk and placed the camera inside. "That's my motto."

Dino slammed the trunk lid. "Quit playing detective."

"Like that's gonna happen," Sydney snickered.

"You're a reporter, damn it. Not a cop."

She held up her palms. Dino had managed to shift gears so quickly, registering ten kinds of annoyance, he'd left her with a bad case of whiplash. "Whoa, you know I only use my superpowers for good."

Dino stiffened. "What's it like in Sydney-world?"

"A lot like yours. I have my ups and downs." Her stomach seized, confused and miffed by Dino's anger. "What's eating you? You came here voluntarily so we could work this together. Ted's the guy you should be peeved at."

Dino cast exasperation aside and replaced it with resignation. "I'm just mad at myself. I can't stop being a cop."

"I know. The city is lousy with them."

Dino pointed at the flash drive. "One of the quickest ways to lose a case and watch a criminal walk, not to mention get on my captain's bad side, is to conduct a search where I had no right to explore—and end up with actionable evidence. Safeguard that thing until I can get a warrant."

Sydney listened with fascination as Dino explained the intricacies associated with *fruit of the poisonous tree*. Evidence tossed. Blah, blah, blah—technicalities. She knew he was blessed with a crime-busting mind. His biggest fault—he was a chronic rule-follower. But she didn't want him to operate any other way.

Sydney nodded at Dino with an unspoken understanding and pocketed the flash drive. "You think Ted is playing me?"

"Playing you?" Dino scratched his chin. "Only way to find out is to dig all the way to the bottom of this case."

37

Back at the TV station, the mood was thick with intrigue as Sydney slipped Piper's flash drive into a USB port, her heart pounding with a mix of anticipation and dread. The dim glow of the computer screen gave the room an ambiance that matched the gravity of her task. She was about to delve into the depths of archived personnel records, files that Piper had surreptitiously downloaded. Those records might hold the key to a conundrum valuable enough to kill for.

Her screen opened to a landslide of seemingly innocuous HR folders. Thankfully, they weren't encrypted or password protected. She scrolled through name after name without a cogent strategy. She cast a frown, then opened Piper Kingston's file. It contained routine employment documents. Sydney skipped to Ted Armstrong and didn't locate anything special in his folder, either. She opened Gavin Lansing's file and discovered a scattering of IRS withholding forms and profit-sharing contracts. Nothing illuminating or the least bit interesting.

Sydney ejected the flash drive and ambled to the altar. "Hey, I met with my primary source again for one of the rabid pieces I promised you."

"'Bout damn time," Olivia said. "What do y'all have for me?"

Sydney detailed what little she knew about the Aeneid hacking operation. "My source also made a lot of wild accusations."

"Believe him?" Olivia asked.

"I honestly don't know. If he didn't do the deed, he can point out who did."

"And I'll bet you get the exclusive."

"Yeah, but he saddled me with a thorny caveat. Says if we air his story tonight—he'll be killed."

Olivia axed a section of her production run sheets with a red marker. "Sounds to me like you have a guaranteed follow-up."

Sydney's mouth slackened.

Olivia glanced up. "Oh, are you serious?"

"Well, yeah. Even if our legal team green-lights my story, his claims are totally unsubstantiated. That violates my strict code of conduct."

Both reporter and producer were keenly aware of the pitfalls in airing unconfirmed information. Most of the time, it came back to bite you in the ass and made the station look foolish. Local news organizations couldn't chance losing market share because of sloppy journalism, regardless of Pete's retraction ideas.

"What if the death threat is a hoax or a misdirection?" Olivia asked.

Sydney shook her head. "I think he's credible. We'd risk exposure if some loony decides to kill Ted, since we had prior knowledge of a threat."

Olivia chucked her pen on the desk. "It's a good piece. I want to air it."

"Look, you'll have plenty of tough choices when you take over after Pete leaves. But this isn't the hill you want to die on."

Olivia turned up her nose with patented heard-it-all-before doubt. "Pete's not leaving."

Dammit, why couldn't Sydney keep her yap shut? She held a finger to her lips. "I'm pretty sure that was supposed to be top secret."

"He's been hinting for a few days. I never thought . . ." Olivia made an elaborate show of adjusting her papers. "Okay, we won't air your piece tonight. But tomorrow, you hit the ground running and find me someone or something to substantiate. Before we lose our exclusive."

38

The morning began with a thud, followed by steady clanking, juddering Sydney out of the luxurious bed aboard the mega-yacht. She pulled on a Detroit Tigers hoodie with the sleeves cut off and moved onto the rear balcony. Sun smacked her face, prompting her to shade her eyes.

Through slotted fingers, she spotted four big rigs with flatbed trailers, systematically loading construction leftovers from a nearby hotel renovation. On the horizon, the Ravenel Bridge's aluminum double diamonds sparkled. Suspension cables connecting the bridge's towers to the roadway deck disappeared into a cloudless sky.

Her stomach rumbled. Not so much empty as simply demanding attention. Sydney moved inside and attempted to make breakfast. Minutes later, she waved a kitchen towel at the smoking leftovers she'd over-zapped in the microwave. She cranked open a porthole, then disconnected the galley's fire alarm. Completing the cycle of misfortune, her phone jiggled with a text from Olivia that read: *DB*.

Sydney punched her producer's number. "Why did you text me so early?"

"News never sleeps," Olivia said. "I need you on location."

"Send an intern. I want to remain available when Dino, the undersheriff, and Mason nail Ted Armstrong today."

"You say the sweetest things. That's just precious. Did y'all even read my message?"

Waving away the stench of scorched fried rice, Sydney reread Olivia's text.

Police often abbreviated *dead body* with the letters DB. Action 7 never used the redundant phrase on air. Instead, they used quaint little lexes like *victim* or *poor schmuck*.

Sydney plunked onto a chair. "Who died?"

"You're kinda grouchy this morning," Olivia hooted. "That was the whole idea I had when I assigned you to check it out. See, you take a peek, then call me with the name of the dead person, and we air a story. You following how this works, or need me to draw you a—"

"Where am I headed?"

"The Golden Crust—Lansing Group."

"Holy shi—pwreck, Olivia. You buried the lede."

"You used to be a whole lot smarter before ole what's-his-name started painting your toenails. Eric will meet you there." Olivia clicked off.

A dead body at Lansing Group.

Action 7 hadn't aired Ted's story last night—so it wouldn't be him. Who could it be?

And what was the dead person's connection to Piper's murder?

She phoned Ted without success.

Then, a bolt of fear struck her and she called Mason. It went straight to voicemail. She hoped that meant he was busy, refusing to believe that he could be the poor dead schmuck at LG.

Sydney placed the burned rice in the galley sink, then dressed. She chose a Bill Blass number with green and blue threads in a subdued pattern. She snagged a Diet Dew and half a bagel from the pantry on her way out, then locked the salon door.

An overnight shower had spawned heavy air. The car labored to cool the vehicle's interior temperature from core meltdown to slightly below four-alarm flop sweat. Moss ringlets dangled from the long-armed live oaks and crepe myrtles lining the marina's parking lot.

She merged into Crosstown Expressway commuter traffic, chomping the bagel. As she crawled over the Ravenel Bridge, she clicked into reporter mode, creating a mental to-do list—interview police for details regarding the dead body, capture co-workers' reactions on camera, and retrieve coroner notes, if available. She ducked around a traffic backup on Johnnie Dodds, raced over the Wando River on the I-526 Loop, then veered off at The Golden Crust's exit.

A glut of police cruisers and the coroner's black van swarmed the vast parking lot. Sydney threw her car into park and cut the engine. Steam rose from the asphalt as overnight puddles evaporated and became outlined in pine pollen's greenish-yellow paste. A rancid odor from the nearby paper mill burned Sydney's nostrils.

She spotted Action 7's mobile television station, the Osprey, and darted between crusted pollen puddles. The Big O was the same Ford E-350 panel van she'd used at Coosaw Creek's hostage standoff. The van had a twenty-five-mile transmitting and receiving radius via a telescoping microwave antenna and satellite dish mounted atop the roof, which could be reached by a five-step ladder attached to the vehicle's rear door. A heavy platform tower also sported four huge floodlights. Good thing the van had secured a primo location, since she didn't see any good snooping-trees to scale.

Eric, her photojournalist, mumbled something and handed Sydney a stick mic. They jogged toward the Azalea Building. Their progress was halted by a stout policewoman with a CPD ball cap pulled so low over her eyes, she had to lean her head back when she spoke. This gave the impression of looking down her nose at Sydney, a figurative gesture the cop used to her advantage.

"Where do you think you're headed?" the officer asked.

"Sydney Quinn, Action 7 News. Here to see Gavin Lansing."

"Press conference in two hours." The officer twisted away, sporting a condescending smirk.

Sydney snuck a glance at the officer's name tag. "Officer Jacobs, where's Lieutenant Bernadino?" She posed the question offhandedly, without knowing who'd caught the case.

The officer pointed over her shoulder. "Talk to Sergeant Temple."

Sydney was familiar with Derek Temple, the police department's public information officer. He modeled a recruiting-poster physique and an unflappable demeanor. But handing him the lead on a DB situation didn't make sense.

She approached a young guy wearing khakis and a light blue oxford shirt with the Lansing Group corporate logo stitched on his sleeve. "I'm Sydney Quinn from Action 7. Do you know why the police are here?"

"Ted's dead."

"Wait . . . What?" Sydney winced. "I mean, tell me more."

Keep it together. Maybe LG had more than one employee named Ted.

But what if her key source and suspect—the man who might have stolen money from everyone and who should've been apprehended that morning—had just been taken off the board?

"Ted Armstrong," the guy said. "Grace called me at home. Told me to hurry."

Fresh pangs of uncertainty washed over Sydney.

But I didn't air his story.

"Sorry for the loss of your co-worker." Sydney offered the stock phrase while she tried to regain her footing. "Would you like to share this information with the rest of the Lowcountry?"

The man's face contorted. "S'pose so."

Sydney remained stone-faced. *They'd* gotten to him, as Ted had feared. But who were *they*?

She flagged Eric and ensured police cars were backdropped in the frame. "Tell me about Ted?"

"He's my boss. Head of programming and software development. We worked together for five years. I can't believe he's dead."

She bowed her head. "Neither can I."

39

Sydney held the stick mic for the LG employee.

"When Grace called to tell me—" His voice trailed off.

Sydney prodded. "What did she say?"

"Grace told me—"The guy hesitated. "Come to the office as fast as I could. I gotta go, Ms. Quinn." He brushed past the reporter.

Sydney turned to Eric. "Let's find another way into the building. I need to speak with Mason Sterling or Gavin Lansing."

Her mind did a high-speed rewind.

Ted had been her prime suspect in Piper's murder, as well as the biznap ransom scheme. *Good riddance* seemed appropriate—but his death cast doubt on those suspicions. Besides, a guilty-verdict-by-press-release wasn't her style. If she believed half of what he'd told her, that meant the architect behind Aeneid, the mysterious superbug, was the person most likely connected to Piper's, and now Ted's, deaths.

A silver Mercedes 350 SL pulled into the CEO's space.

"Sydney Quinn, Action 7 News." She closed the distance as Gavin Lansing exited his car. "What happened to Ted Armstrong?"

Gavin locked the car with a fob. "I'll leave the police to explain, Ms. Quinn. I will say he'll be sorely missed. He was a great computer guy." He tucked his head, then dashed inside.

She skirted Officer Jacobs as the cop worked her stalemate routine on Julia Mayfair and other area reporters. Sydney spotted Sergeant Temple talking to a pair of patrol officers.

"Derek, long time, huh?" Sydney said. "What brings you out at this hour?"

"Come on, Syd. I'm working here. Didn't the uniforms tell you about the press conference?"

Sydney said, "Trying to do my job, too. Let me cut to the chase. I already know who you have in there. And I'm using his name in my piece." She made the declaration hoping to stimulate exclusive conversation.

The sergeant moved between Sydney and the other cops and lowered his voice. "Do me a solid and keep the name to yourself until we notify next of kin."

"Cause of death?" Sydney asked.

Temple spun away without answering.

Sydney called after him. "What detective is heading the investigation?"

No response.

The police department was clearly not getting their money's worth with him in charge of public information.

Sydney tottered to the van. Eric sat at the editing station, laying sound over B-roll footage. He didn't take his eyes off the monitor, but he pointed at his cell phone.

"What did y'all find out?" Olivia's tone sounded raw, even via speaker.

Sydney tossed her pen on the worktable. "Nothing from the police. They're holding a press conference later. But—"

"Who's dead?"

"Ted Armstrong." When the words spurted out, Sydney's spine vibrated like a tuning fork. She pressed the cell phone to her cheek with a shoulder and rubbed her arms.

"You mean laptop guy?" Olivia asked.

"And my key source for the unverified huge story."

Olivia sucked in air. "Did Dino provide anything we can use?"

"He's not here." Sydney disconnected.

Her cell buzzed with a text from the Nail Salon—her code name for Big Jim's Garage. The text read: *2N1T/0100, Adams Run, off 174, $2H*. Translation: She had to plunk down two hundred bucks at 1:00 a.m. for a spot in tonight's dig—an illegal street race.

She wanted in the race. Bad.

Sydney climbed atop the Osprey. The vantage offered an excellent view of the entire parking lot. The Osprey swayed as Julia Mayfair, of Eyewitness 13, climbed aboard, stopping on every other rung to flip her bottle-blonde mane from one shoulder to the other. When she reached the roof, the two rivals exchanged mild insults.

"Nice job on your EMS piece. Put me down for three hundred bucks." Julia's tone was absent sincerity. The gal could nurse a grudge like a skid-row wino. She slid into a folding chair and started preening her nails, purring at the emery board like it was catnip.

The NBC kid from Monday's hostage event climbed halfway up the ladder and gushed. "I think your idea to raise money for emergency responders is superb."

"Flattery doesn't work with her." Julia cleared her throat and tousled her over-processed do. "Now, scram."

"Leave him alone." Sydney turned to the NBC kid. "Anything else?"

"Oh, Miss Sydney. I could go on and on."

"Any chance of stopping you?" Julia nudged Sydney. "Tell him to take a hike, or I'll air footage of you at last year's jellyfish festival."

Their professional spats were usually settled over a cold one and a greasy burger at the Blue Pelican Lounge, but now the NBC kid was caught in the crossfire.

And Sydney wasn't good with ultimatums. "Damn it, Julia, sometimes you piss me off. Lighten up."

The NBC guy took the hint and bolted.

Julia never blinked. "Aren't journalism schools teaching manners anymore?"

"Give the guy a break. You'll undoubtedly be sleeping with him by the end of next week."

"Perhaps," Julia said. "But you didn't have to go all Rambo on me in front of the newbie. Now, what have you heard about the DB?"

"Waiting for the press conference, same as you."

"C'mon. Why do you make me beg?"

Sydney feigned picking her teeth. "Suffice it to say, the situation is stickier than a pot of day-old grits."

Julia put her palms together. "If you have any empathy, toss me a Scooby Snack."

Sydney jumped to her feet and slid down the ladder, thudding to the pavement with less elegance than she'd planned.

Julia hung her head over the side of the Osprey.

"Dead guy is Ted Armstrong. You owe me." Sydney dashed across the parking lot, chasing Mason's BMW.

While members of the press corps had been stuck outside, he'd been able to spend time inside, cloistered with CPD, all while dodging her phone calls.

•

Sydney didn't stick around for the presser. She returned to the station instead, where she divvied up ideas and tasks with Mandy.

Mandy hurriedly scribbled notes. "Slow down. You aren't making sense."

"I know, things sound too crazy."

"They sound just the right amount of crazy. Tell me more."

Sydney wrung an empty Diet Dew can in her hands like a dishrag. "I have to speak with Grace. She knows details about Ted's death. I'll convince her she doesn't need to protect anyone. Including Gavin Lansing."

Mandy flinched. "What do you think happened to Ted?"

"I don't know. CPD didn't bring Dino onboard, which is odd. We need lots more details, dammit."

Olivia strolled by the cubicle. "Sugar Booger, Mrs. Muirfield asked if you'd meet her at the yacht club for dinner tonight. I gave her the impression you'd love to."

"Thanks, it'll be the contract renewal meeting I've been waiting for," Sydney said.

"Don't forget to let her know how your fundraiser is coming

together," Olivia said.

Mandy added, "We're locked in for Monday. Emergency service chiefs have offered a full turnout. An ambulance with EMS, police, fire, SWAT, the fireboat. And of course, fireworks. I reserved Waterfront Park."

"Sounds great. Andy says lots of money is already flowing in." Sydney's cell phone vibrated, and she pinched the phone between her shoulder and ear.

"Sorry I couldn't take your calls earlier," Mason said. "Grace botched the scene. Destroyed potential evidence before calling the police. It's been a total zoo around here."

"Glad you're okay." She wanted to expand on that sentiment, but she cut herself off. "How did Ted die?"

"Coroner labeled it a suicide. Self-inflicted gunshot wound to the head."

Sydney threw a pencil at the partition.

Suicide? No way.

Why would Ted kill himself when he wanted so desperately to avoid being killed by the mysterious *they?*

Mason broke into her thoughts. "Gavin is going nuts over his IPO. He has to deal with two dead executives inside of a week and massive server farm problems. Darn glad I'm not him."

40

lickering blue lights from the cop-car klatch were long gone by the time Sydney and Mandy returned to Lansing Group. And the fleet of media vans had also pulled up stakes, signaling an end to the press conference and their interest in the tragedy that'd occurred earlier.

Sydney left Mandy in the car while she went off, hoping to corner Velma. She zigzagged across black-and-white checkerboard tiles in the Delphinium Building's atrium with the tensile awareness that she was being shadowed. Sydney detoured, hoping to disappear into the vast network of hallways. Her pace quickened as she tried to double back, but the path dead ended. She ducked behind a janitorial cart and spotted Grace pushing open doors.

Sydney trailed her back to the lobby and slid behind a row of potted palms while Grace slipped into the ladies' room. The redhead emerged a minute later, surveyed the foyer, then headed off in the direction of the Records Office. There, Sydney watched her pick the lock and disappear into Velma's place.

Sydney pressed her back to the wall and registered sounds of scraping metal, papers ruffling. No voices. She elbowed open the door. "Looking for something?"

Grace slammed a file drawer shut and seemed to measure her response. "Gavin asked me to locate a record on a former client."

Curious.

"Client records are on the other wall." Sydney pointed at the large signs hanging from the ceiling, denoting various cabinets' contents. "You're searching staff files."

"Explains why I came up empty-handed."

"I'm thinking *red*-handed. How'd you get in? Velma told me this room is always locked when no one is around."

Grace dangled a loop with a full assortment. "I have a key."

Sydney folded her arms and leaned against the edge of a desk. "After the laptop fiasco, Velma changed the locks. She and her supervisor are the only ones with access."

Grace fluttered the backs of her fingers under her chin. "Guess you got me there."

Curiouser and curiouser.

Sydney studied Grace, trying to read between her enigmatic lines. "I watched you pick the lock." She knew in her gut Grace would attempt to walk her in circles. Buying time to work on a plausible storyline. "You work for the head honcho. Why did you need to break in? Besides, doesn't the clutter in this office give you the heebie-jeebies?"

Grace began straightening folders atop the nearest desk.

Sydney said, "What's really going on?"

Grace faked a yawn. "Gavin asked me to ensure we don't have any moles on our team."

"Why?"

"Apparently, a spy in the company won't look good to the Securities and Exchange Commission or potential IPO stock investors."

"Must mean he thinks someone is sabotaging the initial public offering. Or benefitting from insider information."

Grace conceded the possibilities. "Suffice it to say, he'd prefer if you weren't nosing around at the same time."

"Oh, would he?" Sydney wondered whether Mason's undercover assignment was built with an impenetrable backstop to avoid Grace's detection. "And in return?"

Grace looked as though she carried a boulder-sized chip on her shoulder. "I'll answer your questions." She creased her brow into peaks and troughs as perfect as a freshly plowed back-forty. "Correction, only those questions that won't compromise me or the firm."

Sydney recalled Ted's ominous message: *Grace, tell Sydney what you know*. Perhaps this was her attempt to control the narrative. "Keep your friends close, as they say."

•

Sydney fired off a quick text to Mandy, her fingers dancing over the screen with urgency. Moments later, they rendezvoused in the lobby of the Azalea Building. The duo was a study in contrasts—Sydney, with her determined stride and sharp gaze, and Mandy, exuding a calm confidence that surely belied the storm of questions brewing in her analytical mind. Together, they were an unstoppable force, ready to pry open the lid on Ted's unexpected suicide.

As they approached Grace standing at the reception desk, Sydney asked, "Want to play good cop, bad cop?"

Mandy smirked. "As long as I get to be the good one."

With a shared nod, they followed the redhead as she guided them toward the turnstiles leading away from the executive suite and into the bowels of the main building. Grace swiped a card, and the barricade arm released so they could pass. Next, she put her thumb on a small keypad screen, and the glass door in front of them clicked open.

Once they were behind the glass barrier, Grace relaxed, though she continued to speak in hushed tones. "Didn't catch your colleague's name?"

"Mandy Rutledge." She stuck out her hand. "Why all the cloak and dagger?"

"Discretion." Grace turned away without further explanation.

Sydney had never been inside that particular labyrinth of hallways. Less impressive than the foyer and executive wing, and much different from the Delphinium Building where Velma worked. Here, tiled halls were wide, well-lit, unadorned. A series of dots and lined floor markings were explained when a life-sized robot whirred around a corner. The bot resembled Rosie from *The Jetsons*, with a round base in lieu of legs, broad shoulders, and bright green eyes.

"Good afternoon, Grace," said the bot's synthesized voice. "Welcome to Lansing Group—Tom."

The robot rolled past.

"Nice little guy, but not very bright," Mandy said.

"He's the most advanced communications robot in the world," Grace said. "Ted wrote code for him to speak. Tom is the name on the generic pass I used to let you in. It won't show on the master entry log. Besides, I think the bot is delivering interoffice mail, not serving as your welcome wagon." She swiped another card at an unmarked door. "In here—Tom."

Grace herded the women into a conference room with a stainless-steel refrigerator and long, sleek, black-lacquered table. A pyramid of R*Ampd energy drink cans served as a centerpiece. She slid bottles of water with LG labels to the Action 7 duo. "You must understand, I don't believe Ted committed suicide. I'm hoping you'll investigate his death."

Sydney nearly spit water through her nose. "Wha—"

"The guy was a boat junkie, not a self-destructive loony-tune. He recently ordered a new J-21, for heaven's sake."

Sydney leaned back in her chair. "Why ask for my help? Remember, I'm the one who wanted him thrown in jail for Piper Kingston's murder."

"He didn't kill her." Grace stabbed a finger in Sydney's direction. "You can start by asking Gavin about an argument he had with Ted."

Sydney urged her to elaborate.

Grace said she didn't know any details but agreed the exchange had been fiery.

Mandy asked, "Before or after Ted was taken by the police in the apparent laptop theft?"

"Tuesday morning, before the fireworks," Grace said.

Sydney made a mental note, then changed course. "Who was the first person to find Ted?"

"I guess it was me. Phoned the police when I spotted the . . ." Color drained from Grace's features. She took a swallow of R*Ampd to steady herself. "The scene was off somehow. Blood soaked through papers Ted must've been working on. And I spotted broken computer games plus two empty R*Ampd cans in the trash. Very weird, because Ted recycled everything."

"You point those anomalies out to the police?"

Grace lowered her head. "Of course. But I want you to have the same information. They are discounting crucial evidence because they think he killed himself, and they are ready to drop any further investigation."

Sydney picked at the water bottle's label. "I doubt I'll find anything the cops haven't already considered."

Grace hunched her shoulders. "Try. They won't even assign a detective."

"May I see where you found him?" Sydney asked.

She pointed to a desk in the outer office. "Right there."

Sydney nosed around without locating any signs of suicide or murder. The air reeked of pine-scented disinfectant, reminding her of summer camp. "Why'd you clean up?"

Grace leaned against the door jamb. "Where did you get that idea?"

"I protect my sources." Sydney recalled Mason mentioning Grace had interfered with the scene. She assumed the neatnik couldn't help herself. "What happened with the bloody papers?"

"I suppose whoever wiped the desk also dumped the documents. I never touched them."

Either Mason or Grace wasn't telling the truth. He had no motive to mislead, while Grace could be manipulating things in her favor for any number of reasons. Most importantly, to offset the mistake she'd made by tampering—whether intentional or not.

Sydney skimmed multicolored folders piled like a snowdrift on the credenza. Everything seemed inconspicuous, though the space lacked any personal effects. "Is this Ted's private space?"

"A common work area. His office is over there." Grace pointed across the room.

Ted's office was the kind you'd expect for a software guru. A glass wall faced into the pod. His furniture matched the lacquered style of the conference room. An imposing floor-to-ceiling dry erase board, covered with what resembled a mega-complex algorithm, flanked the wall opposite the window.

Sydney waved at the whiteboard's obscure number, symbol, and letter strands. "Homework?"

"Ted is," Grace said, "or rather, *was* a brilliant programmer. I'm told he loved to deconstruct other people's code, searching for flaws or genius."

"Which one is this—garbage or virtuosity?"

"I'm not sure." Grace crinkled her nose. "By the way, any chance Ted gave you some software to hold?"

"Why would he trust me? I was his chief accuser."

When Grace turned away, Sydney quickly snapped a photo of the whiteboard. She didn't know if the gobbledygook was important, but with someone's penchant for destroying potential evidence, she wasn't taking any chances.

Sydney continued searching the office, shoveling through another stack of folders on Ted's desk. She opened drawers, delved through books on shelves, flipped frames on the wall. Ted was a boat junkie, all right. Pictures of sailboats and motorboats were taped every-where. Though nothing pointed to why he'd killed himself . . . or was killed.

Until Sydney spotted an empty personnel folder stashed under the desk blotter, with a name she recognized from the Hack Pack—the notorious Luis Gaston, who'd reportedly died years earlier.

41

Sydney dropped Mandy at the station, promising to return with enough food for the entire newsroom. Palmetto Pizza Kitchen, located in Town Center Mall, was only a few doors from her bank. She located a parking space halfway between the two.

After a few steps on firecracker-hot pavement, sweat beaded in places proper women shouldn't perspire. Sydney wanted to duck inside the bank for a large dose of air conditioning, opting instead for the deserted ATM fronting the sidewalk. She plugged her bank card into the machine and hit the $500 fast-cash button, so she'd have enough for lunch and the dig's entry fee. The screen blinked an unpleasant *insufficient funds* message.

Sydney checked to ensure she was using the proper card, swiped it again—same result.

She tried a third time, attempting to access checking and savings account balances. No funds. An icy wave swam at her. She launched the banking apps on her phone, calling up retirement accounts, investments from LG's brokerage, and a savings account she kept in a Michigan credit union. All of her accounts had been looted, as the black-hat hacker, Dale, had predicted.

She'd been financially eviscerated by an unknown cyber-thief from the dark web.

Sydney phoned Dino. "I've been robbed." Her voice took on a pitch she didn't recognize.

"You okay? Where? What happened? Any witnesses?" Dino's usually unflappable cop tone sounded ruffled.

"ATM, Town Center. No money in any of my accounts."

"Are. You. Okay?"

Sydney shouted, "My money is gone!" Several shoppers turned to stare at her. She dropped her hands by her sides and drew a sharp breath. "My accounts have been raided—retirement, investment, banking—all gone."

Dino was breathing hard, too. "Go speak with the manager. Get them to do what they do. They know the drill."

Sydney disconnected and dashed inside.

Eighteen minutes later, she was a registered fraud victim. The only money in her pocket came from a $1,000 signature loan.

Gavin Lansing nearly plowed into Sydney as she exited the bank.

She hastily recovered to leverage the unexpected encounter. "Are you aware of any problems involving client funds?" She left it open-ended, foregoing any mention that her accounts had been sucked dry and the likelihood his company's computer system was worm infested.

"Everything points to Ted and Piper, Ms. Quinn. Don't blow this out of proportion."

Sydney wanted to scream.

He continued. "I'm a week from the stock offering. Let's avoid investors getting the wrong idea about my firm prior to the IPO."

Sydney quashed an urge to punch Gavin in the nose. Instead, she appealed to his ego. "You could be a big help to me. What do you know about Aeneid? Does it affect your IPO?"

He glanced around. "Not for public record."

"Do you think Ted went rogue?"

"I couldn't possibly know all his demons."

Sydney continued blocking Gavin's path. "How did you and he get along?"

"We were fraternity brothers." Gavin jutted out his chin. "At least for one semester, before I dropped out to form my first company. But I'll bet you want me to say I resented him. This might shock you, but I didn't. As you know, I own one of the largest insurance and financial firms on the East Coast."

"What did you and he argue about Tuesday morning?"

Gavin didn't miss a beat. "Our discourse was quite personal."

"Did you kill Piper?" Sydney stared at Gavin. Not accusingly, but with detached, scientific interest.

He threw his shoulders back and puffed out his chest. "Don't be ridiculous."

"Why not? You had a perfectly good motive."

"I hope you don't talk like that to the police. Now, if you'll excuse me, my banker is waiting."

"I believe the deaths of two executives and other financial woes at your firm will be of interest to potential investors. Especially if I reveal this conspiracy as an inside job. What else are you hiding?"

Even a first-year journalism student knew an inflammatory statement like that might be grounds for a slander suit. Unless she could prove her allegations.

Sydney moved aside. "Out of curiosity, where were you when Ted was killed?"

"You mean when he took his own life?" Gavin reached for the door. "To placate your curiosity, last night I attended a Garden Club meeting. They discussed the fall cotillion. My wife is organizing the event. There until about eleven—ask anybody."

"What about during the timeframe of Piper's demise?"

"I don't recall. Now, if that explanation doesn't work, I suspect you'll create what you need. 'Never let facts get in the way of a good story.' That's your station's tagline, right?" Gavin disappeared into the bank.

Sydney shook her head in frustration. "You have us confused with Eyewitness 13."

42

Sydney called Detective Sergeant Mike Cash, of the Financial Crimes Task Force, her fingers tapping impatiently until he answered. On the other end, Cash's voice was gruff, tinged with the weariness of a man who'd investigated too many financial fiascos. After a bit of cajoling and the promise of a decent meal, he reluctantly agreed to meet at Lotus Garden, a spa nestled in a West Ashley suburban strip mall.

The Zen retreat's reception area was scattered with potted palms and plump furniture. Sydney had to chuckle at Cash's choice for a clandestine meeting, since he was a man more accustomed to spreadsheets than mani-pedis, though she hoped to get the answers she needed. She bounded the stairs two at a time, then dashed the length of the mezzanine. Cash was waiting by the last door.

Sydney surveyed the dimly lit room as she caught her breath. "Interesting place."

The first things she noticed were a massage table, crystals, balms, and fragrant elixirs—tools of the spa trade. The second things that captivated her attention: three computer stations, wall-mounted screens, and the static hum from a tower of blinking servers stacked against the wall—task force tools in an undercover war room of sorts. The spot was an unexpected departure from the stoic federal building, blending inconspicuous serenity with fed-style privacy.

Cash said, "Lieutenant Bernadino mentioned your financial misfortune and asked me to give you a peek behind the curtain." He stroked his chin, perhaps debating how many behind-the-curtain details to offer. "Suffice it to say, you aren't alone. We are experiencing a major breach. This incident goes well beyond corporate embezzlement. More like serious bank and wire fraud. Full extent of the damage is unclear."

Sydney made an audible wheezing noise.

He added, "Cyberthreats pose the most serious economic and grave national security challenge we face."

Duh.

Sydney registered his frustration, though Cash had dodged the fact his team played a potential role in the screw-up, failing to intervene before serious damage occurred.

Deep creases accentuated his pale complexion. "Off the record—we have alarm bells going off in dozens of cabinet-level departments. All national agencies are on high alert to avert further penetration."

"From the Aeneid Trojan?"

Cash made no attempt to hide his surprise. "How do you know about Aeneid?"

"I'm really good at my job." Sydney removed a fresh notepad and dropped her purse on a chair. "I cultivate sources. Sift truth from lies. Find buried secrets and determine their context. In the end, I usually discover more than two sides to a story, especially when I'm directly affected. Then, I report."

"Okay, but we're off the record."

"Not for long."

Cash seemed to mull it over, then flattened his palms on a notebook.

Sydney asked, "How do you explain this . . . problem?"

"Federal systems use 256-bit AES encryption and high-grade intrusion detection systems to monitor networks for suspicious activity. And CISA, the Cybersecurity & Infrastructure Security Agency, takes down large botnets all the time."

"Meaning?"

"Despite the government's best efforts, no one can explain why this hack is so effective." Cash rubbed his eye with a knuckle. "It's been less than twelve hours since acknowledging the bug's existence. Now, Aeneid is fully weaponized. That tells me the most virulent strain of code we've ever encountered is jumping from one system to the next with blinding speed. Whatever criminals or spies are behind the dirty script are able to loot sensitive data, plant more malware, or erase crucial information. The bug also seems capable of stripping large amounts of money from both government and private-client accounts."

"Whew, that's a lot to unpack."

Cash wiped his brow. "Adversaries, like Mr. Armstrong and Ms. Kingston, siphoned a gold mine—as much as $23 billion in US losses already. And hundreds of thousands of infected computers are draining who-knows-what classified data. I don't think I'm exaggerating when I say it's a cluster fu—" He caught himself, then cleared his throat. "I mean cluster frig—of epic proportions."

Sydney sagged onto a stool. "Any idea why they chose a cyber-crowbar to do a smash-and-grab on so many different accounts?"

Cash's face reflected a combination of concern and amusement. "Look, I believe those two were out for pure profit. Yet they also made a giant statement, proving they had the means to get to anyone. Anytime. Anyplace."

"Let me get this straight. You think Piper and Ted masterminded the greatest heist ever?"

Cash nodded.

Sydney had never believed Piper was involved in the gigantic hijacking. She'd invested in her complete and utter innocence. A malevolent side hustle of any size simply wasn't in her character. Ted, on the other hand . . . All the votes weren't yet tabulated.

"Piper and Ted aren't your villains," she said.

Cash blew out a jet of air and slapped his hands on his thighs. "It gets worse."

"How could that be?"

"I received an Interpol communiqué suggesting an invincible malware package—the Aeneid code I suspect is doing all this damage—is being moved on the dark web. I'm operating under the premise Armstrong and Kingston first stole money for themselves using Lansing Group servers outright, then prepared to peddle Aeneid to the highest bidder for an even larger score. I fear their rip-off only serves to solidify proof-of-concept, boosting the selling price. It's imperative we eliminate the scourge and hold them accountable."

Sydney gnawed the inside of her lip with the realization the sergeant was making a huge mistake fingering Piper and Ted. "You and I already talked about the attack having the hallmark of a nation-state or terrorist group that hoped our government wouldn't notice the thefts until it was too late. This has the feel of a perfect espionage operation."

"Perhaps—"

"Riddle me this. Who reaps the scheme's profits since Piper and Ted are both dead?"

Cash said nothing.

Sydney tapped her pen on the pad's wire spiral. "That's where your theory loses momentum. Most logically, another person is intensifying the havoc, stealing money with scant fear of repercussions. But you're right about one thing. He or she likely has their hands on Aeneid and hopes to peddle it. And that person killed Piper and Ted to get the mother code."

Cash cut his eyes to her. "Murder isn't in my charter, but I'll play along. Who do you have in mind?" His question hung as a challenge.

"The Hack Pack is behind this."

Cash folded his arms across his chest and flinched. An infinitesimal grimace, but a squinch nonetheless. His nothing-to-see-here façade was cracking.

"That group is extinct."

"Not based on my research and instincts. Try again."

Cash sucked in a huge gulp of air and held it for a few beats before forcibly exhaling. "Okay, here goes. I discovered an incriminating post two hours ago in an underground chat room—the Hack Pack claimed responsibility for the massive intrusion."

"So, the band's back together?"

Cash ignored her. "That prompted the FBI to open a counter-intelligence investigation. They are hell-bent on pursuing every lead. Whole thing is way above my paygrade."

Sydney steepled her fingers. "Then allow me to fill in the blanks. Ted Armstrong, formerly known as Jake Bishop, was a founding member of the Hack Pack back in the day. I'm confident you already know this factoid because you have access to sealed records. So, don't deny it. Plus, he was your confidential informant. Fellow Secret Service agents probably flipped him twenty years ago. How am I doing so far?"

Cash grinned. "No comment."

"And you also know the other member of the Hack Pack, Luis Gaston, is dead."

"I repeat, no comment."

"That suggests whoever is claiming they are the new and improved Hack Pack is an unknown player."

Cash showed no emotion.

Sydney said, "Let me stop spitballing. Time to bare all. Is the task force tailing anyone special? Wiretaps? Surveillance of any flavor? What about a federal warrant?"

"No. Comment."

She shook her head. "I think whoever is behind Hack Pack 2.0 should be raked over the proverbial coals."

Cash hooked a thumb on his belt and said nothing. He was taking *no comment* too far.

She tried reading him like a fortune teller. Scouring subtle facial expressions or a simple shift in body language. To her trained eye, Cash appeared bored rather than vigilant, which further frustrated Sydney.

She grudgingly steamed ahead. "You planted Ted at LG to

leverage the company's giant server farm. Blink if I'm warm."

"You have a wonderful imagination." His tone was calm and even, as if he had one sleeve stuffed with aces in every suit.

Sydney continued. "Okay, how about this? You aren't really investigating financial improprieties at LG."

Cash audibly exhaled. And another squinch.

Sydney beamed. "Bingo! That means you're in cahoots with Gavin Lansing. Perhaps leasing his server farm for whatever operation you're running in a weird public-private partnership. But once his servers became infected, you realized a serious problematic fumble and had to switch gears. Even went so far as to plant another insider." She meant Mason but avoided blurting it out.

Cash frowned. "Massive servers like LG's serve as a holy grail for black-hat hackers because they have a common processing system and vulnerable access points between clients with less sophisticated security systems."

"Can you dumb down any of that for me?"

Cash pushed out his lips. "Ordinarily, vulnerabilities such as that would leave gaping holes in the company's overall security net. Ted Armstrong employed ironclad, best-in-breed safeguards, but a hacker broke in and created a virtual private network, establishing a secure connection to download their pirated data. See, criminal VPNs often reroute bootlegged information back to the same server they hijacked as a safe place to stash ill-gotten gains."

"Under the last-place-anyone-will-look premise?" Sydney asked.

Cash nodded.

Sydney added, "That takes—"

"A gigantic pair of brass ones."

43

Sydney was gaining momentum and started churning over story points in her head.

Cash gestured toward the server rack leaning against the wall. "Ted provided us with a back door. Told us all about Aeneid's dirty script and said he was writing an app to remedy the hurt. With Ted dead, we're geeking out on killer runs of code, hoping to find his off switch and dismantle the virus. The mountain of work is tedious and time-consuming. And time is our bitter enemy."

Sydney needed to let that information marinate before circling back. "Is Aeneid connected to any ransomware attacks targeting small businesses in our area?"

Cash hiked one leg atop the other knee and plucked at his sock. "I believe Aeneid was initially conceived as a ransomware hack. A simple side hustle, a beta run of sorts, to deploy the virus. Once it successfully creates a twisted network from which to begin extraction, the darn thing continues to replicate and evolve."

"That means Aeneid could sell for—"

"Several billion buckeroos. Give or take." Cash combed his fingers through his hair. "If a hostile nation or terrorist group were to gain access to a destructive cyber-tool like this one, we have to assume they'll strike us without hesitation."

"May I air any of your findings or suspicions?" Sydney asked.

Cash skated over the question. "We're doing everything possible to avoid letting more accounts bleed out."

"I'm concerned about our national honeypot, too. But you have to let me run this story. The public has a right—"

"Our treasury might already be disemboweled. Along with countless corporations, universities, endowments, and foundations.

I can hold you as a material witness." Cash pounded a fist into his palm. "If any of this were to leak out, it'd destroy the economy. Don't you understand, we're on very shaky ground."

"Let's not get all rendition-y. I'm as patriotic as the next gal." Sydney was financially disemboweled too. So, she understood the threat. "Always happy to cooperate with authorities, after you lay your paper on me."

Cash patted the air. "What I meant—"

"I know what you meant." Sydney gave an annoyed wave of her hand. He'd meant to intimidate her, but she was having none of it. "I've been throwing you plenty of curveballs about Piper and Ted's innocence, but I'm prepared to stand by this claim—Ted crafted the virus script responsible for all the hubbub. But he so much as told me he was coerced into writing the malware."

"Interesting. Walk me through it."

Sydney crossed her arms. "Someone with a vicious hold over Ted forced him to do something he didn't want to do. He'd learned from experience, and he chose to create super-secure systems. That tells me he intentionally withheld key elements of dirty code or was working too slowly. To enlist Ted's full compliance, the conspirator kills Piper to force his hand. That's why Ted was eager to craft an antidote for you. He was the only coder who could stop Aeneid. He's been working on the side of the angels for years. That's the kind of man he became, and he paid the ultimate price for his patriotism."

She opened a jar of aromatherapy goo. Spearmint. She helped herself to a sample tube, then continued to paint the canvas. "In summary, the conspirator killed Piper and Ted because that person knows who really gains from Aeneid. For my money, Gavin Lansing or Grace Rogers are plausible characters who put Ted up to this. They're both hiding something."

Sydney based this conclusion mostly on intuition. Along with Mason's statement: *Leave Gavin to me.* And Ted's: *Grace, tell Sydney what you know.*

Cash shook his head. "Your theory is all wet. Ted's death was a suicide."

"No cluster-friggin' way." She pulled a notebook from her purse and thumbed through the pages from her conversations with Ted. He'd mentioned Aeneid without bragging at their first Golden Crust meeting. She felt certain that confirmed his direct knowledge of the virus and attack. Though it didn't exonerate Ted or prove neither he nor Piper was involved in the strip hack or potential multi-billion-dollar sale.

All Sydney had was Ted's assertion he'd been bullied into crafting the dirty script.

Along with a dynamite hypothesis.

Minus tangible evidence.

Sydney restated Cash's position. "An electronic pirate sniffed around LG, used it as ground zero to launch the attack, and now everyone is hemorrhaging money. And you think Ted was the pirate-in-chief, not a victim of someone else's plot."

Cash manufactured a ragged smile. "Look, this is a high-tech game of cat and mouse. We are in a world of hurt since Ted died before he delivered the antidote patch. The blame game has taken a backseat to stopping the bleed. My whole team, and countless others, are lasered in on finding a kill switch to eradicate or at least neuter this parasite. Not to mention, I'd love to get my hands on Aeneid's mother code so I can shoot it. Burn it. Chemically castrate it. Then bury it in a red anthill."

"Add in some deadly scorpions and an active volcano, and I'm pretty sure Aeneid wouldn't pose any further damage."

Then, without warning, an alarm on one of the computers blared.

Three technicians barreled through the door and parked themselves at the consoles. They pointed at screens and furiously powdered their keyboards. Cash sprang from his seat as a ripple of excitement ringed the room.

"What's happening?" Sydney asked, her eyes raking their screens.

Cash said, "Another attempted wallop. The agents are fending off the attack."

Sydney took one last run at something Cash had mentioned earlier. "You said you were searching for Ted's unfinished antiviral application. Where would he stash that source code? On a cloud?"

He made a sharp shake of his head. "Aeneid and the kill scripts are too valuable to risk sending over a network just to be stored on a cloud server. Ted most likely buried them in existing code on a server he controlled—like Lansing Group. That's our focus." Cash held out his hand. "Any chance he slipped you a little black box—open only in case of emergency?"

Sydney hiked her shoulders.

"Long shot. Had to ask." Cash sucked in his cheeks. "You have any idea what you've stumbled into?"

"Yeah, knee-deep kimchi."

Grace had also asked Sydney whether Ted had given her something. That confirmed a potential bad actor was also hunting for the world's most important software. Grace was more interested in recovering Aeneid, while the feds were after both Aeneid and Ted's antivirus to stop it.

Cash said, "Looks like we both trusted Ted to do the right thing."

"Aha, so Ted *was* one of the good guys." Sydney had misread Ted early on, but as new revelations moved the needle, she was flexible enough to alter her perspective. She said, "I'm sensing you won't be implicating Piper or Ted in either the embezzlement or Aeneid schemes."

"I admire your loyalty, Ms. Quinn." Cash blew out a jet of air. "Yeah, they're both off my radar. And for the record, he was with me when Ms. Kingston was killed. One last thing. Since most of your theory is spot-on, I'll authorize you to leak tendrils of the story if you are appropriately vague and non-attributional."

Sydney winked. "Anonymous federal sources are my specialty."

44

Sydney departed Lotus Garden with a barn burner of an exclusive from her second source inside the federal investigation. And he'd confirmed a seismic shift in the current situation.

She mentally broke down the story's main components. Money was being siphoned from national coffers faster than floodwater over a levee. Stopping the disaster rested on finding Ted's application utility, which was in an unknown state of completion or working order. Furthermore, pinpointing where the stolen loot eventually wound up was like trying to harness soap bubbles. Despite those monumental hurdles, at least one huge boulder had been moved uphill, since Sergeant Cash had cleared Piper and Ted of all embezzlement and conspiracy accusations.

While identifying Piper's murderer continued to hold Sydney's attention, a change in priorities was inevitable. Her empty bank accounts mirrored the hollow pit in her stomach.

She was evaluating the gravity of her position when she noticed a lug wrench poking from the driver's-side rear tire of her car. And her T-bird looked like a unicorn had pooped a rainbow all over its finish.

Jeezus, what else could go wrong?

Sydney's heart thumped in anger. She plucked at her cell phone, her finger pausing over Dino's number. Then she pressed her lips together and called Big Jim's Garage instead. She pounded a fist on her thigh as she provided details that some wing nut had stabbed her defenseless automobile and bombarded it with paintballs.

Twenty minutes later, the T-bird rolled onto one of Jim's tow trucks. The driver assured Sydney the car could be fixed and repainted like new.

Hakuna matata—no worries.

Wanna bet?

Without wheels, and preserving what little cash she had on hand, Sydney was forced to hitch a ride on public transportation, rather than calling Mandy, Dino, or a rideshare service.

She slogged three blocks to a bus stop and waited until a bright orange and maroon bus, vomiting black smoke, skidded to a stop twenty feet from the would-be riders. Sydney reluctantly boarded the bus, which reeked of stale fast food.

Clenching and unclenching her fists, she tossed a handful of quarters into the obsolete fare machine. The bus driver, whose hair was dyed a color not found in nature, grinned as she inched past.

Another man rose from a crouch in the aisle and made a mock pucker. Thick eyeglass frames bucked against chunky cheeks. "Smokin' sweet. Channel 7, right?"

Sydney's eyes traced the numeral seven stenciled on her duffel bag and the Action 7 bumper stickers plastered on her briefcase. She forced a smile.

A third gelatinous male of enormous girth rubbed a grimy scorpion tattoo on his forearm. "Channel 13's babes are hotter."

Sydney couldn't ignore the slight. "Whatever you say."

•

By the time Sydney arrived at the newsroom, she was ready to pick a fight with the first person who crossed her path. She kicked open the rear door that studio engineers routinely propped open when they weren't on the air and marched to her cubicle like a vengeful army.

"Dino told me about your money woes," Mandy said. "And your car mishap made the scanner."

Sydney removed her shoes and draped her legs across the recliner's armrest. "I'm not being mean, but how do the crazies always find me?"

"Because you're a cosmic beauty."

"You say that like it's a bad thing." Sydney faked a pout. "I had to ride the bus sandwiched between two lug nuts with an acute case of nothing-to-brag-about."

Mandy offered a mischievous grin. "Allow me to serve as your driver while your car is being repaired. And about money—you know I have plenty to go around."

"That's above and beyond the call. I accept being chauffeured." Sydney went on to explain what she'd learned from Sergeant Cash—that Mandy's own riches could be in jeopardy since Aeneid's malware had infected a slew of organizations. "Give me a minute to decompress, then I'll let you take me to visit Dino."

45

Sydney hopped from Mandy's car at the Law Enforcement Center.

Mandy said, "I'll be back in about ten minutes. Couple of things I need to do."

Once inside, the desk sergeant waved Sydney past. She sauntered straight to the Crimes Against Persons Bureau located on the second floor. Dino was on the phone when she nosed into his office. He cradled the receiver and motioned for her to sit in one of the metal chairs fronting his desk.

"Planted any evidence today, Lieutenant?" she asked.

"Nothing you'll ever find." Dino's stud grin sent a warm spark to her brain. "I have two RiverDogs tickets for tonight. Figure that'll take your mind off your troubles.

She pulled a notepad from her purse. "Thanks for the offer, but I'm meeting Mrs. Muirfield later."

"I get it. You'd rather spend time with the wealthiest woman in town than eat hot dogs in the cheap seats with a lowly public servant."

Sydney chuckled. "I know, doesn't sound like me."

Dino moved around the desk and sat beside her. "Glad you're maintaining a sense of humor, Ladybug. What do you need?" He pointed at her pad.

She shifted, crossing her legs. His gaze danced up her thigh—a coincidence she took great pains to arrange.

Clearing his throat, he asked, "We on the record?"

"I'm fact-finding." Dino's eyes eventually met hers. Sydney almost never used her sexuality to pry information. Now, it seemed like harmless fun. "Ted Armstrong's death?"

"Yeah, that came as quite a surprise." Dino returned to his desk and tapped the keyboard. "Says here COD is suicide."

"Your cause of death is wrong."

He bounced a pencil on the eraser end, while Sydney described her meeting with Grace. Dino asked what evidence the gal had offered to cast doubt that Ted had killed himself.

Sydney said, "Grace mentioned finding empty R*Ampd cans in the trash."

"You think Armstrong was murdered because he forgot to recycle?" Dino caught the pencil in midair. "Ordinarily, garbage isn't a felony. I didn't know the penalty was so severe at Lansing Group."

"I also learned Ted was preparing to leave LG," Sydney said. "And he recently bought a new boat."

"People kill themselves all the time for reasons we'll never understand." Dino resumed bouncing the pencil. "Yesterday, you were mad when I didn't toss him in the slammer."

"I'm all about clean endings. Ted's death isn't how I expected this leg of the story to close. But at least he's off the hook for Piper's murder. Mike Cash vouched for him."

"Your suspicions about him seemed solid. And Ted admitted taking money from LG."

She shook her head. "Cash cleared him of that too."

Dino frowned. "What about the laptop?"

"Ted didn't take it."

"How do you know?"

Sydney grabbed the annoying pencil from Dino's hand and slammed it down. "Because he told me."

"Aw, c'mon." Dino eyed the pencil, made a motion to reach for it, then stretched his arms behind his head instead. "Ted trafficked in half-truths. Wouldn't be the first time that tactic was used as a master plan to dodge incriminating circumstances."

Sydney moved to the window. "Will you open an investigation into his death?"

"Based on what? No physical evidence. Circumstantial motive. And no suspect. I bring that to the deputy chief, and I might as well wave any promotion goodbye."

Sydney mocked Dino. "Wouldn't be the first time a goon committed a murder and tried to stage it like a suicide. Grace Rogers makes a terrific suspect. Or Gavin Lansing. I'm torn between the two. And I know you hate jumping to conclusions without—"

"Proof. Evidence. Corroboration of any kind."

Mandy pushed through the door with bags of food from Waffle House. "Hey, Dino. I wrote ten imaginary tickets on the ride over. Want plate numbers to make it official? Maybe you have a quota to fill?"

"Nah, I'm good this month." He reached for the pencil, bounced it once, and then dropped it in his top drawer. He motioned for Mandy to sit at the table and tore open his bag.

Mandy reached into her purse and pulled out a Diet Dew for Sydney.

Dino said, "Forgot to mention, I met Mason at LG today."

"You and Mandy are working from the same hymnal now. Your thoughts?" Sydney endured a puff of unease awaiting his assessment.

"He's okay, I guess."

Sydney threw her hands in the air. "Well, at least you gave him a chance. Now, let's get technical. I'd like to examine the ballistics report from Ted's death."

"Not sure we have any results yet. It's only been a few hours." Dino jammed a spoonful of hash browns in his mouth before grabbing the phone. "Bring me the Armstrong book. And grab a Pepsi from the canteen, please." He cradled the receiver and inhaled a grilled cheese sandwich. "I do know the gun is registered to Gavin Lansing. When I interviewed him, he told me he kept the pistol in a desk drawer. Only a couple of people knew it, including Ted." Dino wadded the foil wrapper and tossed it into a waste can.

Sydney grinned. "Aha, you did open an investigation."

Dino shook his head. "Only conducted a follow-up because I knew you'd be interfering and badgering me."

"Smart man. Now, did Ted have a contact wound, blowback, gunshot residue? You know, physical evidence supporting a self-inflicted gunshot wound."

He shoveled in the last of the hash browns as a uniformed policeman entered the office and tossed a thin red folder and a bottle of Pepsi on the table. Dino scanned the file and let out a whistle. "Gavin's gun, alright. But the bullet isn't what killed Ted."

Sydney's eyebrows shot up. "Oh?"

"He poisoned himself."

"Poisoned *and* shot. Let me see his tox screen."

Dino passed her the folder. "What do you know about toxicology?"

"There's a cop show on TV every hour. Sort of makes me an expert." Her fingers traced the report. "Says here Ted had chloral hydrate, taurine, glucuronolactone, caffeine, and niacin in his blood."

"Does your prolific TV forensic training help interpret that?"

"Listen, I'm busy. Can you annoy me later?"

Dino rocked back in his chair. "Chloral hydrate is a synthetic sedative or reagent—often referred to as a Mickey Finn or knockout drops. It's also used to treat short-term insomnia."

"Nice time to bust out words from the SAT exam," Mandy said.

Dino remained professional. "Seems Ted ingested a fatal dose. The bullet merely sealed the deal. Those other ingredients are from an energy drink. He may have dissolved the drug in R*Ampd. That'd explain the empty cans Grace found at the scene."

"But R*Ampd is a caffeine bomb," Sydney said. "Ted would never—"

"What if the drink was forced on him?" Mandy asked. "Or maybe he didn't care about caffeine and took the drug to calm his nerves prior to—you know."

Sydney snapped her fingers. "That reminds me. What about Josh? Did he have any sedatives in his system?"

Dino moved back to his computer to search for an answer. He keyboarded more strokes than seemed necessary.

Sydney wrinkled her nose. "It would explain his being knocked out long enough for the assailant to find his golf club, then kill Piper. Where can you get chloral hydrate?"

Dino glanced away from his screen. "The FDA effectively banned the substance in 2012. Somebody either had leftovers in their medicine cabinet or had it shipped from overseas."

Sydney stood. "Ted didn't kill himself. And I intend to prove it."

Dino threw up a hand to fend her off. "Tell you what. I'm gonna open a homicide investigation."

"Accepting my challenge?"

Dino fired off his trademark two-handed index-finger pistols. "That, and chloral hydrate appears in each of Ted, Piper, and Josh's tox reports. It's a co-inky-dink I won't ignore."

<h1 style="text-align:center">46</h1>

Sydney felt energized by the bizarre connection between Ted's and Piper's deaths. And proof of Josh's sedative-induced incapacitation gave credence to her theory of what had likely happened inside Piper's house after he arrived. She phoned Mason and Bob while she and Mandy raced to the VA Medical Center. She hoped the team would be able to solidify ideas about who'd hacked her money, breached the national coffers, framed Josh, and killed Piper and Ted.

As the four settled in Bob's room to conduct their second impromptu murder board of the week, Mason taped fresh newsprint to the wall. He also set an alarm for 4:00 p.m., giving them one hour to cogitate.

"I met with Sergeant Cash of the financial crimes task force," Sydney said. "He confirmed Ted was working with the feds."

Mason winced.

She patted the air, indicating no undercover beans would be spilled, but wanted to pull more information from Mason about his covert LG investigation. "And the kicker, Cash said they were discussing back doors and kill switches at the time of Piper's death."

Bob moved to the newsprint and wrote: *TED'S ALIBI = FEDS.* "That eliminates him from her murder. What else did you learn?"

"LG is cleaned out—no money left," Sydney said.

Mandy added, "Syd's been tapped, too."

"Is that true?" Mason asked.

Sydney nodded, and Bob wrote *FUBAR* under a BIG IDEAS heading.

Mason pointed. "What's fubar?"

Bob licked his lips. "Fouled up beyond all recognition. Or words to that effect. I cleaned it up for the dolls."

Mason's eyes flicked when he registered the omitted expletive.

Sydney moved ahead. "Cash also thinks sniffers, strippers, and Trojans were involved in the big heist."

Bob wrote *STRIPPERS*, then held a finger to his mouth as he choked back a laugh. "Sounds kind of smutty. You sure we're talking 'bout nerdy computer programmers?"

Mason chimed in. "I think Sydney means stripper code."

Bob gyrated like an octogenarian hula dancer. "What do sniffling strippers do?"

"It's a sophisticated technique to steal data or money," Mason said matter-of-factly.

Sydney welcomed his translation and added her own. "As I understand it, the bad code is completely undetectable by software pros. And whatever the code is instructed to do happens in the blink of an eye. The national treasury is also leaking like a colander."

Mason jumped from his chair. "No kidding? Aeneid works?"

Sydney nodded. "Cash is quite sure."

Bob stood ramrod straight at the makeshift board. "We're doomed. What else, maestro?"

Sydney tapped her finger on the SUSPECT sheet. "Let's focus on who would want Ted dead."

Bob said, "I thought he killed himself. What evidence do the coppers have that Ted was murdered?"

Sydney said, "They were initially convinced he took his own life, but the tox screens for Piper and Ted revealed the same incapacitating drug in their systems, which is out of the ordinary. Not some over-the-counter tablet. The obvious connection prompted Dino to change his mind on the manner of death. I think he wants to leverage his way back into the sheriff's investigation of Piper by welding the two investigations together. Though he asked me not to report CPD's original suicide findings on air until he squares things with his chain of command."

After glancing at Sydney's notepad, Bob printed *CHLORAL HYDRATE* on the board.

Sydney eyed her group. "My list is pretty short for those with the means, motive, and opportunity to kill Ted. Focusing primarily on motive, which I believe includes Piper's murder, let's make a case for Gavin Lansing versus Grace Rogers."

Mandy used one of the new leads. "Start with the Hack Pack, since they're taking credit for Aeneid."

Bob copied *HACK PACK* on a score sheet. "Now we're getting somewhere."

Sydney recapped what she knew. "Legend has it, the Pack originally consisted of two people. Luis Gaston died years ago. Jake Bishop changed his name to Ted Armstrong to assuage past notoriety. Now he's dead, too."

Bob faced Sydney. "I see how you baked that loaf, Doll. I'll bet you think a new keyboard criminal simply stole the old name. Not like it's a registered trademark or anything."

Sydney turned toward Mason. "Any ideas?"

He surprised Sydney by snapping to attention. "Brilliant deduction, Commander. Even if the feds don't know who's in the reconstituted Hack Pack, my guess is they've made a profile—organized, well-funded, probably never had any trouble with the law."

Bob sank into a chair. "That rules Sydney out—she isn't well-funded. And it's not me, 'cuz I had a run-in with gendarmes in my youth. That leaves only Mandy and you, Johnnie Applecakes."

Sydney eyed Mason. "Any chance the feds could be wrong?"

"What can I say? Profiling is an inexact science," he said. "Though Gavin and Grace fit the bill."

Mandy added, "I backgrounded Grace. The woman has no history other than her work at LG. She's a ghost."

"I knew she shouldn't be trusted," Sydney said.

Mason ticked off items against Grace on his fingers. "She had access to Gavin's gun. She could've authored the typewritten note for Josh to meet Piper. And she muddled Ted's death scene."

Bob dutifully wrote Mason's points on the suspect sheet. "Johnny makes a swell case against Grace. Someone should apprehend the vixen."

Sydney added, "I also caught her breaking into LG's records office."

"Really?" Mason said. "Wonder why."

Sydney said, "Who knows what goes on in her head."

"What about Gavin Lansing?" Mandy asked. "Only LG employees would have access to Ted's work pod."

"An inside job? How exciting," Bob said.

"Leave Gavin to me," Mason had told Sydney.

When she combined that with Cash's blanket refusal to point a finger at the CEO, Sydney decided that was confirmation that Gavin had been working with the task force. Cooperation meant he was untouchable.

Sydney placated the others, yet withheld Gavin's secret involvement. "Gavin obviously had access to his own gun. He also could've been behind the note to Josh. I'll check his alibi later. But he's probably in the clear."

"What are we missing?" Mandy asked.

Mason's alarm beeped. "Ted's antidote for Aeneid. Finding his code will put an end to the electronic looting."

Sydney asked, "What about street gangs or international hackers?"

"In my opinion, gangs lack sophistication and expertise," Mason said. "But I'll wager the task force is monitoring chatter on any number of transnational players."

•

The Mark Clark Expressway was clogged with commuters crawling their way home to suburban Mount Pleasant neighborhoods. Sydney and Mandy became mired in traffic on the box girder bridge over the Wando River, giving Sydney time to pen her script for the evening broadcast. Her two stories: Ted's *suicide* was based upon earlier information from CPD, and Aeneid's financial rampage included notes from her encounter with Sergeant Cash.

When they finally reached the TV station, Sydney freshened her look for the camera, then strolled to the altar for an impromptu production meeting with Olivia and Pete. Olivia waved the Aeneid script and debated whether they needed clearance from the Secret Service before airing the story.

"Cable news is already alluding to a mystery breach," Pete snarled. "You know I hate cable. And the Dow is down almost two thousand points. Run it." He hopped to the newsroom floor and headed toward his office.

Olivia glanced Sydney's way. "Pete's field ain't ripe for picking, if you know what I mean."

Sydney rarely knew what Olivia meant since she didn't own a Southern-speak decoder ring. "Sergeant Cash only insisted on non-attribution. He won't object to the story as written."

"Then we run it," Olivia said.

Ten minutes later, Sydney toed her mark in Studio Control.

"Syd, standby," Olivia said. "Go."

The red light clicked on, and Sydney lit the dynamite story's fuse. "Even though many consumers have become immune to cyber-breaches, buckle up. An elaborate hacking operation is sending tremors through the global financial world. The latest malware outbreak may have infected millions of computer networks and reached directly into banks, businesses, and other treasure chests, making off with a staggering amount.

"Government agencies and private companies are rushing to secure computer networks following a sophisticated interruption, which managed to exploit existing vulnerabilities. The source of the outbreak is unknown at this time, and authorities won't confirm which government systems have been attacked. But the havoc serves as a mind-boggling reminder—taking the offense, like a criminal enterprise, is a lot easier and cheaper than playing defense.

"One federal official, who spoke on condition of anonymity, stated the confidence-shaking attack bypassed previously impenetrable intrusion detection software with alarming ease. The official cannot, for operational security reasons, disclose any actions they are taking to remediate the intrusions. But suffice it to say, malicious cyber-actors have employed exceptional tradecraft in unleashing this major assault. The threat cannot be overstated. As bad as previous attacks have been, they don't eclipse what is happening this round.

"But who is behind the fleecing of American wallets? My sources tell me the attack appears to stem in part from software developed right here in the Lowcountry. Sydney Quinn, Action 7 News, reporting live from Studio Control."

She held her position until Eric sliced two fingers across his throat. She wasn't due an out-tag since her principle federal source insisted on remaining mum.

After a commercial break, Sydney delivered a lackluster report on Ted's death, maintaining the suicide façade. "Ted Armstrong, age fifty-four, died this morning from an apparent self-inflicted small-caliber gunshot wound. Gavin Lansing, founder of the Lansing Group, where Mr. Armstrong was employed as a software developer, told this reporter Mr. Armstrong may have been distraught over the death of his close friend and associate, Piper Kingston, killed on Monday. No one has yet been charged with that crime. If you have any information regarding either death, please call the Charleston Police Department."

"Roll B1," Olivia said.

Images of Lansing Group's office complex filled the screen, and the CPD tip line phone number crawled across the frame's bottom.

"Nice work," Olivia said in Sydney's earpiece.

"Alert the media. Wait, that's me."

At 7:00 p.m., Sydney sauntered down *Miss Adventure's* gangway to the Ashley Yacht Club. She eagerly awaited dining with Mrs. Muirfield, hoping to hammer down a contract renewal so she could set a closing date on her new home.

Sydney wore a magnolia-print poplin sundress and wondered whether the blue bloods could identify it as a Dolce & Gabbana knockoff. She managed to relax in the lounge for almost two whole minutes before being ordered to abandon ship.

"This is a private club, ma'am," the silver-haired bartender snorted. "Perhaps I could call an Uber to take you someplace more, shall we say—touristy."

"Hey, I've been tossed out of plenty of fine places, but this isn't your night, buster."

When Sydney didn't budge, he tugged the bottom of his vest and snapped his fingers at a nearby waiter. The waiter rushed over, tails from his tuxedo flying behind, and jerked her arm.

"Wait," she murmured. "I'm not a hooker or anything. I live aboard *Miss Adventure*. I have a pass to dine here." She fumbled in her purse.

Lounge patrons stirred. Newcomers weren't a welcome addition in this rarified, highbrow world.

Sydney came from more middlebrow air—squarely in the first row of *meh*. And at present she was dead broke.

Mrs. Camille Muirfield, heiress to the area's oldest rice plantation and owner of the TV station where Sydney worked, appeared beside the waiter. Her tone sounded proper and refined. "Mr. Vicks, I hope there's no misunderstanding. The lady is joining me."

Vicks released Sydney and shot her a dirty look. "My apologies, ma'am. She isn't on our guest list. Claims to reside at the marina."

His contempt stung.

Mrs. Muirfield put one hand under Vick's elbow. "Then, by all means, please send our dinner to her residence. This way, dear," she said in Sydney's direction.

The old gal oozed culture, refinement, and polish.

Sydney led Mrs. Muirfield across the parking lot and down the pier toward Mason's humongous yacht. Three kitchen staff trailed, pushing a cart heaped with a half-dozen silver-domed cloches and table linens. When they arrived at *Miss Adventure*, Sydney pointed to the aft brow.

"Pfft," Vicks blustered, signaling his waitstaff to go aboard.

Mrs. Muirfield reached over and patted Sydney's hand. "And I worried you didn't have a place to call home."

Halfway into the meal, Sydney said, "I hate to mix business and pleasure, but I need to check Gavin Lansing's alibi for the time Ted Armstrong, an important source of mine, died. Gavin says he attended the Garden Club's cotillion meeting last night."

Mrs. Muirfield expressed distaste for Lansing by dabbing pursed lips. "New money. The wife is a spender, too. He's hoping his company's public offering defies gravity in an effort to fund her lavish lifestyle."

"Do you remember Gavin at the meeting?" Sydney urged.

"All I can say is he was there at some point. I have no idea as to his exact comings and goings."

"I see." Sydney grabbed another dinner roll. She wasn't afraid of packing on the carbs. Her version of a diet might appall many, but she was blessed with the metabolism of a linebacker and could down almost anything while still maintaining her slender, TV-friendly shape.

Mrs. Muirfield probed her reporter regarding the world's financial calamities along with a disturbing rumor about her mental state. Sydney crossed her fingers and lied about the latter, certain the rice baroness had caught the whiff of deception in her voice.

Mrs. Muirfield blotted her lips. "Those who aren't familiar with Charleston women suffer from delusions we're pampered coquettes hypnotized by the fatuous. You, my dear Sydney, are tied to a freight train—going places faster than I can dream of. Tell me more about your people."

Answering the dreaded *people* question and being judged by one's place on the social registry was a time-honored tradition in the South. Sydney had prepared a stock answer that had served her well on prior occasions of one-upmanship.

After a bite of strawberry pie, she dabbed her lips, mirroring Mrs. Muirfield. The station owner already knew Sydney was a damn Yankee, so she didn't have to sugarcoat her heritage. "I'm the product of a mixed marriage—dad was from Ohio, and Mom was born and raised in Michigan."

"But what do your people *do?*" Mrs. Muirfield asked.

The follow-up caught her off balance. Sydney rubbed imaginary sweat from her eyelid and picked at the pie's flaky crust, glazed juice berries, and whipped cream topping. Finally, an appropriate reply came to her. "The Quinn clan has always been affiliated with the huddled masses. Simply yearning to be paid."

"I like you. You remind me of myself at your age. A real hellion." Mrs. Muirfield reached for Sydney's hand. "Regarding your future with Action 7 News. I know a wonderful psychologist who specializes in war trauma. I'm surprised how productive you've been thus far without any professional assistance. I'm prepared to offer you a handsome raise—contingent on your seeking help."

"I'm not good at asking for help. I'd rather—"

"I know, dear. You'd rather we sweep the awful mess under the foyer rug." She shook her head. "No more. I'm pulling those rugs away and exposing the mental rubbish that has accumulated in your brilliant mind."

"But—"

"You are worth the effort." It became clear Mrs. Muirfield wouldn't listen to any more of Sydney's excuses. "By the way, I received a call from your realtor regarding an Adger's Wharf property. Nice choice. I'll back your mortgage until they clear up this financial virus nuisance and your insurance inconvenience."

"That's very generous. People in the know are working to stop the losses. Are you certain your money is protected?"

"So far. Though I worry this debacle may interfere with your upcoming fundraiser."

Sydney frowned. "Never considered that."

Mrs. Muirfield shook Sydney's hand, sealing the deal. "I have a check for the first responders in my purse. I'm honored to back any initiative you are fronting."

<h1 style="text-align:center">48</h1>

Sydney recapped the Aeneid story during the late broadcast before changing into jeans and a peasant blouse. She held an ice-cold can of Diet Dew against her forehead. A few seconds later, she popped the top and funneled its contents. Then, she stuffed two bills for the race into her pocket and hailed a rideshare.

Twenty minutes later, she tipped the driver before claiming her Civic for a little illicit, high-speed fun. Her heart hammered as she recalled the recent promise to Mrs. Muirfield to clean up her act.

But she hankered for action and couldn't help herself.

Sydney rechecked Big Jim's message, then entered the address for the street race into the car's GPS. The screen filled with a map for Adam's Run, an isolated stretch of rural road off Routes 174 and 162, the stage site. She sucked in a huge gulp of air and held it until her throat burned. Then she blew out a long breath.

She took her time heading west on Savannah Highway—past overpriced antique shops, marine stores, and automobile dealerships—before arriving at the road leading to Edisto Beach.

By the time Sydney rolled up on the abandoned tomato-processing factory, Big Jim and his fellow organizers had managed to attract thirteen cars. She sized up the field—one tricked-out Porsche, three Camaros, a trashed Mustang, and a cherry 'Vette. The rest were rice burners whose owners often focused on external customization to increase their aesthetic without any effect on performance.

Sydney's Civic was considered a ricer by many, but she'd actually created a *sleeper*—a vehicle with a stock appearance that'd been juiced with high-performance modifications. The Civic's unassuming exterior was designed to deter car thieves, dissuade attention from law enforcement, and fool opponents into underestimating the speed of her ride.

Of the many configurations in street racing, Sydney preferred dig racing. Two cars lined up against each other at a dead stop, as opposed to a rolling start. Then drivers had to *dig* themselves from zero miles per hour to top racing speed.

Sydney pulled her hair into a loose ponytail and tucked it up under a RiverDogs ball cap. She yanked a fistful of napkins from the burger bag and wiped away her lip gloss before pulling the two Ben Franklins from her pocket and stashing her purse under the passenger seat.

Big Jim's three-man race crew was packed behind a folding table littered with police scanners, laptops, and two-way radios. Jim was poking his fingers into the chest of an undersized Hispanic male rocking homeboy jeans, a baggy T-shirt, and purple hair. The guy shoved his hands deep in his pockets, probably to keep from taking a swipe at the host.

"This is the last time I'll tell you," Big Jim shouted. "Keep your fart cannon away from my stage."

"But I have plenty of *dinero* for the race, and it's a great car." He pointed with pride at his Mazda low-rider and its huge exhaust pipes, which served no purpose except to make the car showier. The ride also sported expensive rims probably costing more than the car itself, a neon-yellow body covered in cool aftermarket company stickers it most likely didn't have parts from, and a spoiler looking like something Boeing made for a 757.

Jim signaled his men and they snagged the Mazda with a tow truck.

"Careful, man," said one of the crew members. "This car is so slammed I can barely fit my fist under the oil pan."

"I agree, it's a nice ride," Big Jim said, sarcasm dripping. "You just can't race with me. My guys will give you a lift back to Savannah Highway." He refocused his attention on the rest of the drivers. "Okay, that gives us twelve cars."

An even number meant everyone raced.

Sydney knew they'd draw numbers and be paired against the person holding the same number. She only hoped she didn't draw the Porsche. That German beauty was *blown*, meaning it had an engine with a supercharger to increase output. The result—a super-fast vehicle.

"Don't count Hector's Hyundai," said a high-pitched voice from somewhere behind the table. "He's only a hard parker."

Several young guys snickered and punched each other.

Big Jim traced the voice. "Hector, you built a badass car, but never intend to race the motherfucker?"

A short, stout guy pressed forward. "She ain't ready yet."

A scantily clad woman draped herself over Hector's arm. "Yeah, Hector spent all his money making his car track-worthy, but when race night comes, he'd rather sit here and be a hard parker." She rubbed herself up and down his leg. "Ooh, it's so hard, baby."

The young guys moaned lustfully.

Big Jim ogled Hector's woman, then cleared his throat. "Leaves eleven cars. Anyone else wimping out?" He waited but no one came forward. "Okay—one of you is sitting tonight."

A low groan swam through the drivers.

Jim spread his arms. "I know, I know. You came a long way to run. I'll put five pairs of numbers in the hat, along with a blank. Whoever draws the blank gets his money back and serves as the flagger. You know the routine. The finish line is a few hundred feet beyond a big curve we marked with flares."

Sydney stuck her hand in the hat, hoping to pull a two or three so she could run and get out of there. Drawing a higher number meant an elevated risk of getting caught as the night dragged on. She glanced at the small slip of paper—four. She was racing next to last in the unsanctioned contest.

Illegal street racing transcended age, color, creed, gender, and economic status. Tonight was no exception. She searched the drivers until she found the other number four—the crappy Mustang. She flushed with excitement.

Races were usually a half mile or so and didn't last long. Most cars went from zero to sixty in only a couple of seconds, then needed a few more heartbeats to reach top speed as they passed the dig's checkered flagger. Additional organizers at the end line radioed the winners back to Big Jim so they could be paid. Jim skimmed fifty from each two-hundred-dollar entry fee, leaving dig winners with a pot of three hundred bucks.

In addition to the high, Sydney knew a win would help her dire financial situation.

The first two digs went off without a hitch, and Sydney could hear the squeal of tires from the winner's three-sixty burnouts off in the distance. The third dig restarted a half-dozen times, both drivers jumping the gun, brazenly false starting. Big Jim warned each driver that the next flag would be their last, or he'd keep their money.

They ran a clean race.

Sydney's Civic and the Mustang were finally waved to the start. She nosed her bumper to the line, avoiding eye contact with the Ford's driver.

Black cars. Black road. No allies.

At the starting line, centuries-old live oaks bounded both roadsides. Their canopies entwined, blocking out moonlight from above. The darkness reminded Sydney of Baghdad—an enemy lurking in the shadows.

She flexed her fingers, then tightened her grip on the wheel.

Tension was building—senses on high alert.

49

Sydney fixed her gaze on the flagger—the angry Porsche driver who'd drawn the blank, now responsible for starting the digs. The guy stood between the two vehicles at a distance of about five feet from aligned front bumpers. The flagger went through a series of orchestrated gyrations—head and hand signals to verify both drivers were ready.

When he dropped his arms, Sydney mashed the gas pedal.

The Civic launched forward, tires quickly grabbing hold of the road well ahead of the slip-sliding Mustang. She'd made a fast start, easily pulling ahead, then shifted into high gear for the length of the run. Her headlights gave up trying to illuminate the road, instead flicking at weeds in the ditch. The car clawed momentum, and Sydney smiled at its steady performance.

She checked the rearview.

The Mustang was drawing closer, but lagged about seven lengths, fishtailing out of control, churning up gravel and grass along the roadside.

Ahead, a dozen flares sprouted on the right side, indicating the final turn. She held the inside lane, so she eased off the gas, hoping to hug the unfamiliar curve, then gun it to the finish. She checked the rearview again to locate the Mustang and was disappointed to find it nearly alongside—pedal to the metal despite the impending bend.

The Mustang pulled tight, coming in hot.

When the out-of-control Ford crossed the center line, it clipped Sydney's rear panel. She crammed the brakes as her car spun around, skidding violently to a stop in a cloud of grit and water spray. The Mustang careened off the road into the swamp, coming to rest jammed in a clot of cypress trees.

Sydney tried to swallow, but her throat was dry as lint. She held back a sob with two fingers, then clenched her fist when flashing red and blue lights bounced down the road before pulling to a stop directly in front of her.

High beams scorched her eyes.

Anger and fear were quickly replaced by relief when she recognized Dino's Mustang.

Sydney spotted him sprinting toward her in short, desperate steps, elbowing through a lump of spectators. Another unmarked cop car pulled up behind Dino's, and two guys rushed toward the derailed Mustang.

Dino folded his body into the compact Civic and sucked a few deep breaths. After a beat, his expression smoothed.

Crash etiquette required Sydney to speak first. "I'm fine."

Dino's gaze bored into her. "Oh? Then can I get you anything? French fries? Diet Dew? Handcuffs?"

"What do you want from me? I'm working things out."

Dino seemed unfazed. "Every day is a winding road?"

"Ah, the world according to Sheryl Crow." Sydney's insides jumped. "Is this an intervention, or an arrest?"

"You need help, Ladybug."

"Not until you wipe the pity off your face."

Dino's tone remained even. "This isn't pity. But I am concerned."

"I don't need your help. If you can't accept me the way I am, then you're a person I don't want around." Sydney knew her words were hurtful, but she couldn't seem to hold back. She was cascading down a deep ravine with nothing to slow her fall.

"Don't need my help?" Dino reached over and bound her hands to the wheel with flexible cuffs. "Yeah, you do."

Sydney shifted in her seat when his handheld radio crackled.

A voice said, "Hey, LT. Everybody's okay, but we're going to have to let these yo-yos bounce. I forgot to pick up the warrant. My bad."

Dino offered a wry smile. "Let 'em go."

"What about the car in the marsh?"

"Anybody who crashes a Mustang has to call his own tow."

"Copy."

Dino turned to Sydney and slashed the flexicuffs with a measured swipe of his knife.

She narrowed her eyes in an effort to appear determined, despite reeling from the crash. "He didn't really mess up, did he?"

"These guys are off duty," Dino said. "They owed me a favor."

She understood Dino was throwing her a lifeline and softened her tone. "You're taking an awful risk."

He reached for her hand. "Talk to me."

50

Sydney hated to slice open that particular vein, but she couldn't feel good again until she set the record straight. "I do a lot of things that scare me. Most turn out okay." She let out a purposeful exhale. "Though I worry about what others may think."

"Don't fret—most aren't very good at it."

Leave it to Dino to provide levity in the throes of a meltdown.

Sydney asked, "What about you?"

"Try me."

Sydney flexed her fingers. Tears stung the corners of her eyes. She felt a little self-conscious, but she started describing the horror in Iraq. She rarely gave a full accounting and never added gory details. She always left out the part about the helicopters. And glossed over getting shot.

Yet the end result never varied—good men died.

Sydney closed her eyes and sank into the vivid memory, wanting to get it all out.

Rounds snapped nearby, raining rocks and debris. A barrage of gunfire came from all angles. Enemy rocket-propelled grenades disabled two vehicles.

Her voice weakened to barely a whisper. "Metal shards from the RPGs pinged off my helmet."

Dino didn't say a word.

She'd lost all her swagger—swept away to another time.

Dino listened as Sydney painted the scene for him.

Several Marines narrowly skirted the carnage, jumping from soft-skinned vehicles to escape the flames. Heavy smoke billowed from blown-out windows. Searing heat cut like a saw blade through the dust-filled air and a riot of color.

Sydney wiped her cheek with a knuckle. "I can still recall the god-awful stench from burning flesh."

She'd panned the convoy with her camera to document the ambush, but her eyes chased shadows until she spotted Gunny Walters dragging men from burning vehicles over to the riverbank.

"He found a narrow bend to serve as temporary cover," she said. "We hid behind an embankment and the column of Humvees." She massaged her elbows, recalling the sting of gravel as she low-crawled under the chaos, her camera a heavy lump in her pocket.

Gunny's eyes locked on her. "Syd, I need all hands on deck getting our wounded to the river."

Sydney felt too afraid to exhale. The sight of blood-drenched cammies hit like a prizefighter's uppercut.

Day and night, she was surrounded by those jarheads—the men of Echo Company, 1st Battalion, 24th Marines, 4th Marine Division. They put duty before themselves. Trained to accept the prospect of death at any moment.

For some, their moment had arrived.

She tugged a dozen or so injured men over the embankment until the trench was littered with fallen Marines. Then she sank to her knees and watched a corpsman expertly wrap field dressings on gaping wounds and grisly burns with blinding speed and agility. A numbness washed over her.

Gunny inventoried the squad. "Where's Townsend?"

"Circling the wagons," Sydney said.

She grabbed a packet of bandages, hoping to find a useful purpose. She kneeled beside Hammer, unsure where to start. His uniform was soaked with blood and tissue fragments. Doc, the Navy corpsman attached to the company, slapped her shoulder.

When she glanced his way, he shook his head and lowered his eyes.

Gunny overruled Doc and motioned for Sydney to continue, perhaps sensing her need to engage in something worthwhile. Hammer reflexively clenched her vest when she laced a bandage around the hole in his head where his right ear and cheek should've been. She was thankful his family would only remember his soft blue eyes and bright red hair, rather than bulging arteries hidden behind gauzy compresses.

His hand fell to his side.

Gunny wiped sweat and grit from his brow, then thumbed a shoulder mic. "Tango One, this is Echo Niner. Bad rain delay. Need an umbrella."

"Roger, Echo Niner. Coordinates?"

Gunny's eyes darted across the horizon, registering the unit's location from memory. "Three clicks north of Pebble Beach. Friendlies in the water hazard. Light up the sixth fairway, then pick us up."

"Make bunkers in the fairway. Read you, Lima Charlie."

Sydney choked back the sour taste of fear and said to Dino, "Incoming mortar rounds pounded our position as the attack intensified. Then things really snowballed. More like an avalanche of really bad shit. Everything became a blur."

Fish's cheeks drained when she applied extra pressure to a spurting bullet hole in his shoulder. His eyes met hers with a pleading look.

Sydney held his gaze, ignoring the body parts slopping from his gut. "This'll give you a helluva story to tell when you get back home."

Next, Doc signaled her to tend to a badly burned body. The man's face was contorted in agony.

Gunny squatted beside her and shared his Ka-Bar knife. "Cut BJ's shirt off, but don't yank anything stuck to his wounds. Put his watch in his pants pocket. Wrap these dressings over his arms, hands, and torso. Seal the edges if you can." He tossed a pebble at the corpsman. "Hey, Doc. This man needs an IV, ricky-tick." Then Gunny shouted into his shoulder mic. "Dammit, Tango One, how much longer we gotta play this hole?"

"Hunker down, Echo Niner. Next tee time is less than five mikes."

In the next instant, a mortar concussion knocked Sydney on her butt as another Humvee became a fiery heap.

Sam Townsend's dreadful scream pierced the din. "Help. Me."

Searing frag from the vehicle's steel chassis and makeshift armor tomahawked over their heads and splashed into the river. The TOW missile launcher splintered from its roof-mount and speared into the ground like a javelin. Sydney covered her mouth with a sleeve and joined a pair of Marines sprinting toward the wreckage.

They found Townsend splayed on the road. Shrapnel had blown through his left knee, severing his lower leg. His exposed femoral artery spurted in every direction before Corporal Weston managed to tie a tourniquet.

The Humvee had been swallowed in a crater surrounded by a halo of blackened pavement. Machine gun rounds ricocheted off roadside rocks as they hauled Townsend to the trench line.

Sydney pressed him into the riverbank.

Blood oozed from the sergeant's mouth, and his eyelids flagged closed. He was bleeding out—nothing more anyone could do.

Gunny shoved a rifle in her hands. "We have to hold our position until the choppers arrive. Point the small end down range and squeeze the trigger every ten seconds. Keep your head down and keep firing until I tell you to stop."

Sydney hoisted the weapon over the top of the berm, squeezed the trigger, and counted to ten. She emptied eight magazines before feeling the huge burps of rotor wash from three Cobras swooping overhead. The attack helicopters emptied their ordnance, eliminating the insurgents' withering assault, then corkscrewed onto the highway near the squad's location for an urgent exfil.

As Sydney rose to dash for the safety of a helo, her pack snagged. A bullet creased her flak-vest, sending a white-hot flash of pain through her upper arm. Gunny grabbed the nape of her vest, cut her free, then flung her back into the trench. A split second later, a sniper's bullet slammed into his neck with a sickening thud.

One of the Cobra's gunners silenced the sniper with a flurry of American firepower.

Doc's wet eyes found hers. "Syd, you've been shot."

She drew back to the present. "All my fault—" She wrapped her arms around Dino and wouldn't let go. "Should've been me—"

Sydney ignored the jolt in her shoulder as Doc wrenched her away from Gunny.

By the time the unit returned to the compound, thirty-nine Marines and one reporter had been injured. She never felt Doc insert an IV in her wrist. Moving into unconsciousness, she overheard a physician's assistant say, "Trouble in River City—five angels."

Navy medical staff referred to dead Marines as angels. River City—a phrase which made everyone's bowels curdle—was code to cut off communications from camp and prevent leaking tragic news to family members back home before they could be notified through official channels.

Crandall. Reed. Slater. Townsend. Walters.

For the record, the ambush lasted forty-one minutes.

Stories of heroism and quick-thinking abounded in the tragedy's wake. Members of Sydney's profession conflated what happened at the river. Time magazine christened her TV's Brunette Studette—and even implied she was some kind of wunderkind who'd saved the convoy.

Instead, she'd learned firsthand how deadly routine patrol could be—and bitterly heartbreaking.

Dino remained transfixed. "How have you held this in for so long?"

Sydney choked on her words. "Gunny was married—"

"Ladybug, it was years—"

"I came back, he didn't." She caught sight of her trembling hands. "His death was all my fault."

"Why?"

Sydney began rocking as if in a daze. That was the first time she'd put it all together. "Crandall. Reed. Slater. Townsend. Walters."

"Are you blaming yourself for their deaths?"

"Gunny Walters paid a terrible price to help me."

Dino shook his head.

She wiped her face with the back of her hand.

Though she couldn't articulate it—even to herself—going through the torment again had somehow tripped a relief valve. As though maybe she was ready to finally let it go.

Almost.

She eyed Dino, who was positively the steadiest person she'd ever known. "Look, I have a great job and good friends. But I can't sleep through the night. Two out of three ain't bad."

"Ladybug, you need to realize these memories are eating you alive."

She banged her hands on the steering wheel. "What I realize is, I'm a liar and a fraud. Not exactly the kind of person you want at the helm of the most trusted name in broadcast news." She was fighting herself with bare knuckles. And losing. "People still call me a hero. But a lie is a lie—no matter how often it's repeated or how many people choose to believe it."

"You were shot. People died. This code of silence—" Dino shrugged and appeared to gingerly select his words. She sensed he could finally understand her pain. "It takes a lot of courage to seek help. And you need a professional."

Sydney allowed herself a wounded smile, then buried her face in Dino's shoulder. He smelled like sandalwood and warm herbs, and his strong arm across her shoulders felt like a shield between her and the memories.

"Okay," she said. "Okay."

51

The morning poured in as hot as fresh pancakes off the griddle. Opting against venturing out for breakfast, Sydney placed a delivery order—which proved a stroke of genius, considering she was still frowzy from last night's ordeal. And since both of her cars were enjoying a spa day at the body shop, her transportation options were limited.

She climbed to *Miss Adventure's* pilot deck and phoned Eve Martel.

The realtor sounded downright giddy as she diagrammed the next steps in completing the house purchase. She assured Sydney less than a dozen or so e-signatures were required to move ahead. "Beats having to deliver the ream of paper in a briefcase," Eve said. "You know, I've been at this so long, I even remember when faxing documents sped up the operation. Now, all it takes is a few clicks, and presto . . . you own a visually stunning, culturally influenced, and historically preserved property. I'm simply *vert*, *verde*, *grön* with envy."

Sydney recognized two of the foreign words and deduced they all meant green. More interestingly, Eve's mention of a briefcase reminded her of a piece of unfinished business. She thanked her realtor before disconnecting, then climbed below to rummage for the documents she'd snatched from Piper's house following the standoff.

Once the food delivery arrived, Sydney lined up breakfast and the papers on the aft deck. She alternated forkfuls of pancakes with each page scan. Though much of Piper's paperwork baffled her, the strange documents seemed to indicate the insurance executive had her hands in more than worker's comp claims.

Two hours later, Sydney welcomed Josh aboard the yacht. The timing seemed right to challenge his skills.

He went to work pursuing Piper's document collection. "What am I looking for?"

"I was hoping you'd tell me. It reads like gobbledygook. Or plans for a hostile takeover by rogue lifeforms, for all I know."

"You're funny." Josh scanned the lines with his index finger racing side-to-side. "I'm not seeing battle plans. Rather, this is genius-level computer code."

"You have my attention."

"I'll need time to dissect it. It's written in a programming language I don't recognize."

Sydney's eyebrows shot up, sensing this might be the Aeneid source code or kill switch everyone clamored for. She made Josh vow he wouldn't divulge what he was working on.

He spat into his palm and extended a sodden mitt. "I swear."

Sydney had been a girl for so long, she'd forgotten how her brothers taught her to seal a deal. She followed Josh's lead, then they shook. Next, Sydney taught Josh the girly way—a pinky promise. "Two oaths of secrecy are better than one," she said.

Mandy arrived soon after to drive them to the newsroom. Sydney stashed Josh in Editing Bay 5 while he analyzed the tantalizing and mysterious new code. She also locked a duplicate copy of Piper's papers in the station safe. When she took a seat at her desk, she noticed a small, padded envelope with her name printed on it. No return address. Local postmark. Too small and flat for a pipe bomb.

She unzipped the red strip with theatrical flair, then dumped the envelope's contents: an electronics gizmo half the size of a credit card and a note from Ted Armstrong.

The note read: *Syd, save the world if I'm not around.*

Sydney clamped her eyelids shut as her brain redlined. His words made her shudder. Ted knew he was going to die. And he trusted her enough to send that thing—whatever it was.

She stared at Ted's note again. On the reverse side were a host of symbols and characters that looked like doodles. Then she turned her attention to the green gizmo with silvery raised dots and wondered whether it was a computer chip with more of the valuable code everyone was searching for. Or held the name of a perpetrator. Or both.

Or maybe something entirely different and unexpected.

Sydney dashed to Mandy's cubicle, ready to share the plastic doohickey with her. "What does this plug into?"

"Looks like a semiconductor of sorts." Mandy poked it into access ports on her computer without success. "Doesn't fit any of my peripherals. Probably goes under the hood. Where'd you get it?"

"Ted."

Mandy shook imaginary death cooties from her hands. "Yikes."

Sydney handed her Ted's note.

Mandy shrieked. "Double yikes. Voices from the beyond are plain creepy."

Sydney wrapped the gizmo-thingy with the note and slid both into her pocket. "Maybe bad karma too."

"Karma means I can rest easy knowing the people I treated badly had it coming," Mandy giggled. "By the way, I received a text from my cousin in Columbia. Guess who the W of J&W Enterprises is?" Before Sydney could respond, Mandy blurted out, "It's Moose. His given name is Webb."

Sydney nodded. "Makes perfect sense. He and Ted are business partners."

"Should we tell the authorities?"

Sydney shook her head. "Of course not. Yet."

Mandy opened her mouth, then seemed to reconsider what she was going to say.

"Go ahead," Sydney said. "What's on your mind?"

"Simply playing *what if?*" Mandy wrung her hands and leaned forward. "What if there's a weensy-teensy-bitsy chance you're going about this money mess all wrong?"

Sydney eyed her friend. "I hear what you're saying. But you know me. I'm almost never wro—"

"Should you at least give your law enforcement buds a hint about what you're working on?"

Sydney felt confident the semiconductor delicately wrapped in her pocket was an important clue regarding Ted's viral or antiviral codes. He couldn't have known she'd swiped papers from Piper's house or kept Piper's flash drive from the cops that might also offer further clues as to the code's whereabouts.

Sydney wanted first crack at whatever Josh uncovered, along with the gizmo's contents. However, identifying what device could read the darn thing seemed impossible for someone with her limited tech skills. She conceded that point with Mandy and trundled back to her desk. She left ambiguous messages regarding the microchip for both of her task force sources, Mason and Sergeant Cash.

Time to save the world, she thought.

Tears rimmed her eyes, and she cursed Ted under her breath. "You sneaky bastard."

52

By 1:18 p.m., Sydney was still pacing the newsroom, no closer to making sense of Ted Armstrong's latest clues. She considered her next move—meeting with Moose. As Ted's business associate, he would be in a position to provide valuable insight.

She and Mandy drove to the Geek store, leaving Josh at the TV station under the anchorman's watchful eye. They found Moose in the workshop repairing a processing unit. Computer pieces clotted every surface. Several plastic sandwich bags, all filled with small parts, dangled by zip ties from larger components.

Sydney showed him Ted's green plastic gizmo. "Any idea what this is?"

Moose examined the device, then passed it back. "Basic circuitry. Could plug into anything requiring chipsets, like TVs, lamps, gaming devices, blow-dryers, computers. You get the idea."

"That the best you can do?"

Moose shrugged.

Frustration mounting, Sydney asked, "Who inherits Ted's estate?"

Mandy dropped her purse. "Nice bedside manner, Syd. The man just lost his friend. How about a little consideration?" She extended an outstretched hand. "Hi, I'm Mandy."

Sydney caught herself. Mandy was right. Moose deserved compassion.

After an extended silence, he eyed Sydney. "I'm Ted's sole beneficiary. He didn't have any family he cared about. They disowned him back when he had his little . . . situation. Why do you ask?"

"I'm concerned someone might weave a story that makes you the villain."

Moose flattened his hands on the table. "Oh?"

Mandy asked, "What are you implying, Syd?"

Sydney offered a smile she hoped was supportive. "For example, someone might say you pilfered the LG laptop just so you could peddle your expensive ID Rx candy. Ted found out, so you killed him to cover up your misdeed and inherit his fortune that he made from investments and the upcoming stock offering."

Moose jumped to his feet. "I didn't . . ."

Sydney patted the air with her palms. "I believe you. That's why I'm asking for your help in solving his murder. Now, regarding Ted's *situation*. I spotted Jake's personnel folder on his desk. I didn't recognize the significance at the time, but what if it came out that Lansing Group's software chief had once been a legendary member of the Hack Pack? News like that could jeopardize the price of the company's IPO or derail the stock sale altogether."

Mandy plunged through miscellaneous parts heaped on an open roll-top desk shoved against the wall. "Does that detail make Gavin a legit suspect?"

Moose shook his head. "Gavin knew all about Ted's past. He was killed by whoever tinkered with his code."

Sydney slid a steel chair next to the workbench and took out her notebook. "Tell me more."

A slumping hulk, Moose knitted his fingers in his lap. "We were supposed to get together after work Thursday, but I had a date. Instead, Ted and I met later, around ten o'clock. He tried to convince me an old acquaintance had slammed the firm's code and hijacked the servers. I've never seen him so rattled—sorta scared me."

"What happened next?" Sydney asked.

"Ted started writing fierce Griff Six code on the whiteboard behind his desk. Dude was manic. Making all sorts of logic errors in the language he invented."

"That implied—"

"He was way out of control. I couldn't help him, so I bounced. We agreed to meet yesterday morning and pick up where we left off."

Moose fumbled a bag of parts. "Think he'd be around if I stayed?"

Sydney studied his apologetic expression and swallowed hard. "You may be the last person, other than the killer, to have seen Ted alive."

Mandy continued rummaging through other goodies in the workroom. "Is this a Mattel Football game?"

Moose examined what she was holding. "Good eye—a 1977 first edition. They only made a hundred thousand. Ted didn't like to keep toys in their packages. Believed they were meant to be played with. Or taken apart to learn how they worked. That mess by your elbow looks like game parts too. He must've been tinkering before he was . . ." His voice trailed off.

Mandy inspected the pieces. "Looks like six or seven carcasses here."

Sydney slapped a palm on her thigh. "I'm not interested in electronic toys. Let's return to Ted. What kind of logic problems did he make?"

Moose refocused his attention. "Ted writes complex code, but it's always clean. Even elegant. Junk I saw on the board was sloppy, with none of his usual flair. That signaled to me he was super rattled. Or purposely writing bad code to throw off a would-be copycat."

Sydney tried to avoid appearing glassy-eyed, though it hit her that many of the strange characters from Ted's whiteboard matched those in Piper's papers. More Griff Six, she surmised. Ted's unique computer code.

Moose added, "Coders are extremely competitive. The best ones, like Ted, stylize their programming using unique characters or a special rhythm. Or they embed bold, inert statements or graphics just for fun that won't interfere in the code's function."

"Like a dog spraying a tree to mark his territory," Mandy offered.

Moose's head rocked north and south in agreement. "Digital DNA. A code jockey's signature."

"What was Ted's signature?" Sydney asked.

"Reverse gambit," Moose said. "Ted was famous for crazy security measures in every program. He knew how easy hacking into a system and altering program performance could be. That's why he got so unnerved to find someone had penetrated his servers. Ted thought they were invincible."

"A break-in would unnerve anyone." Sydney rubbed away a chill from her arms. "Ted mentioned you were going to review LG security video for the hours prior to the laptop's recovery. Anything catch your eye?"

He smoothed his chin. "Nothing unusual. Everyone we identified was authorized to access the pod."

"Let's talk about ID Rx," Sydney said. "Why didn't you tell me you owned the company with Ted when I came here the first time?"

"Sounds kind of sick, but you didn't ask. We launched that company about five years ago, I guess. Ted's experience in hacking made him an expert in how to combat it." Moose tightened the metal cover of the cpu he'd finished repairing. "We landed our first client because no other security or restoration company would touch 'em. Even earned the seal of approval from the irs identity theft bureau. That truly inspired Ted. He wanted to leave Lansing Group after the ipo and devote more time to that end of our business."

Mandy held up a handful of plastic game remnants. "May I buy these?"

"Take 'em," Moose said. "And find out who killed Ted?"

"I'll make sure Syd keeps digging."

Sydney knew she wouldn't need any prodding from Mandy. She felt bad enough about accusing Ted of illegal activity. Now, she was deeply invested in seeing this story through to its rightful conclusion.

In the car, Mandy could barely hide her excitement. "This broken stuff is great."

"A trove of geeky goodness?" Sydney asked.

"Just you wait and see."

Sydney's phone buzzed with a call from Mason.

"What am I supposed to do with your cryptic message about a weird microchip that might run a lamp or TV?" he asked.

"I know, not much help," she said, hoping to throw him off.

"Nevertheless, why don't I swing by and take the darn thing off your hands?" His cadence slowed. "My team can determine whether it has any value."

"Monday morning. Then, the gizmo is all yours."

"That's obstruction. And a rotten thing to do."

A smile tugged at her lips. "I know."

53

Back at the TV station, Sydney wedged herself next to Josh in Editing Bay 5. "Any luck finding the RAT eating LG's server-farm cheese?" she asked.

Josh tossed a laugh in her direction. "Not sure how others get any work done 'round here with you always cracking wise."

Mandy handed Sydney a Diet Dew, then passed a can of R*Ampd and a bag of pretzels to Josh. "Yeah, she's a laugh riot."

Sydney frowned, then offered a relevant nugget. "I think you may be looking at code written in Griff Six. Sound familiar?"

"Hmm, Griff Six? That one's new to me, but it's high-level." Josh tore into the pretzels, spilling them on the workstation. "Whoever wrote this is brilliant."

"Yeah. Ted was."

Josh hummed with obvious excitement. "I think I extracted an app buried among what looks to be scraps of compiled binary assembly code."

Sydney didn't want him to stop for an explanation. "Cut to the summation. Is it Ted's kill-switch patcheroo?"

Josh tipped back in the chair. "See, the app was camouflaged. Masquerading among benign script. But I think it has fragments of the self-propagating bot that launched The Golden Crust's spam."

Sydney snapped her fingers. "The free-food vouchers."

Mandy nodded as she munched a handful of potato chips. "Good work, Josh."

"If you yank the bot app out, does that crash Aeneid?" Sydney asked.

He shook his head. "This is just part of a utility. Aeneid is comprised of specific hack script. There's a bigger file somewhere else."

Mandy wiped her lips. "Could you wipe the Trojan if you rebooted LG's system?"

Josh nestled his chin in a palm. "I don't have access. Besides, the backups are probably infected too."

Sydney pleaded, "If you need help, how about going to one of those hacker forum-thingies?"

Mandy placed a hand on Sydney's shoulder. "Doesn't work that way. Any overt attempt to elicit assistance would draw a huge amount of unwanted attention."

Josh pulled a note from his backpack and pushed it over to Sydney. "Here's an example of lines that were repeated several times in Piper's documents. Comingled code that doesn't serve any purpose, as far as I can tell. What do you think?"

The code read:

```
///A7//10/12/17/14//A13//16/18//23/20///
A9///12/14/19/16//A20/23/25/4/1///
///♥@•$©Ω¶8>7P£
%дΨ ▲ ///◊ ► ☼□!@•2<5(*&^%$97136♪ ▲ ‼◊///
///A7//10/12/17/14//A13//16/18//23/20///
A9///12/14/19/16//A20/23/25/4/1///
///♥@•$©Ω¶8>7P£
%дΨ ▲ ///◊ ► ☼□!@•2<5(*&^%$97136♪ ▲ ‼◊///
```

Mandy eyed the character string. "Beats me."

"Hold on a sec." Sydney tossed her notepad on the desk. "Do you think Ted would write the kill code in Griff Six, a unique and proprietary code that almost no one understands, or in a more conventional computer language?"

Josh grinned. "He'd write the kill code to match Aeneid's mother code."

Sydney recounted how Cash's team was scouring LG's operating software with little success. Now that Josh had broken through parts of Griff Six and could at least tell insignificant fluff from gold, perhaps he and Moose would be able to identify Ted's unique code faster than the task force.

Josh squirmed a little. "Syd, I'm all in helping you find the mother code. But I have to come clean—I haven't been completely honest with you."

She didn't like the sound of that. "Oh?"

"The note from Piper. I lied when I said it was typed. The thing was handwritten."

Sydney frowned. "Why would you lie about that?"

"I knew the cops were listening in when you were filming me at Ms. Alston's house."

"Interesting."

•

Sydney lugged a carton of notes down the marina's long pier. Buoyed by Josh's code discoveries, as fragmented and puzzling as they seemed, she and Mandy prepared for an all-nighter. Sydney reasoned that if she could interpret Josh's work, maybe she'd be able to decipher even more. And Mandy was determined to find a home for Ted's gizmo chip.

Sydney ached from exhaustion, and the all-nighter didn't sound like such a good idea anymore. Besides, Mandy announced she'd left Ted's microchip in the station safe. Their plan *B* would consist of a late nosh followed by a good night's sleep.

Mandy worked a switch near the door, but the salon lights didn't cooperate.

Sydney moved past her and crashed into a coffee table, where she opted to ditch the carton. "I'll find a lamp." She probed the outer bulkhead, banging into more things along the way. A dull thud sounded behind her.

The nape of her neck tingled, and not in a good way. "Mandy, are you okay?"

"Nuh-uh, she ain't," said a raspy voice with an artificial corn-pone accent.

Sydney spotted the burning end of a cigarette. And behind it, the shadowy figure of an intruder filled the doorway. That person took a long drag before flicking the butt over the side. The skinny shaft of light through the open door offered scant illumination.

Nicotine-soaked air made Sydney's throat seize. Her mind spooled to chain-smoking Grace, but the intruder was larger and had a deeper voice. *Definitely a man*, Sydney thought. She called to Mandy again.

No response.

Sydney couldn't allow herself to become the next assault victim, even if her Krav Maga training taught her to avoid physical confrontation. She focused on escaping this fiasco in one piece.

She grappled her way through the salon and located the spiral staircase leading to the owner's suite, hoping Mandy wasn't badly hurt. Her bestie needed to hold on long enough for Sydney to get to the wheelhouse and signal police and marina security for assistance.

Slivers of light leaked through a curtain crack in an otherwise blackened suite. The streak cast menacing shadows throughout the room. Sydney negotiated her way past a pile of dirty clothes and raced to the wheelhouse, where she instinctively locked the door behind her. The flimsy lock wouldn't be enough to discourage a determined attacker.

On the flybridge, the pier's LED spotlights aided her search of the cabinets. She found a phone jammed behind rolls of nautical charts, but the landline was dead.

Additional thuds from below caused the hair on Sydney's forearms to stand at attention. It sounded like the intruder was ransacking the salon with careless disregard. Questions swirled. The most pertinent: Was this a random break-in, or a targeted attack? Sydney believed that under the existing conditions, nothing could be considered random.

Powered by high-octane caffeine, she groped the piloting console, flipping every toggle on the yacht's massive dashboard. Little happened until she located the boat's horn. The blast bowled her backward.

Sydney fumbled with the toggles until the horn blared again. She held the button using one hand, found a roll of duct tape below the helm with the other, then improvised. She wanted the commotion to wake the entire marina, especially her Canadian neighbors tied on the starboard side.

Sydney spotted a shadow move through the owner's suite. She climbed out through a window onto the observation deck, crouching three stories above water on a walkway barely ten inches wide. From there, she would shinny down two levels to the forecastle, then sprint the length of the pier for help.

Diesel fumes and other hydrocarbons continued to belch from the rusty tub still running on a generator. Sydney sucked in a breath and held it for as long as she could, while clenching lifelines and flailing with a dangling foot for the stainless-steel ladder hanging across the forward compartment. Sensing the intruder nearing, she abandoned her original plan and edged backward on the walk-around deck heading toward the stern.

Why hadn't marina security, or anyone else for that matter, responded to her manufactured chaos?

When she reached the aft deck, Sydney searched for an object she could use as a weapon. Discovering a long paddle beneath an overturned kayak, she pried the paddle from its storage spot and knew the seven-foot device would be more useful if she could shorten the shaft. She fingered the midsection and found a push-button release that allowed her to break down the paddle into halves, with a fiberglass blade on each end. She gripped one section in her right hand and dropped the other half onto the deck, confident the half-paddle would serve as a capable weapon for both offensive attacks and defensive counters.

Sydney hunkered behind the spa tub, her lips pulled tight against dry teeth. When the door slid open, it became decision time. Fight or flight?

Now seemed as good a time as any to put up a fight. To assert herself and defend Mandy and the yacht.

Sydney had trained for this moment. All those bruises and sore muscles earned on her way to an orange belt had prepared her for a real-world test. She plugged her ears against the blare of the horn and harnessed a physical aggression she'd practiced at the training center, ready to put her unsuspecting opponent off balance.

The intruder inched forward, a handkerchief now covering his mouth and nose. The guy tripped over the kayak, which had slid into his path. Sydney squinted at his hands through the darkness, searching for a gun, knife, or any other tactical weapon. Seeing none, she emerged from behind the spa and advanced.

She swung the paddle at the side of his head, then took several jabs at both knees. He cried out, spewing tasteless vulgarities. Her strikes had been quick and efficient. He collapsed onto all fours in shock and obvious pain, but he wasn't fully incapacitated. He still posed a considerable threat.

The danger escalated when he brandished a handgun that'd been tucked in the small of his back.

Without hesitation, Sydney dove over the port side, careful to avoid slamming into *Three Maple Leaves* moored in the starboard slip. The chill of the river water made her want to quickly resurface and seek refuge ashore. However, she changed her mind when she heard pops, then felt splats from bullets plunking into the water all around her. She pulled herself deeper, hoping to swim out of range. When the shooting stopped, she swam underwater in the direction of her neighbor's stern.

Sydney surfaced beneath the dock, using it for cover. She spotted strobing blue and red lights between the pilings that she suspected came from police cruisers parked at the foot of the mega-pier. In the next instant, the blare of the yacht's horn ceased, replaced by heavy footsteps directly above her.

Dino shouted, "Syd, you out there?"

She banged a fist on an aluminum pontoon to signal her position, then sucked in a breath to duck under a flotation device.

Dino was wearing his trademark black commando pants and long-sleeved black shirt. He leaned over and wrapped his big mitts around her wrists, then dragged her onto the pier. "Saving your bacon is becoming a habit."

Sydney scrambled to her feet. "What about Mandy? Did you find her? Is she okay?"

"She received a nasty bump on the head," he said. "Though she managed to call 911 and tell us you went into the river. EMS just took her to the Medical University's emergency room for examination. She was alert and asking about you before they drove off."

<h1 style="text-align:center">54</h1>

Sydney managed to slosh froth from her mug of hot chocolate onto the salon floor, creating a small, sticky puddle that looked like a modern art piece titled *Oops*. Meanwhile, Dino was outside on the pier, gesticulating wildly as he spoke to a uniformed officer, his animated conversation visible through the tinted window. Between shivers that made her feel like a human maraca, Sydney fumbled for her phone and dialed Nick, Action 7's anchor and Mandy's plus-one.

She tried to keep her teeth from chattering. "I need a status report on our favorite researcher. Is she still in one piece, or has she gone full diva on us?"

Nick assured her that Mandy was fine. "No sign of any concussion. Doc said I could take her home to keep an eye on her. Give Dino my thanks for letting me know what happened."

Sydney sighed in relief, taking another sip of her hot chocolate. "Boy, that's good news. I felt terrible abandoning her to escape topside."

"Mandy told me she faked being conked out so she could watch the creep search the salon. When he went up the stairs after you, she dashed away to call for help. She heard something splash into the water and presumed it was you, since the splash was followed by gunshots. Mandy and I both know you don't own a gun. Even so, better quit your sleuthing, heh?"

"I don't go looking for danger. It has a way of finding me." Sydney clicked off with a dull ache pinging in her head—sympathy pains for her bestie.

Dino returned aboard the yacht and unfolded a space blanket he pulled from one of the deep pockets on his thigh. "Smooth move going over the side."

Lost in thoughts about Mandy, Sydney didn't realize Dino was talking to her.

He touched her shoulder. "Your neighbor gave the dive an eight-point-five. Didn't think you stuck the landing."

"Practicing sarcasm or are you spending too much free time at the Oceanside Comedy Factory?" Sydney continued licking hot chocolate. "And what stinks? I smell rotten eggs. Hope you aren't tracking in garbage."

"Nobody's tracking anything. You're the one doing the Pepé Le Pew. Good gravy, Ladybug, look at you. You have river sludge and pluff mud in your—" He made an hourglass shape with his hands.

"Keep your eyes off my pluff. Did you catch the lug nut who broke in?"

"He was long gone when the first patrol rolled up. My guys are canvassing the marina. By the way, the uniforms had a helluva time turning off the damn horn." Dino studied the yacht. "This crib isn't half bad for a gal with no money."

"Shouldn't you put out a BOLO or go engage in a high-speed chase?"

He sat on the couch. "How's about telling me what happened?"

The lingering odor of nicotine stung Sydney's nostrils. She summarized all she could remember regarding the break-in, the intruder, and the assaults.

Dino mentioned he'd found no forced entry, then quickly moved into interrogator mode. Was she sure she'd locked the door? Did anyone else have a key? What time did she arrive? Was anything missing? He left little time between questions and responses, ultimately concluding she and Mandy had surprised a burglar in the act. But he could be wrong.

Once the detective finished his questions, Sydney reeled off a few of her own. Who were his suspects in Ted's murder? Did he know about an argument with Gavin Lansing? Had he connected Piper and Ted's deaths to the misplaced LG laptop?

"Ladybug, leave the police work to me, and I won't report the news. Let's go, I made you reservations at Francis Marion."

55

ydney pushed a fork through scrambled eggs and stared at the clock in her familiar ninth-floor suite at the Francis Marion Hotel. For the past six hours, she'd channel-surfed, skimmed an assortment of neatly stacked magazines, filed her nails, continued to worry about Mandy, and raided all the snacks in the minibar. She was miffed about the attack but adored the gray sweatpants and CPD T-shirt Dino had provided.

She phoned Mason to recount the break-in.

"Anything taken?" he asked.

"Nope."

"Sheesh, you were lucky you didn't have Ted's microchip. It could've been ruined when you did your swan dive. Are you thinking that's what the intruder came for?"

"Perhaps."

"Then I demand you turn it over to me." After several beats of obdurate silence, Mason sighed and said, "You have anything else somebody would want?"

"Yeah, I think Grace has the hots for you." Sydney disconnected before he could pry any further.

•

A little after nine, Sydney trooped through the newsroom. The weekend producer huddled over the Associated Press computer monitoring Aeneid's prolific spread. A half-dozen interns worked telephones or crammed into editing bays. Additional production assistants monitored police scanners and trolled morning papers hoping to snare new leads.

Pete waved her into his office and closed the door. "I hear you almost got Mandy killed."

Sydney folded her arms and glared. "I'm fine, thanks for asking. Why are you here on a weekend?"

He plunked onto the corner of his desk. "Tell me about it?"

"A deranged lug nut broke into the yacht and conked Mandy on the head. When the police came, they took her to the ER and me to a hotel for safekeeping."

"This shouldn't have happened. I told you to lay off the laptop story." His caustic tone left little leeway for disagreement.

Yet Sydney flared with contempt. "This isn't about the laptop. It ceased being about a laptop when Ted was killed. I'm the only one who never lost sight of the real story. My friend, Piper Kingston, was murdered. That's the precipitating event in a terrible series that merely includes the stolen laptop."

Pete narrowed his eyes. "I could fire you."

She placed her hands on her hips. "You could, but that wouldn't be good for either of us. I tell you, the break-in is a sign I'm onto something. You know, making people nervous. Not bragging—just stating a fact."

He motioned for her to leave.

Sydney returned to the newsroom and poked her head around a partition to explore the curious odor emanating from Mandy's cubicle. Mandy wore oversized protective eye goggles, a leather carpenter's apron hanging below her knees, and thick canvas work gloves. Game parts collected from the Geek store were heaped on her desk.

"What in the world?" Sydney said. "Shouldn't you be home? In bed? With an icepack on your noggin?"

Mandy was intent on soldering two wires. "Hang on, this is precarious."

Nick bobbed around the corner sporting a puckish grin. "Syd, I'm peeved at you. You got my girl knocked up. That's my job."

Mandy finished soldering, then swatted him.

Sydney fumbled her pen. "You have every right—"

Nick went on. "And a rotten influence. Mandy insisted I retrieve this junk after we came home from the hospital. If you think this is a mess, my dining room table looks like a robotics lab."

Sydney reflexively rubbed her head. "You've been working all night?"

"Good thing she didn't have these parts with her on the yacht, huh?" Nick said.

"Yeah, I've been told."

Mandy placed the soldering gun on an aluminum pie tin, then removed the goggles and gloves. "For the last time, I tell you I'm fine." She eyed Sydney. "Remember Ted's microchip?"

Sydney nodded.

"I'm betting it goes into Simon," Mandy said. "He knew you'd purchased one, so he chose a chip from that specific game."

"Genius." Nick, ever the anchor, coaxed additional information from his gal pal. "Now what?"

Mandy snapped the circular plastic casing over the game's electronic innards. "I dissected several processing chips for practice before working with Ted's actual deal. You may recall Simon plays musical tones. And Ted was instrumental in getting LG's robots to talk."

Nick popped with excitement. "Is everyone thinking Ted's microchip will actually tell us about his solution to the whole Aeneid mess?"

Mandy nodded. "I'm hoping this works, or else we may be sunk. Because Ted's gizmo will never come out in one piece." She crossed fingers on both hands. "Ready?"

The three gulped in unison.

Mandy pressed Simon's large red button. The toy blinked a series of lights. *Sans* game sounds or human voices. Nick tried the blue button. Nothing. No lights or sound. Sydney tried the yellow and green buttons, anxious to hear Ted's voice. Nada—no lights or sounds from those buttons either. Mandy tapped the red button again. The flashing red light blinked on and off in a seemingly random pattern.

They exhaled in collective disappointment.

"You tried, kiddo," Sydney said. "Though I have another idea."

•

Sydney grabbed a rideshare to the Veterans Affairs Medical Center, her driver regaling her with tales of his cat's latest escapades, which were surprisingly entertaining. Upon arrival, she bounded the stairs to Bob's room with the caffeine-induced energy of someone who had enjoyed one too many Diet Dews.

The commander was seated at the table, finishing a late breakfast. "Ah, dear Sydney."

She pinched her nose. "What are they feeding you?"

"Cream-of-whatever. I refuse to ask anymore." Bob pushed away the tray. "You look like the devil stole your favorite shoes. Trouble in TV-land, Doll?"

"Ted Armstrong sent me a microchip."

"Dead Ted?"

Sydney nodded. "Mandy worked a little of her magic soldering the chip into an electronic game. But the darn thing only blinks. That made me think of you."

Mason strode into the room wearing an expensive suit and a scowl. "Is that the same chip you supposedly wouldn't fork over until tomorrow?" he asked, visibly irritated.

She flipped her palms up. "So, sue me. Now's a good time, since I don't have any money."

That earned a fractious grin.

Mason said, "I'm sure it's what the thief was after, which means your game is now evidence. I demand you turn it over. Don't make me play hardball."

Sydney was a little surprised Mason wasn't permanently stooped over from toting that giant chip on his shoulder. Federal agent arrogance, she guessed. "Why are you here? Are you following me?"

"Don't be absurd. I . . . Uh . . ." Mason toed the floor. "Came by to see if I left anything from our last visit. I can't find my favorite pen."

Bob seemed to ignore the rift as he shuffled to the closet. He pulled out a flashlight and two large books. "You two can sort things out later. Obviously, the game's blinking lights tell a story of urgent importance."

Mason grabbed a book from Bob and read the spine. "*Great Intelligence Blunders*. Kind of an oxymoron, huh?"

"Ahem," Sydney scoffed. "Bob was a career intelligence officer."

"My bad." Mason returned the book. "Any chance I can redeem myself by learning from a true professional?"

"Only if you keep your big yap shut and switch off the overhead," Bob said.

Mason turned out the lights and settled at the desk.

Bob pointed the flashlight at the ceiling and blinked the beam. "Doll Face, tell me what you see."

"You need new batteries," Mason offered.

"You were supposed to watch and learn," Bob said. "So, zip it."

Sydney kicked Mason. He groaned, then thumbed through the second book without saying a word.

"Doll?" Bob asked.

She stared at the lights. "Morse code, right?"

Bob nodded. "You bring me the toy. And I'll decode the message, if there is one. But there's always a scant chance poor Mandy connected the chip improperly and everything is garbage."

Sydney snorted a laugh. "Sometimes a blinking light is only a blinking light."

Mason flipped on the room's ceiling unit. "And sometimes the flashlight needs new batteries."

"Johnny Jackass." Bob gave him a glower, then tapped his forehead with a pair of fingers. "Everyone knows the Morse alphabet and numbers are composed of a series of dots and dashes. A great many calendar pages have passed since I last interpreted signals. But I was pretty darn good, way back when. I'll bone up using my old books."

Sydney jumped up and threw her arms around him. "I'll have Mandy bring Simon."

"Who's Simon?" Bob asked.

Her eyes misted with a wave of emotion she hadn't addressed from last night's attack.

In the hallway, Mason affixed a hint of a friendly smile. "How's about I save Mandy the trip? I'll swing by the TV station with you and take Simon off your hands."

Sydney shook her head, not falling prey to Mason's attempted charm. If that was his idea of flirting, he was going about it all wrong. But he did force her to revise the plan to get Simon and Bob in the same room so Mason couldn't intercept them. She said, "Not gonna turn it over until I see a subpoena. I'm asserting my First Amendment privilege."

Mason said nothing.

Sydney mirrored his expressionless glare. "I can play hardball, too, Johnny."

56

Back in the newsroom, Sydney opened a Diet Dew, her attention riveted on the poppy seed bagel she'd snatched from VA's cafeteria. She slathered on chive-flavored cream cheese and stuffed a big bite in her mouth.

Mandy returned from delivering Simon and Commander Bob to an undisclosed location. While out, she also picked up Josh. They peeked around the corner as Sydney licked white goo from her fingers.

"You sure onion breath is a good choice?" Mandy asked.

"Breath mints to the rescue." Sydney pointed toward the recliner for Josh.

Mandy leaned against the partition. "You always have a back-up plan. It's your *modus operandi*."

Josh added, "It's Latin for criminal operating procedures."

Sydney lifted an eyebrow. "Did that conk on your head make you start ruminating in Latin and thinking I'm some sort of criminal?"

Josh snickered.

"Not really," Mandy said. "But if you want more, the work you're doing for Josh is *pro bono*, since he's not paying for your services."

"Should I charge? I could use the money."

"Nah, you need the brownie points," Mandy said.

Sydney ignored the good-natured jab. "You sure Bob and Simon are safe?"

"We changed cars so many times, I lost count," Mandy said. "Good to have a huge number of relatives I can call on."

"I'll never make fun of your family tree again."

"Yes, you will." Mandy laughed. "Back to Josh. He's proven his worth again by decoding more of Ted's bizarre repetition strands.

We don't think they match the Griff Six code taken from Piper's documents."

Sydney glowered. "Did you remove secret information from the newsroom? That was risky—"

"No more than our bringing things to the yacht," Mandy said.

"Touché." Sydney tossed a pen on her desk, causing photos to tumble into Josh's lap. "For the record, successful decoding should've been your lede. Keep talking."

Josh said, "I tried everything—Caesar's Shift, Rail Fence, reversals, combinations, patterns, decoys." He seemed distracted by the photos—enlargements taken of Ted's whiteboard in the LG office.

Sydney held up a hand. "And?"

"Ted used complex number substitutions four different ways, but each strand reads the same: *DFKH*. There's also a lot more inert filler—junk code with no purpose but to confuse—in my opinion. What do you think it means?"

"I have no idea." Sydney sorted through a pile of notepads, picked the one she wanted, and flicked pages to find the strand of letters and numbers she'd discovered on the back of Ted's note enclosed with the curious microchip:

///+/–//10.12.17.14//•18//25.1.11.10.21.9//$//•1343//$$///

Sydney added, "I'm really good at puzzles. Let me take a crack at this line using your fancy substitution decryption idea."

"Yeah, you're a linguistic lioness—queen of the haughty vocab," Mandy said. "But you can't balance your checkbook."

"Never felt the need." Sydney scowled as she studied the strand. "This is hard for me to acknowledge, but I don't know where to start."

Josh eyed the notepad, then nudged her from the desk. He scribbled the alphabet down one side of a page and a series of numbers in another column, creating a codex. He moved his fingers back-and-forth over the cryptic strand.

Sydney said, "It's not Braille."

Mandy rubbed her head where she'd been conked. "Let him work without your clever critique."

Josh tore his note-page in half, then slid the page up and down, realigning the halves. "Wowzer, Ted spelled out *DFKH* again."

Sydney gnawed her cheek, half regretting Mandy's injury and half begrudging Josh's decoding success. "Okay, I give. How'd you do it?"

Josh pushed the number and letter pages to Sydney. "Cracking code in any language involves staring at a lot of character packets meaningless to most people. Since I figured the main four letters might be in this run too, it proved easy to line up numbers until they matched. The substitution code is A7."

"Meaning?"

"Align the number seven with the letter *A*. I'll read the rest of the numbers, and you jot the corresponding letter."

"Sounds easy enough. Go ahead."

Josh read the number sequence.

The result: *///+/–//DFKH//•18/SU//EDOC//\$//•1343//\$\$///*

"I think the slash marks indicate a word break," he said.

"These aren't words," Sydney said. "Could it be more of Ted's complicated Griff code?"

Mandy said, "Or a secret-sauce recipe."

Sydney's phone buzzed with an incoming call from Commander Bob. "Anything of value in the blinking lights?" she asked.

"I could be wrong, but I made out the letters K, F, H, and D. Not sure what order they go in or if that's even the right outcome."

"Sorta matches what Josh discovered. Mean anything to you?"

"Not a lick. That Ted was more of a wacky old coot than me. Gotta run, Doll. My cactus-land poker buddy is ready for another beatdown." Bob disconnected.

Josh was running his fingers across the oversized photos of the whiteboard from Ted's office. "Now that I have a better understanding of his coding preferences, I can see what Ted was trying to do here. But he made syntax errors in the executables. This won't work without—" He swiped Mandy's electronic notepad and began drawing symbols with weird number and letter combinations. "By the way, Griff could be short for 'gryphon,'" he offered.

Sydney was awestruck by Josh's speed. "Why?"

"A gryphon is a legendary creature—combination lion and eagle."

Mandy jumped to her feet. "Oh, I get it. Ted's the lion and Syd's the eagle. Our station mascot."

"What's a gryphon's purpose?" Sydney asked.

Mandy snorted. "Guarding treasures and priceless possessions, of course."

Sydney cocked her head. "Gotta admit—Ted had style."

Josh passed the pad to Mandy. "Check my work."

Mandy ran her fingers over Josh's rewrite. "I see." She winked at Sydney and shook her head. "No, wait. I get it." She tapped the screen. "Josh, move this string up here."

He drew an arrow as she suggested. "I think this is more of Ted's missing patch. I'll collate it with the code from Piper's papers."

Sydney gasped. "Can you fix the syntax errors? Does it cut off Aeneid's RAT-head so it stops devouring everyone's brie?"

Josh doubled over. "Jeez, you're hilarious."

"We've established that." She ate the last bite of her bagel. "Anyone ever call you a genius?"

He shook his head. "All the time."

"What else did you find?"

"This fragment here . . ." Josh tapped the photo with authority. "This has to be tied to Aeneid, not the fix. It looks like code for a super-aggressive stripper that rakes giant chunks from every account the virus infects using rapid sequence transfers." Josh continued to move his finger across the garble of code. "Wait a sec. How did I miss . . . Man, oh man. There's a vintage tracer worm concealed inside a mountain of bogus fluff." He pointed to another passage in the photo, then seemed to sense Sydney's frustration. "Tracer worms are often used as electronic trip wires."

"Still not following." Sydney leaned forward. "Can you make the patch work?"

Josh dog-eared corners of several pages from Piper's collection. "In my opinion, Ted left behind good news. Bad news. And terrible news."

"Give me the good news first." Sydney held her breath.

Josh coiled with optimism. "Reverse Gambit."

She blew out the air she was holding in. "Ted's signature? Why is that good news?"

"When these two hunks of code are merged together, you have reference points to more of Ted's nasty script. But this also reveals his stripper code is merely giving the illusion of swiping cash. Ted actually *reversed* Aeneid's executables—nothing's been taken."

"No way. My money is really gone. I'm wiped out."

"I'm telling you, Ted created fake *deposits* to make the thief think he's getting rich, though his virus actually hid the *stolen* money in blind accounts. The only thing the person who coerced Ted into developing Aeneid is getting is an epic dose of smoke and mirrors." Josh clapped his hands. "Ted even coded in a keystroke tracker so he could catch anyone who monitored the hack."

Sydney asked, "Where are those blind accounts?"

Josh tapped a finger on the script. "See here? Ted dumped all the money and stolen info back onto LG's network. He used the Bishop and Gaston files."

"So, he used Hack Pack names—a very clever breadcrumb trail."

"The cool kids call 'em Easter eggs," Josh said.

Sydney eyed him with approval. "That explains why someone tried to pilfer the laptop. Perhaps suspecting Ted stored Aeneid's mother code on it."

Josh said, "Except the files on the laptop are bogus. They are red herrings."

At long last, Sydney understood the laptop had never held the

Aeneid code that could be plucked for sale on the black market. Or any malware code, for that matter. That was why the thief had dumped the device in Ted's work area—as a ruse. She also understood why Piper had downloaded a backup of archived personnel files using Velma's access.

The Gaston and Bishop files were on Piper's hot-pink flash drive. What was the name of the cartoon on Piper's portable device? Sydney snapped her fingers as she made the connections.

Hello Kitty.

Hello. Kitty. Flash. Drive.

H.K.F.D.

Using Ted's reverse gambit logic, that translated to DFKH—matching the clues Ted planted on Simon, his note with the microchip, and in the scrambled text among Piper's papers. Then Sydney recalled when she'd confronted Ted at his house. He told her she had everything she needed—because she possessed the flash drive.

That meant she had Aeneid.

The viral code had to be embedded within the Gaston and/or Bishop folders too. The brilliant, yet foul, program that'd set the nation's financial markets on the brink of apparent bankruptcy had been captured on Piper's butt-ugly flash drive, currently locked away in the station safe.

All of that explained why Cash and his task force agents couldn't find the nasty script anywhere on the server.

She forcibly exhaled and eyed Josh. "What's the bad news?"

"Portions of Ted's reverser code aren't flawless. He probably didn't have time to run a beta. That's why people think they've been fleeced. With a few minor tweaks—"

"Those dog-eared pages?"

Josh slid back in his chair. "Fix and upload, and it'll move money from the blind accounts back to the rightful owners."

Sydney involuntarily flinched. "And the terrible news? As if I need to ask."

"Aeneid's mother code—all of it—must be destroyed. Otherwise—"

"Neck-deep kimchi."

57

With so much at stake, Sydney wasn't prepared to put all of her trust in Josh's debugging abilities. Mercifully, she knew where to get a second opinion. And if things coalesced as she expected, she'd need either Mason or Gavin's help to upload the edited code onto LG's servers, thereby putting an end to the financial nightmare. She phoned Mason from the car, leaving a message saying that she urgently wished to meet with both Lansing Group men.

A little before two o'clock, Sydney and Mandy crossed the Ashley River, exited on Folly Road, and continued driving south another fifteen minutes until traffic thinned. Few cars ventured into gritty Five Forts.

Five Forts, named for its proximity to a quintet of Civil War garrisons, was a patchwork of low-rise apartments and single-family homes occupied by the working class. The 'hood laid claim as Charleston's most crime-riddled area, despite a desirable location on James Island, one of nearly two hundred barrier islands dotting the state's pristine coastline.

Elsewhere in the Holy City, birds were singing, lovers strolling. Sydney imagined children playing in the secret gardens of idyllic Old South mansions while well-heeled mothers danced in a tranquil fragrance of jasmine and gardenia. But not the folks who lived in Five Forts.

Thinking about them gave her the willies.

Sydney parked at the curb of the address her dark-web chat mate had provided. Seeing the place, she rather wished he'd offered to meet on the trawler again. The house was a no-nonsense, weathered-gray, two-story clapboard hovel with little charm or personality. Dilapidated didn't begin to cover it.

The place was a dump.

Clothes hung on a line along the grassless side yard littered with debris as though a carnival had recently moved away. And an aluminum ladder, rigged to a nearby telephone pole with a frayed strand of rope, shored up the crumbling second-floor piazza.

Sydney wouldn't have trusted the contraption to hold up a birdfeeder.

The rest of the street was lined with salt-bitten cinder block homes standing shoulder-to-shoulder with other row houses. Paint crawled off them in jagged fragments—a cliché for creepy suburban decay. To add to the ambiance, two men disappeared behind the house across the street. Twitching blinds in a front window tilted closed.

A tingle shot up Sydney's spine. Talk about creepy.

She was glad Mandy had borrowed a cousin's beater. The rusted Ford Edge was a solid fit for the sketchy Five Forts, the sort of neighborhood where people starting their way up lived alongside folks plummeting their way down the social ladder.

"I think hacking is undoubtedly viewed as a life skill rather than a crime around here," Sydney said. "Lock the doors, kiddo."

She traipsed the length of the crumbled sidewalk to the hacker's front porch, knocked, then waited. She nudged a soggy phone book with her toe, then raised her hand to knock again. A low growl swelled behind her. From the corner of her eye, Sydney spotted the clenched teeth of a medium-sized, pit-style mongrel with a bad attitude.

"Look away, dammit," she mumbled to herself.

The cur crouched at the base of the porch steps, blocking her escape route. Sydney was in good shape from thrice-weekly Krav Maga. But the beast was operating two plays ahead of her and seemed to know it.

Dale opened the door and eyed Sydney, then his poochy. He

leashed the mutt to a post before any blood could be drawn. She exhaled and signaled to Mandy the path had been made safe.

Once inside, Sydney heard the window air-conditioning unit laboring, but the thing managed to crank out enough cool air for the room to feel like the walk-in reefer at The Golden Crust. Electronic equipment and a four-panel matrix of computer screens littered Dale's front room, along with the reek of tequila and faulty plumbing.

Sydney fought an impulse to barf.

After bringing Dale up to speed on her objectives, she requested banking records for her only suspects: Grace Rogers and Gavin Lansing. She agreed to pay him a hundred bucks—blowing up her cardinal rule. "I'll have to give you an IOU."

"I'll do a transfer," Dale said.

"No—" Mandy peered from behind the notes she was reading. "I have cash."

He cocked his head toward the reporter. "Technophobe?"

"No, broke," Sydney said.

Dale cracked his knuckles. "Oh, right. Someone stole your digits. An elegant solution to their problem."

Sydney knitted her hands. "I wouldn't call extortion elegant. Or even stylish."

He roosted at the desk and pounded his keyboard. He wasn't as gentle as Mandy, yet he hijacked the unsuspecting accounts with ease. A confusion of pages spewed from the printer. "You girls want a drink?" He cracked his knuckles again. "There's a new box of wine on the counter."

"Probably a good vintage, but no thanks," Sydney said. "I'm on duty."

Mandy headed to the kitchen to sample the vino.

Sydney took an uninvited seat at the dining table, shoving a week's worth of newspapers on the floor. What Dale's house lacked in cleanliness it made up for in discomfort.

She scanned Gavin's bank statements first. His account revealed several suspiciously large deposits, though the source of the deposits was secreted by special bank codes. Then, the account was drained, presumably by Aeneid, which implied he was not the mastermind behind the heist.

She'd only considered Gavin a suspect because of his nexus to LG's two dead executives. But he'd still have to explain the large deposits.

"Oh, man. This is bad," Dale said. "Or maybe good, depending on your perspective."

"Let's hear it," Sydney said.

Dale continued. "As you know, The Golden Crust's phishing hacker did a pretty good job framing Ted. But the dumbass got sloppy when he or she used Lansing Group's server as a proxy."

Sydney nodded. "Your guys aboard the trawler discovered the electronic trail. Is that the good or bad thing you found?"

"A doozy—the phisher is still using the dead guy's IP."

"Does that prove the phishing scheme and Aeneid breach are related?"

"Oh, yeah."

Mandy drained her glass. "Syd's theory is, Ted was forced to create big, bad Aeneid—the gold standard in cyber-thievery. Stealing keystrokes, money, the whole shebang. Like he once did as a Hack Packer."

Dale blew out a puff of air. "Man, that brings back memories. The Pack pulled a cyber-bank robbery, netting 45 million smackeroos in only a few hours. The rip-off wasn't discovered for weeks."

Sydney said, "I suppose back in the day, when money was only stashed in vaults, it became pretty obvious when a bank had been robbed. Things are even more nasty in the crypto age."

Mandy licked the rim of her glass. "In addition to a hacker still cloaking Ted's address, something else bothers me. Josh thinks money wasn't actually stolen from the infected accounts."

Sydney strolled over and double-tapped the papers she'd handed Dale earlier. "He spotted a flaw in Ted's stripper-stopper doodad. Please double-check his suggested tweaks on the bent pages."

"Ted threw a wrench in the works, alright." Dale began keyboarding as fast as his fingers would allow. His glance darted between the dog-eared pages and the screen. Then he plastered on a wide grin. "Presto. Your guy did a bang-up job interpreting Ted's code. I made a few adjustments. Now all you need is to upload this onto LG's server and launch it to restore everyone's money—like Ted intended." Dale threw a hand in the air. "High five, anyone?"

Mandy sauntered back to the kitchen, refilled her glass from the boxed chardonnay, then gulped it down. She poured another glassful, then shook the empty box.

Dale stared at Sydney in astonishment. "What? No takers? This is epic."

She slammed her palm into Dale's. "You're right. This feels good. Since neither Aeneid nor the kill-switch mother codes were stored on LG's server, that's how we beat the feds to the master fix."

58

ale spun in his chair to face Sydney. "That makes sense, since Ted's software has lines and lines of inert crap outsiders would have to sift through. Your guy had a focal point, then spotted a few anomalies and sifted away the chaff."

"How are we gonna upload it?" Mandy asked. "We don't have access to LG's servers. And time is of the essence."

Sydney checked her phone to see if Gavin or Mason had called. Neither had responded as yet.

She eyed Dale. "You're the best hacker I know. Dammit, you're the only hacker I know. Let's break in and launch the repair patch."

Dale's eyes widened with what appeared to be unabashed pride. Could've been acid reflux; he was hard to read. "My guys suspected it might come to this, so they did a little advance poking around to test LG's firewalls. Gotta be honest, we failed. Ted's security is impenetrable without a password. Any ideas?"

Sydney chewed the end of her pen. "Just spitballing to juice the creative rotor blades. I figure a Ted-style password would have to be made of special characters and numbers. Making it impossible to guess or trip onto."

"And long, too," Dale said. "A password like that would be either super meaningful so Ted could remember it or written down somewhere."

Mandy began pacing the full length of the living room. "My own passwords are elite, but none exceed twenty characters."

Sydney sprung from the dining room bench and snatched her purse. She riffled through notebooks like a blackjack dealer. "Maybe Ted gave us his password." She pointed to the second strand Ted had written on the back of his note and began to bounce with excitement:

///♥@•$©Ω¶8>7P£
%дΨ ▲ ///◊ ▶ ☼□!@•2<5(*&^%$97136♪ ▲ !!◊///

Sydney handed the notebook to Dale. "Coders, like Ted and you, create digital debris wrapped in cyber-detritus that throws us noobs for a loop. I didn't give this a second glance once we decoded Hello Kitty Flash Drive. Ted hoped I'd know what to do when the time came. Now is that time."

Dale said, "We probably only get one chance at this before we're locked out."

"Then don't screw up," Sydney said.

He cracked his knuckles. "Here goes."

"Wait," Mandy shouted. "Reverse gambit."

Sydney gave her pal a thoughtful glance, then cocked her head toward Dale. "Key it in backward."

He scrunched his nose as though she was Looney Tunes crazy. "Why?"

Sydney placed a hand atop Dale's. "Trust me."

He meticulously entered each character, slowing when he came across an odd one or Greek letter. He checked with both women to ensure he'd chosen the proper symbol from a special menu. When all three were satisfied that Dale had replicated the password strand in the exact reverse sequence, he pasted it into the Lansing Group login box.

Dale turned to Sydney. "Your honors." As if to accentuate the obvious, he pointed to the *Enter* key.

Sydney sucked in a huge gulp of air and held it until she felt a sizzle in her lungs. Then, she pressed *Enter*.

Dale's computer blinked twice before the encoded credential was successfully hashed in Lansing Group's servers, giving the access they needed. A menu popped on the screen. He used his mouse to search the drive, folder, and file hierarchy to locate where he thought it best to launch Ted's patch.

Dale's fingers flew across the keyboard. "This might take a minute."

The screen blurred as scores of software lines flicked past.

Sydney was mesmerized by the computer doing what the device was designed to do: read and search humongous data sets as commanded.

When Dale announced all of the antidote code had been uploaded, his screen settled on the LG logo bouncing from corner to corner.

Mandy dropped onto the couch. "You mean it's finally over?"

"Still burning white hot." Dale ticked off three items. "Before you arrived, I found a Chechen buyer nosing around a dark web forum seeking info on Aeneid's sale. Still gotta nab the conspirator who offed Ted and Piper. And Grace Rogers presents a special problem."

"Elaborate on the last item," Sydney said.

"Unlike Gavin, her mainstream financials show no huge deposits. But if she's as smart as you think, she converted everything to klepto-currency and bounced it over hundreds of Tor browsers before hiding it where US authorities and Aeneid can't touch it."

"Sounds like routine criminal activity the task force can unravel."

"Here comes the hinky," Dale said. "Grace's financial history only goes back a year or so."

"*Hmmph,*" Sydney snorted. Her wave of relief at stopping Aeneid's destruction was derailed by thoughts of Grace. "That information lines up with what Mandy discovered when she backgrounded the wily redhead. I have a far-fetched idea about how I can sort out her involvement. But I need to run it by Mason first."

Dale bowed. "Seems Ted put his trust in the right person."

Mandy downed the last gulp of chardonnay. "If you're right about Grace, you might be crossing into troubled territory. Will you take me along for the ride?"

Sydney's cell phone vibrated and she was tempted to ignore it. Instead, she glanced at the caller ID, then at Mandy.

"It's Mason, isn't it?" Mandy asked.

Sydney nodded.

"Go ahead, we won't listen."

Sydney answered the call.

Mason said, "You'll never guess who just showed up at my house?"

"No idea."

"Gavin. You want a piece of him?"

"Absolutely. He's sorta *numero uno* on my suspect list. Either he hired some mulch-for-brains to kill Piper and Ted, or he's being framed by the person who did the dirty deeds." None of that was true, but it sounded good.

"You're adorable when you grab hold of a conspiratorial bone."

Sydney scrawled Mason's address, then disconnected. She signaled Mandy, and they headed for the door, but something drew her back.

She spun on a heel, facing Dale. "Did you know the dead guy?"

"Ted? How would I know him? Why would you ask me?"

"Two reasons. One, he hasn't always been dead. And two, he was once in your unique line of work."

"Nihilistic hackers and crackers avoid socializing in large circles. Instead, we're driven by enormous egos to simply attain notoriety. We exist to explore code boundaries, then extend those limits—just because we can." Dale slid the keyboard away. "Nope, never had the privilege of meeting the guy behind this one."

Since he'd been straight with her so far, Sydney chose to believe him.

59

L eaving Dale's, Sydney hightailed it back to the TV station. After a quick change of clothes, she phoned Dino while en route to Mason's. "Any news about the yacht break-in?"

"We collared a thug in a Spruill Avenue bar," Dino said. "The guy bragged about doing a marina job. We matched his fingerprint to one on the yacht's door."

"What happens next?"

"Booked him on B&E and assault. This particular citizen is a habitual offender. Undoubtedly, he'll go away for a long time." Dino disconnected.

By the time Sydney reached Kiawah Island, the barrier isle hailed as the East Coast's premier golf destination, she knew exactly how she wanted to force her play. She parked the borrowed beater in front of an eight-thousand-square-foot Flyaway Drive mansion—the house Mason had inherited.

She knew he'd coasted through a high life, spoiled by the customary trappings of family wealth. Too much of everything—expensive cars, luxury trips, the best clubs—every whim indulged. Sydney wondered whether he could make it without a strong tether to oodles of money. Though she would've been willing, even elated, to tether herself along for the ride as his Mrs., if his job hadn't pulled him away fourteen years earlier.

Sydney raked a shoe across the beach house's perfectly manicured lawn, then let herself in through the front door. She floated with enough style and elegance to match the surroundings, delighted she'd changed into a designer cream-colored shift dress purchased before losing all her money. Gold studs dotted an overlay of gossamer silk cut above the knees. The creation had set her back a thousand bucks, but the fabric gracefully rearranged itself with every step.

She hoped her spanking-new outfit made the right impression.

Gavin emerged from a side patio dressed in black pants and a sky-blue polo. Mason wore khakis and a peach oxford. When both their slackened jaws dropped to their chests, she knew her blithe *sangfroid* had hit a grand slam.

Mason winked, earning bonus points by not pretending to act casual. "You look incredible."

Gavin mouthed a few words to Mason before turning to her. "Ms. Quinn, what the devil are you doing here?"

Sydney never shied away from her God-given assets. She was smart, pretty, and had a nose for the truth. Three things she couldn't hide. This time, flaunting her beauty seemed like bringing a cannon to a water balloon fight. Even so, she wanted to ensure the upper hand.

"Call me Syd. Sorry to blindside you, but you're a hard man to pin down. Mind if I record this?" She conjured her patented moxie and placed a camera on the fireplace mantel before signaling for Gavin to sit.

"Do I have a choice?" he asked.

Sydney handed him a lapel mic. "You can cooperate. Or we can do things the hard way. How would you like to proceed?"

"No comment." His tone bit with a menacing growl.

Sydney held her ground. "Surely your communications people tell you the public hates when a beleaguered executive says 'no comment.'"

Gavin whirled toward Mason. "Tell her to leave."

Mason skated around the obvious attempt at undue influence. "Hold on a sec. Let's see what she wants. Our Lois Lane is a great listener."

Gavin spun back to Sydney. His glare held a frosty edge. "How long will this take if I decide to oblige?"

She made a mock frown at Mason for using a stupid pet name, then studied Gavin. Image was everything to him. "I'm giving you a chance to set the record straight. In terms of time, about the same as having a molar extracted."

He eased onto the sofa across from her.

Sydney continued. "I won't ask anything about my personal dispute with your firm. I'm more interested in what's happening to others. Like Josh Andrews."

"Who?"

"C'mon, don't play dumb. He's been all over the news. On Monday, the guy held two hostages at Piper Kingston's house."

"Oh, him." Gavin pasted a thin smile on equally thin lips, and he tried to act as cool as the iceberg that'd cleaved the Titanic.

He failed. Though it was fun watching him try.

"Don't insult my viewers."

Gavin glanced around for something to do with his hands. "May I get an iced tea?"

Mason's eyes swiveled between Sydney and Gavin. He threw up his hands and leaped to his feet. "Where are my manners?"

Sydney hooked a thumb toward the kitchen. "While the cat's away, will you confirm you have a government agent working undercover at your company?"

Gavin instinctively nodded. Then, seemingly spooked, he looked like he should run for cover.

Sydney beamed. "No take-backsies. The agent is there to help your firm. Unless you're doing something against the law. Are you?"

"Absolutely not."

Mason returned with three glasses on a silver tray. He poured bottled water into two of them and a Diet Mountain Dew for Sydney into the third.

She offered a long, contemplative stare. "Josh was miffed his benefits were terminated after a private investigator, on your payroll, captured video of him helping his three-year-old son into a car seat.

Do you remember the incident?"

"How can I be expected to recall—"

Sydney held up a palm, then slid a page from Josh's claim file across the coffee table.

Gavin's eyebrows scrunched together as he scanned the entry referencing his ultimate decision. "Where did you get this?"

Sydney jabbed a finger at the page. "Piper recommended continuing disability payments. You overrode her and stopped his benefits. Josh's life has been a living hell ever since."

"Is there a question?" Gavin asked.

Sydney pooh-poohed the smug bastard. "You have an awesome responsibility to ensure our hero first responders receive compensation when they need it. My question, Mr. Lansing: How many other firefighters, cops, or EMTs have had their injury benefits prematurely nixed under your watch?"

"I'm saving taxpayer money. Workers' comp fraud is rampant. The state would be bankrupted if it weren't for aggressive oversight by insurance carriers such as LG." Gavin wiped spittle from his lips with the back of his hand.

Sydney tapped a key on her electronic pad to cue the video from Hank Jenkins, the private eye. She turned the screen so both men could watch. They winced when Josh collapsed after helping his kid.

"This is the first I'm seeing this," Gavin said.

"Then how did you decide Josh's fate without viewing the evidence you paid for? With taxpayer money."

"This must've fallen through the cracks."

"I'll be sure the state insurance board knows about the thoroughness with which you treat your clients. But let's move on." She took a sip of Diet Dew, carefully returning the cut crystal to a monogrammed leather coaster. "Josh was accused of killing Piper. I think you'll agree, he wasn't able to inflict that punishment because—" She tilted her head toward the iPad.

Mason drew in a breath. His reaction seemed unpretentious,

sort of heartrending. "Gavin, can his benefits be reinstated without a lot of fuss?"

Gavin scoffed. "It sets an ugly precedent."

"Standard corporate response," Sydney said. "Put yourself in his shoes. Sheesh, put yourself in Piper's. How many other claims agents' lives are you willing to risk?"

"The proper procedure would be an appeal," Gavin said with irritating bumptiousness.

"A lengthy. Costly. Appeal," Sydney said.

Mason shook his head. "Quit the party-line comebacks. Syd is like a Rottweiler with a sirloin. And she can smell bullshit."

Gavin knuckled under. "Fine. I'll reinstate his benefits."

That was the second time Mason had labeled her a dog with a chewie. This version sounded dangerously close to a compliment. Despite her aversion to his sobriquets, Sydney wore it as a badge of honor.

Returning to the task at hand, she slid a form from her folder. "This makes it official."

Gavin sneered as he signed the document.

Sydney slipped the paper back into the folder. "You can put the hammer down on fraudsters without hurting those who aren't trying to game the system. But emergency workers wounded on the job cannot be overcompensated. We owe them a huge debt." She nodded to gain consensus and liked the direction in which the conversation was heading.

Time to screw prudence and go for the jugular.

60

Asking loads of questions was a force of habit for Sydney. And she knew when to pounce. "Did you know Ted Armstrong was a former Hack Pack member?"

Gavin raised a hand as if he could fend off the incoming Hack Pack inquiry. "I'm not at liberty to discuss the matter. Closed-door congressional hearings and sealed records are sacrosanct. National security and other rot. Besides, the Pack is old news." He pushed the last words through a clenched jaw.

"You are a coward. You'd rather hide behind the law." Sydney's tone took on a whole new level of sarcasm.

Mason was shaking his head, apparently trying to signal her to stop. "Gavin, everyone knows the Pack gained notoriety for electronically infiltrating Defense Department systems. It's a matter of public record."

Sydney waggled a finger. "I'm interested in the non-mainstream particulars."

"Such as?" Gavin asked.

"If the Hack Pack is old news, how come they claimed responsibility for raiding public and private coffers this week? Including LG accounts." She laced her fingers and folded her hands in her lap. "Haven't you been watching the news? Listening to your people?"

Gavin huffed.

"I'll take that as a no." Sydney took another sip of Diet Dew. "Let me lay it out. Your clients have been ripped off right under your nose. Anything you'd like to say to address your lack of pecuniary responsibility?"

Gavin fumbled with his water glass. "No comment."

"I warned you." Sydney affixed her best sideways glare,

determined to wait him out. When he didn't respond right away, she thought maybe silence was his answer. And not the one she expected or sought.

Gavin eventually cracked the quiet. "I want my lawyer."

"Wrong answer."

Gavin balled his fists and leaned forward. "I hate girls like you."

"You mean ones with an IQ larger than their cup size."

"You'll ruin me."

Sydney didn't cave. "Your definition of *ruin* might be different from mine. I've learned you live close to the edge—financially speaking. Yet your bank account recently found itself suspiciously fruitful. Via the Aeneid thefts perhaps?"

"Impossible."

Sydney pressed on, ignoring her fib. "Then how do you explain the large deposits?"

Gavin drew a deep breath and his chin dropped onto his chest. "My company, like my wife, is spending hand over fist. Maybe we expanded too quickly." He tried to raise his head to meet Sydney's glance, but his shoulders sagged. "Anyway, I didn't want to lay anyone off. When you spotted me at the bank the other day—I was there to borrow money." He drew in a breath. "They turned me down. So, I had to liquidate many of my holdings. Even put up my house and boat as collateral, to meet payroll. I thought it'd be noble to keep people working."

Gavin's candor caught Sydney flat-footed.

She started to speak but had to clear her throat. "Let's say you're telling the truth. Would public knowledge of hiring a former Hack Packer adversely affect the IPO and derail your shot at the infusion of money you desperately need?"

"What's that supposed to mean?"

"Ted had ample skill to create the infected malware that is stripping a jaw-dropping amount of money from client accounts. As you know, the Aeneid virus is also plundering national resources. And someone is planning to sell the code on the dark web."

"Mason promised me your interviewing skills were first-rate. I was horribly misled."

Sydney eyed Mason with a sly grin. "Are you Luis Gaston? Perhaps you falsified your death after doing prison time. Came back to retaliate against your frat bro, Ted, who walked away from the Pack scot-free."

Gavin vigorously shook his head. "Of course not."

Sydney pressed forward. "You learned Ted came clean and started dishing to the Secret Service. Maybe he even discovered your hand in the company cookie jar. I'd be mad as hell."

Angry features snaked over Gavin's face. "You have no idea."

Sydney's eyes leveled with his. "Mad enough to kill?"

"I didn't kill Ted. I told you where my money came from." Gavin melted into his chair. "Oh, hell. Might as well spill the whole of it. Worst-kept secret in the company. I knew Ted changed his name. Jake Bishop—the original master hacker," he snorted. "Credited with many infamous super viruses, arrested for hacking into World Bank and Federal Reserve computers. A brilliant programmer."

"So, you hired Ted as what? A public relations stunt to promote his redemption tour?"

"I asked him to oversee company security. Our clients want their money safe from anyone using a modem and a bootleg tracer. I trusted him."

"How'd that work out?" Sydney maintained a poker face as she shifted lanes. "What did you two argue about?"

"Ted told me things were fishy. I wanted him to lay it out for me. But he said he didn't have his ducks in a row, and I had the damn cotillion meeting. We agreed to meet early Friday to discuss the details."

She had Gavin where she wanted him, ready to storm the castle. "LG's server farm. Is that an actual thing or something in the cloud?"

Mason stifled a gratuitous laugh.

Sydney thought it seemed like a fair question. Yet she sensed Mason was mocking her and it didn't sit well. Not one bit.

He redeemed himself with his usual panache when he said, "Syd's always been such a kidder. More like a savvy attorney who asks leading questions to ensure her subject is the star of the interview."

Gavin allowed a sheepish grin. "Our farm is located in a warehouse in St. George. It contains racks of hardware, forming clusters of computer servers supporting the company. How is that important?"

Sydney tented her fingers. "I learned yours is an infected proxy. That's the *fishy* Ted wanted to tell you about."

"Can't be. LG has triple-encrypted, industrial-strength physical and cyber security."

She knew the interview was drawing to a close, and she'd cast a wide net with strategic fibs and blatant lies, mingled with incontrovertible truth, hoping to trip him up and test his veracity. Based on what she'd seen and heard, Gavin wasn't the guy she hoped the state would punish for killing Piper or Ted.

Sydney said, "You have a murderer on your staff."

Gavin leaned forward. "You know who killed them?"

She eyed Mason and held out her empty glass. She didn't want him in the room when she made her final riposte. "May I have a refill?"

"Anything for you, babe."

Once Mason left the room, Sydney said, "I buried the lede— you're being framed. Ted tried to stop the malware but was killed before he could finish his reverse-flipper-ma-doodle code. I hired a guy to complete Ted's work. Aeneid is dead."

Gavin wiped his brow and seemed like he wanted to shriek. "I'll have my assistant—"

"Whoa, no." Sydney waved her hands like an NFL ref. "This is an insidious high-tech horror story. Your server farm is really infected."

"What do you want from me?"

"I have a way for the hacker to steal some fast cash in hopes of trapping her."

Gavin jerked off the lapel mic and squeezed the bridge of his nose. "Her? Who?"

"Grace Rogers, your red-headed assistant."

"I'll kill her."

"That's the spirit."

He didn't crack a smile. "Wait, I'm kidding."

Sydney made an if-you-say-so kind of shrug. "Of course. But she probably killed both of your executives. And I'll bet she's the one marketing Aeneid to the highest bidder."

Sydney slid a folded note with instructions for Gavin to phone her later and mimed hiding it in his pocket. He stuffed the note in his pants, though his expression read somewhere in the vicinity of 'Yeah, right' and 'What the fugazzi?'

Mason returned with a fresh Diet Dew. "Did I hear you say you think Grace killed Ted? That's astonishing." He didn't try to contradict Sydney, another point in his favor. She'd forgiven him for his earlier nickname transgression, though she didn't answer right away.

Sydney moved to the rear of the house and spotted the ocean. As far as ostentatious and inherited luxury mansions went, Mason could do a lot worse. Mesmerized by the rolling waves, she took a moment to recalculate. Critical details were falling into place. Yet her insides felt like she'd been uprooted by an EF-3 tornado and dropped on her head in Oz.

Mason continued to ruminate. "Makes sense. Grace knows where Gavin kept his gun. None of us should trust anything she says."

Gavin protested. "You're both wrong about Grace."

"Remains to be seen. Syd has a knack for exposing . . . you know." Mason steered her toward the front door before she attempted to launch another query storm. He finished his farewell with the world's biggest understatement. "That about sums everything up. I knew you could do it, babe."

Her heart thumped wildly and she elbowed him in the ribs. "No, you didn't."

"Yeah, right. I'd have bet three to one against your pulling this off. But I'm happy for you."

Sydney whispered in his ear. "It all fits with why you were assigned at LG, right?"

Mason said nothing.

Sydney lobbed a final grenade to punctuate her success. "Suppose for a moment I know where to find both Aeneid and Ted's antidote."

Mason leaned against the wall. "Simon? Hand it over."

"You can have the game first thing in the morning. But trust me when I say this is bigger than Simon." Sydney was in the process of reconsidering, about to come clean and bare all she knew about the antidote's upload and Piper's hot-pink flash drive, when Mason interrupted.

"Man, you've been right about Grace all along—I should've listened. She slipped up when she conned Josh into going to Piper's house using that handwritten note."

Sydney grinned. "Pro tip: Never leave incriminating evidence in your own handwriting."

61

Vintage Motown blared from the weight room as Sydney ventured into the jam-packed Lowcountry Rehab Station at the old mall in North Charleston. Dinner must've been Italian because notes of oregano wafted from the kitchen and made Sydney's stomach growl.

Andy Bates was watching TV when he spotted her. "Hey, Syd. Didn't know you were coming by."

She toed the floor. "I'll leave if I'm intruding."

"Safe space, remember?" He bobbed his head as he sized her up, apparently spotting something he needed to treat. "What'll it be—food, beverage, shoulder?"

"Money." Sydney unzipped her purse. "Tapped my usual sources, who were all too happy to share with you guys."

The music shifted to a hip-hop number with a thumping backbeat that reminded her of the deafening roar of Cobras. One helo circled, swooped. Voices crackled over the radio. Then, a barrage of gunfire. The helo barely cleared the rooftops.

Sydney tried to blink away the memory and return to the present. She forced herself to lock her eyes on Andy. Yet her throat dried and she staved off a pant. "Changed my mind. I'll take one of those fruity concoctions you made last time. With a side of talk-me-down-from-the-precipice."

Andy exhaled with a compassion shared by those suffering from traumatic stress. He flagged Danny. "Two triple berry smoothies, Code 3."

Danny flicked his eyes between his crew chief and Sydney. "On it."

Sydney's mind foundered—swirling smack dab into a chute of dangerous thoughts. She'd relived the ambush the other night with

Dino and didn't want to go through it again.

"Crandall. Reed. Slater. Townsend. Walters," she whispered to herself. "The world is a good place. My life makes sense." She released the stranglehold on her purse and eyed Andy. "I feel like I've been hurdled into a vat of moldering kimchi."

"Damn," Andy said. "Doesn't sound good."

Sydney flopped into an upholstered chair. "Step one, I'm a chick with an anxiety disorder."

Andy allowed himself a wry grin, then spoke in a hushed tone. "That puts you way ahead of the curve. Most of us don't realize we have anything wrong." Without bleating, he asked, "What's your vice?"

Sydney shook her head with knee-jerk-like resistance. "Don't have one."

"C'mon, spill it."

She scrambled for the right thing to say. "I used to crave street racing."

"Used to?" Andy's contemplative stare burned into her. Sydney couldn't tell whether he was annoyed. Impressed. Or both. "I *used to* be an enthusiastic drinker," he said. "Now, I'm always teetering on the brink to drink. All it takes is one bad day. I can't even imagine what moldering kimchi feels like."

Danny arrived carrying the smoothies. "Took a chance with extra whip."

"Nice touch, Danny boy." Andy handed Sydney a tall glass and toasted. "Smoothies are a gateway to chocolate chips, but I'll take my chances."

"Need me to stick around? Call for backup?" Danny asked.

Sydney puckered her brow and said, with a hint of sarcasm, "Not like I boosted a Trans-Am from a Mount Pleasant body shop."

"Did you?" Danny clucked. "Nah, you're nursing an inner wound. Makes us do dumb things."

The edges of Andy's mouth wobbled. "Drunkenness was my

dumb thing. Now, sobriety is my superpower."

Danny added, "My superpower is working two jobs. Still strapped for cash. But being a paramedic—man, I love it."

Sydney told the fellas she enjoyed being a journalist. She omitted the part about hellish war images and the god-awful smells tattooed on her brain. "My job gives me a chance to hang out with bozos like you." She straightened. "How flexible are you with your policy on replaying what happened at the hostage scene before I barreled in?"

Andy plucked at his cell phone. "Thought you might ask. So, I downloaded Josh's call." He punched play.

"Nine-one-one, where's your emergency?"

"Need an ambulance—417 Carnegie Road," Josh said.

"What happened?"

"Someone must've broken in. Please hurry."

"EMS is on the way. Can you describe the victim's injuries?"

"She's bleeding. It's bad."

Andy broke in. "We rolled out at 1:36 p.m. Dorchester Road traffic was thick and ignored our sirens. Danny plowed through the median, churning a wake of grass and gravel. I started envisioning the sheaf of paperwork I'd be responsible for if we got stuck or hit another car. But I knew it'd never happen." Andy scratched his jaw, as if weighing how much detail to disclose. "Danny and me—we've been pals since grade school. Stationed together for the better part of our sixteen-year career with NCFD. First, as probationary fire-fighters. Then, paramedics. I'm lucky my best friend is always at my helm." He gave his smoothie a fierce swizzle with the straw. "Once we arrived on scene, I tossed out a number to Danny."

"What was it?" Sydney asked.

"Four thousand-six hundred-and eighty-four."

"Because?"

"That's how many runs we'd responded to." Andy fiddled with a loose cuticle on his index finger. "Josh's call was our four thousand-six hundred-and eighty-fifth, which would put us ahead of the clowns who worked Goose Creek back in the nineties. We were officially the longest-running pair in department history. Wished to hell I hadn't said the call would be epic when we left the barn."

Several minutes of poignant silence passed between them before Sydney let out a spray of laughter.

62

Sydney parked Mandy's borrowed Edge at the downtown Visitor Center, then hailed a pedicab to take her three blocks to the Francis Marion. The oversized tricycle's driver was in his mid-twenties, wore baggy beach trunks, a puka shell necklace, and a neon yellow polo shirt that clashed with his bleached surfer hair. Tanned and lean, he glistened in the twinkling streetlights.

Mandy was seated on a king-sized tufted ottoman in the elegantly appointed hotel lobby when Sydney arrived. They moved toward the bank of elevators and Mandy pressed a button for the top floor. When the lift came to a stop, they wandered past Sydney's most recent suite to another room. Mandy knocked twice. Paused. Then, knocked three times. "We have a secret code. Strictly need-to-know," she said.

"Your spy craft is foolproof," Sydney said. "Who are we meeting?"

"A sworn member of our sleuthing team."

Commander Bob opened the door and glanced furtively down the hallway.

Sydney followed his eyes. "Everything copacetic?"

He motioned the women into the suite. "Ducky."

"So, this is where you stashed Bob. I like it." Sydney spotted Josh. "Good news. Gavin Lansing reinstated your disability benefits. He also agreed to a lump sum payment to cover your gap in coverage. And hacker Dale said you did a fine job cleaning up Ted's code."

"Wow, how can I repay you?" Josh said.

"*Pro bono*, remember?" She ambled toward the massive floor-to-ceiling windows and threw back the heavy curtains and gauzy silk panels, revealing a spectacular view of Marion Square.

Bob lowered himself onto an upholstered settee and smoothed

wisps of white hair. "Take a seat, Doll Face." His voice never quivered with age. "Tell us how you saved the world from financial ruin."

"I needed lots of help." Sydney scuffled with the contents of her purse, finally locating the right notebook. "As I mentioned, Josh fixed the coding errors, Ted's fail-safe. Dale uploaded the patch. And Mandy is single-handedly honchoing our EMS fundraiser tomorrow. My role is more like ringmaster."

Bob flashed a rascal's grin and patted Sydney's hand. "Simply wonderful."

Mandy slid a pair of banker's boxes onto the coffee table.

Sydney pointed. "What are those?"

Mandy scooted Bob's box toward him. "You go first."

He pulled out the Simon game and pushed the big red button, which blinked as before. Then he punched the blue button and was rewarded with more blinking.

Sydney pinched her eyebrows. "That's new. Yet, it doesn't explain why a former hacker/world-class programmer used something so crude to convey a major clue."

Mandy said, "Ted went old-school for you."

Bob passed Sydney a note that read: *DFKH. Don't Show Grace.*

Sydney said, "That's more than you gave me earlier. I'm guessing from the new blue lights?"

Bob and Mandy exchanged glances.

"We spoke . . . ah . . ." Bob stammered. "Before I figured out the second part." He splayed his hands, looking abashed.

Mandy knitted her fingers together. "What we have here is an itty-bitty, almost infinitesimal problematic wrinkle."

Sydney gave them a squint. "What?"

"I no longer deserve membership on the sleuthing team," Bob muttered.

"Why? Your interpretation makes perfect sense, since Grace is our top suspect."

"Because I'm an old fool—"

"Go ahead, spill it. I promise I won't bite."

"It happened so fast," Bob said. "The lady said she was working with you and needed everything I had for an urgent newscast."

Sydney sat forward in her chair. "Who?"

"Julia Mayfair—Eyewitness 13," Mandy scoffed.

"She's no lady," Sydney said.

Mandy added, "Julia suckered Bob into revealing the whole thing, including the new *Don't Show Grace* bit."

"She tricked me." Bob hung his head. "Sorry, Doll. I forgot Julia was the enemy and not with your station."

Bee-yatch, Sydney thought. *Tricked my friend, did you? Thinking he was a common source.*

Even so, Julia had been clever. Had to give her props for that. First, to find Bob. Then to con him into revealing any secret information. Julia possessed a real scoop if she knew what the code meant.

"No worries," Sydney said. "Julia will put two and two together and come up with eight. Anything she reports based on your tip will be flat wrong."

"We're okay then?" Bob sniffled.

"Better than okay—we're a primo sleuthing team. But we should shift you to another room—under an alias."

63

Sydney hefted Commander Bob's suitcase onto the ottoman in his new room, which was conveniently located directly below her suite—perfect for when he decided to blast his favorite marching band tunes at full volume. "There you go, Commander." She patted the suitcase as if it were a loyal pet. "Promise me you didn't pack any contraband snacks."

Bob winked. "Just those suspiciously addictive gummy bears. You know, I never dreamed I'd end up in such an expensive safe house. This room is even nicer than the last one. I'll try not to practice my tap-dancing routine too late."

She laughed, knowing full well that Bob's idea of a wild evening involved a good book and a cup of chamomile tea.

Mandy said, "Bob, the rooms are identical."

He raked his hands through his hair. "Ah, but here, the mini-bar is full."

Sydney said, "Let's shift lanes and try our hand at a high-speed rewind."

"What do you mean?" Josh asked.

Nothing, not even Julia's unethical stunt, could bring her down. She tossed Piper's Hello Kitty flash drive to Mandy. "Since Bob discovered additional information on Simon, I say we take another peek at the personnel files Piper downloaded. Specifically, the Jake Bishop and Luis Gaston folders. I wasn't keen to their significance earlier, so I never searched them. Makes me think I missed something important. Like Aeneid's mother code." Sydney poured herself a Diet Dew from Bob's well-stocked minibar.

Mandy stuck Kitty into a USB port on her laptop and squealed. "Oh. My. God."

Everyone spun toward her as she yanked a page from the printer.

Mandy handed the paper to Sydney as Bob and Josh peered over her shoulder at a copy of a photograph. The color had been washed out from years of exposure, leaving an eerie orange tint to the overtly staged picture of a pair of twenty-somethings striking gangsta poses. To round out their theatrical composition, the duo aimed keyboards at the camera lens instead of guns. And they were surrounded by bricks of cash rather than drugs.

They were witnessing the only known image of the notorious Hack Pack.

Jake. And Luis.

The guy on the left was unmistakably Ted Armstrong, née Jake Bishop. And the youthful figure on the right took Sydney's breath away. The supposedly *dead* Luis Gaston bore a remarkable resemblance to the man she knew as Mason Sterling.

Sydney's stomach roiled with mushrooming seasickness. Make that incandescent rage, coupled with a profound sense of betrayal, as the ground shifted beneath her.

"Oh, Syd." Mandy reached for her friend. "I'm so sorry."

Sydney felt her cheeks warm. She wished bad people came with warning labels because she hated unforced errors of any kind.

Moreover, this photo rerouted her entire theory of the crimes straight down the crapper.

Mason had managed to leverage their relationship to his advantage.

Her eyes found Mandy, who seemed extra-delighted to have confirmation Mason was a skeevy sonovabitch.

Every conversation with him clamored for playback and reassessment.

Then, Sydney mumbled, "Handwritten."

Bob cupped an ear. "Didn't catch that, Doll."

Sydney held up a hand. "Give me a sec."

She mentally flicked through an inventory of tactics one might employ to keep tabs on a quarry. She concluded with confidence that Mason had likely bugged her phone. Accordingly, she used the room's landline to call Dino. She needed him to fact-check an important item in Josh's story. Thankfully, she never had to question Dino's trust and loyalty.

Sydney gasped when he confirmed that evidence-recovery technicians were unable to locate Josh's note, his invitation to Piper's house, in the McDonald's trash where he'd tossed it.

Then how did Mason know the note from the LG receptionist to Josh had been *handwritten* if that piece of physical evidence was never circulated among the law enforcement community? Had Mason made an honest goof or a guilty slip-of-the-tongue?

After she disconnected with Dino, Sydney turned toward Josh. "Are you absolutely certain you only told me about the note being handwritten—no one else?"

"Mandy was in earshot," Josh said with earnest emphasis.

Sydney shot her a glance. Mandy locked her lips with an imaginary key.

That left Sydney with a raw fact she could no longer ignore or make excuses for—Mason was squarely behind Piper's murder, the mega-hack, and Ted's death.

She cleared her throat. "Your invitation wasn't written by Piper."

Josh's mouth dropped open. "You mean the note was fake? Not an invitation from her to discuss my case?"

Sydney fanned her hands like windshield wipers. At that moment, she began martialing her resources to wage all-out war against Mason, rather than relying on her contractually obligated impartiality. "Your presence was artfully arranged by a killer who needed to frame someone and deflect attention."

"Well, that sucks for me," Josh said.

Sydney had nothing to add to that succinct abridgement. "Do you recall anything unusual when you arrived at Piper's?"

Josh took a moment to respond. "I pulled into the driveway

hoping I didn't scratch the Beemer. Went inside and got beaned from behind. No idea who, how, or why." He rubbed his head.

"Beemer?" Mandy shot upright. "Piper's Lexus was parked in the garage."

Josh's eyes sparkled. "I'm certain the car was a BMW. A cherry German ride. You know? Sporty. Expensive."

"You never mentioned the car before," Sydney said.

Josh hiked his shoulders. "Didn't remember until now. Dark Beemer—super cherry."

Mandy tapped her palm on a thigh. "Grace drives a black BMW."

Mason does too, Sydney thought.

They were in this together.

Partners? Co-conspirators? Lovers who'd enjoyed a hearty guffaw at Sydney's expense?

Ted had even coded *Don't Show Grace* onto Simon.

She confronted the realization she'd been used by Mason and Grace.

No question about it. And that didn't sit well.

Now, she had to find a way to get past any hurt feelings and follow the evidence regardless of where it led.

"What else do you have, Bob?" Sydney asked.

He flipped the banker's box upside down, spilling random office supplies, like LG monogrammed staplers, pens, and notepads. "Johnny Jackass left this swag in my room after our last meeting."

Sydney fingered an assortment of flash drives with characters and team logos—purple Baltimore Ravens, yellow Minions, and a black Darth Vader. She shook out a T-shirt with a gold star—the Secret Service emblem.

Based on what she now believed, Mason had doubtlessly bought the shirt at a novelty store.

Bob eyed the shirt's logo and his hands flew to his mouth. "Is your Johnny a secret agent?"

"Uh, not likely." Sydney tapped the old Hack Pack photo and

squirmed. "We can circle back to that discussion another time. Maybe never."

"That reminds me," Mandy said. "Mason showed up in the police blotter on the day Piper died."

Sydney couldn't block reacting to another shocking revelation. "Wait . . . What?"

Bob beamed. "Lucky we're doing a new rundown. More info keeps bursting the pipes."

Mandy nodded. "A North Charleston firefighter spotted Mason on the sixteenth fairway behind Piper's house after cops set up their perimeter." She glanced at Josh, apparently registering his unfortunate involvement in the aforementioned hostage situation. "Oops."

"Don't sugarcoat it. I did it," Josh said. "And I'm sorry."

"Anyway," Mandy continued, "whatever excuse Mason gave was enough for them to let him go."

The corners of Bob's lips curled in amusement. "Johnny must have pulled the ole my-badge-is-bigger-than-yours routine. But I'm guessing from your reaction to that old picture, his badge was a jim-dandy counterfeit."

"You can say that again." Sydney flipped her shoes to the floor and pushed back into the recliner. She took a long pull of Diet Dew.

Bob pointed at the label on Mandy's box. "What's Reverse Gambit?"

Mandy said, "That's the signature Ted used when he wrote computer programming code. The guy put things in reverse order—like Yoda."

"Yoda?" Bob rubbed his eyes as he processed the explanation.

"Jedi Master. Little green fella. Pointy ears."

Bob enjoyed a glint of recognition. "Ah, yes—sleuthing team, we are."

"Yup," Sydney said. "We used that logic to unravel every clue Ted left us."

"Not every clue." Mandy scooped a page from her pile.

"Remember when Josh was showing you how to use a substitution code? We were so focused on HKFD that we dropped the ball on the trailer: *///+/-//DFKH//•18/SU//EDOC//$//•1343//$$///.* When I flip each part between the slash marks, I get: 81 US Code 3431. Followed by a legal symbol and dollar signs."

Bob said, "Anyone besides me still confused?"

Mandy read from her iPad. "Eighty-one US Code is the legal statute concerning Piracy and Privateering, Radio Act of 1927, Acquisition and Operations of Hospital Facilities, and the Federal Employment Compensation Act, among other things."

"Seems sorta irrelevant," Bob said.

Sydney suggested, "How about 18 US Code, Section 1343? Perhaps the numbers aren't transposed."

Mandy entered the new data into her pad. "Wire fraud."

"That's more like it," Sydney said.

Mandy quoted from her electronic notebook: "Whoever devises any scheme to defraud or obtain money by false pretenses, blah, blah, blah, shall be imprisoned not more than twenty years."

64

I n every story, there comes a time when tangents converge on a single focal point, like tributaries flowing into a mighty river. For Sydney, the intertwined tales of Josh, Piper, and Ted had catapulted her squarely atop one such crucial pinnacle. And the moment demanded clear eyes and unwavering resolve. Sydney knew she had to balance the weight of truth and consequence with every step.

Action 7's newsroom vibrated from a typical Monday morning with sounds of crinkling food wrappers, purring printers, and squelching police scanners. To the untrained observer, the situation might have appeared chaotic. Perhaps no rhyme to the scattershot choreography of assistant producers, reporters, and videographers streaking between editing bays, hovering at crowded workstations, or queuing around monitors. But a skilled spectator like Sydney knew better.

Olivia had ordered the entire team in for the early show. An unusual request, though necessary for special live coverage of the First Responder Rehab Center's fundraising campaign on Sydney's behalf.

As cub reporters prepared to head into the field, Sydney tromped into Pete's office. "I'd like to pitch a story."

Pete slammed the door behind her. "The network thinks you're a liability. A loose cannon. A real liability."

"Redundant? Doesn't sound like me."

Cue the eye roll.

Pete said, "I told 'em the reporting you did on the computer glitch was top-drawer. But sheesh—they want me to suspend you."

Sydney's heart skipped. "Fat chance." A suspension would wreck her plan. Especially since she was on the verge of busting everything wide open. "What for?"

Pete seemed to craft something from thin air. "Violating station policy."

"What policy?" The indignation in Sydney's voice surprised her.

"Road racing."

"Oh, you know." Sydney chose to play it cool. "How?"

"C'mon, you have to ask?" Pete scratched the stubble on his cheeks, letting it hang there.

Sydney opted to wait him out, but soon wished she'd chosen a different tack.

At times, a minute rushed by like it didn't want to enjoy the full sixty seconds it'd been allotted. Other minutes seemed to stretch unreasonably longer than their preordained time.

After a few of the latter, Pete let out a sigh. "I still have sources in the police department. Let's hear your pitch."

Sydney presented her scheme to take down the people she believed were behind Aeneid and Piper and Ted's murders, which involved trapping Mason and Grace aboard his yacht. To add a little more icing to Mason's going-back-to-prison cake, she'd first lure them into snagging one more biznap heist. It could be risky. But she thought it'd be hard for them to resist.

Even if they didn't snatch the ransom worm, the task force and local police could build solid cases when, one, or both, bit the Aeneid hook and claimed Piper's Hello Kitty flash drive, which now hosted a harmless copy of Aeneid—so polluted with inert fluff and intentional errors and omissions, nobody could ever sort it out.

Sydney concluded, "I spoke with my Secret Service contact and we're ready to put everything in motion."

Pete shook his head. "What you're proposing is idiotic. I should fire you. But damn spam, Sydney, I hired you. What would that say about me?"

She knew he didn't mean it. He *fired* her all the time. Besides, Mrs. Muirfield had extended her contract. Nevertheless, after Pete retired from Action 7, he could start a side hustle as a motivational speaker. Wink, wink.

"Wait a minute." She braced her hands on her hips. "I'm a reporter. I track leads. Some pan out. Others don't. I have a huge story right here—biting you in the ass." Pete opened his mouth to speak, but Sydney cut him off with a chop of her hand. "Pro tip: I know you're retiring, but now's a great time to man up."

"You've laid out a half-decent plan." Pete's tongue was planted firmly in his cheek as he poured another cup of sludge from his worn Mr. Coffee machine. He took his time adding three packets of sugar and two creams. "Run through it one more time."

Turned out, Pete had been onboard all along.

Good, because he had zero chance of talking Sydney out of it.

She repeated her plan.

This time, Pete poked holes until she'd eliminated any nagging gaps likely to trip her up.

She said, "Covert action like this must remind you of your time in Moscow or Istanbul, huh?"

Pete ran the stir stick around the coffee cup. "Eyewitness 13 broke in with an exclusive. They claimed Gavin Lansing knew all about Aeneid's hack long before it happened. Laid the Treasury breach and Wall Street's crash square on his doorstep."

Sydney made herself comfortable in a side chair. "Gotta love Channel 13. All the news you need, whether it's true or not."

"I didn't think accuracy fit their demographic. Any chance things will go bad for us?"

"Impossible for me to guarantee success. What would constitute an acceptable outcome?"

"For a zinger like this, I need an on-camera confession, witnessed by the Chief Justice, and attested to by a priest."

"What? No live grenades and next-day retractions? I thought that was your revised proclivity for TV journalism—according to dodgeball rules."

"Look Syd, you can be a bastard. I only object to your being a stupid bastard." He tapped his thumb on his lips and grinned. "You're right, the story's a ball-buster. Cancel the suspension. Do it."

Sydney dashed next door to the fitness center and used their landline to call Dino. She still suspected Mason was monitoring all the phones in her orbit, a detail she would use to her advantage. She gave Dino a cryptic go-ahead that served as their pre-arranged code to arm the yacht with hi-def cameras and super-sensitive mics.

When she returned to the station, she strolled to the ladies' dressing room and examined the last remaining garment in her stash. Sydney was contemplating the lightweight, floral-printed blazer and pink camisole when Olivia entered, wearing a fabulous bottle-green dress with a charmeuse bodice.

"Take off your clothes," Sydney said.

"Sugar Booger, I told you, I don't swing that way."

"Everybody's a comedian. I need your dress. *Paa-leeeeeze* let me borrow it."

"Girl, ordinarily I'd say yes. But I've seen how y'all take care of your possessions lately. This one cost me a week's salary. And you don't have the scratch to pay me back."

"I promise on my three Emmys, I'll return it like new."

"Well, I can't let you wear . . ." She pointed at the flowery blazer. "People will think you got humped by an FTD truck."

"Hand over the dress, Shecky."

65

Sydney gave her hair a quick fluff, trying to channel a bit of glamor after slipping into Olivia's precious garment—a piece so cherished it needed its own insurance policy. She sneaked barefoot from the dressing room to her cubicle, tiptoeing like a ninja on a mission to avoid the dreaded carpet static. Once there, she salvaged a pair of faux crocodile pumps, which had seen more action than a soap-opera plot twist. Slipping them on, she felt a surge of confidence, ready to face the day with the poise of someone who didn't sneak around the office in her bare feet.

Mandy rounded the corner and hovered beside Sydney's desk. "Need any help with your piece?"

Sydney passed a scrap of paper with an outline and an SD card. "Time to catch a phish."

She shared the big plan with Mandy before they moved to the main studio. Sydney squeezed herself between the morning show co-hosts. High-octane adrenaline ratcheted inside her.

Throughout the years, concerns over hair and makeup, along with more mundane matters such as camera angle, lighting, and the perfect stand-up location, had replaced sweaty palms and a swirling stomach. For her biggest moments, Sydney also relied on a calm voice in her earbud. Especially when Olivia was directing the segment.

"Okay, everybody, good show," Olivia said. "We're out of commercial in ten seconds. Roll credits on my mark. Mark—opening credits. Nick, standby. Standby, Sydney. Camera 1—the shot is yours. Nick in three, two, one."

Action 7's anchor went to work. "Good morning, Lowcountry. I'm Nick Braydon. Our top story is breaking news from the area's

US Secret Service Financial Crimes Task Force, offering relief to millions of Americans concerned about their life savings and retirement funds being depleted by a malicious computer virus known as Aeneid. Our senior correspondent, Sydney Quinn, first brought you this story."

"Thanks, Nick," Sydney said. "The operation to dismantle Aeneid, the most sophisticated and destructive botnet authorities have ever seen, began when federal and local law enforcement, along with several international police agencies, sought to put an end to the nightmare by modifying computer command codes written by a former cyber-gang member.

"Moreover, Internet black-hat hackers have been rocked by news one of their own had been serving as a Secret Service informant for years, helping build cases against dozens of his comrades. The hacker's exploits made him a cyber-hero until a series of rookie mistakes—such as posting without cloaking his computer identity—prompted someone to tip off authorities."

She was keenly aware her segment drifted over the truth while offering a few flakes of harmless misinformation. She hoped that'd cajole Mason and Grace into a confession without forfeiting public trust.

Sydney continued. "A corrective patch has been deployed. It'll release infected computers from their corrupted network created by a remote-access Trojan. In plain language, government agents continue working to ensure all versions of Aeneid are destroyed.

"The big break came when an anonymous source tipped off the Secret Service to the existence of sophisticated, yet malicious, code. As of this broadcast, the cyber-looting has almost been curtailed. But the criminal who siphoned valuable personal and financial information—and bilked a staggering $100 billion from more than two hundred banks in thirty countries, along with several US government agencies—remains at large.

"Authorities fear the elusive hacker or hackers may never be caught or face federal charges for bank fraud, wire fraud, money laundering, and extortion. In addition to national and international felonies, they are also allegedly involved with two Lowcountry murders, Piper Kingston and Ted Armstrong, which are important South Carolina state crimes."

Sydney dangled the Hello Kitty flash drive. "This is a standard 128-gig USB portable storage device many of us have on hand. My source discovered Aeneid's original malware code on this specific flash drive. If it falls into the wrong hands, devious hackers or thieves could jump-start a new round of robbery. And with US credit limits at a tipping point, it's hard to say what another intrusion would do to our economy."

"Sounds dangerous," Nick said. "What are your plans to safeguard that thing?"

"I have an unnamed source who will soon turn it over to federal authorities."

"Thank goodness this nightmare is coming to an end," the anchor said.

"Standby video and CG," Olivia said in everyone's earpieces. "Cue Sydney."

Sydney held up a palm. "Not so fast, Nick. As one bad bug is eliminated, another takes its place. I've also discovered many local businesses are concerned they may become the next victim of an unknown hack targeting them with specialized malicious software called ransomware, designed to steal keystrokes and hold their operating system and files hostage.

"My sources inside that investigation likened the attack to SolarWinds, referring to a Russian cyber-espionage campaign that spread by infecting common network management software, allowing hackers to compromise millions of usernames and passwords.

"In one such Lowcountry hijack, Lansing Group's CEO, Gavin Lansing, defended his position to abruptly pay millions to a criminal cyber-gang, as he faced down one of the most disruptive ransomware attacks in this nation's history."

Olivia said, "Roll A1."

A clip from Gavin aired. "I had no choice. I feared terrible consequences and a more costly confrontation as I watched the attack unfold. Paying the ransom put the interests of my clients and employees first."

"Cue Sydney," Olivia said.

Sydney said, "That incident offers a rare window into the dilemma faced by the private sector amid a storm of ransomware events that all start the same way—a hacker breaches a company network, encrypts their proprietary data, then demands a ransom to release it back to the owner.

"It should be noted that government authorities urged Lansing not to pay, arguing that giving in emboldens and incentivizes crooks to press forward. The feds warned the company that they had no assurances crypto keys would be provided or even work. Yet we must recognize this attack for what it is—digital extortion and a serious national security threat."

Olivia said, "Roll A2."

Sydney watched the monitor as her wee-hours interview with The Golden Crust's owner aired.

In an elaborate show of emotion, Hugo Dupont pleaded with the hacker to bypass his business and not hit him a second time. The video wiped to Gavin Lansing, whose performance for his two clips had been unscripted and shot in single takes. Gavin contritely recounted how he'd learned his server farm had been infiltrated, becoming a proxy for both the brazen Aeneid and ransomware breaches. In turn, he'd been so moved by Hugo's loss, the chief executive promised to personally pay any ransom if his deli business was attacked again.

"Cue Sydney," Olivia said. "Nick, standby."

Sydney faced the camera. "With no way to stop the ransomware attacks, Lowcountry businesses remain wary and on high alert, hoping they don't fall prey to the insidious hack. Additionally, my sources are quick to state there's no evidence of Lansing Group's culpability for the hacks, as erroneously reported by other outlets."

"Thank you, Sydney," Nick said. "In other news . . ."

While Olivia and the rest of the broadcast team continued to work the remainder of the morning show, Sydney backtracked to her desk.

Dino was the first to phone. "Anonymous source? Your report was full of—"

"Yeah, I know." They were tiptoeing through a script, and Sydney hoped it sounded like Dino was trying to get a rise out of her in case anyone was listening in by illegal means. "I did it purely to aggravate you."

"Must give you great satisfaction." He paused. "You certain you can corral Grace all by yourself?"

"I got this."

"Be careful."

"Always." Sydney disconnected, then swallowed a huge gulp of Diet Dew. Next, she phoned Mason.

He said, "You made yourself a target for every crazy out there. You gotta give me Simon and that darn flash drive. C'mon, no more games."

Sydney tapped her pen to her lips and couldn't decipher whether she'd heard sincerity in his tone or fake concern. She gut-checked the motive of one of her prime targets and forged ahead. "I know you want in on Grace's apprehension, so meet me on the yacht at ten. You can have her and the flash drive." She pumped her fist, then clicked off.

For Mason, overstating his own intellect had been an obvious character flaw.

But underestimating Sydney's—that'd be his downfall.

She thumbed her notes and debated the next move, opting to go off-book. More like jumping into the left-field bleachers, to be specific.

She strode to Editing Bay 5, pulled the shade, and phoned Grace. "If you watched my broadcast, you know what I have."

Grace said nothing.

Her silence made Sydney feel even more convinced Grace and Mason were working together. Sydney planned to snare them both in a two-for-one grab.

"It's all yours," Sydney said. "For a price."

"How much?"

"I leased a G-650 to take you to the Caymans for a meet with a Chechen buyer. His offer is $1.1 billion. I'm not greedy. How does $88 million sound? That'll be enough for my EMS Rehab Center upgrade and cover the cost of the Gulfstream."

"Ha, you're kidding. Always the jokester." Grace's voice sounded tight.

Sydney became exasperated with the redhead. "When have you ever heard me tell a joke?"

"No alarm bells? Red flags?"

Sydney paused before responding. "That was rhetorical, right?"

Brooding silence. Then, Grace glommed onto the bait. "Where and when?"

Hook. Line. And stinker.

Sydney beamed. "Meet me on the yacht at ten. Bring cash."

66

At Vendue Range, Sydney cut over to the Cooper River and rolled past Waterfront Park where the giant pineapple fountain flowed. Emergency service and first responder vehicles were staged for the upcoming fundraising event. An array of tents, chairs, and food trucks had fanned out. One uniformed cop haplessly directed the melee of traffic headed to the spectacular with the precision of a guy who'd graduated last in his academy class.

Sydney checked her watch—nine-thirty.

When she arrived at the marina, she scurried down the pier and dashed up the brow of *Miss Adventure*. She had intended to spend the rest of the day in Olivia's precious Donna Karan, but she didn't want to risk leaving traces of perspiration or spills of any sort. So, she dashed to her stateroom, stripped off the dress, then donned light orange slacks and an orange-and-white striped blouse. Sydney pocketed the Hello Kitty flash drive that Josh had uploaded with gibberish code. For good measure, she placed a second decoy flash drive in a plastic zip bag and slipped it under her bra.

Sydney allowed herself a solemn moment to remember Piper and Ted.

She had to admire them both. Neither had gone down without a fight. And Ted's biggest clues—photographic proof of the old Hack Pack and his odd reverse shazam code—sealed the case.

Her cell buzzed and she fumbled the phone. A text message from Dale read: *Golden Crust's system jacked. Paid ransom using GL$. It's your girl.*

"Hot damn." Sydney forwarded the text to Mason, adding: *Come take her.*

Shouldering her purse, she shoved the cell phone in the back

324

pocket of her slacks and climbed down the spiral staircase without a stab of regret.

325

67

At the bottom of the stairs, Sydney stumbled upon a scene straight out of a buddy cop movie gone wrong: Mason and Grace were locked in a standoff, each brandishing a Smith & Wesson pistol with the intensity of two actors vying for an Oscar.

"Well, this is awkward," Sydney said, trying to lighten the tension. "I see neither of you can tell time." She half-expected them to start debating who had the better aim, but instead, she cleared her throat and added, "Should I grab popcorn, or can we call it a draw?"

"I'm here to take her," Mason said. "Just like your text mentioned."

Grace made a sudden move and Mason fired one round. An earsplitting noise upended Sydney's train of thought. The bullet grazed Grace's arm and she blubbered in pain. Her gun toppled onto the deck.

Grace squeezed her wound and color drained from her face. Sydney thought the wily redhead looked frightened, too, and she couldn't blame her. Gun in the face, bullet through the arm, and all.

What a crock. Don't fall for this act. They are in it together, Sydney reminded herself.

The two felons were staging the little tiff, going to diabolical lengths to sell their con. Eventually, Mason would assert his "arrest" authority and take his partner, Grace, into custody. They probably planned to stroll off the yacht with Aeneid in one hand while lovingly cuffed together. All for show.

Mason scooped up Grace's pistol and jammed it in the front of his trousers. He faced Sydney with an almost distressed expression. "Here, babe. Take a seat. Sorry you had to see me use . . ." He waggled the gun as if he'd never shot one before.

Sydney didn't budge.

Mason continued. "I know you care about people. But you saw her. She made an aggressive move, right?"

Sydney snuck a peek at Grace, then back to Mason.

"I, ugh, don't kill people." Mason examined the gun. "I did it to protect . . . us. Sometimes things get messy." He patted the sofa for Sydney to come to him.

She remained frozen in place as she continued to read the room. The situation wasn't playing out at all like she'd anticipated. Sydney opted to stay cool because that seemed the best way to pull off the charade. The stakes were sky-high, even though the yacht had been wired with cameras, recording devices, and enough sensors to alert all of Charleston's finest.

Mason leveled the gun on Grace. "Time for a confession, dumbass. Tell Syd the boring details."

Grace whimpered, likely feeling what Sydney hated to admit— she was fascinated and repulsed by the ease with which Mason, the man they both were attracted to, could conjure wickedness and consideration at the same time.

Nah, Grace wasn't that deep.

Though Sydney felt certain the gunshot caused genuine discomfort.

Grace continued to press her hand atop the oozing wound, which was making a mess of her clothes and the salon's polished deck. "I discovered . . ." Her face tightened. "Correction. I planted the laptop in Ted's office." Grace's raspy voice hovered on the brink of an open floodgate. "He needed a little prodding to let me in on the big score."

Sydney identified notes of confusion in Grace's story. As if this scene, a false confession, hadn't been rehearsed. She and Mason were winging it.

Sydney needed to steer any spontaneous admissions. "Why did Ted need coaxing? Everyone knew he was already on team Hack Pack."

"The Internet is changing so fast, the feds aren't keeping up. Chinese and North Koreans have us looking like friggin' amateurs. And the Russians—" Grace threw her head back with an anxious laugh. "Can I get a smoke?"

Mason snarled. "Blanket answer—no." He motioned for Grace to sit on the couch next to Sydney.

Sydney cursed under her breath. "The big score—Aeneid?"

"Right," Grace said.

Sydney managed to snake a hand around to her back pocket and jam her cell phone between the seat cushions. She turned her attention to Mason. "How long have you known Grace was involved?"

He winked. "Not until you put me onto her yesterday."

"You're kidding?" Sydney failed to keep any skepticism from her tone.

"Kudos to you for putting a bow around the parts I missed. You'll get all the credit."

Sydney shook off his compliment. "Then why didn't you shut her down last night?"

Mason started to speak. Instead, he moved to the bar to pour a drink. "Either of you need a stiff one?"

Sydney ignored the sexually explicit pun. She felt confident the male cops listening in the tactical van were howling at that frat-boy raunchiness. She asked Grace, "What about Piper Kingston?"

Grace rolled her bloodstained fingers as though she were holding an imaginary cigarette. "She caught me boosting the laptop. Her death was all the incentive Ted needed to tweak his vaunted security on the servers so he could activate Aeneid's malware code." Her *story* was gaining momentum with each lie.

Sydney preferred open-ended questions in an interview, though at that moment, she aimed for a straight yes or no option. "Did you kill Piper?"

Grace didn't answer, instead spinning a sordid tale about how she chose Lansing Group as the place to launch the money grab.

"LG's server farm was a perfect host. Ted's job was to tamp down any warnings that popped up once he corrupted the servers."

Sydney coaxed additional details, coming at Grace sideways. Not following a chronological timeline.

Mason continued to verbally applaud Sydney's work. Doling out compliments at every turn. Even adding plausible nuggets if Grace omitted any details. Sydney hated to admit her invincible truth-o-meter was faltering in proximity to Mason's magnetism.

Grace also added that she was the one who'd framed Josh and planted Piper's flash drive at Ted's house. She further admitted cloaking the email headers on The Golden Crust's phishing attack, making it appear like it came from Ted, and ensured his IP was on the crypto key.

Grace contorted from the gunshot wound, while Mason fawned over Sydney.

Sydney eyed him, then gave voice to the really big question. "How'd Grace do? Any errors in her summation?"

Mason shook his head, yet he skated around what Sydney considered the most obvious point—his own involvement in one or more felonies. When the yacht's big engines turned over, his demeanor veered. He growled into a walkie-talkie, "Move."

This was Sydney's first indication that a third person was aboard to pilot the yacht. How many others were lurking in the shadows? She wondered if Dino had spotted them coming aboard.

She could feel the boat moving away from the pier. Where were they headed? And why hadn't Dino and his heavily armed team already crashed through the slider?

"Hey, I'm supposed to be at the fundraiser," Sydney said. "People will notice if I'm missing. All ashore who's going ashore."

Mason beamed. "Doesn't work that way."

"Oh, I see." Sydney paused to reboot, then snapped her fingers under the pretext his deception had just dawned on her. "Not with the Secret Service, eh, Luis?"

Mason responded with a reflexively turgid shrug.

That move confirmed everything Sydney needed. This time, however, the Earth did not shift beneath her feet. She'd rattled him. "Who else are you working with?"

His smugness waned as he seemed to calculate the odds that he'd wandered into a setup.

Even though they were on the move, time had expired for his clean getaway.

Mason had to understand that Dino and other local law enforcement officers, along with real badge-carrying agents from the Secret Service, would soon surround the yacht. Apprehend the criminals. Save the day.

Sydney eyed Mason with as much disdain as she could muster, refusing to fall for his hypnotic twinkle. "I believe the only thing Grace muffed in her recap was the attribution. My money says *you* did some of those things. Let's clean up her confession and solidify who killed Ted and Piper."

Mason snorted. "Should've figured you'd never go bad-apple on me. When you made that ridiculous offer to Grace . . ." He seemed to distance himself from his partner while closing in on Sydney. "Kitten, you have to believe . . . I never lied. Though I didn't disabuse any of your faulty assumptions. What happens next is on you." He cinched Sydney's hands in front with a plastic zip tie before she could react. The band sliced into her wrists and she let out a yelp. A squall of anger darkened his face as he shoved her back onto the sofa.

Sydney's head snapped as if she'd taken a punch.

Mason's eyes swept left to right around the salon, strafing the walls and ceiling.

She nudged the phone out of sight with her hip, unintimidated. "What are you looking for?"

He was on the prowl. "Where's the damn flash drive?"

"Can you be more specific?"

"The one with Ted's all-important code. Shit has hit the fan thanks to you, but I can still sell Aeneid. Dozens of dirtbag scum on the dark web want it." Mason turned on the salon's TV. He was taking his sweet time, leaving Sydney to conclude he was unaware the marina was swarming with cops—a tactical advantage in her favor.

He said, "While I search, let's watch what your friends are saying about your little fundraiser. Bet you think I'm full of surprises."

Sydney rolled her eyes. "Full of something."

Mason backhanded her with the remote. She tried to slide away but wasn't fast enough. It caught her squarely in the face.

Sydney wiped a sleeve across her nose while forging a strategy to buy a little time without further antagonizing her captor. It didn't make sense to threaten Mason, but it felt damn good to take a stand.

Surely Dino was mounting a rescue and would burst in any minute.

She just needed to string Mason along until that happened.

Sydney slowed her speech. "Grace omitted a few details I'd like to hear from you. Like, why involve Ted? And was it your idea to rip off LG's clients? Seems kinda petty in view of your super-sized score."

Mason gave a flip of his hand. "My skills have deteriorated, so I needed an elite hacker like Ted. Plus, I wanted to be sure he was implicated, as payback for leaving me holding the bag years ago. As Grace said, Ted didn't want to play ball at first. But I needed him to bypass LG's asymmetric encryption so I could crack open the Federal Treasury. Damn, he was good. No one noticed my stealthy dips." He rubbed his fingers across his chin. "As far as the ransomware and LG money goes, well, why not? When you're a greedy sonovabitch, you take everything you can." Mason rummaged through Sydney's purse. "Where's the pink flash drive?"

"I've spoken to the cops about you."

"Quit lying. I intercepted all your calls, you little shit. No one knows I'm here."

Ha, you're wrong about that, dipstick.

Under the circumstances, Sydney should've been terrified out of her mind. Mason was a full-blown psychopath likely planning her demise. Instead, she burst out laughing. Who knew? Maybe that was what terror should feel like.

She clicked her mind back on offense.

You want psycho? I'll give you psycho. She'd reported on the antics of more than one crazy girlfriend and was willing to give their tricks a whirl.

Mason said, "C'mon, babe. I need that USB. Give it to me and I promise to let you live."

<h1 style="text-align:center">68</h1>

In a blink, visions of Gunny Walters poked into Sydney's mind. Ah, those days in Baghdad with her powerful Marine.

Don't go there. Not now.

If Gunny couldn't magically appear with all his artillery, then she didn't have time for any grim thoughts about his death. She couldn't afford to wallow in the past or relive events she couldn't change.

On the other hand, since this was the second time Gunny had made an unscheduled appearance in the past few days, maybe seeking help for her *problem* was a solid idea after all. If she lived through this ordeal.

Mason continued to demand the flash drive.

Sydney felt a little juiced that she'd reeled him in and might actually survive. They glared at each other long and hard. Their hatred sizzled enough to warm the room.

She added another insult. "Your elaborate plan to raid the banks through LG's backdoor didn't work."

Mason spoke with a lethal undertone. "Sure, it did."

"Ted double-crossed you. He wrote a reverse flipper. The intricacies confound me, but techies tell me whatever money you think you stole, Ted ripped back—and left you with only a bad paper trail."

Mason squeezed his eyebrows together and worked his jaw. "I despise reformed criminals. Makes me glad I killed him."

Finally. An acknowledgement for one murder.

Mason jerked Sydney to her feet and centered the steely nose of his gun on her forehead. His index finger slid to the trigger. "Last chance."

"I know you left me in college because you went to prison for your Hack Pack screw-ups."

Mason affixed a savage sneer and backed her against the bar. She felt his hot breath on her cheek. "Shut the fuck up. You never should've gotten involved. This was a matter between old friends."

Jeezus, was he really going to kill her? And for what? Money? How could she have ever loved this man?

Coop would never be abusive.

With that, Sydney felt a wave of calmness wash over her. "How come everyone thinks you died, Luis?"

"Creating an obit and death certificate was child's play."

"So was stealing the money. That means you didn't have to kill Piper and Ted."

Mason's eyes speared into her. "When you started asking about the argument Ted had with Gavin, I suspected Ted was ready to squeal—tell Gavin everything. I had to take extreme measures."

Mason's detailed admission sucked the wind from her sails. She quickly recovered. "Oh, no, dammit. I won't let you lay Ted's murder on me. You drugged him and pulled the trigger." Despite a tinge of guilt, another awful thought sideswiped her. "Was Gavin next on your list? Or maybe you were leaving that one to her?" Sydney cocked her head in Grace's direction.

He lowered the gun from Sydney's head and pulled her close. "There's gotta be another way to solve our little problem, babe," Mason whispered. "Despite your energetic antics in the sack, you still haven't given me what I really want." Mason pushed Sydney away and began pawing through her purse. She edged back to the couch and fished her phone from the cushions. She pressed 911.

Mason opened the salon door and flung her handbag overboard. "You won't need this anymore."

Sydney remained outwardly tranquil despite boiling anger. "Aw, crap. That was a valuable Louis Vuitton knock-off."

Nick Braydon's voice came from the TV. He was reading a script she'd written for the segment. "Officials hope public generosity will subsidize mental health and recovery programs for those putting their lives on the line and coping with crises. First responders from all departments, ambulance strike teams, and emergency dispatchers encounter tragedy each shift. Help comes in the form of finding the good in everyday activities. Overriding negativity by scheduling positive experiences. And ensuring responders understand their sense of purpose."

Sydney refocused her attention on Mason. "Why'd you shoot Grace? Aren't you partners in this heist?"

He shook his head. "Jeezus, Syd. You've had the facts wrong from the jump."

"Enlighten me, then." Her lips curled in disgust. "I can't believe I swallowed that bull about you being a federal agent."

Mason barked an ugly laugh. "I tried to tell you there aren't any federal agents working undercover at LG."

Grace raised her chin in defiance, though her face remained taut with pain. "Wanna bet?"

69

Sydney felt a surge of voltage jack through her, equal parts surprise and curiosity, as Grace's stunning revelation began to crystallize. It certainly explained why Mason had shot her. They weren't partners or co-conspirators after all.

Sydney eyeballed the redhead, unsure what kind of federal agent she could be. But it didn't really matter as long as Grace had dropped a truth bomb.

Mason's cool evaporated. "What the fuck are you saying?"

Through gritted teeth, Grace set the record straight. "Let me spell it out for you. I showed up for this meeting to make sure you'd be caught. And believe Sydney when she tells you—Aeneid doesn't work." She winced when she glanced at her arm. The sleeve was soaked now, and blood continued leaching between her fingertips.

"Of course, it works. I have plenty of crypto-loot as proof." Mason glared at Sydney. "The head . . ."

Sydney collected herself. "Upstairs, on your left. Sheesh, it's your own damn boat. You think you'd know where the johns are located."

"No, dumbass," Mason hissed. "I'll bet that's where you stashed the flash drive."

He sprinted up the stairs.

With Mason out of the room, Sydney's mind stoked with alternatives. She could either wait for him to come back empty-handed—and surely die. Or get off the boat.

Grace, wan and woozy, moaned in agony.

Sydney's gaze followed the red droplets splashing onto the deck. Time to extricate themselves. Otherwise . . .

Sydney didn't want to think about the possibilities.

She tugged the self-proclaimed federal agent toward the aft

balcony. At the slider, Sydney scanned the horizon. Neither Dino nor a SWAT rescue team was anywhere in sight.

Mason raced into the salon before the two could escape off the yacht.

Sydney improvised—shooting her arms out like a cobra. In one fist was the benign flash drive she'd jerked from her pocket. As Mason reached for it, Sydney lunged to block his wrist, wrong-footing him. But his weight dropped on her when he tumbled. The flash drive scuttled across the deck.

Mason's pistol swept Sydney's cheek.

Grace kicked feebly at his legs, though Mason managed to wriggle away. He yanked Sydney's hair, then his left fist hooked around with blinding speed. With her hands bound, Sydney had no chance to deflect the explosive punch before he clocked her in the chops.

Blood gushed from Sydney's mouth and nose. "Damn you." Her voice held an unforeseen measure of defiance.

Nick's voiceover continued on the TV. "Being a first responder is stressful. Departments experience high turnover, critical shortages, and training shortfalls. Your pledge will go directly to supporting the center dedicated to private group therapy, peer support, and individualized rehabilitation, comradery, and recreation."

The yacht slowed.

A voice squawked on Mason's portable walkie-talkie. "We're in position."

"You have the instructions." Mason snatched the flash drive off the deck and jammed it into a laptop he'd positioned atop the bar. "You're plucky, kitten. I used to like that side of you." He scanned the bogus script Josh had created, oblivious to the sham. "Once I sell Ted's code, I should clear a billion in walking-around money. I need it too, because my father squandered my inheritance. The Kiawah mansion and this yacht are leased."

He pocketed Hello Kitty, then dumped the contents from a small yellow envelope into a can of soda.

What a waste of Diet Mountain Dew, Sydney thought.

"Drink this—for fun." Mason yanked Sydney's hair again, tipping her head back with only a split second for her to register the impending disaster.

She clenched her jaw, drawing her lips tight. Mason jabbed a thumb into her cheek, forcing her to open her mouth if she wanted to relieve the excruciating pain.

Sydney tightened her throat as best she could to avoid swallowing the adulterated concoction. "I've never had this much fun thrust on me in such large doses." Then she sputtered away what remained of the drink once Mason freed her head.

She suspected the Dew had been laced with the same chloral hydrate found in Ted's R*Ampd—the same substance with which Mason had likely used to dose Piper before whacking her with the four-iron. The guy wasn't very imaginative, though the drug's effects were immediate.

Sydney must've swallowed more than she thought. Blood ebbed from her head, and her vision grew fuzzy around the edges. Her skin prickled, and she sensed a sickening loss of feeling in her fingertips.

Tender memories of her life flitted through a drug-addled mind. Weekends spent with her brothers learning about baseball and cars. Her sister teaching her to apply mascara so it didn't clump. Dad, helping to pick out a prom dress. Mom, crying at the airport before she boarded the plane for Iraq. And of course, Gunny Walters.

Mason's voice brought her out of the memories. "Your sign-off is gonna be a bang." He tugged on a dry suit. "You'll be the top story one last time—if they can find any pieces of you. You see, the boat is rigged with explosives."

Sydney believed him. He was too much of an arrogant prick to bluff. She glanced around the yacht. Mahogany, plush carpet, paintings. Beautiful. Striking. Too bad the darn thing was going to blow.

And if that happened before she and Grace could abandon ship, they were screwed.

"Shoo thon't met way miff this." Her slurred speech caught her off guard. She didn't drink alcohol, so that'd never happened before.

The chloral hydrate-induced euphoria began to feel like a magical thing, yet Sydney knew she couldn't spend another minute circling the drain. With her mind all gauzy and stupid, she bent over and forced a coughing fit to whittle away the mental confusion.

"The first fireworks are the most dramatic and picturesque," Nick's voice on the TV said. "Here we go."

70

The engine noise from a Zodiac rigid inflatable boat roared to life, slicing through the air with the urgency of a rock concert's opening riff. Moments later, the horizon was illuminated by the initial round of fireworks, bursting into vibrant colors that danced across the sky like a painter gone wild with a cosmic palette.

Mason pinned Sydney with his gaze and aimed the gun at her head. "My ride is waiting."

Time was up. She and Grace were going to die.

The yacht's anchor splashed over the side, rocking the boat, and sending the smug bastard's shot errantly through a sofa and into the bulkhead.

Sydney marshaled enough energy and coordination to lever herself and catapult forward, pile driving her head deep into Mason's stomach before he could re-aim. His gun bounced off a chair and skidded under a tiled occasional table.

Mason scrabbled to his feet, holding his midsection. The air had blasted out of his lungs and he had trouble recovering from the impact. Sydney lunged again, this time landing a rewarding foot to his groin that sent him doubled over in a pain he wouldn't soon forget. Mason squealed like a maimed animal, one hand clutching his prized sporting goods section.

Consciousness fading, Sydney stumbled toward the aft deck, where she'd parked Grace crumpled in a pile. The salon door crashed open before she could tug the wounded agent over the side.

Another gunshot ricocheted off the stainless-steel railing.

Sydney dove under a patio table, but it toppled over, crushing her ankle. She let fly a spate of obscenities and flagged her hands in defeat. She tried to keep the desperation from her voice as she moved over to shield Grace. "Shtop. That frash thrive is a flake. Ted's thipper coze on 'nother flasthpff drive."

"You're lying?" Mason sneered with hideously crazed eyes. "Where?"

"Upstairs. In dwain fipe." Her fat, swollen lips puckered with distaste.

Mason gripped Sydney's arm. "Show me."

A grotesque crunch from her mangled ankle rocketed pain through her entire body. Sydney clamped her mouth rather than howl. "Can't climb shairs in mith condish. Suite C, under sthink. The pipe ifff only hand-smightened."

Mason shoved Sydney and stomped her ankle with his jackboot.

She refused to shed a tear, though the sting was worse than when she'd been shot in Iraq. "Thuck you." Sydney folded over and vomited.

"You have a misguided sense of cockiness," Mason said, before darting up the stairs.

Sydney tried to shake the blinding tremors. She was a jangle of nerves and wasn't about to let him put a bullet in her when he discovered the drainpipe was empty. She envisioned Julia Mayfair's lede—*Sydney Quinn, senior Action 7 News reporter, died today in a tragic accident aboard her dirtbag ex-boyfriend's leased yacht.*

Nope.

She wouldn't give Julia—or Mason—the satisfaction.

Sydney dragged Grace to the swim platform. Grace drew a fishing knife from inside her jacket and clumsily sliced off their plastic handcuffs. She'd either found the knife before Sydney arrived, or this was part of her personal armament.

Grace handed Sydney the knife, then made a sharp intake of breath. "I can't swim."

Well, crap.

Their situation was more hopeless than Sydney had feared.

If they jumped over the side, she'd have to keep them both afloat while hopelessly drugged, then swim to shore with little help from Grace.

But the boat was rigged to blow.

So, staying aboard was out of the question.

Mason flew out the door toward the women as they inched to the platform's edge. He was moving at full speed.

Arching.

Attacking.

When he neared, Sydney's hands quivered from primal fear. She set aside the terror and reached up, snagged him by the collar, then stuck the knife into his shoulder. He cried out as he cravenly lunged for the safety of the escape Zodiac that had maneuvered alongside.

He was leaving them stranded aboard a yacht packed with explosives.

Intuitively, Sydney knew she didn't have time to process alternatives. She hurled Grace overboard into the river, then took several deep breaths. Lots of air. She was gonna need it. She toppled overboard and began fighting the current as she searched the frigid waters for Grace.

Sydney dived under but couldn't see a darn thing. She reached out in every direction to locate the government agent. After several failed attempts, her fingers brushed against cloth. She grabbed hold of Grace's arm and attempted to jerk her up. Sydney made three desperate bids to surface with the flailing woman. Wet clothes, among other things, continued to drag them under.

They'd sink to the bottom if Sydney couldn't break the surface on her next attempt.

A surge of panic-fueled energy coursed through her, and with a flurry of mighty kicks, they crested into the sunlight. Both women gasped for lungfuls of clean air as they bobbed in the waves.

Stone-cold river water had proved a sufficient remedy to gain a squinch of equilibrium despite the throbbing in Sydney's ankle and the toxic chemicals leeching through her carburetor. Without know-ing how much time they had before the explosion, they needed to create distance between themselves and the doomed yacht. Sydney coughed to clear her lungs, but Grace's useless wriggling yanked them under again.

She must be flooded with adrenaline, Sydney thought.

Not good for a gal who was bleeding profusely.

As Sydney wrestled Grace into a rescue swimmer's hold, the agent's body gradually grew limp.

Dino, where are you?

In her mind's eye, Dino was racing to her backed by the entire Coast Guard.

But the only sound she registered was her own panting. She began furiously kicking away from the yacht, federal agent in tow. Sydney's arms sagged as she pulled against Grace's helpless torso.

Keep going.

They were barely a hundred yards away when the yacht's bone-jarring explosion sent out a stampeding rip current that towed them down into murky darkness.

71

Sydney's cramped legs were failing, but she managed to kick to the surface, jerking Grace's head above the whitecaps. Thankfully, Grace didn't have any strength to fight back. Nearby, fiery gasoline, no longer contained by humongous fuel tanks housed below deck, produced immense heat. Flames danced atop undulations in the river, prompting new concerns.

The two women gasped in vain, struggling to find a clean breath in the suffocating and polluted air. Sydney's vision, already blurred from the chloral hydrate, was further distorted by billowy black smoke, making her completely lose her way.

Despite their predicament, Sydney sensed getting towed under had likely averted serious injury from being struck by flying debris from the massive explosion that had destroyed the luxury yacht.

Obliterated was a more accurate description.

Sydney grabbed hold of an expensive chunk of light blue flotsam as it drifted by. Grace mumbled an indistinct "thanks" as Sydney maneuvered them further away from the flames in case a secondary explosion or other surprise awaited them. Fatigue and fear finally overcame her, and Sydney surrendered to the sweeping current, never realizing how close they'd come to extinction.

·

An unknown amount of time passed before Sydney felt her knees scuff against the muck along the river bottom, a gritty reminder of the precarious situation she was in. Clinging to the debris raft with one hand, she held Grace's head above water with the other, her muscles burning from the effort. The scene was like something out of a survival thriller, with Sydney playing the dual roles of heroine and lifeline. Each second stretched into an eternity, the river's current tendering a relentless challenge as she'd fought to keep them both afloat.

They'd washed ashore near Waterfront Park, though much of the shoreline was obscured by tall reeds. The twelve-acre tract, situated between Vendue Range to the north and Sydney's dream house on Adger's Wharf to the south, had historically been home to several shipping terminals. On this occasion, the park was playing host to a significant encampment of news vans, cameras, lights, and reporters covering her fundraising extravaganza.

Sydney sucked air in greedy gulps. It took several minutes for her lungs to feel like they were functioning properly. She was mired in pluff mud, yet a voice in her head told her, *Keep moving.* Every muscle spasmed as she scrambled upright on ruined legs and feeble ankles. Wet sand caked her feet.

"Land ho, Grace. Time to find a hunky paramedic to tend to that nasty hole in your arm." Sydney listed hard to port, gleefully recognizing her absence of slurred speech. She draped an arm around Grace's waist for support.

Grace forced a weak laugh. "Damn, I could sure use a cigarette."

Sydney offered a shaky smile. "Why don't you vape like the cool kids?"

Grace drew in a shaky breath. "A hunky EMT . . . Sounds pretty good, too. You saved my scrawny butt."

Sydney offered an impish grin. "The very least I could do after trying to pin two murders and Aeneid's theft on you."

Sydney dragged her mauled right ankle along the oyster shell-crusted shore. As they limped toward the park like newborn fawns trying to navigate their first steps, a couple of thoughts crossed her mind. First, they'd been more than lucky to reach *terra firma* in one piece. Second, she'd never be able to repay Olivia for destroying her precious Donna Karan dress. And lastly, where the hell were Dino and Sergeant Cash when she needed them?

The two were less than fifty yards from the comfort of Action 7's mobile van when the seagrass parted and an angry Mason burst through, blocking Grace and Sydney's path. He'd shed the dry suit and was bleeding profusely from the stab wound Sydney had inflicted, along with multiple shrapnel lacerations from the explosion. Sydney shouted for her co-workers and other reporters until her throat seized.

Grace fell to her knees. "You're under arrest, asshole."

Sydney admired the wily redhead's pluck.

"I don't think so." Mason rammed into Grace like a bull, and her head cracked hard against jagged shells.

Sydney threw herself on Mason's back as he tried to lasso Grace's arms. He grabbed a shank of her hair, trying to pull her off, but Sydney managed to jab a thumb into his eye socket, then yanked Grace's gun from the front of his pants. She scrambled to her feet while Grace remained laid out.

Why had Mason hung around and come after them again?

Did he hope to keep Sydney and Grace from exposing him? Sheesh, the guy couldn't take a hint? He was in big trouble with the law and should've skedaddled when he had a chance.

Mason dropped on all fours and panted. "You won't kill me on live television." He cocked his head toward Eric—whose camera was aimed in their direction. Mason eased to his feet, smarmy-looking eyes drilling through Sydney.

The rest of the assembled media contingent raced toward them, thrashing about, still trying to reconcile the explosion and the unfolding scenario.

Sydney leveled the gun, the red laser sight from the anodized matte-black pistol pointed at Mason's chest. She flicked off the safety with her thumb. *Don't make me do this.*

Nick edged behind Mason, but Mason spun, seizing the anchorman. He flung Nick to the ground with a fistful of tailored shirt. Nick shouted a string of expletives as he yowled in pain.

Sydney's finger tensed on the trigger. *Please don't make me shoot you.*

Mason lunged for her, and the gun bucked in Sydney's hand.

Once.

Twice.

Blood mushroomed from the pair of entry wounds in his chest.

Dino, Sergeant Cash, and two uniformed cops charged toward the commotion. One cop kneeled beside Mason, felt for a pulse, then shook his head. Another kneeled beside Grace to inspect her wounded arm. He keyed the mic attached to his ballistic Kevlar vest and signaled for EMTs to respond to his location.

Sydney handed the gun to Dino before yanking out Nick's IFB and shoving it in her ear. Next, she grabbed a stick mic from Eric. Her nerves prickled with a thousand needles. The realization that she'd actually killed Mason, or rather Luis, landed like a punch to the solar plexus. She gagged and spit out a mouthful of bile.

"Olivia, don't give her a hot mic," Pete shouted through the earpiece. "Look at what she's wearing. Jeezus, we'll get a huge FCC fine for sure."

Eric's camera trained on Sydney.

She wiped the edges of her mouth with the back of her hand. She peered into the faces of her friends and colleagues to assure them she was okay. "This man . . ." She swallowed hard, then willed herself to manufacture a stoic reporter persona. "Luis Gaston, AKA Mason Sterling, killed Piper Kingston and Ted Armstrong. He also attempted to steal billions from the federal government, international banks, and many other personal accounts." She could add more detail and context, but she opted to throw it back to an associate who wasn't fighting shock, anger, and a tinge of sadness. "This is Sydney Quinn, reporting live. Back to whoever is anchoring Action 7's coverage of this exclusive."

"Damn spam, Olivia," Pete said. "You're fired. But keep the cameras rolling. We finally scooped those bastards at Eyewitness 13."

72

After shooting Mason, Sydney had spent the rest of that afternoon retching the remnants of his drug-laced cocktail from her system. Doctors had successfully mended Nick's broken collarbone with two screws and patched the bullet wound on Grace's arm. Both were expected to make a full recovery.

Coop had phoned her at least a dozen times. Sent scads of flowers and chocolates. And apologized he couldn't be there because he was working undercover with a white-collar arson-for-profit group outside of Atlanta.

Now, two days later, Sydney pulled Mandy's sock-monkey sheets and a matching comforter over her head. Her arms and legs hurt. Her back and shoulders ached. And her surgically repaired ankle had been packed in a fiberglass cast. Aside from all that, she felt great and should've returned to her hotel room yesterday.

Mandy stood at the foot of the bed. "There's a bright side, Sparky."

Sydney threw back the covers and arched an eyebrow.

"You never have to question whether you missed out not having Mason in your life." Mandy handed her a Diet Dew and grabbed a truffle from one of the open boxes. "That should free you up to address how you really feel about you-know-who up in Charlotte."

Sydney sat up and took a sip. "Hallelujah."

"Grace told me she'd never known anyone so cruel, so selfish. She called Mason a total jerk." Mandy bit into the truffle and smiled. "By the way, all the networks have phoned."

Sydney peeked at Mandy with one eye. "Job interview?"

"Interview—talking head shows. And one last item. Pete wants you in his office by nine-thirty."

Sydney glanced at the Betty Boop clock on the nightstand in

Mandy's guest room. One hour to get ready. "I have nothing to wear," she said. "And the yacht explosion totaled Olivia's precious DKNY."

"Yeah, she knows. Not sure what the tariff will be on the loss of a Donna Karan." Mandy removed Sydney's favorite Chanel suit from the closet. "But . . ."

Sydney said, "How did you know—"

"Grace reminded me you'd dropped it at the cleaners." Mandy climbed on the bed. "She's a very interesting gal. When did you learn she was a federal agent?"

Sydney took another pull of Dew. "Came as a complete surprise when she revealed herself. I should've picked up on Ted's reverse shazam—*Don't Tell Grace*. I figured he was implicating her, rather than leading me to an ally. By the way, I never asked what agency she works for. Any idea?"

"She's an IRS Criminal Investigator," Mandy said. "Grace told me she was the one who'd spotted trends in area ransomware heists. That's why she inserted herself at LG to work with Ted, with Gavin's approval, of course. She tried everything she could to discourage you off the case, but since you stayed with it, she knew you'd be an ideal accomplice."

"That's a helluva *ta-da*," Sydney said.

"Things almost came unglued when a few LG employees caught wind the feds were nosing around. That's why Gavin pressured Grace for the press conference, using a misplaced laptop as a ruse." Mandy started to pace in tight circles. "Grace respected Ted's coding prowess, but she never liked his double-whammy script. She thought if he electronically recaptured the money Mason sent to his offshore account, how could she prove the guy's embezzlement? Or tax fraud . . . and so on. Ted obviously ignored her—and still ensured the proof existed."

The doorbell rang.

Mandy said, "That's for you."

Sydney eased out of bed. Her feet felt funny when they touched the floor, and the cast tilted her off balance. She knew she had to use crutches.

Dino filled the doorway and studied her. "Ladybug, you look like crap."

The expression on his face caused Sydney to grin. "I'm sensing that was a compliment."

His eyes came alive. "Look, I know you've endured a lot lately. But I gotta lay a little something else on you. And it won't be easy to hear."

"Forget it. I've fallen on enough land mines for a lifetime."

He eased onto the corner of the bed. "I found a way for you to rewrite your personal narrative."

Sydney sat beside him. "That pickup line is so old, it has whiskers."

Dino's voice was soft, reassuring. "I located Corporal Ace Weston, formerly of Echo Company."

Sydney placed him immediately. *Home: Boyne Falls. Wife: Alma. Two kids: Ben and Alex. Blessed with a wicked sweet tooth and an unending supply of Twizzlers.*

Dino said, "The corporal remembers the Taliban firefight almost as clearly as you, Ladybug."

Sydney drew a knee to her chest. "Why dredge up the ambush? I don't want to—"

. . . Recall a pain I'll regret for the rest of my life.

Dino put his hand on her head and stroked her hair. "The corporal told me he'd been torn up about the death of your gunnery sergeant for years—until he finally spoke to Gunny's wife. The corporal knew he was the one who'd signaled you to move to the helo before Gunny was shot and killed."

Sydney wiped her eyes. "Not my—"

"Not your fault." Dino gripped her by the arms.

Mandy swam into the room and sobbed. Snot shot out of both barrels. "Not Syd's fault."

"It takes courage to admit you need help." Dino offered an

outstretched hand. "I'm here. Always. Code 3—lights and sirens."

Sydney stuffed her hands into his.

Casting aside ingrained recollections and shame would never be easy. But she felt up to the challenge. "How'd Mason's confession play? Did you hear everything before the bomb went off?"

"State and federal prosecutors are having a field day. Should be able to close their cases associated with the two murders and fraud." Dino held her gaze. "When did you first think he was dirty?"

Sydney ticked off items on her fingers. "He slipped when he mentioned Josh's *handwritten* note. Plus, Mandy said he was at Piper's on the day she was killed. He made the police blotter. And Josh spotted Mason's car in Piper's driveway. The Beemer disappeared before all the fun started."

"And the crown jewel—Ted's Hack Pack photo." Mandy popped up with excitement. "But there's one thing I need clarification on. Did you actually try to sell Grace the Aeneid software?"

"I knew my phone was tapped, so I figured if I kept my focus on her, then Mason would come along for the ride. Even though I admit I thought they were working together."

Dino said, "Had to scrape Mike Cash off the ground when you called that audible on the final play. Get this—he wasn't read in that Grace was working undercover. He thought you were really going rogue."

Sydney grinned. "On the left hand—Secret Service. The right—an IRS agent. I'm guessing Cash got schooled on multi-agency task force management. What about Grace's ransom discoveries?"

Dino said, "It's her job to help businesses test their system vulnerabilities so they can avert identity theft. She shows them what might happen unless they do a better job protecting their online goodies. She was able to return the ransom money Ted and Gavin paid." He sucked in a gulp. "Ladybug, I'm really sorry we couldn't find you in the water. I had uniforms surround the yacht prior to the ceremony. Unfortunately, they chose to trail Mason's dinghy after you left the pier. When the onboard cameras caught you and Grace going over the side, I sent another crew to pick you up. But the yacht blew—"

"And you became lost in foamy surf," Mandy said.

Dino's smile flickered like an old lightbulb about to blow. "We launched the helos, then I staked out Action 7's mobile location in hopes you'd find your way home."

Sydney smoothed the fabric of her favorite suit. "The rest, as they say, is television history."

Dino stared at her. "All these years, you've been caught between Iraq and a hard place."

Mandy groaned. "C'mon, Dino."

He winked. "Dad joke?"

Mandy turned to Sydney. "I'll meet you at the station. Nine-thirty. Be on time."

After she left the room, Sydney faced Dino. "I jumped to faulty conclusions regarding Ted. I know you hate that."

"I hate it because it's an all-too-human response." He jerked a thumb toward himself. "Don't tell anyone, but I do it too."

"Are you saying we're human?"

"Suck it up, 'cuz I won't repeat it."

Sydney grinned. "Thanks, I guess."

Dino said, "Your Thunderbird has been repaired, Ladybug. Keys are on the counter by the door. But I'll be your chauffeur until your ankle heals."

73

Sydney hobbled into the station manager's office at precisely nine-twenty. She resented the crutches, which not only wrinkled her suit, but also slowed her down. And *slow* never suited her.

Pete appeared riveted to a ream of paper almost an inch thick. He pointed to the printout. "Ratings are in. We blew them away."

"Lousy choice of words, boss," Sydney said.

Pete jiggled coins in his pocket. "What can I say? I'm fired up."

Sydney scrunched her face.

"Sorry. I haven't seen numbers like this in a long time. Your story was a real piss-cutter, even before your slimy blouse thing."

"My thing?" she mouthed.

Talk about distilling an event. The looting, the shooting, the explosion—forever labeled in the annals of Action 7 News as simply *Sydney's slimy blouse thing.*

TV was indeed a sound-bite jungle.

Pete moved to the credenza, poured a cup of coffee, and scooted a chair out for his top reporter. "You took a chance waving that flash drive around during your segment. Wasn't part of the plan we ironed out."

She eye-checked him before responding. "I ad-libbed."

"The ole bait and switch. You hoodwinked the crook." He took a sip and brightened. "Damn spam, I knew that when the stakes were at their highest, you'd be at your best. And more good news, the county solicitor won't be charging you for the . . ." He cleared his throat. "Said you clearly fired at the bozo in self-defense."

"Remember, you only objected to my being a *stupid* bastard."

"More than a pretty face. Exactly what I told Grace Rogers when she mentioned you were working with her to apprehend that ruffian. Said you'd been sworn to secrecy. That takes a set of lady plums, Syd." Pete resumed flipping through the ratings printout. "Decide on Mrs. Muirfield's offer yet?"

"Depends—"

"I know she wants her new chief investigative reporter to seek professional help. Says she'll be with you every step of the way. Just one caveat—no more street racing."

"That's easy, my foot's in a cast."

"What's it gonna be?"

Sydney made an audible exhaling sound. "I'm looking forward to being a big fish in this weird wee pond."

Mandy shrieked and yanked open the door. She bounced in, followed by Olivia, who toted a small gift bag.

Sydney removed a four-leaf clover paperweight from the bag. "Chief Investigative Reporter."

"We know," Olivia said. "Pay's the same as before, but people will disrespect you less."

"Including you?"

"It's a job title—not magic beans."

Mandy bounced up and down. Sydney tottered on one leg with her.

Bouncing was the feminine equivalent of rapping knuckles or bumping chests.

Olivia fanned her face with a stack of papers. "I hate to break up whatever this is, but two guys are in the newsroom waiting to see you. The big one says he's poochy's dad. I think that man needs more fiber in his diet, if you know what I mean."

"Send 'em in," Sydney said.

Dale Lawson had crammed his refrigerator body into a black Armani suit and a crisp white shirt, no tie. He'd also cut and groomed his hair. Josh Andrews wore LG's trademark crisp light-blue oxford and khakis.

Josh said, "Thanks for my new job, Syd. I owe you."

Sydney drummed her nails on one crutch. "You know how it is. Gavin Lansing didn't need much convincing he could use a guy with your unique skills."

"Well, butter my butt and call me a biscuit," Olivia said. "Syd, through all your tribulations, you never forgot the whole mess started with Josh and Piper."

"Hey, pump the brakes on the celebration," Mandy said. "Everyone's been made whole except Sparky, since her money was hijacked by someone on the dark web, not Aeneid."

Josh grinned. "Actually, Dale is a genuine member of the Secret Service. He operates as a white-hat hacker. He corralled Syd's money long before anyone could drain it."

Sydney gave Dale a nod. "Explains why Cash told me that we'd provided valuable information regarding The Golden Crust—a lead connected to Aeneid his group didn't have."

Mandy patted her stomach. "All this happy news is making me hungry. What say we—"

"Head to Waffle House." Sydney grabbed her purse. "I need something scattered, smothered, and ooey-gooey covered."

ACKNOWLEDGMENTS

Crafting a mystery novel is analogous to piecing together an intricate puzzle that is rife with impossible roadblocks. It takes a great deal of help to find the edges from which to launch. First and foremost, massive thanks to the makers of Diet Mountain Dew for crafting a delightful elixir.

High-fives to my neighbors for not calling the police during late-night brainstorming sessions in which I loudly debated plot twists with myself. Your patience is as enigmatic as my storylines.

I openly recognize Google Search for answering bizarre questions like "How long does it take to dig a six-foot deep hole?" or "When do blowflies lay eggs?" without alerting any authorities.

Cheers to my fellow mystery novelists whose books I devoured in procrastination—your work was both enlightening and an excellent distraction from writing mine.

A special nod to spellcheck for flagging most of my typos—but leaving enough so the editors could enjoy their own sleuthing experience.

A tip of the beret to the many wonderful people I've met at book signings, conferences, truck stops, and fast-food joints. Too numerous to name—I thank you all.

Despite eagerly accepting encouragement from a host of sources (horoscopes, fortune cookies, Magic 8 Balls), I am truly grateful to those people who filled my cup throughout this journey and are singularly influential in defining who I am. From you, I received reassurance, optimism, and additional ice-cold elixir doses (see above) that inspired me to forge ahead. You are weird and wonderful. And your unwavering belief in my dreams is my greatest source of strength.

Special shout-outs to:

My brilliant editors, Jaden, Emily, and Erika, whose keen eyes and insightful feedback transformed this manuscript into a tale of suspense and intrigue. The way you identified hidden threads, corrected grammatical boo-boos, then laced everything into a cohesive narrative is nothing short of magical.

Hannah (Books Fluent) and Jackie (Books Forward)—I toast your sharp insights and tireless dedication.

The incredibly talented voice actor, Daryl Mayfield, whose artistry breathes soul into my characters through his remarkable performances. Your work is truly cherished, and I'm immensely fortunate to have found such a gifted collaborator.

Sgt. Chris Stinson, Charleston Police Department's Public Information Officer, who fielded all my crazy questions.

Linda L. Kontos and Peter T. Kontos, who generously shared their time, talent, and expertise to create cover art, photos for my website (wendygeeauthor.com), and several headshots for this and future works.

The Lewes Public Library staff and Friends, whose wealth of knowledge and willingness to assist in my research have been indispensable. Your quiet sanctuary also provided the perfect backdrop for creativity to flourish.

Candace C. Vessella (my Navy bud) and Adrian Nakayama (a wonderful human being). A million and one hugs for being shareholders in the Triple Crown club! I am beyond grateful for you both.

My Delaware group, whose spirited discussions have been instrumental in refining every twist and turn. Your camaraderie and support are most appreciated.

Janice Dumais and Debbie Johnson for their extraordinary advice and efforts regarding all things technical (while also providing an uninterrupted supply of the aforementioned elixir).

Clay Stafford and his remarkable Killer Nashville conference and staff. He continues to provide endless inspiration and exceptional guidance.

Finally, I salute my brilliant readers. Your passion for mystery and adventure fuels my imagination. Thank you for delving into the unknown with me, for it is your curiosity and enthusiasm that bring these stories to life.

www.ingramcontent.com/pod-product-compliance
Lightning Source LLC
Chambersburg PA
CBHW061303190726
48288CB00002B/325